KURDISH SCAVENGERS
CACHE OF NERVE GAS IN IF
THEM TO KURDISH FIGHTERS IN TURKEY.
THE SPECIAL OPERATIONS BEDLAM ALPHA
TEAM MUST SECURE THE WEAPONS
BEFORE THEY CAN BE USED.

In their daily struggle for survival, Iraqi Kurdish scavengers uncover a cache of chemical weapons. They offer the weapons to Kurdish rebels in Turkey and Syria to assist in their quest to free an imprisoned leader and create a unified homeland. After receiving a tip from an unlikely source, the newly formed Special Operations Bedlam team is called to arms. Can the team recover the weapons before it's too late?

"The Kurdish Connection—a compelling read. A story of friendship, danger and intrigue."—*Ann Everett, Amazon Best Selling Author.*

"... Randall's authentic voice adds a powerful push to keep a reader turning the pages." —*Janet Taylor-Perry, author of The Raiford Chronicles, The Legend of Draconis Saga, and April Chastain Intrigues.*

"Topical - Engaging - Intriguing – Powerful ... A real page turner."—*Rikon Gaites, author of Mummy's Little Soldier and Darius Odenkirk.*

"... Randall Krzak brings his wealth of experience living in this troubled part of the world and his military knowledge to bear in this exciting story..."—*John L. DeBoer, author of When the Reaper Comes.*

"... a journey full of history, suspense, intrigue, and action...a MUST READ for all!"—*Les Stahl, Retired* NSA Executive.

"... Readers need to fasten their seatbelts for a fast-paced tale made believable by a writer who knows what he's writing about."—*Preston Holtry, author of the Morgan Westphal mystery series and the Arrius trilogy (forthcoming).*

"A behind the scenes story, ripped from today's headlines deepening the reader's understanding of an ancient strife ... filled with the sights and smells of the market place and secret meetings, the reader is admitted to the secret heart, the desperate longings of those that must fight and win, or see continued subjugation by their masters..."—*Oliver F. Chase, author of Camelot Games,* Levant Mirage, Blind Marsh, and Marsh Island.

THE KURDISH CONNECTION

RANDALL KRZAK

Moonshine Cove Publishing, LLC
Abbeville, South Carolina U.S.A.

FIRST MOONSHINE COVE EDITION FEBRUARY 2017

ISBN: 978-1-945181-06-1
Library of Congress Control Number: 2017931619
Copyright © 2017 by Randall Krzak

Cover images public domain, cover and interior layout by Moonshine Cove staff.

iv

To my wife Sylvia, my true flower of Scotland,
And to our son Craig, of whom we're very proud.
There's no doubt I have the best family in the world.
Thank you for loving me.
I love you both.

About The Author

Randall Krzak is a U.S. Army veteran and retired senior civil servant, spending almost thirty years in Europe, Africa, Central America, and the Middle East. His residency abroad qualifies him to build rich worlds in his action-adventure novels and short stories. Familiar with customs, laws, and social norms, he promotes these to create authentic characters and scenery.

He penned *A Dangerous Occupation*, a winning entry in the August 2016 Wild Sound Writing and Film Festival Review short story category.

Randall holds a general Master in Business Administration (MBA) and a MBA with an emphasis in Strategic Planning both from Heriot-Watt University, Edinburgh, Scotland.

He currently resides with his wife, Sylvia and five cats in the United States. In addition to writing, he enjoys hiking, reading, candle making, pyrography, and sightseeing.

Randall is currently developing a sequel to *The Kurdish Connection* titled, *Dangerous Alliance.* His creative enterprise delved even further into the treacherous sphere of the drug cartel in South America, expanding the manuscript, *A Cartel's Revenge,* into an upcoming series.

Find out more about Randall and his upcoming stories at
http://randallkrzak.com

Acknowledgment

A very special thanks to Les Stahl. Without his prompting, this story would never have been told.

To Gene and his staff at Moonshine Cove Publishing, LLC, for giving me an opportunity to share my work and for the guidance throughout the publishing process. Thank you for the journey.

Many thanks to those who helped me along my journey, including: Charles Brass, John L. DeBoer, Ann Everett, Rikon Gaites, D. Gesalt, Sly Jones, Mike Jackson, Michael Kent, Sylvia Krzak, Baylee McCoy, Tom Oldman, the Alpha to Omega Review Group, Claire O' Sullivan, Craig Palmer, Connie Peck, the Roundtable Pals, Janet Taylor-Perry, Janet Reid, Thomas M. Roberson, Mark Terribile, Amy Thompson, the Sunset Thriller Group, AJ Wallace, as well as other reviewers from The Next Big Writer and Scribophile.

.

Other Works

Dangerous Alliance
Note: This is book 2 in the Bedlam series, *The Kurdish Connection* is book 1.

United Nations' sanctions are crippling North Korea. China has turned her back on her malevolent partner. The North Korean military machine is crumbling, unable to function. Oil reserves are minimal and the government seeks new alliances.
Cargo and tourist ships are disappearing along the Somali and Kenyan coastline at an alarming rate. Speeches abound, but inaction emboldens Al-Shabab to seek their next prize: Kenya. The terror organization controls land but requires weapons.
Bedlam Bravo team leader Colonel (Ret.) Trevor Franklin leads the small international team into East Africa. Tempers flare as the team is embroiled in a political quagmire. The axis must be stopped to avert an international crisis but at what cost?

A Cartel's Revenge
(Bruce and Smith Chronicles Book 1)

A Colombian drug lord watched her profits diminish over the years. Unable to increase market share because of a shrinking consumer base and a new international competitor, she form an unholy alliance.
Olivia Moreno, head of the Barranquilla Cartel, struck a deal with a regional leader within the Revolutionary Armed Forces of Colombia. Little did she know but she initiated her own death warrant. FARC had an unknown support group who wanted a foothold in South America – Islamic State.
Forced to flee, Moreno is captured by a small CIA team. Fearing for her life, she spins a tale about using her money and manpower to destroy ISIS. Laws and rules of engagement mean nothing to her, only her life and family matter.
Will team leader AJ Bruce strike a deal to turn the tables on ISIS and stop them from launching a concentrated attack on the United States? Or will they be too late? If successful, will Moreno's reward be total control of Afghanistan's poppy fields or will she be doubled-crossed?

THE KURDISH

CONNECTION

Prologue
March 1988

Two weeks after the attack on Halabja, Dersim Razyana, an eighteen-year-old engineering student, returned from Beirut to the remains of his hometown—to bury his parents and two brothers.

His childhood friends, seventeen-year-old Ismet Timur and sixteen-year-old Hawre Vandad, were also victims of Saddam Hussein's regime. Ismet suffered horrendous burns over his face, upper body, and arms. His lungs seared by chemicals, Hawre became weak and developed a persistent cough.

Despite their injuries they numbered among the few survivors.

Halabja, a peaceful city of 70,000 inhabitants in Iraqi Kurdistan was surrounded by mountain ranges on three sides, the Sirwan River to the west, and less than ten miles from western Iran.

Forty-eight hours earlier, bombardments shattered the city's peace. Continuous pounding by Iraqi artillery reduced many homes to rubble and destroyed the infrastructure.

The earth shook with each barrage. The screams of the injured penetrated the putrid stench of the dead and acrid, billowing smoke. Many suffocated in the toxic air. Cries of grief over the mangled bodies of loved ones rose everywhere.

Rocket and napalm attacks resumed on the third day, March 16, 1988. Fires raged out of control and residential areas collapsed. People hid in basements or crawled under teetering concrete slabs.

The softening of Halabja had ended.

That evening, sounds burst over the city—jet engines and strange whistling noises like metal falling to the ground. "Gas!" someone yelled. Others picked up on the warning and shouted at passersby. People panicked, trampling one another in vain to find safety.

An aroma, not unlike sweet apples, mixed with the pungent odor of rotten eggs spread across the city. Birds fell from the sky. Insects curled up and died. Cats, dogs, livestock, and then humans sank to the earth.

Waves of Iraqi aircraft flew over the doomed, dropping sarin, mustard gas, and other chemical agents.

Those fortunate enough to be outside the immediate blast area fled. If they owned a vehicle, they drove. If not, they ran. The nearby mountains provided temporary escape as refugees fled into Iran. Those who couldn't became statistics.

More than five thousand died that day, and during the following weeks and months, thousands more joined them due to secondary infections and lack of sustainable medical care.

After burying his family, Dersim sought out his friends. He searched everywhere but couldn't locate them.

"Check at the hospital." A masked worker paused his search through the rubble to speak with Dersim. "The authorities transported many injured people to Zakho."

***

Dersim made the trip to Zakho's hospital, arriving two days later. He spoke to several nurses, all too busy to waste time on a healthy person. A male aide recognized Dersim's frantic face as belonging to someone searching for relatives.

"Try room four. Many from Halabja are there."

The stench reached Dersim before he entered. A room designed to hold ten patients held twice that number. He went from bed to bed, stopping at each one.

In the far corner, he spotted them, crammed into the same bed. They appeared to be asleep.

"Psst. Ismet. Hawre, it's me, Dersim."

Filthy bandages covered the injuries to Ismet's face and upper body. Hawre, whose face appeared almost normal, except for burns around his mouth, opened an eye. "Dersim." He pushed aside an oxygen mask and stretched a shaking hand out to his friend.

"Dersim. I … knew you'd find … us."

"How's Ismet? He seems bad."

"Yes." Hawre coughed several times before using the oxygen once more. "They keep him ... sedated. So he ... will heal."

"No more talking, my friend." Dersim grasped his arm and replaced the mask over Hawre's face. "Rest."

Hawre drifted off.

"Sleep, my friends. I'll be here for you."

As his friends dozed, Dersim's thoughts wandered.

What's our future? How'll we persevere?

Chapter 1
Thursday, December 30, 2010

"You must swear by Allah never to say a word of what I'm going to tell you. If you promise, come to me. Now. At my house. Swear by Allah, or disaster might occur. This is the *most important secret."*

***

Dersim Razyana stretched his left hand toward the dun-colored rocks for balance as he inched around the exposed artillery shell. Once past, the breeze forced him to pull his tattered coat tighter around his body. Although bright and sunny, the morning wind carried a hint of rain from the nearby mountains.

He trudged through the soft sand caught in crevasses and climbed over a small ridge, an area without trees or any animals, yet only an hour's walk from his home. Dersim squeezed through the rusted barbed wire enclosing an abandoned military compound. Rows of derelict buildings stood like silent guards waiting for their leaders.

A once-impressive parade ground now housed the rusted hulks of forgotten vehicles. Miniature sand dunes stretched from the trucks, like fingers, with random shriveled weeds where some forgotten plants once achieved a foothold. Only the occasional call of a passing crow interrupted the silence.

"Come on, you two," Dersim said. He spoke in Sorani, a Kurdish dialect. "Don't take all day. There's scrap to salvage and sell."

Ismet Timur and Hawre Vandad, his friends for more than thirty years, stared at the shell. Streaked with rust, the shell was about seven inches in diameter, and at least two feet long. The men sidled by and joined Dersim.

Dressed in frayed clothes and wearing American-style baseball hats, they continued to move farther away. Of average height, the three men were wiry and strong despite their weathered appearance.

"Don't worry about the shell." Dersim raked his hands through his wavy black hair while he waited.

"Should we—" Hawre broke into a coughing fit. A gust of wind blew sand into his face. He took a piece of cloth from a pocket and wiped the grime away. "Should we try to remove it?"

"No. Through Allah's blessings, we've always returned home without injuries. I don't think any of us are reckless or desperate enough to tempt fate."

"Dersim's right. We don't need to risk our lives."

"Pray to Allah for more good fortune today to end the year." Hawre sank to his knees to offer a prayer before a convulsion ravaged his body.

They often traveled up to one hundred kilometers from Halabja searching for anything to salvage. The Iran-Iraq war had ended twenty-two years before but the once-fertile land yielded a meager living for the three scrap dealers. Together they spent many long days picking through the rubble of war-torn villages and the countryside, examining the insides of abandoned and derelict buildings.

Today, though, they continued to scavenge on a hillside east of Halabja, not far from the Iranian border. Dersim and Hawre loaded Dersim's dilapidated Turkish BMC truck with salvage they had identified during the previous three days. The truck sagged on broken springs. Cracks spider-webbed the windshield and the paintwork was so faded it became difficult to recognize any of the original colors. Dersim maintained the engine and other moving parts in superb working order, at least, when he obtained the necessary components.

Fifty yards away, Ismet screamed and waved his hands. Long-legged and built for running, he left the loading to the others. Dersim spotted Ismet, cringed, and ducked behind the truck.

"Hey!" Ismet whistled. "Dersim! You coward. Come here."

Dersim raised his head and scowled. "By the grace of Allah, don't yell! I thought someone was attacking us."

"Check this out. Wait 'til you see. I can't believe our luck." Ismet locked his hands behind his head and danced his version of the Kurdish Chapi. He pushed his left foot forward twice, stepped back twice on his right, while throwing his right hand upward, moving in a circle.

Dersim hurried to his friend, who stood with a broad smile on his dust-covered face near a collapsed wall by the hillside. The wall hid the entrance to a large cavern, and Ismet had dug around the opening, making a space big enough to squeeze through.

"What did you find?" Dersim bent down, pushing giant cobwebs aside for a better view. Through dark shadows, he made out a well-worn, dust-covered floor beneath stacks of crates.

"Ismet, go to the truck and make some torches. Use the oily rags in the back and grab a few pieces of wood."

Once Ismet returned, Dersim lit a torch, and they crawled inside.

"What did I say? I sensed we'd find treasure." Ismet whooped with delight.

Unlike many other areas they uncovered, concrete paved the massive grotto area. Dersim and Ismet walked between rows of crates stacked ceiling high, marveling at the potential value. Once they reached the end of the cave, Ismet spotted steps carved into the rock and lit another torch.

They descended a long flight of steps to a deep cellar. A hoard of military supplies stretched beyond the light of the torches. Their gaze fell on boxes of uniforms, boots, emergency food rations, tents, and medical supplies.

Ismet hoisted a small box of boots over his head, a grin still on his face. "We're rich, we're rich. Allah has blessed us."

"Let's check this out before you count your money." Dersim waved a hand in Ismet's face to bring him back to earth. "We've found other stockpiles suitable only for scrap."

"This must be one of Saddam's hidden bunkers. I can't believe our luck."

***

Hawre leaned against a pile of rubble to ease his stiff limbs, shuffled a foot in the sand, and kicked a few stones while he guarded the main entrance. A gust of wind blew grit into his face, which he cleaned with a dirty piece of cloth.

"Allah has blessed us!" He overheard Ismet's muffled shout and entered the cave to join the others.

***

"Ismet, you and I'll sort through the items. Hawre, please go back outside and warn us if anyone comes near." *I hope he's a better watchman than he's a scavenger. I wonder if his illness is getting worse.*

Departing, Hawre launched into another coughing fit. He wiped his mouth with his rag. Before putting the cloth back in his pocket, he saw bloodstains, more than last time.

Four hours later, Dersim and Ismet completed their inventory of the cave. Dersim stretched his weary back. "How many uniforms?"

"I stopped counting when I reached one hundred."

Dersim gasped. "What?"

"Brand new. They're all from the Iraqi Army. At least two hundred pairs of boots, too."

"I found hundreds of boxed meals and many cases of bottled water." Dersim pointed down the corridor. "Must be at least fifty to seventy boxes of medical supplies."

"These items are worth a fortune! And we still must count the weapons."

Together they stacked the weapons. Ismet estimated at least fifty Kalashnikov AK-47 assault rifles and seventy-five Glock pistols. Dersim tallied the boxes of ammunition, one for each weapon, and over one hundred 7.62mm magazines.

Along one wall, hidden by a discarded tarp, they found another stack of wooden crates. Dersim pried open the first one with a small crowbar.

Crack!

The dry wood shattered as he forced the lid open, sending splinters and dust into the air. A damp odor wafted from the container. Moving aside an oily cloth, the contents appeared.

Grenades! What a find.

The squeak of nails forced out of their holes and labored breathing filled the air. An odor of mildew mixed with the tang of lubricants and aged pine made breathing difficult. When he finished, he counted ten crates filled with grenades, while another ten contained plastic explosives.

Ismet kept repeating, "We're rich," as he worked.

Dersim mumbled. "You realize we must keep this quiet? Control yourself and be careful where you wave your torch. You might set something on fire and blow us up."

Gravel trickled into the cave entrance and echoed throughout the chamber. The two men froze.

His heart racing, Dersim whispered, "What was that?"

Wide-eyed, Ismet shook his head.

The next sound, Hawre coughing, flooded Dersim with frustrated relief. "Hawre," he said. "Go back to your post. I told you before, pay attention. We don't want anyone to sneak up on us. You'll be able to view everything later."

Hawre shuffled back outside to the wall and sat down. He pulled his wooden prayer beads from a pocket and recited the ritual prayers of the Tasbih to praise and glorify Allah.

While Dersim opened the crates, Ismet found a large steel container secured by an old padlock. He forced the lock with a chisel and hammer from the truck and found six more boxes, each larger than those holding the grenades and explosives. A hand-painted Iraqi flag covered the side. Across the top, a single word written in Arabic script: DANGER. He called Dersim over.

Curious to find out what they contained, they opened the boxes, one at a time, using slow, controlled movements.

"Ismet, be careful with those tools."

Ismet reached down to pick up the pry bar and wrapped the end in a rag. "Sorry, Dersim."

Each box contained nine canisters, wrapped in protective padding. Dersim pulled one out. "Ever come across one of these before?"

Ismet shook his head and pulled another one from the protective covering.

Dersim peered at the faded writing on the canister he held. The mixture of letters and numbers meant nothing to him. He waved the canister at Ismet. "Do you understand what this is?"

Ismet pointed at the label. "Skull and crossbones mean one thing—danger."

Dersim nodded. "We must be careful. Come. Let's move the stuff to the front of the cave."

They made more than a dozen trips to move the treasure to the cave's entrance. During one trip, Dersim found Hawre asleep against the wall. "Hawre, wake up! We need you to pay attention."

He gave instructions to Ismet when he returned. "When you go outside, scout the area in case Hawre missed anyone trying to sneak up on us. I caught him sleeping."

Ismet came back a few minutes later. "I found Hawre bent over making a terrible hacking sound. Is he getting worse?"

"Perhaps. I told him to go back to the doctor, but he refused. No idea how much longer he'll be able to work with us."

Dersim made a decision once they placed the weapons and munitions by the opening.

"The truck isn't large enough to take everything in one trip. Let's take the weapons first because we'll receive more money for them. We'll leave everything else inside until we return. Hawre, you must remain to keep your eyes on things."

Exhausted from the exertion of hauling their hoard to the surface, Dersim and Ismet gulped water and took a short rest. Anxious to leave, they finished loading with a renewed sense of urgency before anyone spotted them.

Stashing their find on the truck, they concealed everything under a load of scrap metal. The two men covered the load with large beige tarps and tied them down with coarse ropes. Dersim walked around the vehicle, double-checking the ropes and glancing around, searching for trouble.

No one. Must be my nerves.

Hawre stayed behind to guard the remaining treasure. They waved to him as they departed on the dusty forty-minute journey to Dersim's walled compound on the western outskirts of Halabja. Other than a couple of donkey-drawn carts and some wild dogs, they controlled the road.

As they approached Dersim's property, an elderly man trudged along the edge of the road, struggling under a load of chopped branches tied together with a piece of rope. He set the load down and waved.

Dersim waved back and slowed to a stop. "Allo, Ahmed. How are you today?"

"Tired, Dersim, but still breathing. It appears you've done well." He pointed at the covered load on the back of the truck. "What did you find?"

"The usual. Old tires, sheet metal, wooden crates. Even some copper."

"Good for you." The man bent down, grabbed his load, and pulled the rope over his shoulder. "Later. Tell Xalan I said hello."

"I'll do. May Allah watch over you."

Dersim nosed the vehicle ahead. Ismet jumped out of the cab and opened the gates, and Dersim pulled into his back yard. They unloaded the truck and covered the weapons with the tarps, weighting the edges down with chunks of concrete.

The men hurried back to the vehicle and returned to the compound. Collecting Hawre and the munitions, they drove back to Dersim's residence arriving as dusk fell. Two people stood by the pedestrian gate. As they drew closer, Dersim recognized them—nosy neighbors.

"Allo, Dersim. Where's Xalan? I came over an hour ago. No one answered. May I come inside and wait for her?"

"Allo, Rana. She took the children this afternoon to visit her parents. They'll be back tomorrow."

"Ah. Okay. Thank you." They headed toward their compound, glancing back at Dersim and the others as they did so.

When he pulled into the compound, he parked next to the house. "Let's move everything inside."

Dersim reset his simple but effective alarm system while the others hauled the stash into the house. Set four feet from the wall, Dersim maintained a rope-linked series of cans, half-filled with stones and broken glass. When disturbed, the contents rattled. During the still of the night, the disturbance couldn't be missed inside.

Dersim lifted a trap door hidden by a carpet under the sofa in the front room. "Hand the crates down."

The men worked together in silence. Noise not unlike the horn on a train shattered the night. The men froze.

The horn sounded again. A deep rumble shook the house.

"The guy lives down the street. He drives a big truck for a Zakho company." Dersim smiled, understanding the fear shown on Ismet and Hawre's faces. "Every time he's back he shows off."

By midnight, they secured the munitions in Dersim's bolthole, built to protect his family in an emergency. He set one of the unknown canisters aside. His cousin might understand the writing.

***

The next morning, Dersim wrapped the canister in a blanket and went outside. He placed the package in the back of his truck and hid the bundle beneath scrap metal. There would likely be police or military checkpoints along the way.

He hopped into the truck and headed toward Erbil, the capital of Iraqi Kurdistan, where his cousin Egid lived. Now a pharmacist, Egid spent several years in the Iraqi military and might tell him about the canisters.

If the security people take the baksheesh, perhaps they won't inspect the cargo. Dersim hoped he brought enough money for bribes at checkpoints along the route.

As Dersim downshifted to climb the next steep part of the road, the engine groaned. His eyes scanned for potholes, and he swerved back and forth to miss the larger ones. The vehicle shuddered every time he misjudged. He uttered a brief prayer. "Tires don't puncture, brakes, don't fail."

Reaching the apex of the steep climb, he inched the vehicle along, past an occasional boulder hanging over the road. He began the treacherous downhill stretch toward Erbil.

The brakes squealed as Dersim tapped them to keep the vehicle under control. A large grinding noise came from the back—the scrap iron slid back and forth while he rocked the vehicle to avoid the largest potholes. At last, the road leveled out again, and he boosted his speed.

Dersim knew he was approaching Erbil by the familiar gray smog of wind-blown dust and ash from soft coal fires lingering over the city. He wrinkled his nose at the pungent stench and tasted the coal dust permeating the air.

He approached one of the permanent security checkpoints outside the city. A burly mustachioed guard dressed in a khaki uniform waved a red flag, signaling Dersim to stop. "Where are you going? What's in the back?"

"I'm taking this scrap metal to the market."

"There's a fee for using this road."

Without a word Dersim handed over an envelope he prepared in advance. The guard grabbed the envelope, took a quick peek, and waved him along.

Dersim drove to the Erbil bus station and parked. He called his cousin when a pay phone became available.

"Egid, it's Dersim. How are you, Cousin? I hope all is well."

"Hello, what a surprise! Where are you?"

"I'm in Erbil with a load of scrap to sell. Do you mind if I stop by when I'm done?"

"Of course, happy to see you again. Come after I close for the evening. We can talk and not be interrupted."

"Good. Until tonight." Dersim returned to his truck and drove to the junkyard to sell his salvaged metal.

When he arrived, Egid ushered him inside the store and closed the door. They went into the back room where Dersim unwrapped his prize.

Egid examined Dersim's bundle. "*Bxo*—shit! Where'd you find this canister? It's dangerous stuff!"

"I suppose. I spotted the skull and crossbones and was careful. What's inside? Fertilizer or poison? We found several of these and plan to sell them."

"I can't be sure, but—see these letters and numbers? They're chemical formulas. Based on what I can make out." Egid picked up the canister and studied the writing. "*Sagbab*—son of a dog! I think this contains a chemical agent used in Saddam's gas attack on Halabja."

Dersim's heart pounded, and his eyes grew wide as he stepped back from the table. He remembered returning to the village after the attack, finding his family—parents and two brothers—dead. His best friend, Ismet, scarred for life, his upper torso, arms and face disfigured. The stench of decaying bodies had overwhelmed him and the screams of the injured and those in mourning haunted him. He shook his head, trying to erase the memories while tears slipped down his face falling to the floor.

"Uh … okay, thanks." Dersim paused, rubbing his chin. He let out a long sigh. "What do you think we should do? Perhaps we should take them back to the compound and bury them deep in the ground."

"Dispose of them. Don't mess with these canisters. Nothing good will come to you. *Dayk heez*—son of a bitch." Egid ground his teeth together and shook his head as he continued to inspect the canister.

Dersim witnessed the doubt in Egid's eyes. "You're right. They're too dangerous."

Dersim spent the evening with Egid. After a quiet meal, they retired early. Dersim tossed and turned throughout the evening. Visions of his parents and brothers swirled through his mind, tormenting him. At last, he fell into a restless sleep

The next morning, Dersim headed back to Halabja. Before departing, he wrapped the canister in heavy padding and secured the container in a sack of grain purchased with the money raised from selling the scrap.

Waving to Egid, he drove away, all thoughts on the previous two days and their unbelievable discovery. *Do I put the canisters back in the ground as I promised Egid? We might make good money for the metal, and not tell anyone what's inside.*

"Damn! What do I do?" Dersim slammed his hand on the steering wheel. "Think." *A lot of money to be made if we're smart. Do we keep the weapons and ammunition, and sell the other stuff?* "Allah, guide me!"

Dersim paid little attention during the return trip, rocking the truck back and forth as he dodged around the worse stretches of the road. His concentration centered on their find and the dilemma they now faced.

"That's it!" *Something I've always wanted to do. We can still raise money to feed our families. Perhaps … we'll also help our people. Create our own destiny.*

Dersim went straight to the post office when he arrived in Halabja. He used the outside pay phone to call his cousin, Babir, in Zakho, to check if he'd a sufficient supply of goods for him to transport to Turkey to sell.

"Happy New Year, Babir!"

"The same to you, my brother."

"You won't believe what we've found."

"Tell me. What did you find?"

"You must swear by Allah never to say a word of what I'm going to tell you. If you promise, come to me. Now. At my house."

"Why the mystery? Tell me!"

"If you can't swear to Allah, disaster might occur."

"All right, Dersim, all right. I swear by Allah to keep what you say to myself. I'll come as soon as I can."

"This is the most important secret. Ever!"

Chapter 2
Halabja, Iraq
Wednesday, January 26, 2011

Winter weather delayed Babir's travel to Halabja. Severe rainstorms, interspersed with occasional sleet and snow, caused havoc on the roads. On Wednesday, the forecast hinted at clear blue skies for the next few days.

Babir fished around in his back pocket for his battered cell phone to give his cousin the good news.

"Dersim, it's Babir. The winter storms are over, and at last, I'm on my way to inspect your find. I'll be with you late this afternoon."

"Remember, to swear—"

"Yes, yes, I remember. I swear by Allah."

"Good. See you later."

By the time Babir arrived at Dersim's home, the sun had dipped to the horizon. A high wall, made of cinder blocks with an outer covering of unpainted concrete, surrounded the house. The dusty and sandy street housed similar compounds. Dersim's two-story dwelling towered above the barricade. Babir noted a fresh coat of lavender house paint. A large cement water tank, the same color, perched on the corner of the flat roof, with a Kurdish flag flying from a short mast.

Babir rapped on the door. No answer. He raised his hand to knock again.

Click.

A young boy, about nine years old, with black hair, large brown eyes, and two missing front teeth eased the door open.

"Yes?"

"Hello, are you Qesem?"

"Yes ... who're you?"

"I'm your father's cousin, Babir. Don't you remember me?"

Qesem shook his head. "Papa! Papa! Someone for you."

Dersim came into the hallway. "Thank you, Qesem." He ruffled his son's hair as he approached their guest. "Tell Mama, Babir's arrived."

"Yes, Papa." He ran to find his mother.

"Welcome, Babir. Come inside." They shook hands and hugged before Dersim led the way into the living room.

"What happened to Qesem's front teeth?"

"Football. He played goalie. A boy missed the ball and his foot smacked into Qesem's mouth."

"Ouch." Babir grimaced after hearing the news. "The kick must have hurt."

"Yes, blood everywhere, too. Please, take a seat. Xalan will bring us food and drink."

They sat on plush, armless, low-back chairs, upholstered in purple and yellow floral fabric. A moment later, Dersim's wife brought a large tray into the room and placed the platter on a side table. Qesem and a young girl trailed behind her.

"Hello, Xalan. Thank you for having me here. Been a long time since I last came to Halabja." Babir smiled at the charming girl with long black hair and dazzling blue eyes. "Who's this pretty little thing?"

"This is Pakan. She's now six."

"The last time I visited, she was learning to walk."

"Xalan, thank you for the refreshments. Please take the children into the kitchen. Babir and I must discuss business."

Once alone, Babir pointed at Dersim with an open right hand. "So what's the big secret? Why couldn't you tell me on the phone?"

"Last month, when we searched near the old military compound, Ismet stumbled across a stockpile of hidden weapons."

"Not unusual. You've found weapons before and taken them to Turkey to help our brothers."

"True. But … we uncovered many strange canisters covered with unusual writing. We didn't understand what they contained, so I showed them to Egid."

"Did he know?"

Dersim glanced around the room and leaned closer to his cousin. "He … he thinks they're chemical weapons."

Stunned into silence, Babir's mouth dropped open. "You … found … what?"

"Egid believes the canisters are left over from Saddam's gas attack on Halabja in 1988."

"How many did you find?"

"Forty." Dersim heaved a sigh and stretched his legs in front of him. "He said most displayed the same writing, a chemical formula. Four bore different inscriptions."

He didn't explain everything to Babir. They stored a dozen more in the attic. Dersim learned long ago not to share everything they found, even with family.

"Where are they now? What do you plan to do with them?"

"They're below your feet—in the cellar. I'll show you later. First, we need to discuss what to do with them. Ismet and Hawre will be here soon and they must be involved in the decision."

They sipped tea and ate stuffed grape leaves, hummus, and sweet dates while they waited.

After they had finished, Xalan entered and cleared the dishes away. Dersim's mustache dipped in his drink as he took a sip. Unaware, he smirked at how cautious Babir stroked his goatee out of the way before eating and drinking. *City dweller. My cousin's become an urbanite.*

A knock on the outer door startled them. Xalan let a small gasp escape as she covered her mouth.

"Shhh, Xalan. Go into the kitchen. We don't know who's outside."

Dersim rose from his seat, crept to the edge of the window, slid the corner of the curtain away, and peered outside. At least two people, perhaps more. Dersim wiped his palms on his sleeves as he tried to determine their identity.

Someone shifted and the moonlight made recognition possible.

"Relax, it's Ismet and Hawre. Qesem, please let them in."

Qesem returned a moment later with the two men. "Can I stay, Papa?"

"No, Qesem, I'm sorry. Not this time. Help Mama clean up in the kitchen."

After everyone shook hands, the four men huddled together and discussed the previous month's find in low tones.

"We'd earn much money for the canisters." Dersim stroked his mustache and chin, deep in thought. "But I'm not sure selling them is a good idea. We won't control whose hands they end up in."

"What do you want to do?"

Before Dersim answered Babir's question, Ismet jumped to his feet, knocking his chair back as he ripped his shirt open. "Look at me," he said. His eyes filled with anger and his breathing became ragged. "If those canisters contain the same stuff, this is what can happen." Deep scars crisscrossed Ismet's upper torso, arms, neck, and face. As the chemicals burrowed deep into his body boiling his tissue away, he'd ripped at his blistering flesh, trying to release the agony.

Hawre's habitual pallor grew paler as he hacked a loud series of coughs, followed by heavy wheezing. He gazed at his old friend, and placed his hand on Ismet's wrist. "Sit down, Ismet. Sit." He guided the still shaking Ismet into his chair.

The two men locked eyes, sharing each other's pain. The attack occurred twenty-three years ago, but they relived the tragedy every day, something others would never understand.

"Remember what happened to Hawre," Ismet clasped his friend's shoulder in support. "People called us the lucky ones because we survived the massacre. He's dying and struggles all the time. Is this the legacy we want to leave others?"

"Hawre, what do you think?" Dersim shifted in his chair.

"I'm not sure. If we sell them, we'll earn money. Isn't that enough?"

"On the drive back from Erbil, I prayed to Allah to guide us. He told me we needed to help our people. But how?" Dersim's head dropped to his chest for a moment before staring at the others. "Should we sell the weapons and hand the money over, or should we provide them to the PKK?"

"What?" Ismet wrinkled his eyebrows and frowned at Dersim's suggestion.

"We must help all Kurdish people, not only the ones in Iraq."

"I agree with Dersim. We all believe one day we'll live in a sovereign Kurdistan. Only one person can make this happen— Abdallah Baziyan."

"But he's in a Turkish prison." Ismet nodded, running a hand across his scarred neck.

"True. However, the Council will guide us. They want him released. No one is better suited to unify Kurdistan." Babir glanced at his watch. "Almost midnight. Are you going to show me your treasure?"

"Yes. Help me move the sofa." Dersim stood and shifted an end table out of the way. Babir and Ismet pulled the sofa away from the wall.

Lifting the trap door, Dersim flicked a light switch over the stairs, and the men climbed down.

"By Allah's blessings. What a find." Babir's eyes gleamed as he gazed upon the crates. He turned in a half circle, taking in the entire hoard.

"May I take a peek at a canister?"

"Of course." Dersim walked to the back of the room and lifted a cover. He pulled a canister out and handed it to Babir.

"No, no. I only wanted to look." Babir raised his hands to ward off any further approach by Dersim and backed toward the stairs.

"I don't think we can decide on our own, but if Allah spoke with you, he'd speak with the mullahs, too. Once I return to Zakho, I'll talk to Mullah Mala. Let him decide. I'll call you when the meeting is arranged."

"Okay. We'll do as the mullah suggests."

***

Two weeks later, Dersim made the 397-kilometer trip north to Zakho. The road, with more potholes than asphalt due to the winter storms, made for a slow journey. Each bump sent a bone-jarring wave through his body.

"Umph. Hope the road improves soon. Can't take much more bouncing around. Won't be good on the vehicle, either."

An uneasy drive through the mountains turned treacherous when Dersim lost control of his truck on a steep downward curve covered with black ice. With the sudden loss of traction, his vehicle skidded close to a thin, rusted guardrail. Veins popped out on his forehead, and his knuckles whitened as he clenched the steering wheel with one hand and grabbed the clutch with the other to downshift while pumping the brakes.

"Stop, stop!"

Dersim veered into the guardrail.

Screeech!

The tires gripped the shoulder and the truck shuddered to a halt, one wheel dangling over the cliff's edge. He jumped out of the vehicle and stared down a 500-foot drop. His body shook at the realization he might have died.

"Praise be to Allah. I thought I'd go over the cliff this time."

Easing the vehicle back, inch by inch, until all four wheels regained solid ground, Dersim continued his journey, albeit slower.

Once on a level section, he stopped on the shoulder. As the road improved so did his spirits.

He ate a couple of green apples as he sang a song by the Kurdish musician, Ali Merdan. Dersim had memorized most of Merdan's songs, but Xalan forbade him singing in the house.

"Dersim, I realize you like to sing, and I like music, but your voice ... is not so nice."

***

After he reached the city, Dersim drove to the store Babir owned with his mother's cousin, Gewran. A trio of bells on the wall announced Dersim's entrance. The shop was quiet—no customers to be seen—and almost closing time. The chimes subsided as he glanced around. Dersim walked down the main aisle, with clothing on one side, and textiles and carpets on the other. Babir stood behind a counter made from an old oak door.

"As-salaam alaikum." Babir grasped Dersim's hand and gave him a hug. "Welcome."

"Wa alaikum salaam."

"A good journey from Halabja?"

"Boring, although security guards stopped me at two checkpoints, both outside Zakho. I showed them my papers, and after a brief glance inside the truck, they let me go. They didn't ask for baksheesh. A curve had a patch of black ice and I almost went over—a bit unnerving."

"Praise Allah you're safe. Come, let's drink tea and eat. We'll meet Mullah Mala and the others this evening. Gewran will join us, too."

***

Perspiration appeared on Dersim's forehead and his face became flushed as the time for the meeting approached. His fingers beat a tune on the chair's arm.

Mullah Mala Sindi Ismail Osman used to be a member of the Kurdistan Democratic Party. He often delivered impassioned sermons at the Zakho Mosque supporting Kurdish unification.

Dersim hoped he wouldn't make a fool of himself in front of such a renowned man.

Babir and Dersim strode along the cobblestone streets to a store near the Delal Bridge, built during the Roman Empire. The sign above the storefront read *Dry Food Emporium* in Turkish, Kurdish, and English.

They wove through narrow aisles stuffed with a hodgepodge of bins and barrels containing Iranian pistachios, dried hot peppers, various spices, and dried fruits. The aroma of garlic, saffron, and mint floated through the air.

Dersim's heart pushed further up into his throat. Bile rose in response to the aromas he enjoyed, but today they assaulted his senses. His face paled.

Aware of his discomfort, Babir stopped and put a hand on Dersim's shoulder. "Relax. Not far now. We're meeting with our spiritual leaders, but your find makes you an equal."

Dersim took a deep breath and nodded. "I'm ready."

They entered the storeroom at the back. The closed external shutters darkened the windows. A single bulb dangled from the ceiling.

In the middle of the room, a large oval table took center stage, surrounded by nine straight-backed chairs with plump cushions. Carafes of fruit juice and plates of baklava were positioned at strategic locations around the table.

Gewran, Mullah Mala, and five other mullahs waited inside. Mullah Mala, a stern-looking man, wearing a patch to cover an empty right eye socket, welcomed Babir and Dersim into the room.

"As-salaam alaikum."

"Wa alaikum salaam." Dersim and Babir both gave a slight bow as they spoke.

"Please be seated. Babir told me about your interesting find."

"Yes, Mullah Mala. My friends and I found a stockpile of regular and chemical weapons."

Everyone stopped speaking, waiting for the mullah's reaction.

***

"Allah Akbar!" A shocked expression appeared upon Mullah Mala's face at Dersim's words before he controlled his emotions. *Did Saddam still possess chemical weapons when the Americans attacked in 2003?*

"Are they in good condition? Are they safe? Is anyone else aware?"

"They seem sturdy and are well hidden. My cousin, Egid, a pharmacist, examined them. Before coming here today, only six knew about the canisters: Ismet, Hawre, Egid, Babir, Gewran, and myself."

"Many nights I've prayed for the release of Abdallah Baziyan so we may unite our people." Mullah Mala pointed at Dersim. "Your find might be the key to his freedom. Once he joins us, we'll be ready, with a man possessing the necessary charisma and leadership to unite all Kurds together in our common cause—the creation of Kurdistan."

Shouts of *'Allah Akbar!'* and *'Baziyan!'* reverberated around the room. The bearded mullahs seemed to come alive as the chants continued.

Mullah Mala gestured for quiet. "Well done, Dersim. No longer will we suffer at the hands of others. We must do everything we can to break Baziyan out of prison."

Dersim nodded at the mullah's wisdom but remained silent.

Mullah Ahmed, a small, thin man, stood to address the others. "This'll lead to a great day for the Kurdish people. We'll require a workable plan, one that won't turn the international community against us.

"Should we try to negotiate with America? Give the chemical weapons to them and in return, the American president must pressure the Turks to release Baziyan. Having the weapons would vindicate Burns and make him a saint. We should demand America's help in creating the Kurdish state."

From the back of the room, a man stood and stepped forward. His bulk towered over Mullah Ahmed by at least a foot. The heavyset man stroked his long, white beard. "I agree with Mullah Ahmed. My first thought is to use everything at our disposal, yet we must recognize the fact most of the world forbids the use of chemical weapons. Perhaps their use isn't in our best interest. Remember what happened in Halabja—over 5,000 died. Would a threat of their use be enough or should we bargain with the Americans?"

"Thank you, Mullah Barzan. Your counsel is wise and must be considered." Mullah Mala acknowledged Barzan's comments with a slight nod.

"We'll meet again in three weeks in Mardin to lay out a plan with our Turkish cousins. They must participate." Mullah Ahmed turned to Dersim. "Please bring the special weapons to Mardin as part of your normal shipment. It'll be easier to keep them hidden in the area while we prepare for our fight. Go to Ali Baba's Third

Class Family Restaurant near the bazaar. You'll be guided to the meeting's location."

"Yes, Mullah Ahmed. I'm acquainted with the restaurant from my regular deliveries to the market."

"Very well. Dersim, you and your cousins may leave now. We've more to discuss."

***

Babir, Gewran, and Dersim headed back to Gewran's apartment above the clothing store. After making tea, Babir joined the others. "Gewran and I'll soon acquire enough excess goods to sell. We can use the supplies to hide the weapons when you take them to Turkey. Everything will be ready."

"Are we doing what's best? The mullahs are taking over. Should we follow Mullah Ahmed's suggestion and deal with the Americans?"

"Relax, Dersim. They'll decide what to do. We've done our part."

"Okay." Dersim tilted his head to the side as he decided. "You're right. I'll return in three weeks and bring Ismet and Hawre with me. Will you come to Mardin with us?"

"No, we'll stay in Zakho and keep the stores open. You know the market and the border guards must recognize you by now with all the trips you've made. Mullah Mala and the others don't need our input. They and the Turks will create the plan. Make sure you're part of their decision. Make us proud."

***

As Dersim returned to Halabja, he thought about the turn of events in his life since they uncovered the chemical weapons. He almost drove off a cliff, met one of the most ferocious mullahs in Iraq, and became involved in discussions regarding the future of the Kurds.

Ismet and Hawre oppose selling the canisters. Babir and Gewran want them for political maneuvering. What do I want? What's best for my family?

Dersim continued to ponder over his fate. Realization came to him.

This is Allah at work. I'm his instrument to provide his message to the mullahs. I'll do his bidding. But I still don't understand how he wants the chemical weapons used.

31

Chapter 3
Zakho, Iraq
Sunday, February 20

Three weeks later, Dersim returned to Zakho with Ismet while Hawre remained in Halabja, too sick to travel. Dersim promised to keep him apprised of their progress.

On their arrival at Gewran's store, Ismet stayed with the truck while Dersim went inside. Gewran remained busy with several customers inspecting the array of handmade carpets, lifting them to the light at the windows, and haggling over the prices. Dersim took a seat and enjoyed the ongoing discussion over the vegetable dyes used to color the wool and about the quality of the carpets.

Time passed as Gewran dealt with them, commenting about his generosity and people taking advantage of him. He shepherded the last customer out and closed the door.

Gewran approached Dersim, shaking hands and giving him a hug. "Welcome back, Cousin! Babir will be over from next door soon."

"Okay, thanks. Ismet is outside. We brought some of the goods, so we didn't want to leave the vehicle unattended."

Pots and pans above an inner door clattered as Babir brushed past, entering through the hatch connecting the stores.

"Hello, Dersim. I saw Ismet, where's Hawre? I thought he was coming, too."

"Hawre's illness is worse."

"May Allah return him to good health."

"Yes. I hope and pray for an end to his suffering." Dersim shook his head, a grimace on his face. "Where can we put the truck so Ismet can join us?"

"Drive behind the stores and go to the large green warehouse. I'll meet you at the front door." Gewran grabbed a large key ring from the table and headed to the back door.

***

After driving to the warehouse and locking the vehicle inside, Gewran, Dersim, and Ismet returned to the store. Babir had tea waiting for them.

"To your health," Babir said. "And our future."

They all lifted their cups and drank. Dersim drained his cup and set it on the table. "Now we must discuss business. During our meeting with Mullah Ahmed, he asked us to bring the entire weapons stockpile to Mardin."

"You're right." Babir nodded and extended an open right hand toward Dersim.

"Ismet, Hawre, and I discussed this. We don't believe we should take everything to Mardin at once. We even considered not taking any weapons until after the meeting. What if the Turks cut us out of the planning and action after we give them the weapons? What could we do? Nothing."

"What did you decide?" Babir shifted his eyes between the two men.

"We brought some." Dersim ran his hands through his thick, black hair. "The weather is still cold, and the security guards hurry their checks so they can return to their shelters. During warm weather they take longer, creating a greater possibility the weapons might be discovered."

"What did you bring?" Gewran poured more tea for everyone.

"About half of the weapons," Ismet said.

"What about the canisters?" Babir asked.

"We brought all of them, leaving the remainder of the weapons in my bolthole."

"They should be happy with what you give them. You're giving them the weapons they need. Come, let's eat. You depart early in the morning for Mardin." Babir reached back for a small envelope. "Oh, I almost forgot. Ismet, Mullah Ahmed gave me this letter for you. He wants you to go to Syria while Dersim goes to Mardin."

Ismet opened the envelope and removed a single sheet of paper. After a brief glance, he handed the letter to Dersim. "Can you please read this? My eyes are bothering me."

Dersim nodded and read the letter. "Mullah Ahmed wants me to drop you off in Silopi, and you're to head to the border crossing and find a truck driver named Kadir, who will take you to Al-Bab. You'll be given further instructions when you arrive, but they want you to go to Aleppo afterward." *I wonder what Mullah Ahmed is up to?*

"Did he say why?" Ismet scratched his scraggly beard, which hid most of his scars.

"No, but I assume you'll meet with some of our Syrian brethren. We wanted to control what happened with the weapons, but the moment we met with the mullahs we became subordinate to them." *Shouldn't he wait until we've met with the Turks before splitting us up?*

***

The following morning, the four men checked the weapons and special cargo snuggled on mattresses in the truck, adding extra padding to protect the chemical weapons. They piled the remainder of the truck as high as possible with goods for the Turkish market, including towels, sheets, bolts of cloth and dried food products. After wishing Dersim and Ismet luck, Gewran and Babir waved them off.

Dersim headed toward the Turkish-Iraqi border. Snow-capped peaks glimmered in the morning sunshine. The day promised to be warm.

Experience taught him good weather didn't mean smooth roads. As with the route from Halabja to Zakho, potholes littered the highway to the border. They bounced over the uneven surface and swayed as Dersim swerved to miss the deeper holes.

After several miles into the journey, they slowed to a crawl. Scattered from one side of the road to the other, small piles of stones created hazards.

"What're the rock piles for?" Ismet pointed at a tall stack near the front fender.

"They're used to mark broken-down vehicles. Most of the time, drivers leave the piles behind, creating traffic hazards. Once I missed a stack and ran straight over the stones, puncturing a tire. As long as they're spotted in time, no problem."

Dersim and Ismet joined the long line of vehicles waiting to pass through the Ibrahim al-Khalil checkpoint. The Turkish guards appeared vigilant. Most times they carried their weapons slung over their shoulders, but today the guards pointed their rifles in the general direction of the vehicles as if expecting an attack.

"What's taking so long?" Ismet fidgeted, glancing in the mirror on his side of the vehicle and out the driver's window. His face grew pale as the wait stretched out.

"Relax, Ismet. Something spooked the guards. We need to be calm and act natural."

"But, Dersim, our load … what if they discover the weapons?"

"Shhh. Be quiet. For both our sake."

"Look! They're searching the vehicle ahead, pulling stuff out." Ismet became agitated as he witnessed the guards unloading part of the van in front of them.

"Nothing we can do. Allah will protect us."

An hour later, a guard motioned for Dersim to pull forward for inspection by two Turkish border guards.

A burly, bald man, with a mustache covering half of his face, wearing the red stripes of an *uzman cavus*, or corporal, stepped forward. He glanced at their papers and the falsified cargo manifest, before handing them back to Dersim. "Out of the vehicle. Come with me."

The three men went to the back. The corporal climbed up to check the load. "What're you carrying?"

"We—we're carrying textiles and foodstuffs from Zakho to sell in the Mardin markets." Dersim pretended to be nervous for the guard's benefit.

The corporal made a cursory check, opening a couple of boxes. Dersim glanced at Ismet, who grew paler and bounced from one foot to the other.

"Relax," Dersim said. "These checks are normal."

Ismet gave a weak smile. "I'll try, but what if he finds the stuff?"

Dersim shook his head. "Shhh. Don't worry. Everything's about money, and this'll be over soon."

A few minutes later, the guard climbed down from the back of the truck, gazed around, and stared in their direction. Dersim glared back. *No matter how many times I come through this checkpoint, they always expect baksheesh.*

Without a word, Dersim slid an envelope out of his pocket and handed it over. The guard thumbed through the wad of Turkish lira. "You may go."

Dersim nodded. He turned away, and they headed back to the cab. *Of all the times for a vigilant guard, it'd be while we're trying to cross into Turkey with something special to hide.*

"I almost passed out when he said to step out of the vehicle and come with him." The color in Ismet's face returned as the potential danger of the situation passed.

"Most of the time the guards hold out their hands for the envelope. I wonder why the extra scrutiny?" Dersim waved a hand in dismissal. "Not sure why the extra guard came snooping, but he left soon enough. Of course, the guard with us concerned me more."

Recovered, Ismet breathed a deep sigh. "*Bxo*—shit! I hope we don't go through another checkpoint."

The drive to Silopi took over thirty minutes and passed without incident. They continued to discuss possible ways on how to use the weapons to break Baziyan out of prison.

"What will be the best way to free him?" Ismet rubbed his chin as he pondered the possibilities. "Perhaps, storm the prison gates and rush in, or attack from a distance with RPGs and force our way?"

"Ismet, I'm sure the mullahs will create a plan. We might speculate all day and not be close to what they want."

Once they arrived in Silopi, Dersim drove to the bus station. Ismet collected two bags from behind the seat. "May Allah guide you in Mardin."

"And you in Syria. Hope you find Kadir without any difficulty. May Allah protect you."

Dersim waved farewell and proceeded toward the E90 highway for the journey to Mardin, which would take a little over three hours.

***

At one p.m., Dersim parked near the Mardin Bazaar and headed across the street to Ali Baba's restaurant for something to eat while he waited for his contact. He took a window seat to watch for anyone tampering with his truck. Two men came in and signaled him. He recognized Mullah Ahmed, a committee member from Zakho. Dersim paid his bill, left the building and followed them to his truck.

The three men climbed into the cab. Mullah Ahmed introduced the stranger. "This is Aram. After we drop off Babir's goods in the bazaar, he'll guide us to our meeting location."

The bazaar bustled, horns blared, vendors hawked their wares, radios played a variety of songs. Bright-colored canopies created shade for the stalls, while along the edge of the bazaar, old wood buildings stood like sentries. Freshly painted buildings of pastel colors mingled with those needing repair.

Dersim drove along the cobbled street. Every driver remained on alert as children ran everywhere while goats and sheep wandered around, looking for anything edible.

"I love the bazaar." Dersim inhaled, sucking in the smells. "Always an adventure. The whiff of roasting chestnuts and cooking meats always sets my mouth watering, even after I've eaten."

Aram nodded. "Yes, everything's available, from sweet dates to hand grenades. Whatever you want can be acquired here for the right price."

They pulled up to a large warehouse on the edge of the bazaar. Two workers stood ready to receive Babir's legitimate goods. Aram scrounged a chair from a nearby stall for Mullah Ahmed.

After unloading Babir's goods, they placed a second tarp and new supplies on top of the hidden load. Dersim, Aram, and Mullah Ahmed returned to the cab. Aram became their guide.

"Head toward Mardin Castle. I'll tell you where to turn."

They drove in silence toward the tenth century castle, perched high on the hill above the city. The castle's reddish brick and stone seemed pristine while some areas succumbed to ravages of time. "Turn right at the next street and continue until you come to a long loading dock behind a row of shops."

Dersim maneuvered along a narrow, cobblestoned street and stopped by a wooden loading dock near some steps. While he and Aram removed the tarp from the back of the truck, Mullah Ahmed went up the steps and into a shop.

Three men came outside and helped them unload the truck and place everything in a storeroom. Before they left the shop, Dersim grabbed a canister and put it in a burlap bag Aram gave him. Mullah Ahmed shut and locked the door.

Aram arranged for food and drink, as they would remain in the store until evening. After the shops closed around eleven p.m. and the streets became quiet, Aram guided Dersim to a back room in a building across the street.

They entered an old three-story structure with broken windows, covered with peeling paint and graffiti sprayed by local soccer team supporters. As they made their way to a large back room, they maneuvered around stacks of damaged furniture and litter. Inside, a long varnished table, with polished wood resembling glass, took center stage. Ten men, including the three Iraqi mullahs, sat at the table. Mullah Mala, the firebrand speaker from Zakho, greeted Dersim. "Welcome. Join us and I'll introduce you."

"Thank you, Mullah Mala. I'm honored to be here."

A tall, heavyset man with black hair, a long black beard, and piercing dark eyes stood. "This is Mufti Mehmed Salih Tanreverdi. He's the mufti of Diyarbakir Province and our honorable host for this evening."

"Welcome, young Dersim. Mullah Ahmed tells me you made an astounding discovery."

Dersim's eyes widened, and he trembled. The mufti, considered one of Abdallah Baziyan's closest friends and his most important advisor, thrust out his hand and gave a warm smile. Dersim took the proffered hand and stammered, "I-It's a special honor to meet you, Mufti Tanreverdi." The mufti took Dersim by the arm and introduced him to several men, each representing one of the adjoining provinces.

During the introductions, Dersim continued holding the burlap bag by a thick strap sewn into the fabric. Mullah Ahmed noted this and pointed at Dersim's hand. "Is this the special weapon?"

"Yes." Dersim placed the package on the table and extracted the cylinder.

Everyone spoke at once as they examined Dersim's treasure. All eyes focused on the simple, gray-colored container with unknown symbols. No one moved forward to touch. The men circled around the table, scrutinizing the canister from all angles. Questions abounded from those staring at the device.

"How does the canister work? Doesn't seem much different from an olive oil container. Will the contents kill our enemies? Are we safe?"

After they had appraised Dersim's find, they took their seats. Dersim covered the canister.

A knock on an inner door brought the discussion to a close. Several servants brought in platters of food, pitchers of water and ayran, the Turkish yogurt drink. After a light meal of rice pilaf and grilled vegetables, the debate continued.

"Dersim's discovery will aid our campaign for a new Kurdistan nation." Mufti Ismail stood and leaned on the back of his chair. "Turkish government organizations would be good targets, but we must minimize civilian casualties, even foreign ones, if we want international support for our cause."

"Strong hands with leveraging power can achieve their goals. We need to pick worthy targets, even foreigners or places frequented by them." Mullah Omar crossed his arms after he finished speaking.

A few heads gave slight shakes to his suggestion but they remained quiet.

Mullah Ahmed raised his hands for quiet. He turned to Dersim. "Where's Ismet? I thought he'd be here, too."

Dersim glanced at him, eyebrows lifted, a frown upon his face. *You gave instructions for Ismet to travel to Syria. So why ask where he is?*

As Mullah Ahmed stared back, he gave a slight nod and a wink. Dersim realized the mullah was putting on an act for the others. Uncertain about the mullah's plan, he went along, for now.

"He's on an information mission in Syria. Before coming here, Ismet, Hawre, and I discussed what we might do to help the cause."

Unhappy with this turn of events, Mullah Ahmed berated Dersim. "Why didn't you ask me first? I'd have agreed because it's right to involve the Syrians. But I should have been informed of your intentions. In the future, do as you're directed and leave the thinking to me and the other religious leaders."

Continuing the apparent charade, Dersim dipped his head and apologized. "I'm sorry we didn't consult you, but we wanted to do our share to support the cause. When he finishes, Ismet will come to Mardin."

Although he appeared unhappy, Mullah Ahmed acknowledged their good intentions caused their rashness. He relaxed back into his chair and nodded, accepting their actions.

Did I make a friend or an enemy? Dersim pondered. *Wait until he finds out I only brought part of the weapons. I'll be an enemy, for sure!*

Everyone agreed with Ismet's trip to Aleppo. Mullah Abdul stood and addressed the others. "We must garner further support among the Kurdish people. Last week I returned from a visit to the Médecins Sans Frontières offices in Aleppo and Al-Bab. We should either threaten the foreigners or take them hostage."

"Taking foreigners hostage or even killing them might encourage some of the wavering Kurds to join the fight." Mufti Ismail returned to his seat. "However, attacking them would also paint a negative picture of us with the West. We must tread with care regarding foreigners."

Mufti Tanreverdi kept silent throughout the discussions. He stood and all eyes followed him as the room quietened. Before speaking, he ran a hand over his beard. "Our primary objective is to free Baziyan. We need him to unite the Kurdish people. Any further comments?"

"We should hit every provincial capital along the southern border from Hakkâri to Adana." Mullah Nasruddin, a nervous man, rocked from foot to foot as he spoke. "This'll cause panic and might encourage more Kurdish involvement after they witness positive action against the Turks."

Mullah Ahmed glanced toward the ceiling, shifting his gaze upon the assembled religious leaders, searching their faces. He gave a slight nod. *"Balê—yes."*

Emboldened after Mullah Ahmed's reluctant approval for their plan and the apparent acceptance of him at the meeting, Dersim stood. "We should divide the weapons, grenades, and explosives into small caches and hide them in different locations. I think the chemical weapons should be distributed in strategic areas, for ready access when they're needed."

Dersim, at first was uncertain of their reaction, the lack of expression on their faces. No one spoke a word, which encouraged him to continue despite his nervousness. "I suggest we hide them in historic locations. Should the security forces find out about the weapons they're less likely to locate them. They would assume stockpiles would be placed near potential targets. Who'd suspect historic areas to be attacked?"

Several of the leaders nodded approval. Mullah Ahmed also acknowledged his suggestions, with a hint of a smile.

Dersim thought *time to be bold.* "I want to be involved in placing the chemical weapons. Without our discovery, we wouldn't be here today." *This way, I'll control the canisters, so the zealots don't create a disaster for us.*

"Enough!" Mufti Tanreverdi thumped his hand on the table. "The moon's rising and we've been debating for hours. Now is the time for action. I've means to communicate with Baziyan. I'll convey to him what took place today, and advise him of the special weapons. Once he agrees, we'll act. Continue your preparations until you hear from me."

One-by-one, the mufti locked eyes with everyone. He filled his glass from a water pitcher, raised it, and took a sip. "Further discussions will occur over the coming days. Although I'm reluctant to use chemical weapons, if need be, all weapons will be considered. Assuming we do this in the right way, the international community will support our efforts. If we push too far, our undertaking will backfire and Kurds will be more subjugated than ever before."

Mufti Tanreverdi's eyes narrowed as he studied each man in the room. "Our first task is to free Baziyan. Under his guidance, we can proceed to our final objective, a united Kurdistan, even if it means war."

Chapter 4
Fort Myer, Virginia
Sunday, March 6

CC woke to the *William Tell Overture* playing near his ear. He rolled over and scooped up his smartphone. "Yeah?"

"Confirm full name."

"Craig Cameron."

"Code phrase."

"Tatties, neeps, and haggis."

"Identity confirmed. Proceed to Bedlam." The line went dead.

"Great, I start the day talking with an automated voice system."

He shook the cobwebs from his head and stared out the window. The sky remained dark, but the stars twinkled and a sliver of the moon glistened across the heavens.

He glanced at the clock—four a.m. CC propelled his muscular six-foot-two-inch frame out of bed and splashed water through his reddish-brown hair and mustache. Dressing in civilian clothes he shot out the condo door, hustled down the two flights of stairs to the garage, and hopped into his late model Ford Explorer.

He drove through the busy streets of Arlington, Virginia, lined with blocks of juxtaposed condos, joining other commuters heading to work at this early hour. The streetlights rolled past, bearing silent witness to his journey to Bedlam Headquarters—BHQ.

What am I doing? No common sense. Should've gone into archeology after the army. Now I'm rushing around in the middle of the night. Damn!

CC snapped a salute as he passed Arlington National Cemetery. Whenever he traveled by, he always honored his fallen comrades.

He stopped at Fort Myer's front gate, and the scrutiny began. He squinted, and half raised his arm to ward off a sudden beam of light in his face. I.D. check. Vehicle check. At last, a brisk wave of an arm from an unsmiling guard motioned him through.

He followed the road to a faded gray, three-story brick warehouse hidden in the trees near the rear of the base. After exiting the car, he began the second round of security. *Damn, why can't they embed a chip in my ass and skip the repetitive shit? One zap with a scanner and done.*

"What a waste of time. Don't you guys remember me from last week?"

Stony silence met his comment. When the robot-like, gray-uniformed guards completed their checks, one motioned him to a blue door, which clicked open as he approached.

Once inside, instructions on a flat-panel monitor directed him to the main conference room. Alone in the hallway, downlighters snapped on and off as he proceeded. He pushed the door open and stepped into a room covered in beige Soundsoak acoustical panels and subdued lighting. Someone sat at the main table, but fresh coffee on a small metal table beckoned him, and he spied a pile of pastries. Pouring himself a steaming cup, he grabbed a chocolate glaze and sauntered to the front of the room.

He sat at the long conference table next to Georgia White, Bedlam's logistics whiz, talking on the phone. While he waited, he ate his donut and sipped the black java without scalding his lips.

Georgia finished her call and turned toward CC.

"Morning." She gave him a big smile.

"Hey, Georgia, what's going on? I thought we didn't meet again until tomorrow afternoon."

"How'd you like the wake-up call? I wanted to test the new automated system. The voice provides instructions as soon as the software confirms your identity."

"Yeah, well, the creepy voice scared the bejesus out of me."

"We'll find out what the others think about the system. We might switch to a sexy voice to motivate everyone."

"Yeah, that would work. But I think their arrival would be delayed."

"A female voice is Toni's suggestion, so take it up with her, she's the communications guru. Once the other team members arrive, we'll be opening a video teleconference with Admiral Blakely."

"Are we going operational?"

"I don't know. He instructed me to recall everyone." Georgia said. "Still, aren't you glad to be doing something more meaningful than catching shoplifters at the mall?"

CC winced, accepting how drastic his life changed in a few short weeks. Every day, he waited for the mail, hoping for a positive reply from the CIA. Desperate, he accepted a menial job at the mall to pay the bills and soothe his aching ego. Just when the day-to-day grind of the routine job bored him, a new challenge presented itself.

General Michael Jones, his former commander and now the Chief of Staff of the Army, had contacted him and urged him to join a new organization. They met at a quiet bar in Annandale, Virginia, where they discussed the matter.

After ordering a couple of local craft brews, General Jones came right to the crux of the meeting. "CC, with your intelligence background, this is the right thing for you. We're putting together a small international organization of former military and intelligence personnel. The teams will work behind the scenes in conflict areas. I informed Admiral Blakely, Chairman of the Joint Chiefs of Staff, you'd be a good candidate to lead the first of three teams. Interested?"

"Who'll be my boss?"

"All contact will be through Admiral Blakely. He'll keep other oversight group members apprised of any activities."

"I appreciate your support, General. Can I think about the offer for two or three days?"

"We must know soon. Today's Monday. Call me by Wednesday."

CC realized, after a few hours of deliberation, he missed the excitement and danger of being a Delta Ranger. He had completed undercover assignments in Somalia, Afghanistan, and Iraq. After fifteen years of deployments, training, and action he became an adrenaline junkie, hooked as bad as any addict on skid row. No wife, no kids to worry about. He called the general. "If the offer's still on the table, I'm in."

This new challenge would be the biggest of his life. Not only did they consider him for this covert team, but they also wanted him in a command position, a prestigious honor. He believed he was the right choice to lead the group's first team, Bedlam Alpha.

His operational team would be lean—five members including him. Everyone came with the requisite backgrounds, experienced in undercover roles, decorated for bravery and courage under fire. Skilled in various martial arts, they had used these abilities in real-world situations.

***

CC remained lost in thought until a ruckus occurred near the donuts. Charles Edwards, Ph.D. and Antonia "Toni" Turner, Ph.D., teased each other over who should eat the last raspberry jam-filled donut.

"Morning, doctors. What about splitting the donut with me?" CC chuckled at their antics.

"Morning to you, too, and find your own." Charles took a big bite, raspberry jam clinging to his mustache. They laughed as they sat across from Georgia. Together, they would be the primary support element for his men. He continued the friendly sparring as the remainder of the operational team arrived.

Once the team grabbed coffee and donuts and joined them, CC introduced Georgia, Toni, and Charles.

"Hey, guys, time for you to explain who you are."

A black-haired, brown-eyed man stood to his full height, well over six feet and addressed the others.

"G'day, mates. I'm Jake Martin. After dropping out of Uni, I joined the Australian Army. I like to work alone, and someone shoved me into the Special Air Service Regiment. Did time in Iraq and Afghanistan. Earned a few trinkets. That about sums me up."

"Aye. Thanks, Jake. Who's next?" CC scanned the remaining team members as they all stood at the same time. "Like your enthusiasm. Let's go in order where you're sitting."

The shortest of the men at five-feet-eleven-inches, a muscle-laden man with close-cropped brown hair and hazel eyes remained standing.

"Well, y'all, I'm William Campbell from South Carolina. Call me Willie. I became one of them there Navy Seals for a spell when the CIA convinced me to volunteer for this outfit. Seems a better deal."

Everyone chuckled as Willie sat and the next team member, tall, blue-eyed blond-haired with chiseled features jumped up.

"I'm Dr. Benjamin Kingston. Call me Ben. Only my parents refer to me as Benjamin. I worked as a physician for several years before joining New Zealand's Security Intelligence Service. Someone suggested I sign up."

The last of the team remained seated. An inch taller than Willie, he sported short black hair and blue eyes. "I'm Aiden Johnson from Montreal. Until being offered the opportunity to enlist with this group I belonged to the Mounties."

"Aye, thanks for introducing yourselves. If you need a fill-up, grab what you want now before we talk with the admiral."

Once everyone settled at the table, Toni initiated the VTC link to Admiral Blakely's office at the Pentagon. When the admiral appeared on the screen, the room silenced.

"Good morning. Sorry for starting your week so early. I've spoken one-on-one with most of you, but this is the first time as a group. I apologize, but I thought we might spend more time together before we deploy Bedlam Alpha."

"Nae problem, Admiral." CC raised his right hand and gave a thumbs up. "We're ready. What's the situation?"

"Several groups of Turkish and Syrian Kurds are uniting to oppose their respective governments. Sympathetic Iraqi Kurds stumbled upon one of Saddam Hussein's old weapons caches in the Halabja area. The stockpile included chemical weapons, although it's unclear if these are functional weapons, including a delivery system, or only chemical agents. The Iraqi Kurds offered the weapons to these groups to support their uprisings."

"Where did this information come from?" Jake scribbled notes on a legal pad.

"A classified source. We believe it's genuine. Should these weapons be used against the Turkish and Syrian governments, there would be an immediate and catastrophic response against the Kurds." The team members glanced at one other but remained quiet. After scanning his notes, the admiral continued.

"The response might be worse than the 1915 Armenian Massacres. Likewise, should either government learn of the Kurdish plans, reprisals would be swift. This true of the Turks, who've had their fill of Kurdish problems. It's also an issue in Syria, as shown by the recent atrocities committed by pro-Syrian government forces against their people."

Ben raised his hand in the air. "Admiral, haven't the Turks and Kurds been fighting with each other for years?"

"Yes. The Turkish military initiated operations against Kurdish rebels in eastern Turkey over thirty years ago. After rumors the Turks used chemical weapons against Kurdish militants, it seems plausible the Kurds might try to retaliate if an opportunity arose."

"Did anyone confirm those rumors, Admiral? I read about them but don't remember if they were verified." Ben sipped his now-cold coffee, glancing at the others who shook their heads.

"Not to my knowledge. We believe the Kurdish groups will conduct simultaneous operations, starting any day. Intelligence indicates the Turkish military will resume their spring offensive. Since Syria is in a state of utter turmoil, there's no telling if the Syrian Kurds will be willing to wait."

The admiral paused before giving the team their orders. "Bedlam Alpha's objective is to locate and recover the chemical weapons and disrupt the Kurdish plots without either the Turkish or Syrian governments realizing the threats. I don't need to describe the ensuing catastrophe should the Kurds use their arsenal in either of those countries, Iraq, or Iran."

CC heaved a big sigh. *Well, I wanted out of the day-to-day grind. I got my wish!*

Chapter 5
Fort Myer, Virginia
Sunday, March 6

The Bedlam team reassembled in the conference room after a short break. Armed with their notes and a few maps, they resumed their planning.

"Everyone's had a chance to review the material the admiral sent over. I want to outline the data and compile a needs assessment." CC walked to the map projected on the screen, showing northern Iraq, Syria, and southeastern Turkey. "What do we know?"

"First, someone found the weapons near Halabja." Aiden used the fingers on one hand to highlight his comments. "Two. Kurds in three countries are involved in the plot. Three. The Turkish military will begin their annual spring offensive soon, eh?"

"Aye, good points. Anyone else?"

"Unrest continues to increase in Syria." Willie raised a thick hand in the air as he spoke. "This would create a perfect environment for adding to the ongoing chaos."

The others nodded in agreement, while Toni finished typing, split the screen, projected their comments, keeping the map visible.

CC reviewed the outline and nodded. "Aye. Good enough for now. We can revisit this later. Now, what are the unknowns?"

Ben stood and paced. "What did the cache contain? If they found chemical weapons, what kind? Are they ready to be used or do they require installation in a delivery system?" He resumed his seat when he finished speaking.

"Is there a specific target or multiple ones?" Jake asked. "When will they strike? How many are involved? Is the source providing reliable information? Last thing we want is to take action based on inaccurate information."

"Aye, we need more data about the source, too. I dealt with several situations based on little intel, but the source proved reliable." CC scanned the outline before continuing.

"We'll ask the admiral for more details about the source. He might not reveal anything further, but at least he'll be aware of our concerns."

"One way to obtain more information would be to go to the starting point." Jake pointed at the map. "Halabja. We need to develop our own sources."

Georgia cleared her throat getting their attention. "What supplies will you need?"

"Communications gear and tracking devices." Aiden glanced at Toni. "Means to detect the chemical weapons."

"Okay, we're moving on the supplies." Georgia made notes on a clipboard. "I'll take care of flights, rental cars, and hotels once your destinations are determined."

"Aye. We should start our deployment in all three countries at the same time and shift as necessary. We'll also need follow-up support once we're on the ground. Thoughts?"

When no one replied, CC continued. "Okay, seems we're all in agreement and ready to move forward. Toni, please reconnect us with the admiral."

Toni re-established the VTC link with Admiral Blakely's office. "Good afternoon, ladies, gentlemen. I trust our time apart was fruitful?"

"Aye, Admiral. Using available data, we'll adopt a three-pronged approach to Turkey, Syria, and Iraq. Gaps exist in our intel, but we're ready to detail our plans, including materiel and support requirements."

"Excellent." Admiral Blakely nodded. "Before you proceed, I want to cover a few things. First, the Intelligence Community is out of the loop regarding your operation. Few people are aware you exist. Once you deploy, you'll be on your own, but we'll try to obtain additional local support."

"Why is that, Admiral?"

"Leaks in the system. Classified information is slipping into the hands of foreign sources. Until I'm convinced this isn't the work of a mole, I want this operation on a strict need-to-know basis."

"Aye, understood, Admiral. We'll do our best."

"Additional intel surfaced from a second source. The Iraqis moved the weapons into Turkey and are meeting with Turkish Kurds in Mardin. It's possible they'll stockpile their weapons in at least two historical areas: the Cappadocia region and near Göbekli

Tepe, not far from the Syrian border. We don't know if Syria will be a feint and thus not involved in the overall Kurdish operation."

"Do y'all think it makes sense to attack historical locations?"

"Aye, Willie. They might not attack but spreading the word would cause confusion for the Turks trying to decide what to protect."

The admiral coughed, attempted to speak, and coughed twice more. "Sorry. According to the source, their objective is to free Abdallah Baziyan from a Turkish prison. He's the leader of the PKK—Kurdish Worker's Party—and led uprisings against the Turkish military.

"We think this group may attack military installations between Adana and Diyarbakir, or even try for a strike on Ankara. This would spread the Turkish forces across a large area and make things easier for prying Baziyan from prison."

The team glanced at each other and shook their heads as they digested the admiral's news.

"Aye, Admiral. Anything else?"

"Yes. They might make demands upon us, trading the weapons for the release of Baziyan and support for an independent Kurdish state. We're afraid if they push this, and we're unable to meet their request, they'll use their arsenal and begin a rampage of reprisals throughout the region. This might mushroom into an atrocity."

The admiral stood and disappeared from the screen. When he returned, he held a piece of paper and wore a foreboding expression.

"Gentlemen, we need you moving ASAP. I received another update from a source. He's unsure what will occur, but in ten days something will happen."

"Admiral, any recognized events of historical or religious significance in nine days?" Jake's eyebrows pointed toward the ceiling as he listened to the briefing.

"March Sixteenth—Halabja Day, the day all Kurds commemorate Saddam's bombardment of the city with chemical weapons."

Complete silence enveloped the room. The clock appeared to stop as if sensing impending doom.

"Well, shut my mouth." Willie blushed at his outburst. "Sorry, Admiral."

Everyone chuckled as the tension eased. Even the admiral cracked a brief smile.

"Gentlemen." The admiral scowled at his watch. "Almost 1400. I want an updated plan based on this new information at 1800." He broke the connection.

***

During the next four hours, the group discussed travel options, deployment areas, and supplies. Hurried phone calls to vendors requested necessities, printers spewed revised plans, and the clicking of keyboards filled the room.

A few minutes before their deadline, the room fell quiet. "Well done, everyone." CC nodded, acknowledging their efforts. "Toni, please contact Admiral Blakely's office. We're ready to continue."

The team waited in silence. CC stood by his seat, arms folded across his chest. The others remained seated, focused on the map.

Admiral Blakely's face appeared on the screen. "Good evening, men, ladies. Fill me in."

"Aye, Admiral. Bedlam Alpha is ready to deploy." CC swept his arms across the room to encompass the team members. "I'll run through our revised deployment strategy."

CC took a deep breath. "Jake will head to northern Iraq and Ben to Syria. Willie, Aiden, and I'll proceed to Turkey. We'll be in London tomorrow night and will proceed to our respective destinations."

He motioned for Toni to project the map on the screen. CC pointed to each location as he spoke. "Jake, under cover as a freelance journalist, will head to Halabja since he speaks excellent Arabic. He'll follow the path of the Iraqi Kurds into Turkey to pick up anything new.

"Ben will use his medical expertise in Syria, where he'll link up with *Médecins Sans Frontières*, or Doctors Without Borders. They're expecting him at their office in Aleppo. His passable Arabic should help him deal with the locals."

He made sure Admiral Blakely had no objections. After a hand motion from the admiral, CC continued. "Willie and Aiden will go to Cappadocia as tourists. Since the area is at least 100 square miles, Aiden will check out the underground locations, and Willie can prowl through the towns and tourist areas. We can modify their search efforts as they investigate.

"I'll join an active archeological dig at Göbekli Tepe, thirty-five miles from the Syrian border. The principal archeologist is German, Professor Konrad Schiffer. He's been directing excavations at Göbekli Tepe since 1995. So far only about five percent of the site is uncovered, so plenty of hiding places."

"This gets the team moving—good planning." The admiral jotted on a pad of paper. "We're still unsure what type of chemical weapons the Iraqis uncovered or what delivery systems they'll use. We're working to identify other potential contacts for you. In the meantime, you'll be going in cold."

"Nae problem. Once we're on the ground, we'll notify Toni or Georgia, who'll keep you informed. They can also pass along any new intel."

"Anything else?"

"Aye, Admiral. Georgia, Charles, and Toni located communications equipment, miniaturized tracking devices, and chemical detectors. I'm sure—"

"The comms gear will arrive later this evening, but the team will depart before we receive the other items," Georgia said. "Request approval to forward packages to our embassies or consulates for the teams to collect."

"Permission granted. Proceed with your plans. If nothing new by 0500 tomorrow, your mission is approved, giving you time to make your flight. Any last questions?"

"Aye, sir. Would you provide us with more information about the sources?"

The admiral tapped the side of his cheek with his forefinger. A deep breath sunk into his lungs. "They're well-placed and maintain first-hand contact with those who found the weapons. I can't provide any further detail."

"Thanks, Admiral. This shows how reliable they can be and how much trust to put in their intel."

"Well done." Admiral Blakely disappeared as the screen darkened.

"Okay, guys, let's go over everything one more time."

They spent the next hour going through their plan. Satisfied with their preparations, CC glanced around the table. "Any questions?"

After a round of headshakes, CC cut them loose with a final order. "Make sure your individual research is complete and we'll meet at 0400. Good night, gents."

Laughter erupted as the four men left. CC grabbed his belongings and returned to his office down the corridor. After unlocking the door and switching on the lights, he sat and booted his computer.

If the Kurds planned to attack the Turkish military, they might try to hide their weapons in multiple areas to minimize discovery. CC pulled up a map of Turkey on the computer screen and studied the locations of the larger cities.

The schematic identified large concentrations of Kurds in the Diyarbakir, Sanliurfa, and Mardin areas reachable from northern Iraq. "Assuming Göbekli Tepe doesn't show any promise, I'll head to Sanliurfa, the closest of the three locations."

At 2300, CC powered down the computer, locked his office, left the building, and returned home.

He tossed and turned as his mind kept ruminating over the day's events. CC thought about other missions and the men he'd lost. It occurred to him this deployment was no different, albeit a smaller team.

Although not a religious man, it never hurt to pray.

Dear God, please help me do the right things at the right time leading this team. Keep my men from harm. Protect them from the perils we'll face and guide us to a successful outcome. Amen.

Chapter 6
Fort Myer, Virginia
Monday, March 7

CC entered Bedlam Headquarters at 0330. The aroma of fresh coffee and the sounds of laughter greeted him as he strolled into the conference room. He helped himself to the coffee, and joined the rest of his team.

Georgia, Toni, and Charles stumbled through the doors a few minutes later, laden with backpacks and supplies.

"Morning, CC." Georgia flicked her head, a blond ponytail swishing across her shoulders.

"Morning. What's this?" CC covered his mouth to hide a smile appearing at the sight of them struggling to reach the table without dropping anything.

"A backpack for each of you." Georgia said. "All the tools you wanted."

Charles dropped three of the packs on the table. "Each one contains two satellite phones, a laptop, a hand-held trace detector, and a dozen tracking devices."

"I thought the detectors and tracking devices would be sent after we arrived." CC scanned through a list in front of him and made several annotations.

"That's what we thought." Georgia pointed toward Toni and Charles. "They worked their magic throughout the night and received everything two hours ago from commercial suppliers. The only items we must send are the Glocks, tasers, and CBRN breathing masks. The other stuff seems harmless enough disguised as a camcorder and accessories, so there shouldn't be any serious scrutiny."

"Great work, everyone. Anything else?"

"A folder inside each backpack contains new tourist passports, tickets, inoculation records, hotel and rental car reservations, various currencies and contact instructions." Georgia ticked the items on her pad as she explained.

"Excellent. Sounds like we're ready to rock 'n roll."

A low thump of drums filled the room. Everyone glanced around, checking for the source.

"What the hell?" Puzzled, Jake turned toward the sound.

Toni laughed. "My notification. Someone wants a VTC."

CC glanced at the clock. "0415. Must be the admiral."

Toni pressed a few buttons on her console, and Admiral Blakely appeared on the screen. Unlike previous teleconferences where the admiral wore full uniform, this morning he had donned civilian clothes and seemed tired.

"Good morning, folks. More intel." The admiral stifled a yawn. "The chemical canister is about the size of an olive oil container or larger than a half-gallon milk jug, gray, and weighs five kilos. The device can fit in a backpack and contains sarin, in a liquid state."

Silence greeted this new information. The team stared at one another, the earlier joking gone, and everyone's expressions grim.

"Bugger that," Jake shook his head. "The same stuff used in that Japanese subway attack in '95. Killed a dozen people and thousands more suffered."

"Admiral, how many canisters are we looking for?" CC grimaced and rubbed his forehead.

"Perhaps forty, according to the sources. The good news is the Kurds don't possess a delivery system. But if they open those damn things, there'll be a major catastrophe."

Again the room became quiet. Only the clicking of the keyboard from Toni's fingers typing the minutes broke the silence.

CC closed his eyes for a moment. "Aye. Sarin, a clear, colorless liquid which can be added to food, drink, or released into the air."

"Yes." The admiral straightened in his chair. "If the Kurdish rebels use this stuff—well, success is mandatory. I briefed the President, and your mission is a go. Good luck, and Godspeed." The screen went blank.

"Aye, now we know what we're up against." CC pursed his lips and frowned.

"Great." Aiden tossed his hands in the air. "Anything might be a target, eh? How do we find this stuff?"

Murmurs of agreement followed his comments.

"That's why we rushed obtaining the detectors." Georgia arched her shoulders up and down. "You'll find the canisters with the slightest trace."

"Listen up." CC glanced at the clock. "Almost 0445. Grab your gear and be at the loading dock in thirty minutes. Charles will bring a van and transport us to Dulles."

Half an hour later, everyone met at the dock. Once they stowed their gear and grabbed a seat, CC turned to the others. "Georgia, Charles, or Toni will keep us advised of any changes. Let's find those canisters."

***

At 0925, their United Airlines flight departed Dulles, twenty minutes behind schedule, bound for London. After a late breakfast, CC glanced around the interior of the plane before he opened Georgia's folder. The first item contained a single page:

Contact Instructions – Memorize and Destroy

1. Daily SITREPs are required, even if NTR.
2. Contact via encrypted satellite phone (voice and text) or laptop (Skype and email). Email is the preferred method to minimize mistakes.
3. Designated call signs:
•BHQ—Alpha
•All Team Members—Zulu
•CC—Haggis
•Jake—Aussie
•Ben—Kiwi
•Aiden—Mountie
•Willie—Rebel

He smiled at the hand-written note underneath.

Sorry guys, no time to allow you to pick your own call signs. Charles came up with them. Don't forget to destroy these pages, it's water-soluble paper. Good luck. Toni.

CC scanned the rest, equipment details, procedures for dealing with sarin, local maps, further PKK background information, and Incirlik Air Force Base access instructions. He put the folder away for later review, adjusted his seat and shut his eyes.

Next thing he knew, the overhead lights bathed the cabin in bright light. The purser instructed everyone to put their trays away and return their seats to an upright position as they descended into London.

Thirty minutes later, the passengers disembarked and headed either to the baggage claim area or other departure gates. The team stepped into a secluded corner, away from scurrying passengers.

"Well, guys, we're on our way." CC stretched, trying to work the kinks out of his back. "Ben, Jake, good hunting."

"Many thanks, boss," Jake said. "Good luck to everyone."

***

The following morning, CC checked out of the Dedeman Hotel in Diyarbakir, Turkey. Before unlocking his Ford Focus rental car, he checked in the wheel wells and underneath the frame for hidden explosives. Not finding anything obvious he unlocked the door, climbed in, and examined the penciled route on a map.

It'd take at least three hours to reach Göbekli Tepe, assuming he didn't take a wrong turn. CC put the car into gear and settled back for what he hoped would be a relaxing journey through the Turkish countryside.

On a decent road, he sped by villages and open countryside. Men and boys tended to cattle and sheep while women weeded fields of wheat and corn, the crops stretching toward the brilliant sunshine. He came around a blind curve and slammed on his brakes.

"Holy shit." He weaved through a herd of cattle ambling along the road.

Three hours later, he came upon a breathtaking sight stretching out in front of him: Göbekli Tepe. Ancient walls and pillars unearthed during previous excavations covered the hillside.

He pulled into a general parking area near several tents. Noticing his arrival, a white-haired gentleman headed his way.

"*Willkommen* to Göbekli Tepe. I assume you're Craig Cameron?" The portly fellow reminded CC of Colonel Sanders from Kentucky Fried Chicken, although black streaked his white beard. "I'm Professor Konrad Schiffer."

"Aye. Good to meet you, Professor. Please call me CC. Göbekli Tepe is a spectacular site."

"Ja. I am honored to lead the excavation work. Please, call me Konrad. We don't stand on ceremony. Too many people with titles to be so formal."

CC grinned. "Okay, Konrad. Many thanks for allowing me to join the team."

"Let me take you for a short tour and I'll introduce you to some of the others. Afterward, I'm sure you'll be ready for something to eat and perhaps some rest after your long journey."

"Aye. Sounds good. I want an early evening so I can establish a routine as fast as possible."

"Such enthusiasm! You'll start with everyone in the morning."

They walked around the excavation, with CC making mental notes of areas to examine when opportunities arose. As they strolled along the perimeter, CC peered into sunken areas where recent digging uncovered massive T-shaped pillars. Temporary shelters covered the most fragile areas to protect them from the elements.

"We believe this area contained a temple, about seven thousand years older than Stonehenge." Konrad waved his arms across the expanse in front of them. "We've found indications a large wall surrounded the temple."

"Did anyone live here?"

"*Nein.* Only for worship. The nearest river is three miles away, and people lived by the water."

"Aye, makes sense."

"Let's head to the canteen."

They arrived at the canteen tent. Konrad grabbed two cold Cokes and beckoned CC to follow him. Within a few minutes, he met several members of the thirty-person international team, who originated from South Africa, Germany, France, Italy, Spain, Canada, and the host country, Turkey.

After a leisurely dinner with the group, CC headed to his tent. Before climbing into his bunk he sent a short email to BHQ.

To: Alpha
From: Haggis.
In position—smooth sailing thus far.

***

Aiden and Willie missed the connecting flight from Istanbul to Nevşehir, the closest airport to Göreme, their first destination in the Cappadocia region. After an uneventful visit to Istanbul's Blue Mosque and a quiet flight the next morning, the men checked out rental cars at Nevsehir's airport.

They arrived at the Kelebek Cave Hotel about an hour later.

"Whoa—lookit yonder!" Willie gazed at the open expanse from the hotel's steps, providing a panoramic view across Göreme and beyond.

"Yeah, amazing, eh?" Aiden pointed at some fairy chimneys formed by erosion and chiseled by wind and rain. "I hope we've rooms inside one of those, eh?"

"Georgia sure outdid herself with this hotel. C'mon, let's check in."

They registered and went to their rooms in one of the fairy chimneys. After dropping their luggage on the beds, they returned to the main lobby for a glass of raki, both adding a splash of water before relishing the unsweetened, anise-flavored spirit.

When they finished their drinks, a member of the hotel staff waited to take them on a tour. "Welcome to Göreme. I show you good time. Come, this way."

Before crashing for the evening, Aiden sent a short email.

To: Alpha
From: Mountie and Rebel
In position. Thanks for a fantastic hotel.

***

Jake identified his departure gate and went to the duty-free area. Knowing from previous Iraqi travels that Western cigarettes were useful for bartering, he purchased eight cartons, stuffed them into his bulging backpack, and headed to the gate.

At 0815, Jake's flight slammed onto the runway. The pilot sped to the gate area as if his life depended on a speedy arrival. Jake surrendered a carton of cigarettes while clearing customs.

With time to spare before his departure to Sulaymaniyah, he found a quiet corner and sent a short email.

To: Alpha
From: Aussie
Touchdown in Green Zone, awaiting next journey.

Jake's flight arrived on time, and he waited with three other Westerners for a taxi. They would stay at the same hotel, the Sulaymaniyah Palace, the best in the city.

A banged-up taxi slid to a halt and the four foreigners squeezed into the vehicle, bags and suitcases shoved into any available space and tied to a roof rack. The cab took off with a squeal of tires, a huge cloud of smoke marking their departure. One of the foreigners screamed. "Slow down. Watch out. You'll kill us!"

The driver weaved across every lane of traffic and even the sidewalk to avoid several sheep. Jake, sitting in front, closed his eyes and prayed the journey would be over soon. A few minutes later, the taxi screeched to a stop in front of the hotel. Wide-eyed passengers bailed out, thankful to be alive. Jake took everything in stride, having lived in Baghdad, but he too relaxed when they arrived at their destination.

To: Alpha
From: Aussie
Arrived. Shaken and stirred.

***

As Ben's flight descended into Aleppo International Airport, he hoped his MSF contact, a Canadian doctor named David Johnson, would be waiting for him.

After a chaotic wait for his luggage, the conveyor belt lurched and ground to a halt—his luggage nowhere to be seen. He went in search of help.

Finding someone who seemed to work in the baggage hall, Ben spoke in hesitant Arabic, "Can you help me? My luggage didn't arrive."

"Come with me. Fill out form. We find."

Ben completed the form and handed the paper back to the man, who gave a brief glance. "Perhaps two or three days, luggage be here. Come back later."

He thanked him and when Ben exited the baggage area, he noted a large, red-haired man, holding a placard with his name. He had dark circles under his eyes and seemed frazzled. His head shifted back and forth as he glanced around.

"Hello, I'm Ben."

The man jumped at Ben's voice before turning to face him. "Welcome to Aleppo. I'm Dr. David Johnson—just call me Dave."

"Are you okay? You seem exhausted."

"Not getting much sleep." Dave said. He lowered his voice. "Lots of unrest in the city—constant gunfire and blaring sirens. I sleep when possible. Enough of my problems, goes with the territory, for sure. Where's your luggage?"

Ben explained.

"Don't worry." Dave tossed his hands in the air. "Happens all the time. We've stuff you can borrow."

They left the building and headed to a battered white Toyota Land Cruiser with MSF emblazoned on the doors and hood. The streets contained more potholes than pavement, and the constant jarring forced Ben to grasp the panic strap. Dave maintained a running commentary about everything they passed.

About an hour later, Dave turned down a narrow street and stopped in front of a once-white two-story building in Aleppo's Old Quarter. A small MSF sign was displayed on the door, with several MSF vehicles parked nearby.

"Welcome to MSF Aleppo," Dave's voice boomed. "We'll find you space on the second floor to drop your backpack, and grab breakfast before the locals knock on the door."

"How many people come every day?"

"Depends. Friday is the religious day of the week, so we don't encourage patients except for urgent or emergency cases. Otherwise, 75-100 people at this building. We try to reach out every other day into the surrounding neighborhoods and nearby villages to offer our assistance."

"Sounds like a packed schedule. Does everyone work seven days a week or is there personal time?"

"We work a five and a half day schedule, which leaves time for getting around the city and the countryside for those who want adventure. A few of the staff use the time off for sleeping, watching movies, reading, or sunbathing."

"Well, I'm the adventurous type, so I'll want to travel around." Ben yawned and twisted his shoulders to remove a kink. "What's my schedule for today?"

"After we eat, we'll sort out your sleeping arrangements, tour the facility, and introduce you around. If you're worn out by jet lag, you can crash. Otherwise, we'll take you out to some of the outlying areas."

"Okay, sounds good. I think we better keep moving before I fall asleep."

"Come on. Time for breakfast and introductions."

A few minutes later, Dave and Ben filled plates with scrambled eggs, beef sausage, cheese, olives, and bread. Heading to a table, they sat and Dave introduced Ben to four of the staff.

After breakfast, they headed upstairs to Ben's sleeping quarters, next to Dave's room. Dropping off Ben's backpack, they began a tour of the remainder of the building.

Ben didn't ask any questions but kept note of things to inquire about later. After the facility tour, he told Dave he'd reached saturation point and needed to rest.

"No problem. I'll check with you later about dinner."

"Many thanks for meeting me and showing me around. I'll ask plenty of questions when I'm more alert."

Ben took his leave from Dave and went up to his room, where he sent a brief email.

To: Alpha

From: Kiwi

In position—Baggage MIA. ETA two to three days.

As Ben closed his computer, a huge explosion shattered windows and rocked the building. The lights dimmed, then glowed so bright he thought they would explode before everything went dark.

"What the hell was that?"

Chapter 7
Mardin, Turkey
Wednesday, March 2

Mufti Tanreverdi scanned the room, eyes settling on Dersim, and motioned him forward. Once he reached his side, the mufti put his arm around Dersim's shoulders.

"Dersim received horrible news early this morning and came to me. I must inform you his childhood friend, Hawre, is no longer with us. He—"

Cries of anguish erupted. Dersim slipped from the mufti's grasp, tears streaming down his face. He fell to his knees. "Hawre … Hawre …."

Several men rushed forward. They guided Dersim to a chair and helped him sit. A man brought a glass of water. Others came, mumbling prayers and condolences, placing hands of comfort upon his shoulders.

Mufti Tanreverdi raised his hands. Everyone followed his lead as he quoted from the Qur'an.

After a moment of silence, the mufti walked over to Dersim. "I'm sorry for your loss."

"Thank you, Mufti Tanreverdi," Dersim said. "He couldn't live with the constant pain any longer. He took his own life."

Soft murmurings of prayers echoed around the room as Tanreverdi spoke to those assembled. "We must always remember to honor our comrades." He paused, his eyes running across the faces of the men packed into the room. "Hawre is our latest casualty."

**

During the two weeks since the group met in this same room, the mufti and his cousin, Afran Bengin Zirek, another key Baziyan advisor, often disappeared for private consultations. They mulled over the use of the armaments Dersim and his friends provided and weighed the arguments presented by the other religious leaders, before reaching a decision.

Mufti Tanreverdi now stood and gazed at those assembled. Everyone wore similar clothing, black, gray, or brown trousers, white shirts and dark-colored jackets. They returned his stare, anticipation of his edict etched upon their faces.

"With Allah's blessings, we'll scatter Turkish forces and create chaos. We'll target government facilities between Mardin and Diyarbakir, near Sanliurfa, in Cappadocia, and along the Turkish-Syrian border."

Shouts of agreement echoed throughout the room. Tanreverdi waved his hands to calm the group before continuing. "We'll also target military installations or police facilities. I'm reluctant to target the Cappadocia area because of numerous foreign tourists, but won't rule anything out if we can minimize civilian casualties."

Afran stood, signaling his turn to speak. "Despite constant conflict with the Turks we don't possess an independent homeland, nor control our own destiny." He slammed his hand on the table.

"What happened after Baziyan's capture in 1999? We became meek and declared a ceasefire."

Heads nodded at his words and several men stomped their feet in approval.

Afran's voice crescendoed. "We've always held weapons, many captured from the Turks. Fighting is in our blood. But, we lost our will. Our Iraqi brothers have once again stirred the fire inside our hearts. Let us begin anew!"

He raised a clenched fist in the air as everyone stood and applauded. After the noise had subsided, Mullah Omar leaped to his feet. "Eloquent words. What about the chemical weapons?"

Several individuals nodded, but no one spoke. The atmosphere grew tense as Mufti Tanreverdi let the silence linger. "During our initial discussions, the use of the chemical weapons became a contested issue. We want to create a united Kurdistan, and we'll need international support.

"I'm reluctant to say this, but I agree with placing these weapons in strategic locations. They'll not be used against the military. For now. If we free Baziyan but don't gain support from the United Nations, we'll threaten to use them."

The applause grew louder than ever. Almost everyone rose to their feet, cheering and clapping their hands. Everyone, except Mullah Omar, one of the Iraqi mullahs, who remained seated, head bowed.

Once the meeting ended, Mufti Tanreverdi pulled Dersim aside and introduced him to Afran. "Come with us. There's more to discuss."

They entered a nearby room where tea and baklava awaited. Dersim sat while the others helped themselves. Tanreverdi pointed at Dersim and the refreshments. "Your efforts honor the Kurdish people. You'll be involved in placing the chemical weapons in selected locations. We want canisters in two of Cappadocia's underground cities and one near the Uchisar Police Station."

"May I ask, why these locations?"

"I'm against the use of these weapons." He made a wide sweeping motion with his hands. "You witnessed the devastation they cause. Underground cities provide an opportunity to threaten tourist areas if required but minimize the possibility of accidental discharge. The police station is also a historical site so we can compound the threat."

"Yes, I understand what the weapons can do."

Afran, sat back, propped his ankle over a knee and spoke. "We took you at your word when you voiced your desire to be involved. You'll be responsible for placing the grenades and plastic explosives in two areas. One is the foreign archeological site at Göbekli Tepe, and the other is the border post at Akçakale."

"Why these sites?"

"We expect little support from our Syrian brethren, but these locations are within their reach. An attack on Göbekli Tepe would make international news while Akçakale is one of the major routes between Turkey and Syria. Closing this access would create panic and mayhem on the Syrian side due to their current civil unrest."

"We've selected two of our closest aides to assist you." Tanreverdi pulled at his long beard. "Serbest Pawan Rohat and Merdem Karza Dimen will accompany you. They frequent the areas where you're going and are trustworthy. You'll meet them in the morning."

***

After prayers, Dersim, Serbest, and Merdem loaded several crates into the back of Dersim's truck and concealed the deadly cargo with bolts of dyed cloth, fluffy towels, and colored blankets. Two crates held grenades, four contained plastic explosives while long boxes concealed the AK-47s, pistols, and ammunition. Separate cartons held the chemical weapons, wrapped in cloth and packed in plastic containers, providing extra padding during the long journey.

A large tarp thrown over the freight and secured, they hopped in the truck. Dersim threaded his way through the narrow streets of Mardin. Upon reaching the E90 highway, he headed east toward Sanliurfa.

As Dersim drove, he cast sideway glances at his new companions. *I understand the mufti and Afran trust them. But who are they? They must earn my trust. What if their purpose is to test me?*

Two hours later, rounding a sharp curve, red and blue flashing lights greeted them. A Tonka truck lay on its side with the cargo scattered across the road. Four police cars, an ambulance, and a fire truck surrounded the scene. The stench of diesel permeated the air. A police officer waved for Dersim to stop.

He slammed on his brakes but hit a patch of spilled fuel and skidded. The back of the truck slewed, the steering wheel almost slipped from Dersim's hands.

"*Bxo.*"

The police officer, eyes wide, froze in place for precious seconds as the vehicle veered toward him. Dersim tightened his hold on the steering wheel until his knuckles turned white. He pumped the brakes and downshifted. The truck's tires gripped the asphalt and came to a stop inches from the petrified man.

"What're you doing?" he said. "Aren't you aware there's always a checkpoint here?"

"Sorry, officer, but I'm from Iraq and don't always travel this far."

"Where are you going? What're you carrying?"

"We're transporting textiles from Iraq and Mardin to Sanliurfa."

"Let me check. Everyone down. Bring your papers."

The three men followed the officer to the back of the truck. The officer stuck his hand out for the documents. He studied Dersim's passport and the others' Turkish identity cards. "Where's the bill of lading?"

Dersim handed over the manifest, trying to still a shaking hand. *Do we run? Where would we go?*

After reviewing the document, he handed the papers back to Dersim and climbed into the truck. Air brakes squealed as a double tractor-trailer careened around the curve, its driver avoiding the stopped vehicles and the spilled load.

The tractor tipped on to the left side wheels as it swung out on the curve until the tires gained purchase on a stretch of dry road—the trailers' weight helping to pull the vehicle back down. The behemoth came to rest with its bumper kissing the back of Dersim's truck.

"Your lucky day," the officer gave Dersim a stern appraisal before rushing away. "I'll remember you. Move."

Dersim nodded, climbed into the cab, drove back on to the road, and maneuvered around the accident to continue their journey. As he drove away, Dersim glanced in the side mirror.

"Appears he made note of the license number," Dersim said. "Won't do any good. They're fake. When we reach a good spot, we'll take them off and install a new set. I had extras made in Mardin."

Thump! Dersim laughed as the tires crunched over the remains of a barricade, grinding the wood to splinters.

Serbest squirmed in his seat. "I thought we'd run him over and end up in jail!"

"Wouldn't happen." Merdem patted his side. "This will take care of anyone snooping."

"We caught a lucky break. Let's hope no more surprises."

As Sanliurfa came into view, Serbest was seated by the door with his elbow resting on the window's edge, a hand against the side of his head. "I know a good place to hide the weapons. Take the next turnoff, which leads through rolling fields to a small forest surrounded by large hills. Except for shepherds tending their flocks, it's vacant."

They bounced over ruts hidden in the ill-maintained track, overgrown thorn bushes scraping both sides of the truck.

"There's the cave." Serbest pointed to a small opening about a meter above the ground. "From the entrance, we can see in both directions, and wait for an opportune time to strike."

When Dersim stopped the vehicle, the men climbed out of the vehicle, stretched, and scouted around the area. Satisfied they were alone, Serbest suggested their next move. "We'll put a small weapons stockpile in the cave for use against either gendarmerie headquarters or the provincial governor's office building."

They inspected the area from different directions, but the cave's entrance wasn't visible. Satisfied, they shifted some of the textiles to reach the hidden load. Afterward, they hauled the arsenal from the truck to outside the cave. Merdem climbed the boulders and waited for Serbest and Dersim to hand everything to him

Finished storing the weapons, Serbest and Merdem concealed the entrance with old branches and leaves while Dersim swept away their footprints with a broom stowed behind the seats in the truck.

They headed into Sanliurfa to eat and spend the night. In the morning, they planned to continue toward the Cappadocia area, one hundred eighty miles away.

***

With dusk approaching, a shepherd entered the cave. He used it, too, when smuggling or hiding from Turkish authorities. The shepherd spotted the disturbed branches and leaves, now scattered at the back.

What's this? Something worth taking?

Chapter 8
Cappadocia, Turkey
Thursday, March 10

"Allah-o-Akbar"... God is Great.

The call to prayer resounded from the nearby mosque, shattering Willie's sound sleep. Two minutes later, the telephone rang.

"Good morning you lazy rabble-rouser. Rise and shine. Shall we begin the day, eh?"

"Morning, Canuck. Guess the singin' musta woke you, too. Meet you in the lobby in thirty."

Willie and Aiden ate a hearty Turkish breakfast of boiled eggs, cheese, olives, and toasted day-old bread, washed down with Nescafe.

"What's our first destination, eh?"

"Afore going to bed last night I read up on one of them there open-air museums. I think Göreme should be top of our list."

"What's an open-air museum?"

"We'd call it a national park or summit like that. Full of caves, old churches, and fairy chimneys. What the heck is a fairy chimney?"

"I think they're also called tent rocks. We call them hoodoos." Aiden spotted the waiters move toward a new group of tourists. He lowered his voice. "We'll take in the sights and check all the nooks and crannies where a package might be concealed, eh?"

"If y'all are finished, let's move." Willie spoke in a normal voice, as a waiter wandered by and asked if they wanted anything else.

They collected their backpacks and supplies from the rooms and jumped in Willie's vehicle for the short drive to the museum. After they had paid the admission, Willie bought a detailed guidebook before rejoining Aiden. "Did y'all catch everyone staring at us?"

"Not many foreigners here this early, so I guess we're a 'local' attraction for them. I read about the Turks being curious, almost rude, in the way they scrutinize outsiders. Be harder to determine if we're under surveillance, eh?"

Inside the museum, Aiden and Willie oriented themselves with the guidebook and spotted an imposing rock structure on the left, a former convent. Ten ancient churches were spread throughout the museum, with dozens of caves and small valleys to explore.

They approached the first church by climbing a black metal ladder bolted to the rocky surface. Dim inside, lit by the sun's rays filtering through the doorway and cracks in the rock, they stepped back into intense sunlight after their visit. Both men needed a couple of minutes for their vision to adjust before scooting down the ladder.

"Man, those frescos are incredible," Aiden said. "I've seen other wall paintings from this period, but these are the best, eh?"

"Yeah. Didn't spot anything else of interest to us."

"If they're all like this, we'll be finished soon."

Over the next three hours, they did the rounds, following tourist groups through the remaining churches. As the morning continued, the lines to enter the churches grew longer, and the two men sweltered in the blazing sunshine.

"Let's take a break." Aiden pointed to a quiet corner shaded by poplar, black pine, and Cappadocian maple trees. "Those trees will help cool us off, eh?"

They perched on small rocks, draping their rucksacks along their legs, grabbing water bottles and oranges.

After a long swig of water, Aiden belched. "I think there are a few places we should inspect with the detectors, eh? The Dark, the Buckle, St. Barbara's Chapel, the Snake, St. Catherine's Chapel, and the Basil Churches all with plenty of nooks and crannies."

"Perhaps, but we should do the Snake and the Basil first."

"We also need to check out the Nunnery."

Paths crisscrossed the three valleys, leading to numerous caves. By 1700, they finished a cursory check of a dozen accessible caves, including one so cramped they crawled most of the way.

Willie wiped the perspiration from his forehead on his sleeve. "Y'all get the picture these people were tiny? I kept bangin' my shoulders and head on the walls. Thought I might get stuck."

"Yeah. I'm glad you squeezed through, I didn't want to push you."

"We need access to the places closed to the public."

"How? We're supposed to be tourists."

"C'mon, ya big Canuck. Remember? The ticket place advertised in Turkish, German, French, and English, about private tours. They cover the main churches and caves, and some of the closed-off areas. We'll sign up and check 'em out. Like a tourist but smarter."

"Good idea. We'll arrange one for this weekend. Appears to be a night watchman, with a separate security booth unoccupied during the day. Not far away from a promising area for an evening visit, eh?"

"Yep, got a glimpse." Willie cocked his head to the side and nodded. "Tomorrow night or Saturday evening. We'll have a better idea about what to investigate further."

"Right. Back to the hotel and a beer or two before dinner, eh?"

Once they returned to the hotel, Willie squeezed the Fiat into the last narrow space in the now-full parking lot. Grabbing their backpacks, they headed upstairs to their rooms.

He inserted his key. Without turning the handle, the door eased open. "Shoot. Not locked." Willie's eyes narrowed to crinkled cracks. "I'm sure I had locked this before we left."

Aiden checked his door. "Mine's the same. Perhaps room service didn't lock up once they finished, eh?"

Willie stepped inside and turned on the light. "What the hell!" He moved in a circle through the shambles, his forehead puckered. "Looks like a bomb hit this place."

He bent down, scooped clothes from the floor, and tossed them on the overturned bed. Willie glanced around the room, shaking his head. "What the—? Someone's ripped open the cushions. Stuffing everywhere."

Willie pivoted on a heel and marched into the hallway. *Good thing we carried our equipment with us. Wonder if someone's on to us?*

Aiden strode out of his room, gritting his teeth, his face red with rage. "*Ça a pas d'allure!*"

"Would y'all use English? I can't understand your Frenchy stuff."

"Sorry. It makes no sense. Everything's tossed around. Shampoo dumped in the sink and shaving cream sprayed on the floor. The window was left open. Nothing to take, eh? All the important stuff right here." Aiden patted the backpack slung over a shoulder.

"Same here. Nothing in the room but clothes and toiletries. Wonder iffen they was after drugs?"

"Perhaps. We better complain at the desk. Like innocent people."

The two men returned to the lobby and went to the front desk where a clerk sat reading a magazine. He appeared to ignore them, so Willie banged his palm on the counter, causing the man to jump. "Call the police. Our rooms were ransacked!"

"Ra-rans … wha?" the clerk asked.

"A thief, a robbery."

The police arrived an hour later, sirens blaring and lights flashing. The manager met the officers and accompanied the group to the rooms, shooing other guests away while he wailed and clutched his hands to his chest. "This never happened before. Look at the damage. Who will pay?"

"We don't think anything's been taken, but until we clean up we won't know for sure, eh?"

The police officers poked around. They asked Aiden and Willie a few questions, spoke with the manager, and left.

The manager turned to them. "Other rooms are okay. If nothing's missing, they can't do anything. They offered to send a junior officer to sit all night in case someone returns. Our security will also be here."

"No, not necessary to station anyone outside. We'll clean things up and try to relax. But a beer would be kinda nice." *The last thing we need is additional eyes posted right outside.*

"I'll send some boys to help with the mess. When you're finished, please come to the lobby. I buy you a drink."

***

An hour later, they returned to the lobby and sat in big, comfortable chairs, a hand-carved wooden table between them. The manager rushed over, followed by a boy carrying a tray. "Please accept our apologies. I can't believe this happened." He motioned the boy forward, took two Efes beers from the tray and a plate of appetizers, and set them on the table. "Please tell us if you want anything else."

"We're okay for now, thanks." The manager waved the boy away and returned to the desk area. Aiden turned to Willie. "Enough excitement for one evening, eh? Wonder who entered the rooms and what they wanted?"

"Not sure. Did we miss something or someone?"

"Don't think so, but this place is packed with tourists. Turkish security officers might monitor the area. There's a huge drug problem, and they probably scrutinize foreigners to cut down on illegal narcotics, eh?"

"So much for having an easy time as tourists." A lackluster smile crossed Willie's face. "We need to be more alert."

"Yeah. Let's call it a night. I'll send an update on today's events, including this evening's excitement. Meet you here in the morning after prayer call, eh?"

Once back in the room, Aiden sent his email.

To: Alpha

From: Mountie and Rebel

Began mission—Nothing overt at museum, more time needed. Rooms ransacked—nothing missing. Surveillance possible but unconfirmed. Advise whether to continue mission or abort.

***

A dark-haired man sitting in a corner of the lobby lowered his newspaper and stared at Willie and Aiden as they explained their problem to the clerk. Beady-eyed, with a drooping mustache, he resumed reading, the paper hiding a smile on his face.

Sometime later, when Willie and Aiden finished the beer and snacks provided by the manager and returned to their rooms, Beady Eyes folded the paper, shuffled to his feet, and went outside, his job done for the evening.

Chapter 9
Göbekli Tepe, Turkey
Thursday, March 10

CC slept through the prayer call undisturbed. Konrad woke him after seven a.m. for breakfast. They strolled through the camp to the canteen tent and greeted the others. After filling their plates from the buffet, they claimed an empty table.

Stuffing feta cheese and beef salami between two slices of Turkish bread, Konrad broke off a large piece and crammed the savory sandwich into his mouth. After he had swallowed, he warmed up with his favorite topic. "Göbekli Tepe might be the world's oldest known religious structure."

"Aye, a real historical treasure. I'm looking forward to working on the dig." CC peeled the shell from a hard-boiled egg, added a dash of salt and pepper before taking a bite.

"Ja. We've been working here since 1995. We might dig another fifty years and only scratch the surface. This may be the most important archeological discovery ever."

After they finished eating and worked their way between tables to the exit, a gust of wind caught the side of the tent, and the flap fluttered before falling still.

"A bit windy, ja?"

"Ach no, you should visit the Highlands."

"Let's find Jürgen Müller. He's digging on a fifth stone circle. You'll work with him."

Konrad and CC climbed a slope to where a man knelt, sweeping away soil with a small brush. Around him, haphazard piles of stone stood where part of a wall had been uncovered. He glanced up as they approached.

"Jürgen, this is Craig Cameron. He goes by CC. He'll be working with you."

The man stood, gaunt and towering over CC and they clasped hands. "*Willkommen.* I hope we'll discover something to keep Konrad busy and away from us."

"Thanks. I'm thrilled to be here. What would you like me to do?"

"Grab a trench shovel and clear debris from what might the top of a structure." Jürgen pointed to the tools and to a small depression where he'd been working. "We must go slow, so we don't cause a cave-in, ja? We will dig closer to the stone, make a grid, and switch to hand shovels."

Konrad shouted at the two men. "I'll leave you to your exploration."

They waved as CC grabbed a shovel and joined Jürgen. Six inches of a massive stone had been unearthed. He loosened more soil, tossing each shovelful over the edge of the depression.

"If this structure follows the pattern of the others, we should end up with a circle, ja? The tallest T-shaped pillar so far is eighteen feet high and weighs at least sixteen tons."

"How many colonnades do you think we'll find?"

"Hard to tell, but we'll have a basic idea in a few weeks. Let's continue clearing away the debris and expand out from this pillar to find the next one."

CC dropped his shovel and helped Jürgen around the column, utilizing small trowels and several hard and soft brushes to sweep away the particles. When their knees became stiff, they stretched their legs and used several mason's lines and leveling staffs to measure out from the pillar.

During a brief respite, CC took digital photos using a telephoto lens.

"*Was ist los?* What are you doing? No time for pictures. Back to work, ja?"

"Aye, in a moment. Konrad gave me permission to take photographs."

Jürgen shook his head, a frown on his face, but didn't speak.

Three hours later, Jürgen and CC took a break for lunch when they observed others heading back. They grabbed something for later and returned to their dig. A few minutes later, Jürgen yelled in German.

"*Ach, mein Gott!*" He switched back to English. "CC, we've found another pillar! I can't believe our luck. In excellent condition, too. There are animal carvings around the exposed area."

"Fantastic, Jürgen. Show me." CC rushed over and together they examined the carvings.

A sheepish grin appeared on Jürgen's face. "My excitement made me too hasty earlier. Would you take photographs so we can show the others at dinner?"

"Aye, nae problem. Should we take measurements? Afterward, we can calculate where the others might be by measuring between the colonnades."

They determined their structure was smaller than the other excavations. "Take more photos, CC. *Mein Gott.* This configuration appears to be oval-shaped rather than circular like the others." A huge grin smothered Jürgen's face. "*Sehr gut.*"

They continued working throughout the afternoon. Tired, hungry, and thirsty, they plodded back to camp, covered head-to-toe with dust and sand. After a lukewarm shower to cleanse the grime away, CC changed and made his way to the canteen.

"Shh." Jürgen put a finger to his lips. "We won't say anything tonight about our find."

After dinner, CC excused himself. "Ach, I need some air. See you in the morning."

CC returned to his tent in the fading sunlight, uploaded the photos and sent a short update.

To: Alpha

From: Haggis

Photos of surrounding area attached. Request assistance in spotting areas to survey.

He shut down the computer, grabbed his backpack, and hiked along the camp's perimeter away from where he and Jürgen had worked all day. He planned to investigate a potential hiding place he spotted in a photograph.

*** *

CC rose early the following morning, eager to dig. He reviewed yesterday's photos of the excavation's perimeter so he could take overlapping snaps. Last night's stroll had not been unproductive, as he'd ruled out one possible location.

When he entered the canteen, Jürgen sat at a table in the corner, remnants of three boiled eggs center stage on his plate as he spread jam on his toast. He wiped a hand across his beard to shake loose any crumbs as CC approached. "*Guten morgen.* Are you ready for another exciting day?"

"Ach aye. What's the plan?"

"We'll continue where we left off. I want to make additional comparisons with the other structures to confirm sizes. We know ours is different."

After CC gobbled a slice of toast and grabbed two eggs to put in his pocket for later, the men headed back to their dig. They worked well together and soon located a huge stone. CC snapped photos of their latest find during a break. He also took more shots of the surrounding area, undulating hills, low bushes, and scrub trees when Jürgen's back was turned.

While snapping away, he spotted a small depression on a nearby hillside with a shallow path leading in the general direction. *If I get the chance tonight, I'll check this out.*

Jürgen worked on what turned out to be a T-pillar, believed to be near the center of the structure, about fifteen feet high, with a circumference of twelve feet. As Jürgen cleared away soil and debris from the sides of the pillar, he spotted a figure. "*Gott im Himmel!* Might be a lizard."

"Excellent work. Let me give you a hand so we can examine the carving." Huge grins appeared on their faces as CC snapped new photos.

After several hours of careful dusting and scraping with a set of dentistry tools, they confirmed the figure resembled a lizard. CC also found another carving with a lion's features.

Almost noon, they broke for nourishment. They rejoined the others and told them of the discovery, with everyone sharing in their excitement.

Lunch finished, as the men climbed back up the hill, CC spotted a slender, dark-haired man. Dressed in baggy pants, loose-fitting shirt, and floppy hat, he appeared to be another Turkish worker, but the backpack slung over his shoulder seemed out of place. He turned in a circle as if trying to gather his bearings, and rushed away. CC kept an eye on the man until he disappeared.

A short time later, the man reappeared near the depression, but no longer carried the backpack. *Hmm, I wonder what's up. Something to investigate.*

***

The day soon passed. They found additional carvings of lions, foxes, snakes, and waterfowl. Jürgen surmised they found another section of the wall supporting their find.

During dinner, Konrad produced a few bottles of raki to celebrate the day's success. CC declined, but after continued prodding, accepted a glass and toasted the others. "Here's to everyone's continued success and good hunting for tomorrow." When no one appeared to be watching, he emptied his glass under the table.

Jürgen, well-oiled from the raki he began drinking before dinner, lurched to his feet, thumping the table as he held on to his chair to steady himself. He drew himself up to his full height and gave a garbled speech.

Everyone laughed as Jürgen plopped in his chair, his head dipping to the table's edge. They ignored him as discussions continued about the findings and possible new grants.

Once the party broke up, people headed back to their tents or out for an evening stroll. CC returned to his tent, grabbed his pack, and set off to examine the suspicious depression.

Using a penlight, he found the path and strode up the hill, checking around for prying eyes before continuing.

The ground leveled out and dipped. *What's this?* CC squatted and examined a small mound of fresh earth. He scooped more away, a small gap appearing, so he enlarged the opening and scrambled inside.

After crawling about ten feet, the space opened, and CC scrambled to his feet. He used his light to search the area and found a backpack. A stack of small wooden boxes leaned against a wall.

CC snapped several photos before using a Swiss Army knife to open a box. *Grenades!* A second one contained several blocks of plastic explosives.

He turned his attention to the pack, bearing a small Kurdish flag sewn into the upper flap. The contents included several detonators, three Glocks, and six magazines. Inside a round cardboard container was a detailed hand-drawn map of the area. A second sketch appeared to be a military installation or a prison, with several buildings surrounded by a high fence, guard towers, and two gates.

CC replaced everything, checking the photos to confirm the position of every item. He covered his tracks and made his way outside. Closing the entrance, he continued his walk.

When he turned in for the evening, CC made notes of his discovery and sent a detailed report.

To: Alpha

From: Haggis

Found weapons cache—grenades, plastique, detonators, pistols. Also, a backpack bearing a Kurdish flag. Two drawings (see attachments). One a map and the other a possible military installation or prison.

CC turned out the oil lamp and climbed into his bunk. *What's the target, Göbekli Tepe? Is the diagram for a military base or a prison? Where?*

Chapter 10
Aleppo, Syria
Friday, March 11

Allah-o-Akbar! Come to prayer. Come to success.

Ben woke before Adhan, the Muslim pre-dawn call to prayer. Darkness loomed in the early light, he flipped on the lights, stretched and yawned as the muezzin's recording extolled the faithful to pray.

Light filtered through space at the bottom of the room's door. In the dimness, he inspected his surroundings, a bed, chair, small desk, and a wardrobe.

He spotted a piece of paper on the concrete floor. Curious, he climbed from the bed as the call to the faithful sounded again.

Prayer is better than sleep. Allah is Great! There is no god but Allah!

The loudspeaker attached to the nearby mosque's minaret broadcast toward the MSF building. Ben covered his ears as he glanced at his reflection in the mirror when he passed the open bathroom door. "Kia Ora, mate. Aren't you glad you woke before the wake-up call began? You'd be plastered against the wall. You're a quiet bloke this morning."

Ben left the bathroom, picked up the paper, and read. "From Dave … Good. Food—I'm famished."

Outside the door, he picked up a tray and set it on the small table in the corner. Ben ate a large portion of fruit and *Manoushi,* a soft and fluffy bread, and washed the meal down with a warm diet soda. Fortified by the refreshment, he showered, dressed in clothes borrowed from staff members, and headed downstairs.

Ben stepped into the reception area where Dave sat in an overstuffed chair, waiting for him. "Good morning. "Hope you enjoyed your rest, for sure."

"Morning. Jet lag got me last night, but I woke feeling like a new man. Many thanks for the food."

"No problem. The least I could do after your two-day trip. I wanted you to assist with some of the treatments today, instead we'll go to Al-Bab, a small city about twenty-three miles northeast of Aleppo."

Pointing at the food-laden table in the adjacent room, Dave continued. "Grab more and we'll go, for sure? We run a small clinic out of the Hotel Dar al Kanadil."

"No, I'm good. May I bring my camera? I like to take shots of my travels."

"Not a problem. But no photos of government buildings, soldiers, police officers, or anything that seems important. You'll be arrested if someone catches you."

"Thanks for the tip. Anything I should take?"

"Extra clothing and comfortable shoes. We'll stay at the hotel this evening, and there might be time for exploring the area."

Forty-five minutes later, Dave and Ben left the MSF building and followed the M4 signs directing them to Al-Bab. Unlike the jarring ride from the airport, the two-lane road was well paved, and Ben felt relaxed and concentrated on the scenery rushing by the window.

The landscape remained the same at first—dusty fields, sparse vegetation, and the occasional shepherd with a flock of sheep or goats. Green fields of indeterminate crops grew in the distance. As they continued along the M4, large groves of olive trees—one of Syria's most important crops—stretched from the highway into the distance.

Once they arrived in Al-Bab, Dave drove around to show Ben various areas of the flourishing city of 150,000 inhabitants. Leaving the M4 and entering the city, the streets became narrow, crammed with trucks, buses, cars, with occasional donkey-drawn carts and wandering pedestrians. Whitewashed buildings jostled for space, with small stores embedded among apartment blocks.

When they arrived at the hotel, Dave parked in the lot, and they went inside.

A tall, thin man with grayish hair jumped to his feet behind the check-in desk and rushed to greet them. "Welcome back, Dr. Dave! Good to see you again. Who's this with you?"

"Hello, Abdel. Meet Doctor Ben, who arrived in Aleppo yesterday. He'll be assisting me. Ben, this is Abdel Mahmoud, the hotel manager, and a good friend."

The men shook hands. "Welcome, Ben. Please tell me if I can do anything for you."

"Thank you, Abdel." Ben glanced around the lobby area. "This seems a pleasant hotel."

"The best in Al-Bab," Abdel said. He placed his right hand over his heart to reaffirm his words. "Almost all foreign visitors stay here. Let me take you to your rooms and we'll serve refreshments before a tour of the hotel."

After they drank a cup of strong Syrian coffee and sampled the dates, Abdel led Ben through the hotel.

When they finished the tour, Abdel took Ben to the MSF area. "The MSF are special friends. We give free space for clinics, and they give medical care to the staff and their families. We don't charge for the rooms but recommend a small donation for any meals, which is given to the needy."

"Thank you for the tour and the warm welcome. Now, I must help Dr. Dave."

***

The day sped by as many people required medical care, ranging from minor ailments to broken bones, and a couple of cracked skulls. After they had finished, Dave planned a snooze by the pool. He suggested Ben ask Abdel for directions to the best shopping area in the nearby souk.

Confident he would locate the bazaar, Ben collected his backpack and headed out the door. In a few minutes, he entered the market and browsed. Carpets, copper and brass pots, silk scarves, semi-precious stones, and jewelry covered display cases and tables in every direction.

A cacophony of voices mixed with music blared from several stalls. The scent of numerous spices and grilled meat made his mouth water. Several shopkeepers tried to steer him to their wares, but he shook his head and spoke in his limited Arabic, "Thank you. I want to browse first."

The shopkeepers nodded at Ben's use of their language and beamed. Aware he bungled most of the words and phrases, they seemed to appreciate his efforts.

Thirsty, he stopped at a small café and ordered a Coke, a Syrian coffee, and pastry. While he snacked, a small man with a scarred face came up to him and asked for some money. As Ben dug in his pockets for loose change, the proprietor came over to chase him away.

"Wait. What happened to his face?" Ben asked the proprietor. "What can I do to help? I'm a doctor. My Arabic is poor, so would you please translate for me?"

After a rapid exchange with the man, the café proprietor snorted.

"He says he came from Iraq and escaped with his life when the Iraqi military attacked Halabja. This sounds far-fetched."

"What's his name?" He waited while another quick exchange in Arabic took place.

"Ismet Timur."

Continuing to use the proprietor as an interpreter, Ben pressed him for information about what happened in Halabja and received permission to take photographs of his injuries. Deep scars crisscrossed Ismet's chest as if something clawed his skin. The disfigurement continued up the neck, spreading across his face.

The three-way conversation completed, Ben departed, taking care to leave a small tip. As he walked away, he glanced over his shoulder. Ismet remained stationary, his hands clenched into fists, an expression of undisguised anger contorting his features.

Ben continued his journey back to the hotel. Sensing someone might be following, he took advantage of storefront windows to check for surveillance. The street, almost empty of pedestrians, provided an eerie sensation, like one of the horror movies he watched as a kid.

Nerves took over. He checked over his right shoulder, and his left. Ben picked up his pace, crossed to the opposite side of the street and back again. Perhaps an overactive imagination, but he swore he'd glimpsed a shadow matching his pace. He shook his head, reminding himself he wasn't twelve anymore, and boogiemen didn't exist.

At the hotel, he went to his room, and took a shower, before going to the lounge. Several chairs and sofas were scattered around the room. In one corner, a dilapidated pool table stood, covered in dust.

Ben spotted Dave reading a newspaper and joined him to describe his trip to the souk.

"I met an Iraqi Kurd named Ismet. Horrific scars."

"Yeah. He's been a regular visitor to the clinic for the past two weeks, for sure. He said he received the injuries in a gas attack on his village years ago." Dave shook his head. "Impossible to comprehend what humanity inflicts upon another. I've witnessed many injured people during my time in this part of the world, but Ismet's injuries are the worst."

"I want to suss things out and help the poor guy if he returns. Must be something we can do to relieve his pain."

"I'll help, too." Dave pointed to several guests heading into the dining area. "Dinner time, for sure."

After a simple but filling meal, Dave and Ben headed back to their rooms. Ben booted up his laptop to compile his daily report.

To: Alpha

From: Kiwi

Began cover duties today in Al-Bab. Return to Aleppo tomorrow. Met an Iraqi man from Halabja who called himself Ismet Timur. Heavy scarring on his face, arms, and chest from Saddam's chemical attack on the city. Coincidence or first contact? Photos attached.

Once he turned out the light, Ben stared into the darkness, reviewing the day's events. *Is Ismet a survivor of the attack? Why did he seem so angry when I left? Did I imagine someone followed me back to the hotel?*

***

Across the street, a short, thin man dressed in a black didashah, with a red and white shumaq huddled in the shadows, watching and waiting. He adjusted the shumaq around his neck to keep the evening chill at bay. *Where are the foreigners?*

Chapter 11
Sulaymaniyah, Iraq
Friday, March 11

Jake left his hotel and took a taxi to Karaj Halabcha, to catch a bus for Halabja, his first destination. Once he arrived at the station, he joined the long ticket queue. Working his way forward, he listened to food vendors hawking their delicacies.

At last, his turn came at the window. In halting Arabic, he requested his ticket and paid. "How long will the bus take to reach Halabja?"

The ticket agent stared at Jake. *Crazy foreigner.* "It depends. On a good day, about two hours. Today, who knows? Allah will decide."

"*Shukran*, thank you."

The passengers already seated stared as Jake boarded and talked about him, not realizing he understood their suspicious whispers. He found an empty spot toward the middle of the bus and watched other travelers while eavesdropping to pick up the rhythm of the Iraqi dialect.

"Look at the foreigner—he must be taller than a door." An elderly lady nudged her companion.

"Oh, but he's got nice black hair and those eyes—brown and dark like the best coffee beans."

"But his nose. You see its shape? Broken more than once if you ask me."

Jake rubbed his nose after the last comment and the two women turned to face the front of the bus. *Nothing wrong with my nose. Got in the way of too many kicks before I mastered Tae Kwon Do.*

The bus made several stops along the route, giving Jake an excellent opportunity to photograph the barren fields and distant mountains. Two hours later, as the bus approached Halabja, he spotted a large stone monument on the left.

A tap on his shoulder made him twist around. A short, bald man wearing 'bottle cap' glasses leaned over from the seat behind. "Forgive me, but I sensed your interest. The monument is in memory of those who died during the chemical attack by the Iraqi military in 1988."

"How many?"

"Over five thousand. All the birds and animals died, too. Horrible." The man's head shook and drooped as he spoke. "I still suffer from bad dreams."

"Thank you for telling me."

When they arrived at the bus station, the man said goodbye and scurried away. Jake held back, the last to depart. He thanked the driver and asked when the bus would return to Sulaymaniyah. "Be back by four p.m. I leave right after. If you need something to eat and drink, around the corner is a good place."

"Thank you. I'll return as soon as I can."

"I'll hold the bus a few minutes in case you're late. No more than fifteen." Jake figured the driver made the offer in hopes of a tip.

He glanced at his watch—about 1130—and headed to the café the driver recommended. He ordered rice and cooked vegetables, along with a bottle of water. The only foreigner in the place, their scrutiny made him uneasy.

An old man walked up to his table and peered at him with obvious interest. "Welcome to Halabja. Are you American?"

"G'day, mate. No, I'm Australian."

"May I ask what you're doing here?"

"I'm a freelance journalist for *The Daily Telegraph* and the *Brisbane Times*. I wanted to come to where the attack took place and write about the survivors."

"I am a survivor, and I'll give you my story. After you are finished with your meal, I'll take you to meet some others. They may tell you." He shrugged. "They may not."

"Thank you."

As he stood, Jake wondered if this was a chance meeting or a set-up. Either way, he needed to trust his instincts, which told him to follow the old man.

A short time later, Jake and the old man, who gave his name as Agrin, left the café and headed down the street. Jake made note of the route to find his way back.

Five minutes later, Agrin pointed to a small building damaged by rocket shells and bullets. At one time painted white, it was now gray and dirty. Motioning for Jake to follow, Agrin led the way inside. A dozen men, each with some disfigurement sat around the perimeter of a large room. They played backgammon on six small tables.

The room fell quiet.

"This *sayyid* is Mr. Jake, a journalist." Agrin ushered Jake forward. "He's agreed to tell the story of the attack on our village, so we must tell him."

The room erupted as everyone spoke at once. An elderly man with one eye and an empty socket jumped to his feet. "Why should we tell our story? Will he give me a new eye?" He slapped an open palm on the table. "Will he bring my family back? Nothing will be done."

Several men nodded at his remarks. Another rose, much younger with a deformed left arm and sporting a claw-like hand. "I think we should tell our story. Look at me—born after the attack. It's not only about those who died. What about the thousands who came later and still suffer?"

More heads nodded, but some of the men, including the one-eyed man, left the building.

"I'm sorry, Mr. Jake." Agrin wrung his hands in apology. "I thought once they met you, all would want to tell their stories."

"I understand this is difficult. I don't have much money, but I'll pay for each story." Jake calculated the potential cost. "I'll give each man twenty American dollars for his story. About twenty-nine thousand Iraqi dinars."

Several shook their heads and left. Agrin, the younger man with the deformed limb, and two others remained. They all talked at the same time.

Jake whistled and waved his hands in the air. "We've time, so if each man tells his story, one by one, everyone will speak. May I take notes?"

Almost two hours had passed before the last person completed his tale. Jake took multiple pages of notes and skimming back through, asked some questions. He also asked to take photographs of their injuries, to which they all agreed.

The atrocities suffered by these men and their families were horrendous. While he might empathize with them, Jake couldn't lose sight of his true mission. "Does anyone know of Abdallah Baziyan?"

Agrin spoke to the others in rapid-fire Arabic, making it difficult for Jake to follow. When the others nodded, he turned back to Jake. "By reputation. Two men in the village know more. We'll tell you—for twenty dollars."

Jake laughed and countered Agrin's price. "I can't pay that much. How about ten dollars—each?"

"We agree—first the money."

Jake handed each man thirty dollars, twenty for their story and ten for information about the two men. Their eyes gleamed. They wouldn't earn this much in a month.

"Thank you, Sayyid Jake. The men are followers of Baziyan and like all Kurds, want an united Kurdistan. Sometimes, they seem to want freedom at any cost."

"How I can contact them?"

"Ismet Timur was disfigured because of the attack," the man with the injured arm said. "I think he went to Syria."

"The other man is named Dersim Razyana," another said. "He was away when the attack happened, but he lost his entire family. Dersim went to Turkey two weeks ago with a load of supplies for the PKK."

"Three months ago, Ismet and Dersim scavenged near one of the abandoned military facilities nearby," Agrin said. "Another man named Hawre worked with them. He bragged about uncovering some of Saddam's weapons. He said these would help create a new Kurdistan."

"Thank you all for sharing your experiences. I realize this has been traumatic for you to do so. I'll try to track these men down, and if they're willing to talk, I'll add their information to my article."

"Thank you, Sayyid Jake, for listening to us." Agrin nodded in appreciation. "We've tried to tell our story before, but few wanted to listen. Most still don't."

"They'll listen. They'll read what I write. I must go now so I can catch the bus back to Sulaymaniyah. I hope I can find Ismet and Dersim, and talk with them. When I have everything together, I'd like to come back to Halabja." *Although I won't come back unless I must.*

"Check for Dersim in Zakho. He went to meet with other Baziyan supporters," someone said. "I think Ismet went to Aleppo."

"Thank you again. Now, I must dash to the station."

Jake hurried back, arriving in time to board. He glanced around as he waited his turn and spotted the one-eyed men who left the backgammon room without cooperating with him. The man spoke with a tall, barrel-chested man, waving his hands in animated gestures. The man nodded once and boarded, sitting two rows in front of Jake.

Two and a half hours later, Jake returned to the Sulaymaniyah Palace Hotel. He spoke to the driver before he left the bus. "Thank you for waiting. Here is something for your trouble," handing him a few Iraqi dinars.

Jake went to his room and compiled his report.

To: Alpha

From: Aussie

Visited Halabja. Paid four men to tell me their stories. More money gave me the names of two Baziyan supporters who found some of Saddam's weapons three months ago.

First name—Ismet Timur. Injured during the attack. Scars cover his face, chest and upper arms. Seems to be a happy-go-lucky type. Headed to Aleppo.

Second name—Dersim Razyana. Absent from the village during the attack. Lost his entire family. Black hair, black eyes, slender build. A serious-type who, along with Ismet, found the weapons. Headed to Zakho.

Will proceed to Zakho in the morning. You owe me one hundred twenty dollars—American.

***

The barrel-chested man followed at a distance and waited outside when Jake entered the hotel. Once the lobby emptied, the man went inside. With no one at the desk, he skimmed the guest register.

"What are you doing?" The clerk, a thin, young man, closed the register.

"Give me the foreigner's name. Now."

"No, I can't tell you." The clerk said. "No. I can't."

"I must know his name. He left something on the bus."

The clerk shook his head but remained silent.

Whipping out a long knife, the man reached over and grabbed the clerk's arm.

"Give me the information—or lose the arm."

The clerk gasped and grabbed a piece of paper. In shaky handwriting, he wrote:

Name: Jake Martin
Nationality: Australian
Profession: freelance journalist

"Not so hard, was it? Forget you saw me." With a last wave of the knife, the man disappeared into the night.

Chapter 12
Cappadocia, Turkey
Friday, March 11

"Y'all get everything stowed away last night?" Willie took a sip of his coffee and grimaced. "Oh, God, the coffee's a mite strong."

"Took me over two hours to stash everything and climb into bed." Aiden flipped the pages in a tourist brochure. "Found a bug, tucked in a corner of a lampshade."

"Was the critter one of them full spectrum things?"

"No, audio only. I cursed up a storm about the shambles. Don't want whoever planted the device to realize we're on to them, so I'll leave the bug alone and not say anything to blow our cover, eh?"

"Good idea. I found one, too. Under the coffee table. Went outside and put the varmint on a passing car."

The headwaiter pushed the dining room doors open until they locked in place. The men headed inside and grabbed a table in the middle of the room. Once they finished breakfast, a waiter brought more coffee.

The constant babble by the guests created good cover to discuss the day's trip to the Zelve Open Air Museum. Willie spoke in hushed tones in case of eavesdroppers. "Shall we take the camcorders with us?"

A waiter sauntered by, so Aiden read from a brochure. "I think we should. Zelve once housed one of the largest communities in the region. An amazing cave town, honeycombed with dwellings, religious and secular chambers. People lived in Zelve until the 1950s when the cliffs became dangerous due to erosion." The waiter disappeared, and Aiden dropped the brochure. "It'd take all day to explore, so using the camcorders should speed things up, eh?"

***

They grabbed their backpacks and headed outside. Aiden glanced around the empty parking lot. "We should switch cars."

"Why do ya think that, Canuck?"

"After what happened yesterday, perhaps your vehicle picked up a tail, eh?"

Willie gestured in agreement, and they walked to the back of Aiden's Hyundai Getz. After opening the trunk, the keys slipped from Aiden's hand. Before picking them up, he checked underneath for any telltale signs of disturbance.

"Seems clear. Let's go, eh?"

Aiden set off, keeping an eye in the rearview mirror while Willie people-watched. They took a few detours, arriving at Zelve as the first visitors entered the museum. Aiden joined the line to buy tickets and a guidebook. Willie scanned the perimeter for an easy way to enter at night as he checked out a nearby souvenir stand and grabbed several bottles of cold water.

The men entered Zelve's first valley, and wandered around the uneven landscape, following paths between the trees and rocks.

Willie pointed to an area of exposed chambers. "Appears the outer walls gave way."

Aiden shook his head. "No wonder the government closed this area to tourists. Wouldn't take much for the rest of the cliff to collapse, eh?"

While Aiden spoke, Willie fished around in his pack. "I've turned the camcorder on with the highest sensitivity." *I hope the detector inside works as advertised.*

"Me, too. Zelve will be difficult to search. If there are any hidden packages, the camcorders might spot them."

"Look at all the crags and pinnacles. Plenty of places to check. We can explore all the caves, nooks and crannies we want—other than the areas marked closed."

Aiden and Willie spent the next five hours working through Zelve's three valleys. Empty living quarters carved into the rock dotted the canyon faces, testimony to a bygone era.

They climbed through numerous tunnels, encountering dozens of passageways, blind paths, and areas used for protection against attacks. They enjoyed themselves, snapping loads of photographs. However, the detectors remained silent.

By early afternoon, they found a pleasant spot at the base of several large boulders to rest and eat the goat cheese and cucumber sandwiches provided by the hotel. Fatigue caught up with them from all the climbing, but they wanted to finish their Zelve excursion in one day.

Willie stopped in his tracks and turned around.

"Ya smell that?"

Aiden grinned, recognizing the familiar aroma. "Come on, Willie, lead us on, eh?"

"Let's head down the path between the trees."

They rambled along, heads twisting from side to side. Willie kept muttering, "Stronger, stronger—the nose knows!"

In front of them, a dozen foreigners leaned against various rock formations and a few trees, looking like Woodstock rejects. Music played in the background while they passed around joints and wine bottles.

"Hey man, wanna join us? How 'bout a hit?"

"No thanks, man." Willie raised a hand to keep distance between them. "We're just checkin' out the scenery. Y'all have a good 'un."

"We will, my man, we will."

Willie and Aiden retraced their steps back to the main path.

"Not what we needed. A bunch of misplaced hippies, eh?" Aiden said.

"I don't know—might have been fun."

Their excitement faded and after another hour of crawling around fallen rumble and through dusty tunnels and caves, they halted their search and headed back to the car.

Once back at the hotel, Aiden and Willie went to the bar for a cold Efes beer. Afterward, they returned to their rooms for a shower and a snooze before dinner.

Two hours later, they discussed their plans for the evening over dinner. A nocturnal visit to the Göreme Open Air Museum on the agenda, they would use both detectors again.

European and North American tourists packed the large dining hall, the noise almost as loud as Niagara Falls. Waiters rushed between the tables with heavy platters of food and drink.

"I want night photos for my collection," Aiden said, for the benefit of any eavesdroppers. "Forgot last night because of the excitement."

"I think we should take the camcorders and the digital cameras. No telling what we might capture."

At 2200, Aiden and Willie strolled around the hotel grounds to check if anyone followed before climbing into Willie's car and weaving through the streets of Göreme. He parked the vehicle down the road in a public parking lot. Closing the doors with a soft click, they ambled toward the museum.

As they approached, Aiden spotted a small glow in the window of the security booth. He nudged Willie and veered away. They clung to the shadows as much as possible, moving toward the fence some distance away. Willie crept on his toes, avoiding any branches.

They found a spot hidden from the security booth. Aiden checked the fence for alarms and electrification while Willie stood guard. Not finding anything hazardous to their mission, they climbed over.

A moonless night, they snapped on their penlights. The soft red glows emitted by the lights couldn't be seen beyond thirty feet.

Getting their bearings, Willie pointed. "To the left—there's the path to the Snake Church."

By 0200, they completed their search of the churches, checking every possible hiding spot without a single beep. Willie and Aiden took a short break and headed to the caves.

The first five caves, all with low ceilings and narrow tunnels, came up negative. They trudged to the last one, entering a long, sloping entrance running deep into the hillside. They continued following the corridor, slipping and sliding on the wet floor caused by seepage.

"I'm getting an occasional beep on the detector," Aiden said. "Nothing constant but appears to be coming from the right side of the tunnel."

"Yes, mine flickered a few times."

"What's that stench, eh?"

"Dunno, but sure is ripe."

Five minutes later, the tunnel opened to the right with an opening four feet above the floor. Aiden climbed up, his detector beeping with urgency. He crawled further inside and yelped. Realizing his mistake, he covered his mouth and mumbled, "Found what triggered the devices. Unless the Kurds are using natural materials, this ain't what we want."

"What'd you find?"

"Bat guano. If I remember my science studies, large quantities of guano trigger false readings on many detectors, caused by the concentration of nitrates and ammonium oxalate. I think the odor fooled the detectors, eh?"

"Well, isn't this a crock! Time to head back to the hotel."

About twenty minutes later, Willie pulled into the hotel's parking lot. They slipped into their rooms for a couple of hours of sleep, agreeing to meet downstairs for breakfast before the dining room closed at 0900. Aiden sent back their daily report and switched off his light.

To: Alpha

From: Mountie and Rebel

Zelve ruled out. Nocturnal visit to Göreme bat cave gave brief excitement—guano fooled the detectors. Churches zilch. 'Another one bites the dust.'

***

Beady Eyes followed Willie and Aiden back from Zelve in the afternoon. He found a good spot to monitor the hotel and made note of their late night excursion. He didn't need to follow—a small package took his place.

Once they returned to their rooms and turned out the lights, the man picked up his phone and speed-dialed his boss.

"*Efendim*—sir. Tayfun here. Subjects passed near a hippie group at Zelve. No apparent contact or transfer. A late night trip will be analyzed after retrieving the package. No extra luggage noted."

After his report, he started his car and drove away. Someone else would take his place in the morning.

Chapter 13
Mardin, Turkey
Friday, March 11

"To a new Kurdistan." Everyone repeated the words and downed their raki.

Dersim wanted revenge against anyone who opposed Kurdish sovereignty. After what happened to his family and now to Hawre, retribution ruled his mind.

He gazed around the table at the twelve men chosen by Serbest to carry out the upcoming attacks. Many had suffered under the Turkish or Iraqi regimes. They sat in a dingy, ramshackle bar with walls held up by the adjacent stores on the western outskirts of Mardin. Owned by a PKK supporter and closed until lunchtime— the perfect meeting place.

He sat at the head of the large, rectangular table. "We placed canisters in two of the underground cities and one in a drain near a Turkish police station in Cappadocia. We wanted to place more in the area, but we followed Mufti Tanreverdi's instructions." *I think using the canisters, even as a threat, is a bad idea. For now, I'll do as I'm told.* "I agree with attacking government targets. Should foreigners be injured or killed, we'll consider them casualties of war."

"You might be right, Dersim, but remember Mufti Tanreverdi wants to minimize unnecessary casualties among foreign tourists." Serbest's brows knitted in a frown. "We don't want to create a negative picture in the West regarding our struggle. We'd be vilified by their press as terrorists."

Dersim glanced at Serbest but ignored his comments. "We took a week transferring weapons and other supplies to locations within Cappadocia, Sanliurfa, Göbekli Tepe, and Akçakale."

"Where's Merdem? I thought he returned with you." The speaker waved his right arm in the air, metal pincers in place of the hand he lost in a firefight with a roving Turkish patrol.

"He stayed in Sanliurfa." Serbest glared at Dersim for attempting to control the meeting. "He wants a job at the Göbekli

Tepe excavation so he can gather more information on the foreigners."

"Did you hide canisters at Göbekli Tepe?" another asked.

"No. Near Sanliurfa. As agreed upon before we left Mardin, I placed plastic explosives and other weapons in a cave near Göbekli Tepe. We also hid some near a Turkish military outpost on the Syrian border."

"Well done." Several individuals nodded, rapping their knuckles on the table.

"However, there could be bad news. When I checked on the stockpile in Göbekli Tepe, a foreigner working on the excavation might have spotted me."

"We always anticipated something like this." Afran rubbed at the patch over an eye lost in a Turkish attack the previous year. "This is the reason for spreading our supplies throughout the area and not keeping them in one or two locations."

"Mufti Tanreverdi gave us the flexibility to do so, as long as we carried out his instructions." Serbest thrust two fingers in the air to emphasize his points. "Someone must return to Göbekli Tepe, and move the weapons to another location."

When Dersim and Serbest finished their report, several others provided updates on their activities. These men handled placement of additional weapons and explosives in surrounding areas.

After the meeting ended, Dersim and Serbest strode outside. Dildar Zagros and Belen Azad joined them.

"Dersim, you're hurting because of Hawre." Serbest put a hand on Dersim's shoulder to acknowledge his pain. "Keep to the plan— don't do anything rash."

"I … it's tough. I miss him." Tears welled in Dersim's eyes. "It's not only about losing Hawre—it reminds me of my parents and brothers."

Serbest grabbed Dersim by his shoulders and gave him a big squeeze. "Honor their sacrifice and do what's right."

"Yes, I must. Thank you, Serbest, for being a good friend. We'll meet again soon."

"Allah be with you."

They shook hands and Dersim climbed into the cab where Dildar and Belen waited. Dersim started the engine and drove away.

"May Allah be with you and guide you." Serbest prayed as they disappeared around a corner.

***

Dersim first met Dildar and Belen several years before when he brought goods to the Mardin Bazaar. Laborers, they helped truckers unload their vehicles for a small fee. Dersim remembered their first meeting—they handled his goods with care, and he bought them a soft drink to show his appreciation for their efforts.

"Thank you for the drink—the work we do is hard, and we're always hot." Belen saluted Dersim with his bottle.

Dersim recognized their use of Sorani when speaking to each other, the same dialect he spoke. "Where are you from?"

"We both grew up in Wazol."

"Yes, west of my village, Halabja."

"You've witnessed the destruction caused by Saddam's troops." Dildar's head bobbed. "They almost flattened our village, so we came here to find work."

"Yes." Dersim explained about the loss of his family.

"Perhaps one day we'll have our own nation and not be at the mercy of others." Belen's chin jutted as he brandished a fist. "The PKK are right—take the fight to others."

"I agree—back home too much talk but no action." Dersim continued in a whisper. "This is why some of the money from selling our goods will be given to help them."

This was the first of many discussions regarding their support of the PKK freedom fighters, or as the Turkish government referred to them—terrorists.

***

Dersim trusted Dildar and Belen with his life. "We told the mullahs we uncovered forty canisters. I made a mistake, and I'll take some back."

"How many?" Belen cocked his head.

"Ten. Any more will be difficult to hide."

"What'll you use them for?" Dildar inhaled a sharp breath.

"I haven't decided. Perhaps bury them deep in the ground so they can't be used."

"Upon our lives and those of our remaining family members, we'll keep this secret among us." Belen placed his hand over his heart, affirming his pledge.

98

"I'm confident you, Dildar, and Ismet will support me when the time comes." *I wish we never found the canisters—nothing but trouble.* "Keep an eye out for any Turkish military or gendarmerie units. We must stay away from them."

Both Belen and Dildar nodded, focusing their attention outside the vehicle.

Since Dersim's truck was a routine sight on the roads in Mardin Province, the group believed he should move supplies around the area. Dildar and Belen assisted Dersim with shifting additional dry foodstuffs, weapons, and ammunition into strategic locations for future operations.

According to Afran, the attack against the Turkish military would start in about three weeks. This timetable might change, depending upon enemy operations and their own plans.

Away from Mardin, Dersim drove to the market areas of several small Kurdish villages. After the first stop, word spread to other locales about their pending visits. At each village, the three men left the vehicle and walked through the market. In the meantime, a constant stream of people walked past the rear of the truck.

Several men jumped into the back with donations or to share with others—weapons, ammunition, medical supplies, and food— all for the cause. Some gave an abundance of financial support, others whatever they could spare.

An elderly woman approached Dersim as he returned to his vehicle. She held out her wrinkled, arthritic hands. "This is all I own of value. My husband's—the Turks killed him." On one palm lay a gold watch. In her other hand, she held six small gold coins, still attached to red ribbons, customary gifts given to couples on their wedding day.

Tears filled the eyes of the three men. "Thank you. Your sacrifice today will help us all tomorrow." Dersim cupped the woman's hands in his own as he accepted her offering.

"Beware, young man, when you approach the next village. A Turkish sympathizer is visiting."

"Thank you, *Daya*—mother, for the warning."

Dersim, Belen, and Dildar returned to the truck and drove around the next village to avoid the possible Turkish spy.

Once the men filled the vehicle, they headed west toward Sanliurfa. They would follow the highway south to the Syrian border, stopping in Akçakale, to leave another stockpile.

Dersim also planned a return to Göbekli Tepe to relocate the weapons. *I hope I don't run into the same foreigner again. If our paths cross, I'll kill him.*

Chapter 14
Göbekli Tepe, Turkey
Saturday, March 12

CC rose before dawn and slipped outside. An early morning calm surrounded the camp, a wisp of white smoke wafted above the canteen. Shades of ebony, crimson, and gold gave way to a deepening cobalt sky as the sun's rays burned away the night. A lone golden eagle circled high above, scanning the ground in search of food.

The cook must be up by now. CC sniffed. *Nothing cooking yet—but the fire seems almost ready.*

CC veered away from the canteen, and moving in slow, deliberate steps to avoid disturbing anyone, made his way through the camp and climbed the hill. As he reached the crest, he crouched, keeping a low profile in case anyone took advantage of the stunning sunrise.

He reached the cavern's entrance and glanced over his shoulder. Confident no one had spotted him, CC noted the shrubs blocking the way remained undisturbed. He pushed them aside and entered, turning his penlight on to scan the space. The crates and the backpack sat in the same locations.

Now to track this stuff before someone moves it. He placed one of the 'Track in a Pack' devices into the bottoms of the two wooden crates he opened during his first visit. Another went inside the backpack, under the bottom insert. CC selected three other packages at random. He removed the contents, wedged units into the base of the crates, and repacked them.

I need more of these devices. A dozen won't be enough at the rate I'm using them.

Satisfied with his work, CC backed out the entrance, shifted the bushes into place, and stopped.

A gentle swishing sound caught his attention. Glancing over his right shoulder, branches on a nearby bush ruffled in the still air.

The flapping of large wings erupted as the bald eagle launched itself toward the heavens, a rodent dangling from one of its claws.

Aye. Good idea to grab breakfast, once my heart stops pounding. Turning, CC worked his way back to the camp.

The place quiet, he strolled to the canteen. Upon entering, the cook, a short, wiry man with gray hair, struggled to raise the huge coffee pot.

"Let me help you." CC grabbed one side of the urn, and together they placed the pot on the stove. "It's heavy. Why try to do this on your own?"

"Thank you, Mr. CC. You moved the pot yesterday. I thought I could, too."

"Before I came, who helped you?"

"No one. I put big pot on stove. Fill small pots with water. Dump in big one."

"Aye, much safer. So what's your name?"

"Cheap Charlie."

"Huh? How'd you earn your name?"

"I used to sell brass, copper, carpets, other tourist things. Foreigners said my prices too cheap. Someone called me Charlie— I thought good name for business—Cheap Charlie's."

"What happened to your store?"

"Sold stuff too cheap, go out of business."

CC laughed and patted Charlie on the shoulder. "So, what's for breakfast?"

"Every day same—Turkish."

About twenty minutes later, Jürgen entered the canteen. "*Guten morgen*! Are you ready for another exciting day up the hill?"

"Coffee first. After a quick bite, I'll be ready."

The morning passed without a single discovery despite the removal of at least a ton of soil and debris. Tedious manual labor, but vital to uncovering new archeological treasures.

"CC, we'll need three or four more supports installed this afternoon along the wall to prevent any collapse, ja?"

"Aye, dinnae want anyone hurt."

"After lunch, I want to dig a few exploratory holes to determine how far the wall stretches."

***

Konrad approached CC while he ate. "I'm heading into Sanliurfa to collect supplies. If everything arrived as requested, we'll celebrate with fresh German wurst and schnapps for dinner. Would you like to go?"

"Aye, and if possible, I'd like to look around."

"We'll make time. We'll spend most of the afternoon. Once we collect the supplies, I want to take a break and visit the bazaar in the Old Town."

"I'm ready. Let's go."

Their first stop was the local airport, a small facility catering for domestic flights from Istanbul, Izmir, and Ankara. The road took them near the runway, where a Turkish Airlines flight taxied into position for takeoff.

"Konrad, is this a busy airport?"

"*Nein*, averages eight flights per day. Between one p.m. and eight p.m. no takeoffs or landings unless a plane is behind schedule."

Once inside the small terminal building they strode to a desk in the corner handling cargo. Konrad confirmed their supplies were ready. The clerk handed him the requisite manifest clearance papers for him to sign. "Take these and drive around back. Go to Door Six. Someone will help you."

They followed the clerk's directions, sidestepping forklifts and small airport trucks hauling cargo into the storage depot. Men carrying clipboards shouted and pointed to the drivers, urging them to their destinations.

The two men found someone to show them to their consignment, and soon they loaded the supplies into the vehicle. Konrad wiped his perspiring forehead with a bandana. "When we're finished, we'll go to the bazaar, ja? I want to pick up some additional local supplies. Things to help make the excavation site more comfortable."

Konrad paused as a workman approached with a handful of papers. He signed again for delivery of the shipment, and they climbed back in the truck.

"We'll stop for ice tea or a soft drink at the market. Unlike other parts of Turkey, finding alcohol in Sanliurfa is almost impossible."

"Nae problem. I'd settle for an iced tea." CC used a shirtsleeve to sponge away the sweat dripping into his eyes as the temperature continued to climb. The built-in thermometer on the dash registered over ninety, far above the average for the time of year.

The rest of the afternoon passed too fast. Returning to the vehicle, they departed. The truck's swaying on the dusty rode lulled CC into a light sleep, with the occasional horn waking him.

When they returned to Göbekli Tepe, Jürgen rushed up to the vehicle. "*Schnell! Mein Gott.* A Turkish workmen has been injured in an accident."

Konrad and CC jumped out of the cab and rushed up the hill behind Jürgen. Dust rose above the workmen trying to remove large stones out of the way where a large section of the wall had collapsed, pinning a laborer. Men shouted frantic orders, as the injured man screamed in pain.

Planks shoved into the loose earth created a dam around the trapped person as workers used their hands to scoop soil away. At last, they freed the man, a final scream when someone tugged on his arm. Two workmen supported him as he teetered on his feet, blood mixing with dust trickled from a gash above his right ear.

The man mumbled a few words and a nearby rescuer jumped into the hole. He pushed soil around until he uncovered a strap. Working the harness free, the man pulled a backpack from the cave-in.

Workers assisted the injured laborer into a vehicle for the trip to the Sanliurfa Hospital. A worker tossed the man's backpack in with him, the same type and color as the one CC discovered in the cave, including the small Kurdish flag sewn into the flap. As the door closed, he scrutinized the man's face but did not recognize him.

Jürgen watched until the vehicle disappeared in the distance. "CC, do you know the injured man? I don't remember him working with us before."

"Aye, I wondered the same thing. I dinnae ken."

They found Konrad inside the canteen. "We don't know who the injured man is." Jürgen brushed a hand across his head to remove bits of soil lodged during the rescue.

Konrad spotted the Turkish foreman entering the tent and called him over. "Ahmed, who's the injured man?"

"Sir, he began this morning."

"I didn't realize we required additional men."

"He's a cousin of one of the others, filling in for him while he's away sick."

"Who's out sick? You didn't mention anything this morning."

"I forget his name. I'll find out and tell you later."

Ahmed left. Konrad turned to the others with a puzzled expression on his face and glanced back at Ahmed's retreating figure. "Hmm. Strange. This is the first time Ahmed hasn't kept me informed. He always comes with a list of things, including any changes to the work roster."

Konrad drummed his fingers on the table. "I think we need to tighten security around the dig. I'll talk with the local police chief and request background checks for any new workers."

CC suspected this new addition to the Turkish workforce of an ulterior motive for stepping into the sick man's shoes. Whatever he planned would have to wait until the man returned to work.

The rest of the day proved uneventful. With no new discoveries and an injured worker, the mood in the canteen remained subdued. Without the usual banter, people returned to their tents after eating.

CC went for his customary walk. He stayed away from the cave, as he preferred to keep an eye on the stash from a distance.

Returning to his tent, he checked the tracking devices on the portable monitor. All six remained stationary. Finished, he composed his evening report for BHQ.

To: Alpha

From: Haggis

Emplaced trackers stationary. NTR.

Request additional tracking devices. Send to Sanliurfa Airport addressed to me c/o Göbekli Tepe Excavation Team. Add six flash memory cards, extra rechargeable batteries, and a charger. List contents on customs form as camera supplies.

Injured local workman at site today. Believed to be Kurdish. Possible connection to weapons cache, but needs to be confirmed.

If the injured man returned, CC hoped to get his name and photograph to add to their list of suspects. Perhaps snap pictures around the dig and capture the man's profile at the same time.

Is Ahmed part of the Kurdish team? I'll need his full name and any other information about him for an independent check.

Chapter 15
Al-Bab, Syria
Saturday, March 12

Ben washed, dressed, and headed downstairs where Abdel, the hotel manager, greeted him. "Good morning, Ben. I trust you slept well."

"Good morning, Abdel. Sweet as. The bed is comfortable."

"Earlier this morning, a scar-faced man asked to meet with you. Said he talked with you yesterday. I told him to come back after eight."

"Yes. Called himself Ismet."

Dr. Dave entered the room with a bounce in his step. "Good morning, gentlemen. I seem to sleep better here than in Aleppo, for sure."

"Good morning."

"Let me bring coffee and tell the kitchen to prepare breakfast." Abdel led them to a table before scurrying away.

"Dave, remember Ismet, the guy I told you about last night? He came this morning and wanted to talk with me. Abdel instructed him to come back later."

"Yeah, he tried the same with me. When I first met him, he returned the next day, asking for additional medicine. No problem meeting with him, as we won't depart right away."

After they finished breakfast, Abdel cleared away the dishes and brought Dave and Ben copies of *Syria Times*, an English daily newspaper. Soon after 0830, Abdel escorted Ismet to Ben's table, and when asked if he wanted coffee, Ismet shook his head.

"Abdel, would you mind translating for me? Ismet speaks little English, and my Arabic is worse."

"Of course, my friend." Abdel sat at the table. Dave excused himself. "I'm heading to the souk for supplies."

Ismet spoke. Abdel waited for him to pause and turned to Ben. "He asked for more pills for his pain. He also wants you to help him."

"Yes, I can provide more if he needs them. Dr. Dave told me which ones he prescribed. I'll need to examine him first."

Ismet glared at Ben as Abdel translated. He unbuttoned his shirt to expose the purple-red scarring extending from his neck to his waist. Separate scars covered part of his face and around his right eye. As he stood, Ismet trembled, gasping for breath.

"These appear to be caused by mustard gas. Does he have eyesight problems?"

Abdel asked this question, and Ismet nodded.

"He can button his shirt. Before I provide the medication, what kind of help is he looking for?"

After another exchange in Arabic, Abdel said, "He wants your help to tell the world the Kurdish people deserve their own country, and shouldn't live under anyone else's rule."

Ben leaned back in his chair, forehead puckered. "I'm not sure what I can do about the Kurdish people since I'm a doctor, not a politician. Abdel, ask him where his people would establish their country." *I wonder if Ismet is aware of the weapons.*

"He says they will take land from the occupiers." Abdel shifted in his chair and held a brief exchange with Ismet without translating. Ben, not giving away how much he understood, realized Ismet's defiant tone made Abdel uncomfortable.

"How'll they manage this?"

"The Kurds will send a message to the world."

"How?" Ben crossed his arms, wearing a deadpan expression.

"Wait and you will learn."

"What message?" Ben asked. "You must tell me. Otherwise, I can't help."

"He says to survive, they search for things to sell. They found a great treasure, which will make the West listen."

"What did they find? Gold? Oil? What?" Ben cocked his head. "I have friends who work for the government. Without knowing the Kurdish message, I can't help."

Unhappy with his response, Ismet shrugged and fell silent. Ben realized the conversation ended and rose to his feet. "If Ismet will wait a moment, I'll grab the prescription."

He returned a few minutes later with a small bottle. Ismet thanked him and said he hoped they would meet again.

Later on, when Ben caught up with Dave in the hotel's clinic, he mentioned Ismet's request.

"Guess because we're from the West he thinks we can help, for sure."

"I suppose, but his approach was strange."

"Perhaps. If you're ready, let's collect our gear and head back to Aleppo."

About an hour later, Dave parked in front of the MSF building and helped Ben unload the vehicle and carry everything inside. Afterward, he took Ben to the clinic and helped set up.

***

The rest of the day passed without incident. Ben learned MSF procedures and assisted with patients. He dealt with an elderly man in severe pain who needed a dentist, not a doctor, a young boy who fell and scraped an elbow and both knees, and a teenager looking for a magical cure for zits.

At last, the final person left and the workday ended. Ben joined the others for dinner in the crowded MSF dining room. After checking out the offerings at the buffet table, he filled a plate with meat, beans, and rice, and grabbed a seat next to Pierre Girard, a doctor from Paris, whom he met the previous day.

"Ben, I'm going to the souk in the Old Quarter if you want to come along. It's one of the largest covered markets in the world. I go at least once a week to rummage."

"Sweet as. I'll go.

***

The size of the market, Suq al-Medina, amazed Ben. They meandered through hundreds of stalls, stopping to inhale the mixed aromas coming from large sacks of spices. Venders touted their wares, urging customers to buy before stocks depleted.

Ben and Pierre veered right into a small alleyway. The stench assaulted them.

"*Excusez-moi.* Wrong way. This is the meat market."

"Horrible stench." Ben gagged and covered his nose.

"*Oui*, but prices are good. Our cook comes here."

They returned to the main path through the souk. Pierre pointed to several displays. "Why don't we buy some dates and pistachios to share with the others?"

"Good idea. Let's get oranges, too."

Ben and Pierre examined every stall they passed. At last, they found one with the items they wanted.

"Ah, my friends, come this way. You need something. I have many things." A small man wearing a stained apron, with a perpetual nod hurried forward, an orange in one hand, a knife in the other.

"Try. Fresh and juicy." He split the orange in two, offering a piece to each man.

Ben and Pierre bit into the tangy fruit, juice running down their chins, smiles etched on their faces.

"Two dozen." Ben reached for his money.

"Wait, *mon ami*. Remember, here we bargain first." Pierre turned to the vendor. "How much for twenty-four oranges?"

The man scratched his chin and screwed his eyes shut. "Two hundred forty lira."

Pierre thrust his hands in the air. "We don't want all your oranges. Fifty."

"Oh, sir. What about my family? Two hundred."

Pierre pulled a face, glancing at Ben. "One hundred fifty. Throw in some dates and pistachios."

"Sir, you drive a hard bargain. I agree." The stall keeper wrapped their purchases and they continued their stroll.

As they passed a café, Ben pointed at an empty table. "Let's grab a table and have a coffee and pastry. My treat."

"Fantastic idea."

They sat at the outside table for some people-watching. Around them couples strolled, a child cried. Stray dogs roamed in search of morsels, a nearby vendor tossing a piece of bread to one.

Pierre talked about a patient he had treated when Ben spotted a familiar looking man not too far away. Another man approached and they soon appeared to be in a heated conversation.

As the two separated, Ben glimpsed the first man's face. Ismet. He didn't appear to recognize Ben, at least didn't let on. Ben became curious and concerned. *Is Ismet following me? Why?*

"Pierre, don't let him catch you looking but do you recognize him? The one with the scarred face."

Pierre scrutinized two young Arab women walking past as only a Parisian could. He attempted to keep his eyes on them while scanning for the scarred man.

"*Oui.* He's been hanging around the MSF building for a few days. Just stares—a fixated expression, which is pure evil."

"Yes. What's he doing?"

"He turned and left."

A short time later, Pierre and Ben left the café and headed back to the MSF building. "Thanks for taking me along, Pierre. A good way to end the day. Good night."

"*Bonne nuit*, Ben."

Ben returned to his room and composed a report to send to BHQ.

To: Alpha

From: Kiwi

Ismet Timur came to the hotel in Al-Bab. Asked for help to convince the world the Kurdish people should live in their own country. Said they found something when scavenging which would make everyone listen.

Spotted him tonight in Aleppo while visiting the souk. Not sure if he's following me or a coincidence. Will procure local weapon. He might bear watching.

Ben glanced at his watch—2200. *Wonder if Dave's still awake?* He slipped out of his room and noticed light coming from under Dave's door. He knocked.

Dave opened the door. "What's up? You okay?"

"Sorry to bother you so late. Can we talk for a minute?"

"Sure, come in. Want something to drink?"

"Thanks. I'm fine. Listen. Wanted to mention, I saw Ismet tonight—at the souk. Not sure if he's following me, but I have an odd feeling."

"Pierre stopped by earlier and told me. I wanted to talk with you in the morning. With things getting worse in the city and now with a possible stalker, I'll increase the building's security, for sure. I asked MSF for additional funding."

"Good idea. I stopped because I want a pistol. Better to be armed if Ismet comes around again."

"As a rule, I'd say no. We're supposed to be in the life-saving business, but as long as you're discreet, I'll take you to a place tomorrow, for sure. Other doctors are now armed. I bought a weapon last week."

"Thanks, Dave. See you in the morning."

Ben returned to his room and thought again about the day's events regarding Ismet. Might be a coincidence, but he doubted things might be so simple.

Is Ismet an innocent war casualty? Did he exaggerate about finding chemical weapons?

Chapter 16
Sulaymaniyah, Iraq
Saturday, March 12

Jake strolled through narrow streets to the Sulaymaniyah bus station, a modern facility compared with some of its ramshackle neighbors. Several battered buses waited for passengers. "G'day, mate. How much for a ticket to Zakho?"

"Twenty dinars."

"Okay, how long will the ride take?"

The agent hit a button on a machine by his elbow and the voucher printed.

Jake handed over the money while the agent continued. "A long way to Zakho, one hundred eighty-nine miles. Many, many stops, and will take about six hours."

"Thanks for the information."

"The trip will be hot and dusty. I recommend buying fruit and water to take with you. There's a stall at the corner."

"Thank you, I will."

The man glanced around and lowered his voice. "My cousin can take you to Zakho. It'd be much faster, four hours. Special price for you, only two hundred thousand Iraqi dinars. If you pay with dollars, one hundred fifty."

Be quicker, but can the 'cousin' be trusted or is this a set-up to rob a naïve foreigner? Jake shook his head. "No thanks, mate. I'm in no hurry. Curious about the length of the trip, but I'll take the bus."

The agent frowned, disappointment etched across his face. "As you will. Good luck."

Jake purchased oranges and bottled water at different stalls and returned to the station as the bus arrived. He took a seat at the rear, hoping to stretch out. Moments later, the bus belched smoke, backfired, and crept from the station. *No wonder the journey takes six hours. At this rate, it'll be a miracle if we arrive in Zakho.*

The bus continued its agonizing crawl north and west while Jake reviewed his notes from Halabja. *If my information is correct, Dersim entered Turkey about two weeks ago.*

***

The bus trundled into Zakho's station after 1400. Jake thanked the driver and veered to a taxi stand. "How much to the Delal Bridge?"

"Special price today. Twenty-five dinars."

"Too much. Fifteen."

The driver hesitated and countered Jake's offer. "Eighteen dinars. Final price."

Even though the price seemed astronomical, Jake agreed. Five minutes later, the taxi stopped a short distance from the bridge. Jake fumed as he handed over a twenty-dinar note. "I want my change."

The taxi driver grinned and dropped a few small coins into his outstretched palm. Jake slammed the door, stomped to a nearby bench to gather his bearings, and blow off a little steam.

Agrin's directions were correct. A few minutes later, he entered a street filled with small businesses, children running around while their parents hawked electronics, kitchen utensils, and other wares. Adjacent to one another stood the stores he wanted.

Window displays bore testimony to their merchandise, with various dry goods stacked in one window and textiles draped over metal racks in the other. The signs over each dingy, gray concrete storefront bore the names of Babir Parez and Gewran Werdek, matching those he received in Halabja, Dersim's cousins. Once Jake entered the dry goods store, everyone stopped talking and stared. "*Masa'u Al-khair,* good afternoon. I wonder if someone might help me."

A small man with a long, ragged scar on his arm stepped forward. "*Al-khair An-nur,* hello. Welcome to my store. Come this way, and I'll show you our best line of dry food."

He guided Jake toward the rear of the store, away from the others. "Would you like some pistachios? Arrived today from Iran."

"Thank you, mate, half a kilo."

"Would you like anything else?"

"I'm looking for someone. Are you acquainted with a man named Dersim Razyana?"

"How do you know Dersim? Who are you?"

"My name is Jake. I'm an Australian journalist. Agrin from Halabja sent me."

"How can I help?"

"Where is he? I want to speak with him about what happened to his family in Halabja."

"Come back tonight at eight and we'll talk. If I'm satisfied with your answers, I'll tell you where to find Dersim."

Jake thanked Babir and headed back toward Delal Bridge. He planned to eat and review his information before returning.

***

After he had returned to the store, Babir placed a 'closed' sign in the window, ushered him inside and locked the door. Jake glanced around, wary. He spotted someone else at a table in the corner. The man appeared older than Babir, his mouth deformed and twisted into a constant grimace. He motioned for Jake to sit. "I am Gewran. My cousin Babir says you want to speak with Dersim. Would you like tea?"

"Hello, I'm Jake. Tea would be super."

"How you find us?"

"I'm an Australian freelance journalist and met a man named Agrin in Halabja yesterday. I'm writing a human-interest story on the Halabja massacre. He took me to meet several survivors and I learned Dersim lost his entire family in the attack."

Jake rubbed his nose, canted his head, sneezed, and stole a quick peek. *Locked front door. Thin bars on the windows. Perhaps a back way out?*

"They mentioned he came here about two weeks ago. I hoped you might tell me where he went. His story would be one of the main pieces of my article."

"Yes, Dersim is our cousin, and his family died in the Halabja massacre." Babir glanced at Gewran before continuing. "He came two weeks ago, following his normal routine. Dersim sells our products in Turkey. He owns a large BMC truck, and delivers goods for us."

Jake perked up and smiled. This confirmed what he learned in Halabja. "Is Dersim here or did he go to Turkey? Anyone with him?"

The cousins stared at each another. Gewran gasped and struggled to speak. "Yes, another man. Bad face, many scars. Hurt in Halabja attack. Lost all family."

"Do you remember his name, perhaps Ismet Timur?"

"Yes, Ismet." Babir rubbed his hand over the dark stubble on his chin. "Dersim said they were going to Turkey, and Ismet would continue to Syria. The Iraqi-Syrian border crossings closed a long time ago."

"Do you remember anything unusual? Agrin hinted Dersim used his scrap metal collection to conceal contraband, perhaps black market truck parts, and cigarettes."

Again, the cousins exchanged glances. Babir nodded. "Perhaps from time to time to earn extra money. Why?"

"Agrin mentioned some boxes. I wondered if Dersim brought them here. He said they were important. Perhaps they contain more evidence of atrocities committed against your people. His information would be crucial to my story if this is true."

Babir stared at the floor, at the ceiling, and back to Jake. "Six or seven boxes. I asked about the contents, but Dersim shrugged and wouldn't say. Ismet bragged the contents would make people take notice of the Kurdish people."

"This bravado. He talk about fighting against Turkish military." Gewran threw his hands in the air. "We never p-paid attention to his ranting. Sometimes, he gives supplies to the P-PKK, but we all do."

"Before departing, they hid the boxes under a load of our goods. We never asked again," Babir said.

"Did either of them mention where Ismet would cross into Syria and where he planned to go? Perhaps I can catch up with him later."

"I not like Ismet. Think he a big hero, going to save Kurds." Gewran yawned, his face further distorted. "Ismet want to sneak into Syria. Meet Kurdish p-patriots. I think he smokes much cannabis, confuse his mind."

"Dersim takes our goods to a trader we use in Mardin," Babir said. "He planned to drop Ismet off in Silopi. He wanted to go to Aleppo."

"Thank you for the information."

"We don't want our cousin in any difficulty." Babir frowned. "Perhaps you'll talk some sense into him. As far as Ismet goes, I think he's trouble."

Gewran and Babir invited Jake to eat with them. Afterward, he headed to the Hotel Jamal, located on Zakho's Main Street.

Once Jake reached his room, he fired up his computer and prepared a report.

To: Alpha

From: Aussie

Arrived in Zakho. Met two men who confirmed they're Dersim's cousins: Babir Parez and Gewran Werdek. Request background checks.

Dersim and Ismet departed for Turkey two weeks ago. Six crates buried under a regular load of goods. Contents unknown. Ismet bragged this would make people listen.

Ismet heading to Aleppo to meet Kurdish patriots. Will proceed to Mardin.

While waiting for the computer to shut down, Jake turned out the light.

Where's he taking the crates? What do they contain? Did Ismet take any weapons with him?

Chapter 17
Fort Myer, Virginia
Sunday, March 13

To: Zulu

From: Alpha

New intel from boss man. Halabja Day still a go. Good news. Kurds fighting among themselves over using chemical weapons. Unspecified action still expected—target(s) unknown at this time.

Additional tracking devices en route. Haggis, collect as requested. Mountie and Rebel, package sent to the Nevsehir Airport in your names. Kiwi, your shipment will be going to Aleppo Airport c/o MSF.

Charlie's still working on Göbekli Tepe photos and the maps. Ruled out local prisons. Background checks continue on Dersim, Ismet, Babir, and Gewran. Details will be provided ASAP.

Chapter 18
Mardin, Turkey
Sunday, March 13

A cool evening breeze swept into the room through the open window. Mufti Tanreverdi pushed the chair back from the cluttered desk and closed one of the heavy wooden shutters. Before doing so, he glanced down the valley across the city. *Soon. Our struggle will resume.*

His room was on the male side of the house, in a compound with twelve-foot-high walls, set back from the street. With twenty rooms, the dwelling was an impressive structure, carved into the rock, and built to last an eternity. In addition to this bedroom, another area was reserved for his use, containing a desk and round table.

I hope we made the right decision. Allah is on our side. He will guide us down the right path if we stray from His wishes.

***

Two days before, Mufti Tanreverdi had met his host, Mufti Ismail, as well as Mullah Abdul from Sanliurfa, and Mullah Ahmed from Zakho. Also present were Afran, his cousin, and Serbest, an advisor.

Halabja Day was five days away, and he'd promised to deliver a specific target list the evening before. He had met with them to hear last-minute recommendations, along with the inevitable arguments regarding the chemical weapons. These didn't matter—he had his instructions. He knew where to strike.

"Thank you for joining me at short notice. Ahmed must return to Zakho for the Halabja Day memorial, so we need to make our decision. I want to keep the chemical weapons hidden for now. To use them right away will undermine our cause."

"I think they should be used now to show we're coming from a position of strength." Abdul glared at the others, his arms crossed. "What better time than Halabja Day?"

"That could also backfire, my friend." Ahmed cast his eyes around the room, noting several nods. "Have we not learned from Halabja?"

Abdul stood and slammed his hand on the table. "Enough! Should we hide behind our women or display our determination to our enemies?"

"I think the right target and day must be chosen if we use chemical weapons." Mufti Ismail rose as he spoke, leaning on the table with both hands, pinning the eyes of each man. "Halabja Day is not the right day."

Tanreverdi sat with his right hand under his chin, resting his elbow on chair's arm. His index finger stroked his mustache and scratched the tip of his nose, his head nodding to an internal voice. "Afran, Serbest—my young friends and trusted aides, what do you say?"

"Mufti, I think … they should be used." Afran scrutinized the others, searching for support. Only Abdul nodded at Afran's declaration.

"Mufti, I've given this careful thought." Serbest stood and walked around the room, ignoring the others. He turned, walked back to his seat, and placed a hand on the back of the chair. "I don't want to use them … unless there's no choice. We must think of our people, no matter the outcome."

Tanreverdi conversed in low tones with Ismail before addressing the others. "We'll break for lunch. When we've finished, I'll announce my decision about the chemical weapons and which targets we'll attack."

***

Two hours later, the dishes were cleared away, and the men returned to their seats. The room grew still. Tanreverdi stood and raised his hands. The others followed, waiting for the mufti's prayers. He began:

"O you who believe! Stand out firmly for justice, as witnesses to Allah, even as against yourselves, or your parents, or your kin, and whether it be against rich or poor: for Allah can best protect both. Follow not the lusts of your hearts, lest you swerve, and if you distort justice or decline to do justice, verily Allah is well-acquainted with all that you do." (The Qur'an 4:135)

"Or think you that you'll enter Paradise without such trials as came to those who passed away before you? They were afflicted with severe poverty and ailments and were so shaken that even the Messenger and those who believed along with him said, "When

will come the Help of Allah?" Yes! Certainly, the Help of Allah is near!" (The Qur'an 2:214)

"No disaster strikes except by permission of Allah. And whoever believes in Allah—He will guide his heart. And Allah is Knowing of all things." (The Qur'an 64:11)

Finished, Mufti Tanreverdi sat. The rest followed. A period of meditation ensued. After giving everyone time to complete their personal prayers, the mufti stood again.

"The chemical weapons will not be used on Halabja Day. We don't want to use them on such an historical date."

"Why not?" Abdul jumped to his feet, his eyes shooting daggers. "Now's the time to begin our own historical march—to a united Kurdistan."

"Enough! I've spoken in a roundabout way with Abdallah Baziyan." Tanreverdi pointed for Abdul to sit. "Do you think I make these decisions in a vacuum? We want him freed, but not at the cost you're willing to pay."

"I meant no disrespect, Mufti." Abdul returned to his seat and gazed around the room. No one would look him in the eyes. "But Baziyan has been in prison for twelve years. How long must we wait?"

"Each year, the Turkish military resumes their attacks on us during the spring. This year, we'll take the fight to them." The mufti walked to a map of southern Turkey taped on the wall.

"Here. A new target. We'll attack Batman." He shook his hand, index finger poised in the air. "Not the city, but nearby to the south. The Bati Raman Oil Field—Turkey's largest and most productive oil field."

Silence enveloped the room as the occupants stared at the map. A head nodded. A second one.

"Only one target?" Abdul raised a hand in the air, bewilderment appearing on his face. "What will that do? I thought we had a list. Why not Diyarbakir, their military stronghold?"

"We are not trying to win a war in one day. This is the beginning," Tanreverdi said. He threw Abdul's suggestion back at him. "Why not Diyarbakir? You provided the answer—it's their stronghold. The oil field makes perfect sense—damage it and their military will struggle to obtain the fuel to move their tanks and fly their planes. We'll use our mobile weapons. Like the Americans during their Revolutionary War with the British, we'll strike and fade into the forest, only to resurface elsewhere."

At last, all nodded, even Abdul.

Serbest returned to the table, poured two fingers of raki into six glasses, and topped them with water. He placed them on a tray and returned to the group.

"Afran will lead the attack. The Turks taught him how to use explosives during his two-year mandatory military service." Tanreverdi waved Afran over. "Now he can show them what he learned."

Everyone crowded around Afran, slapping him on the back and shaking his hand. Serbest handed each person a glass. Tanreverdi raised his hand as his voice lifted into the air. "To Kurdistan." The others echoed his toast and everyone drank.

"Our meeting is over. Thank you for sharing your views. May Allah watch over us." Tanreverdi shook each person's hand as they departed. "Afran, Serbest, please stay a moment."

When the room cleared, the mufti returned to the table and motioned for Afran and Serbest to sit.

"That was hard work. I'm surprised the meeting went well." He breathed a sigh of relief, leaned back in his chair, and placed his hands behind his head. "Baziyan's message arrived this morning. I don't know what I'd have done without his instructions."

"Mufti, thank you for the honor of leading the attack." Afran bowed his head toward the mufti. "I pray I'm up to the task."

"You'll be fine, Afran. Remember, this isn't a suicide mission. Set your explosives in as many places as possible and come back."

"Yes, Mufti. How many men can I take?"

"Take no more than twelve. This is the opening volley in our new struggle. There will be more to come."

"Yes, Mufti. I'll do as you suggest."

"You may go, Afran. May Allah guide you and those who go with you."

"Mufti, what about me? Do I go with Afran?" Serbest glanced up with hope in his eyes.

"No, Serbest. I need you for another task. While Afran is taking care of this business, I need you to look into Mullah Ahmed. Something isn't right about him. I'm not sure what it is, but from our first meeting I've had a premonition."

"Yes, Mufti. I will do as you ask. I also have a concern about Dersim. Since Hawre's death, he seems unstable."

"Do you think he'll abandon our cause? Or worse, give us away?" Concern etched across the mufti's face, deep lines appeared in his forehead as his eyes narrowed. "Where's he now?"

"He should be somewhere near Sanliurfa, hiding weapons, food, and water. I told him we'd start our attack in about three weeks. When he's finished hiding the stockpiles, he'll return here. He should be back Tuesday."

Tanreverdi stared at the ceiling as if seeking divine inspiration, closed his eyes, and nodded—a decision made. "Have someone keep an eye on Dersim. If you think he'll betray us—you know what to do."

Chapter 19
Cappadocia, Turkey
Monday, March 14

Aiden and Willie began the day with their usual Turkish coffee. They sat outdoors on the veranda where they could talk without interruption.

"It's time to switch hotels," Aiden said. "We've been here since Tuesday."

"Good idea. With the break-ins and the bugs, we should move on. Where to?"

"I found a small hotel in Avanos, about five miles away. The Duru. There are twenty rooms on one level. There isn't a formal restaurant, but there's 24-hour room service and a bar/lounge area. The best thing is the location: at the intersection of three streets, which provides plenty of options for coming and going."

"Works for me."

"I planned our surveillance detection route. Where's the map?"

They ate breakfast, grabbed their stuff from the rooms, and checked out. Aiden left the parking lot first, followed a few minutes later by Willie.

The men drove around the Cappadocia area, doubled back, and stopped at several scenic spots, before entering Avanos two hours later. They approached the hotel on different streets and met at the check-in desk.

Willie glanced around—no one near. "I didn't spot any tails."

"Hard to tell with all the locals staring at us. Still, we're here. Let's get our rooms and meet in the bar in about half an hour. Don't forget to check for critters, eh?"

Aiden leaned against the bar with a cold Efes beer in front of him when Willie appeared. The bartender asked Willie what he wanted. "The same and pistachios."

"Took you long enough. Fall asleep?"

"The room was clean. I took a shower first."

"Mine was clean, too, but I wanted to check out the rest of the hotel." Willie dropped a brochure on the table. "Pick something you want to see. I want to go to Cemil's."

The team spent the afternoon prowling around the tourist area. They watched artisans hand painting pottery, depicting local scenery and Islamic symbols. The two men came across a young girl with nimble fingers weaving a wool carpet on a loom. An hour later, they stopped at a small sidewalk café for an apple tea. The afternoon passed without obvious signs of surveillance.

During their last stop before dinner they perused Cemil Galip's Pottery Shoppe. He handcrafted the pottery in the storefront. The display area was located at the rear and carved into the rock. To the right a small alcove widened into another chamber. Willie stared at the ceiling. "Ugh! Look at all the hair! There must be thousands of donations. Imagine a customer parting with their hair, name and address just to be part of a hair museum."

"Yeah, won't see me joining the collection!"

"Cemil won't be asking for your hair, he's only interested in female locks, eh?"

They bought a few trinkets and drank local red wine with Cemil. Willie bought several thimble-size pottery cups, excellent for wine tasting. Aiden cast his eyes upon a large glazed wine jug, embossed with grapes and leaves. After a couple servings of the rich and flavorful red, they switched to a fruity white wine bottled in Nevsehir.

Afterward, they headed to a restaurant Cemil recommended overlooking the *Kizilirmak*, the Red River. The guys devoured an enjoyable meal and headed back to the Duru Hotel.

Willie jerked his head around. "Might be my imagination, but did you notice a car pulling out behind us?"

"No, but this afternoon I felt strange tingling sensations, as if someone was staring at me. Paranoid, eh?"

***

The operatives met in the lobby the following morning. This would be the first time they had split up, and each needed to be aware of the other's plans.

"I'll scout around Ürgüp. If possible, let's meet for lunch," Willie said.

"I'm going to the Mazi underground village first. It's about eleven miles from Ürgüp. If I finish early, I'll also hit Kaymakli."

After breakfast, they headed to their vehicles and left the parking lot with Aiden leading the way. As they approached Ürgüp, Willie flashed his lights farewell and turned off while Aiden continued to Mazi.

Following the signs, Aiden ended up at the base of a large cliff. He saw a cave opening, one of the entrances to Mazi. He parked the car, grabbed his backpack, and headed to a teashop across the road from the cliff. "Is there a fee and guide available for the underground city?" he asked the proprietor.

A wizened man stepped forward. "I'm Ishan Cavdar, the guide. No entrance fee. Here, you'll need this." Ishan handed Aiden a flashlight as they headed across the road and up an incline to the entrance. "This is one of the most authentic underground cities in Cappadocia. There are four entrances and multiple levels. Now and then tourists come here, unlike the larger underground cities where many go."

"I hope to visit the underground cities. I'd been to Cappadocia before but ran out of time and didn't see any of them."

"You should enjoy all of them, but first let's take you through Mazi. If you look on the right, this is where the church was located. Later we'll see the barns and the winery."

"Barns? Did the people living here bring their animals inside?"

"Yes, to protect their livestock from invaders. The same thing could also be done at the other underground cities, but this one had more areas carved out for stables."

"Interesting. Was that large circular stone used to close the tunnels?"

"Yes, with one stone the rest of the city could be blocked to invaders as the four entrances all lead to this main chamber. Now we'll head to the winery where you'll see a tunnel above, used to bring the grapes from the surface."

Before entering Mazi, Aiden reached into his backpack and turned on the detector. He heard a faint beep. He reached inside and turned the detector to vibration mode.

Ihsan took Aiden through the remainder of Mazi and pointed out the near-vertical shafts used to move from one level to another. Aiden took numerous photos, and after the tour thanked Ihsan for his help, giving him a small tip.

When Aiden returned to his car, he realized two hours had passed since he entered Mazi. He called Willie. "I'm on my way back. Where are you?"

"I found a decent place for lunch in Ürgüp. It's near the town square and is called the Ziggy Café."

"Be there in about twenty minutes."

***

When the two cars parted earlier that morning, Willie continued into Ürgüp to have a look around. Ürgüp is one of the main tourist destinations in the Cappadocia region. Willie didn't think the Kurdish rebels would attempt to hide their weapons here, but it was necessary to check and rule it out.

As Willie strolled through the streets, he turned his detector on with an earpiece plugged in. All remained quiet as he walked, looking into the various stores and shops. There were numerous hotels and nightclubs carved into the rock formations and many caves, which were converted into residential homes. His exploration came up empty.

When Aiden arrived at the restaurant, Willie sat munching on some dried nuts and drinking an Efes beer on one of the café's three outside terraces overlooking Ürgüp. Willie pointed to another beer waiting on the table, and Aiden helped himself.

"Looks like Ürgüp is a bust from a mission perspective." Willie shook his head and flexed his shoulders to work out a kink in his neck. "But I enjoyed seeing the sights and playing tourist."

"Well, I want to go back to Mazi tonight. Every so often, the detector vibrated while I followed the guide. Since I didn't come across any bats, and the guide didn't mention any, perhaps there's something of interest, eh?"

"Okay, we can go together this evening. After we eat, I'll check out Uchisar. If everything is negative there, I'll return to the hotel."

"I'm going to the Kaymakli next."

Aiden's drive to the Kaymakli underground city entrance took about twenty minutes. According to the guide, there were four levels open to the public with about 100 tunnels. To this day, local inhabitants used part of the city as cellars for storage and as stables. As in Mazi, there were numerous hiding places in the four levels, so it was possible the weapons were in one of the two locations.

Since several groups of tourists prowled through the various levels, Aiden turned on his detector but left it in his backpack, resorting to the earbuds for notification.

Three hours later, Aiden called it quits. There hadn't been a single beep. He wondered if it'd be worthwhile to come back during the evening and try to enter via one of the access points used by the locals. Fraught with its own problems, he'd have to enter someone's property and find an access point. This was something to discuss later with Willie.

Willie headed to Uchisar. As he approached, he saw the rock citadel towering above the town. The citadel itself was full of caves, first used as dwellings, and some were still occupied. There were several churches and numerous dovecotes used to house pigeons. The local farmers collected the pigeon droppings and used it as fertilizer in the nearby orchards and vineyards.

He parked his vehicle in the town square and hiked up the hill to the citadel where he intended to start his search. After paying the entrance fee, he wandered to the top of the citadel. From this vantage point, he could see for miles—countless fairy chimneys stretched in each direction. It was an awesome sight to behold as there wasn't another landscape anywhere to match this one. The chimneys were large, hollow vertical formations, varying in shape from ramshackle huts with haphazard roofs to exotic mushrooms and even symbols of fertility.

During his visit, Willie activated his detector, but as with Aiden's, it was quiet. On his way back down the steep incline, he noticed a Turkish flag blowing in the breeze. As he approached, he saw it mounted on top of the local police station.

This would make an interesting target. The Kurds could trap tourists inside the citadel and threaten to blow it up. Or attack the police station itself, which would cause panic and disruption to the tourist industry.

Willie continued his meandering through Uchisar and enjoyed the sights and sounds. All of a sudden, the detector beeped. In a crowded area, he couldn't pull the detector out of his backpack to see what triggered the alarm, so he returned to his vehicle.

He opened up his backpack in the car and checked the alarm condition. The detector registered minute traces of sarin. *Damn! Perhaps one of Saddam's weapons. I need to try to pick it up again.*

Energized by the discovery, he retraced his steps back to the Citadel. The detector remained silent despite Willie's painstaking check in broad daylight. He needed to return after dark to see if he could pinpoint the source. Excited and anxious, he retraced his entire route through Uchisar to see if anything else registered.

***

Finished with the day's search efforts, Aiden and Willie met at the House of Memories Restaurant and had an enjoyable meal of köfte, chicken kebabs, rice, grilled vegetables and local red wine.

Willie explained about his discovery.

"Well done, Willie! We need to pinpoint the sarin's source, eh?"

"Agree. We'll use both detectors. We'll be able to cover a larger area, and determine whether they both record the same results."

Since they needed to wait until much later to begin their search, the two men took advantage of being at this particular restaurant, which offered plenty of authentic Turkish food and culture. They took part in a group dance lesson with the owner and his family. Out of breath, Aiden and Willie returned to their table. They finished their meal with Turkish coffee and baklava.

When it was dark enough for them to conduct their search, Willie pointed out the way to the citadel and the tourist area. They sauntered in the stronghold's direction, ensuring their detectors were on and their earpieces in place.

Two hours later, they brought their search to a halt. Whatever had activated Willie's detector no longer registered. They were stymied by their inability to locate the cause.

The team returned to their vehicles, parked on the edge of the square near a Turkish governmental building. As Willie opened his car door, the detector went crazy. "Aiden! Aiden! Look. The detector's going nuts."

Aiden came over. He'd turned his detector off, so he switched it back on. Straight away it began to ding, the meter pegged. "Look, Willie! Mine is picking it up, eh?"

They walked around the area to hone in on the source. No matter which direction they went, the readings were strongest next to Willie's car. Aiden dropped on his hands and knees to look underneath. He saw a drain cover and pushed his detector on top. The device emitted a high-pitched squeal. "Willie, it's under your car! Move it forward."

Willie moved his car away and grabbed some tools from the trunk. They checked their detectors again, and both registered sarin gas.

They looked at each another. Willie spoke first. "Are we in danger? The meters are going nuts, this doesn't look good."

"Remember during the briefing at BHQ the scientist explained these detectors can register even minute traces from a well-sealed container. I don't think we've to worry too much, but let's get the masks."

They checked for anyone watching their movements. After donning their masks, Willie and Aiden worked together to remove the storm drain's cover. Shining a light into the hole, they saw a ladder going down about twenty feet. At the foot of the ladder lay a tan backpack.

"I think only one of us should go down," Aiden said. "In case it's leaking. I'll go. If something happens, get away fast and notify BHQ."

"Okay, be careful."

Aiden descended the ladder, watching the meter. Stepping down next to the backpack, he scanned it with his detector. "No change in the readings. I'll open the bag, eh?"

As he opened the backpack, Aiden recognized a Kurdish flag sewn into the flap. *Well, we know who's playing about. Let's see what's inside.*

Aiden peeked inside the bag, and there was one item inside. "Bingo! We've found a canister."

"Tag it and let's get out of here in case the owner comes back."

"I'll add a tracker to the bag, and be right up, eh?"

Ten minutes later, they left the parking lot and headed back to the Duru Hotel. Willie stopped at the bar to pick up a couple bottles of Efes and headed to Aiden's room. After verifying no one was watching, they entered and drank a toast to their discovery.

After finishing their beer, they composed a short status report.

To: Alpha

From: Rebel and Mountie

Persistent search efforts paid off. Identified location of a sarin gas canister in a backpack emblazoned with a Kurdish flag. Bag is tagged and stationary. Please advise whether continue tracking or grab now.

***

The thin man made note of their return to the hotel. He hadn't followed them during the day, per his boss's instructions and had been instructed to remain near the hotel throughout the night to keep an eye on them. Waiting at the hotel for their return seemed a waste of time if the boss wanted to find out what the men were up to, but he did as he was told.

Chapter 20
Göbekli Tepe, Turkey
Monday, March 14

CC woke up late and took a long, hot shower before breakfast. When he joined the others in the canteen tent, the ongoing discussion centered on Jürgen's wall discovery.

"I think it's a temple wall." Jürgen pointed at the excavation schematic. "If this was part of the perimeter wall it should protrude from the original boundary and several structures would surround it."

Konrad nodded his agreement. "Ja. The best thing to do is to put extra hands into this area. If we confirm Jürgen's hypothesis, then we'll continue using more personnel to uncover the wall. If not, they can return to their regular work areas."

The canteen emptied as everyone headed out to begin the workday. CC drained his coffee and motioned for Jürgen to wait. "Any word on the injured worker? I hope he's okay."

"The doctor released him from the hospital late last night. I saw him earlier, talking with Ahmed, the Turkish foreman. I told Ahmed the man can work with us today if he's up to it. He seemed to be a hard worker."

"Okay, he can help me." *It'll make it easier to keep an eye on him.*

As they started up the hill toward their excavation zone, CC spotted the injured man and approached him. "How are you feeling today? Did the doctor give the okay for you to return to work?"

"Good morning," the man said in passable English. "I'm much better today. Allah be praised, my head is hard, so I only needed a few stitches. No concussion."

"Good to know. I'm CC. What's your name?"

"I'm Merdem Dimen."

"Nice to meet you. Today we'll work along the wall, but every time we clear about four feet, we need to put in a support beam, so the wall doesn't collapse."

A hint of moisture filled the overcast sky. CC and Merdem worked well together, with smooth and careful strokes of the shovels along the line of staggered markers, which indicated the hypothesized location of Jürgen's wall.

Both men were quiet—the only sounds were shovels biting into the sandy soil and grunts as they tossed the earth to the side.

Thunk! Merdem's shovel bit into an immovable object. He tossed the shovel down and scooped soil away with his hands. He jumped to his feet.

"Mr. CC. Come quick!"

"What's the matter? Did you find something?"

"I did—look."

CC peered into the small depression. A skull rested at the bottom of the hole. A human skull. There was plenty of black hair and sun-darkened skin attached. Empty eye sockets peered back, and the mouth was frozen in time, a grimace stretched across the face.

"What do we have here?" CC widened the hole to get a better look. As he pushed the soil further away, he found an arm. Then a hand. A foot—all arrayed around the head.

"Merdem. Quick. Get Jürgen."

Merdem scurried away and came back with Jürgen and Konrad. Ahmed and a group of Turkish workers followed, alerted to Merdem's call for Jürgen.

By this time, a swarm of black flies enveloped the head. The stench was unbearable. CC pulled a bandanna from his back pocket and tied it around his mouth.

"Ahmed, contact the police and tell them what we've found." Konrad gagged and moved to the side, the remains of his breakfast mixing with the loosened soil.

"Yes, Mr. Konrad. I'll get them."

An hour later, two police vans and an ambulance approached the excavation, emergency lights flashing. CC explained in English what happened, with Ahmed translating. The policemen added new stakes and red and white tape emblazoned with '*Polis—Dur*' around the crime scene.

Through Ahmed, the senior police officer requested everyone leave the area, except for Konrad, CC, and Merdem.

"How was the body found?"

CC pointed at Merdem and himself. "We were digging along the buried wall when we unearthed the head. As we cleared dirt away, we found the other body parts."

"Did you move anything?"

"Only the soil. Once we realized what we found, we stopped."

The police officer turned to Konrad. "Do you recognize the person?"

"*Nein*. Never saw him before."

While the officer conducted his interview, crime scene investigators continued to uncover the body. One yelled, "Sir, the whole body is here—but in pieces."

He nodded and snapped his notepad shut. "I want the names of everyone working here. I also need a copy of all foreign passports."

Konrad nodded. "We'll get them ready for you as soon as we can. Is there anything else?"

"No. But I might be back."

***

At long last, the morgue attendants placed the remains in a black body bag and headed to their van. Silence descended over the excavation.

Once released by the police, Merdem said, "I'll be gone part of the afternoon. I must go back to the hospital for a check-up."

"Okay, I'll let Jürgen know. Will you be back today?"

"I should be back by midafternoon."

***

Merdem returned from the hospital a few hours later, sporting a new dressing on his forehead. "They gave me a thorough examination and a bigger bandage. The nurse said some soil was still in the wound. Other than a good cleaning and more painkillers, the doctor said everything was okay."

"That's good news, Merdem." CC clasped his shoulder. "Dinnae push yourself too hard today."

"Okay, but I can still work. If I don't, the foreman won't pay me."

"I want you to take a short break every thirty minutes. The ruins have been here for centuries, so taking our time to uncover them won't matter. We'll work in another area, away from where you found the head."

With the morning's excitement causing a delay, the team worked until sunset and stopped for the day. CC headed back to camp while Merdem joined the other Turkish workers, who had their own campsite.

***

After eating dinner, CC went for his customary evening walk. As he reached the hill's summit, he could see the depression marking the tunnel's entrance in the setting sunlight.

All of a sudden, the depression changed shape and seemed to move. CC zigzagged in a low crouch as he continued heading toward the tunnel. He stopped, listened, and looked around, before moving forward. It appeared no one was paying attention. He repeated his cautious movements several times, weaving a circuitous route. Still no sign anyone was watching.

When he drew closer, CC could see the branches disguising the tunnel's entrance were pushed aside. He continued to move forward, remaining in the darkest shadows. Clinking noises came from inside.

CC maneuvered into a better location for monitoring the entrance. As he placed a foot down, it caught on a root. He yanked it away—big mistake. Small rocks held in place by the root cascaded down the hill.

The noises in the tunnel stopped. CC held his breath. All was quiet except for the chirping of crickets.

CC heard movement. Without warning, a man burst from the tunnel, put down a backpack, and replaced the branches over the entrance. The man took out a small flashlight and directed the beam over his handiwork. He made a few corrections and started down the hill.

When the man turned around, CC almost gasped. *It was Merdem!* CC's suspicions were confirmed. The man was working with whoever placed the weapons and explosives. He watched Merdem head to the Turkish campsite and waited in case he returned.

An hour later, with no further sign of Merdem, CC entered the tunnel. He went to the back where he'd discovered the backpack and the boxes.

The backpack was gone, indicating it must have been the one Merdem carried when he left the cave. CC looked at the boxes. When he moved the top two aside, they seemed lighter. He pried the top off the first one. It had been filled with grenades. Now half were missing. He opened the second one, only to find half the plastic explosives had also disappeared.

CC replaced the top on the second box and checked the others. They appeared undisturbed. He brushed away the marks he'd made and left.

Where's Merdem taking the explosives? What's his target? Is that the last we'll see of him or will he be back?

CC returned to his tent and sent a status report.

To: Alpha

From: Haggis

Injured workman named Merdem Karza Dimen. Suspicions confirmed. Merdem visited weapons cache. Backpack, grenades, and plastic explosives missing. Target(s) unknown. Request priority background check. Dismembered body found in excavation. Identity unknown. Will advise any new info.

***

Merdem returned to the tent he shared with another Turkish worker. He took everything out of the backpack and laid it on his bed. Weapons and munitions were divided into two piles, returning one to the backpack he brought from the tunnel. Everything else went into his knapsack, except for a loaded pistol, which he stuffed in a pocket. He hid the first bag under his bed, and then picked up the second one and headed into the night air.

Merdem worked his way out of the campsite and headed to the area excavated the previous year. Early that morning, he'd hollowed out several places to place the plastic explosives. Working with extreme care, Merdem inserted detonators into the plastique. He placed them in hollowed-out niches and covered them, leaving a small part of the fuse showing.

Once finished, Merdem returned to the Turkish campsite and joined some of the others who were relaxing with a couple bottles of raki. He stayed with them until they finished the bottles, then made his way back to the tent, a big smile on his face, pleased he'd accomplished the mission undiscovered.

Tomorrow Merdem planned to show up for work as normal. No one would know the difference. Only the dead guy knew his true reason for being there—that's why Merdem had killed him.

Chapter 21
Aleppo, Syria
Monday, March 14

The following morning, Ben rose early and booted up his laptop. A new email from Alpha topped the list. He scanned the contents and sat back in the armless chair.

Background checks still underway on Ismet. Ben slammed his hand down. *It's got to be the same guy. Sure, there could be many Ismet Timurs, but how many exhibit facial scars caused by the Halabja attack?*

Pulling up Jake's last email, Ben compared the descriptions with the photos he took and felt certain it was the same man. He'd sent his pictures to Jake but no response yet. If Jake thought they had a match, this could be an important breakthrough.

Ben closed his laptop and headed downstairs for breakfast. Dave sat at a table by himself. After filling a plate, Ben joined him. "Morning. What's going on?"

"Not much. I'm on my second cup of coffee, getting charged up for the day, for sure."

"Remember, I mentioned my meeting with Ismet in Al-Bab? Last night when Pierre and I visited the Souk al-Medina, I'm sure I spotted him."

"Yeah, most likely. I've seen him there myself. He also hangs around the clinic. It didn't occur to me that his behavior might be unusual, so I didn't mention it."

"Well, I'm not sure if it's unusual or a coincidence. I find it curious he'd seek treatment from the MSF in Al-Bab and then show up here. Being in Aleppo may be nothing by itself, but the fact you saw him near the clinic makes me wonder what his game is, that's for sure."

"I guess. But that's your area—I'll keep my nose out. Oh, after we finish with the last patient we need to go on a trip. The airport called. Your bags showed up."

"Don't they deliver?"

"Nope. They expect us to pick them up, and they'll want a hefty reward for finding your bags."

"Figures. Corruption to the core."

"Once we collect your bags, we'll pick up the item we talked about last night, for sure." Dave glanced around, but none of the local staff were in the room. He lowered his typical booming voice to a loud whisper. "I made arrangements before you came downstairs."

"That's great. I'll feel better with my stuff and that piece of equipment."

After breakfast, Dave and Ben headed upstairs, where several patients waited for treatment. Ben took the first patient, a man who looked to be about ninety, into an examination room.

"What can I do for you today?"

"Huh? How are you today?" The old fella cupped a shriveled hand around one ear.

Got the message. "No. What do you want? Is there pain?"

"Yes, yes. Pain."

"Sit down and I'll check you over." Ben pulled over a stool and listened to the man's chest with his stethoscope.

"Cough."

"No, no cough."

"I want you to cough." Ben demonstrated what he wanted. Ten minutes later, he completed his examination.

"Where's the pain?"

"Plumbing." The old geezer cracked a toothless grin and laughed.

"Do you have a problem going to the bathroom?" Ben mimicked using the toilet.

"No, no, no. Have woman. Need via."

"What?"

"Need via grass."

"How old are you?"

"Ninety-one. My woman is eighty-nine. She says get via grass from doctor."

"I think she meant Viagra."

"That's it. She read in magazine. We make babies."

Ben cringed at the picture that came to mind. He scribbled on a piece of paper. "Go to the nurse outside. She'll give you one tablet. Come back next week." *If you're still alive.*

The next few patients had routine maladies, typical of those surviving on a poor diet and living in squalor. After handing out a variety of medications for dysentery, hepatitis, and dehydration, the waiting room emptied.

Dave walked in. "Lunch time. Let's eat and we'll head to the airport after we finish, for sure."

They filled plates and sat with Pierre and several other doctors.

"Is anyone going to the souk tonight?" Ben asked.

"Yes," Pierre said. "Would you like to join us?"

"Sure, if it's not any trouble."

"We'll meet in the lobby at 1900."

"Okay, thanks."

After they finished lunch, Ben and Dave headed for a vehicle for the hour-long trip to the airport. As with Ben's inaugural travel through the city, Dave seemed to find every pothole. The jarring made it almost impossible to talk but Ben had matured and no longer required the panic strap.

Occasional gunfire echoed across the city during their journey. Dave shook his head. "Unrest has been heating up for several months, but now gunfire seems to be part of the norm, for sure."

"Is that why you authorized weapons for your team?"

"Yes. Under normal circumstances, we'd never be armed— we're noncombatants. But we can't rely on the locals to guarantee our safety."

Dave spun the wheel, slid ahead of an oncoming truck and entered the airport parking lot to the accompaniment of the truck's horn.

"Do you need a hand with your luggage?" Dave squeezed the vehicle into a small parking spot near the terminal's entrance.

"No, I should be all right. Be back as quick as I can."

Ben worked his way into the terminal through a mass of humanity striving to exit the building. Once inside, he looked around for luggage claim. He stopped a porter and asked for guidance. The man pointed at an ill-lit, glass-enclosed office. A sign explained *Closed for prayers.*

The clock on the wall read 1430, so Ben leaned against the office door to wait. Ten minutes later, a young man limped toward him, carrying a bunch of keys. He grinned at Ben, several teeth missing.

"Hello. You want baggage, yes?"

"Yes. Someone called and said my bags arrived. Here are the claim tickets."

The man used a key and stepped aside so Ben could enter. "In that room." He motioned to an inner door. "Go ahead and check. When you find, bring to the desk."

Ben moved what seemed like half the luggage in the room before he spotted his bags. He yanked them free and went to the desk.

"Claim tickets please." After a slow comparison of the numbers on the luggage and the claim tickets, the man nodded.

"Yes, right baggage. Five thousand Syrian pounds."

"What?"

"Five thousand pounds. Each bag."

"That's robbery."

"No robbery—fee for finding luggage. No pay, no luggage."

Ben did a quick calculation. Ten thousand Syrian pounds was about forty-six dollars. He pulled the money out of a pocket and handed it over.

The man beamed and stuck the money in his pocket. "Me help carry luggage? No charge."

"No, that's okay, I've got it."

When Ben returned to the vehicle, he explained what happened to Dave, who laughed.

"Yeah, the fee is crazy. I think they search for foreign names on the luggage tickets and pull some aside as 'lost'. Then they wait a few days and let the owner know their baggage arrived and claim their fee, for sure."

Ben tossed his bags in the back and climbed into the passenger seat as Dave took off. Reaching the road, he took a quick left, almost clipping the front of a taxi. Ben just closed his eyes—and prayed.

Twenty minutes later, Dave pulled off the highway and drove to a large, gray concrete building that had seen better days. Most of the glass was missing from the window frames. The concrete was pockmarked in many places, the roof on the verge of collapse.

"Here's the place. Let me do the talking." Dave got out of the vehicle, grabbed a small box, and walked toward a half-open door. Ben caught up to Dave as he put down the box and pushed the door open enough to enter. A loud squeal pierced the air as the door rubbed across a rusted metal frame.

"Who's there?" A large man, dressed in local clothing but wearing Western tennis shoes, approached. As he walked, his earrings danced to each step. Over his shoulder rested an AK-47.

"Dr. Dave. Remember I wanted another pistol?"

"You bring package?"

"Yes. Everything you asked for."

Dave reached outside, grabbed the box and set it on the floor. He used his foot to slide the package toward the man.

The man pulled out a small package that had been tucked behind his back and tossed it at Dave, who caught the package with both hands.

"Here is pistol, bullets, magazines."

Dave nodded, and they backed out the door. As soon as they got in the vehicle, Dave started the engine and left.

"What was in the box? You didn't ask me for any money." Ben opened the envelope and shook out the contents, a used but serviceable 9mm Beretta, thirty rounds of ammunition, and two magazines.

"Didn't need any money. He wanted Western cigarettes, Swiss chocolate, and adult magazines, for sure."

Ben endured another wild but uneventful ride back to MSF Headquarters. When they returned to the building, he went to his room and further examined his new weapon.

***

Just after 1900, four MSF staffers and Ben, now armed, headed to the souk. Everyone was in a joyous mood. They planned to eat at a family style restaurant, prowl through the souk, and perhaps end up at one of the smaller restaurants, which featured local musicians.

Almost everyone had an enjoyable evening, both during the meal and listening to the music. A guy who tried to sing in English but couldn't quite pronounce the words had everyone laughing. They headed back to the MSF building around midnight. Ben didn't enjoy himself since he had been preoccupied with trying to spot Ismet.

Ben sat to compose a short message to headquarters.

To: Alpha

From: Kiwi

Baggage in possession. Now armed. No sign of Ismet. NTR.

After sending his report, he looked for new messages. The one he wanted was top of the list.

Chapter 22
Zakho, Iraq
Monday, March 14

Jake checked his email while having his first cup of coffee. There was one.

Aussie, please review the attached photos. I took these of a guy I met in Al-Bab. He said his name was Ismet Timur from Halabja. Wonder if he's the Ismet you reported on? Let me know. Thanks. Kiwi

Jake opened the attachments and stared at Ismet's face. No doubt, his Ismet and Ben's was the same guy. The descriptions he obtained were a perfect match. He emailed the entire team.

To: Alpha

From: Aussie

Examined Kiwi's photos of Ismet. The descriptions I received in Halabja and Zakho match the scarring on Kiwi's photos. Believe we've now confirmed the identity and location of one of the Iraqi Kurds who came across Saddam's chemical weapons. Please advise next steps.

After a filling vegetarian breakfast, Jake took a taxi the eighteen miles to Silopi. They waited in a short queue at the border. After Jake presented his passport and journalist credentials, they entered Turkey.

Once in the Silopi town center, Jake paid the taxi driver and walked over to the bus station, where he purchased a one-way ticket to Mardin. He was told the bus would leave in an hour, so he wandered around the town center to kill time.

The bus was in better physical shape than the one he took to Zakho and moved much faster. Once he'd boarded, the driver said, "Welcome. It'll take us about three hours to make the trip to Mardin. Depends on any PKK attacks and extra roadblocks or road closures instituted by the Turkish Army."

"Thank you. I hope it's a quiet trip, and I'll be able to get some sleep."

He was dozing off when the bus came to a screeching stop. There was lots of shouting, both inside and outside of the bus.

Several screams also echoed through the bus. Someone translated for Jake. "The driver said he came upon an army checkpoint, which wasn't there yesterday. He ran over a guard's foot who was standing too close."

Two stern-looking Turkish privates boarded the bus. "Papers," demanded one of them. Seeing others pulling out their Turkish identity cards, Jake took his passport from his backpack and offered it to a soldier. The guy scrutinized the passport and limped toward the driver and berated him, causing the driver to cower. Anger spent, he slapped the man across the head, handed Jake's passport to the other soldier, and left the bus. The private returned the passport to Jake and said in broken English, "Welcome Turkey. Have good holiday."

The private continued his search. Once satisfied, he departed. Two other soldiers moved the barricade aside, and a sergeant waved the bus forward. Before they moved, the driver spoke to Jake. "The soldiers were very interested in you."

"What did they want?"

"Western foreigners are rare visitors to this part of Turkey, and draw interest. I told them you boarded in Silopi, and they seemed satisfied. The guy yelling at me was the one I almost hit. That'll teach them to put up a new roadblock on a blind curve."

***

Around 1330, the bus pulled into the Mardin bus station. Jake thanked the driver and joined the other passengers. He went to a nearby shop and asked about a hotel room. The shopkeeper took Jake down the street to the Artuklu Kervansaray Hotel.

Jake dumped his stuff in the room and headed to the Mardin Bazaar. Gewran and Babir said Dersim always took their goods there, but they didn't specify where. He walked around the bazaar to acquaint himself. Jake began at one end of the busy market and inquired about Dersim.

"Hello. I'm looking for a man named Dersim who delivers goods from Zakho." He repeated his patter numerous times, as he went from stall to stall. "Do you know him?"

Most of the stall keepers shook their heads, but at one stall, Jake noticed there seemed to be special interest in what he said.

"No." The man stared at Jake. "I don't know any Dersim. Try the stalls on the other side of the bazaar."

***

Jake thanked him and headed in the direction he pointed. In the meantime, the man kept staring at Jake, pulled out his cell phone, and made a short call to Aram, who had escorted Dersim to his meeting with Mufti Tanreverdi.

"There's an Australian asking questions about Dersim. I told him I didn't know anyone by that name and sent him in the wrong direction."

"Keep an eye on the him. Report back when there's something noteworthy."

***

Jake continued asking for Dersim and met with the same negative response. Toward the end of the bazaar, someone said they knew him.

"Why are you looking for Dersim?"

"I'm a journalist writing an article about the Halabja survivors. My inquiries in Halabja led me to his cousins in Zakho. They told me Dersim came here. I want to include his story in my article."

"It's about two weeks since he last came. After dropping off his cousin's goods, he always goes to visit his friends who work in a shop near Mardin Castle. I don't remember the name, but ask around when you get there."

Jake thanked the man and headed toward the castle area. Behind Jake, a young man tagged along.

Following the directions, which weren't the best, Jake found the street near the castle with some difficulty. As in the bazaar, he inquired about Dersim. Most of the shopkeepers shook their heads, but at last Jake found the shop.

"Yes, he's a friend of mine. However, he isn't in Mardin right now."

"Do you know where he went?"

"No, I don't. He spends a day or so here, and either heads to Diyarbakir if he's more goods to drop off or returns to Iraq."

"Okay mate, thanks for your help. If you talk to him, tell him I'd like to interview him for my story about Halabja."

Jake left the shop and explored Mardin Castle. He didn't know whether he should head to Diyarbakir or stay longer in Mardin in case Dersim returned.

After visiting the castle, Jake headed back toward the hotel when a young man bumped into him. "Excuse me," he said. The man continued walking away from Jake.

Jake gave the man, who appeared to be in his mid-twenties a once-over. *I saw him at the bazaar. He was also the same man who ducked into a store as I glanced in his direction before I entered the one by the castle.*

After eating in the hotel restaurant, Jake went for a short walk. When he came out of the hotel, Jake spotted the man who had bumped into him. He'd picked up a tail. *Is the man working for the Turkish government or is he a PKK sympathizer?* Either way, he had to lose him.

After his walk, Jake returned to his room. He pulled out his laptop to check for new emails. No response from Bedlam regarding his earlier message. *Thought they might want me to assist Ben and capture Ismet. Only two days left.*

While he reviewed the teams' emails, he pondered his next move. Decision made, he emailed BHQ.

To: Alpha

From: Aussie

Visited Dersim's regular haunts in Mardin. No sign. Someone suggested he went to Diyarbakir so will follow.

Picked up a local tail, about twenty-five. Will shed ASAP.

Once done, he closed the laptop, climbed into bed, and shut out the light. He wanted to leave early the next morning.

***

The man following Jake didn't belong to the PKK. The Turkish government knew him as Lieutenant Derin Koray, and he worked undercover in the Mardin Bazaar. After completing his mandatory military service, Lt. Koray's mission was to monitor activities of potential PKK sympathizers, for his true employer, the Turkish National Intelligence Organization.

Lt. Koray remained in the shadow of a building across the street from Jake's hotel. He had line-of-sight to Jake's room and remained in place until the lights went out. He pulled out his phone and pressed a speed-dial number.

"Suspect appears down for the night. Will resume coverage in the morning."

Chapter 23
Al-Bab, Syria
Monday, March 14

Ismet rose long before prayer call. He went through the ritual purification before going to the nearby mosque. Prayers completed, he returned to his rented room in a shabby-looking guesthouse. The price was right with no questions asked.

Fixing a breakfast of bread, honey, and cheese, Ismet washed the meal down with a cup of strong tea. As he ate, he reflected on how his life had changed since they stumbled across the weapons at the derelict Iraqi military compound. His life as a scavenger seemed a lifetime ago.

We exist in a bitter world. Now I'm involved in creating Kurdistan. Did Allah choose me?

***

It had been almost three weeks since Dersim dropped Ismet off at the bus station in Silopi. He found the bus to Nusaybin, loaded his luggage in the overhead rack, and tried to sleep during the seventy-mile journey, which would take two hours.

Ismet left the bus in Nusaybin and found a taxi driver to take him to the al-Qamishli border crossing. After asking several truck drivers for a ride into Syria, one named Kadir agreed. "Yes, I'll take you. Say nothing to the authorities as we cross. I'll do all the talking. Do you have any money? They might need to be persuaded."

Ismet hid his luggage in the back of the truck and jumped into the cab. "Thank you. Here is some money. If you don't need it for crossing, keep it for yourself as payment for taking me."

"I make the trip from Turkey into Syria every week. The past few times it's been taking longer and longer to go through the crossing. The problem isn't on the Turkish side, it's the Syrians."

"Why?"

"The Syrians are arresting people trying to leave the country. They're fleeing because of the government's crackdown on civil unrest."

"Will there be any problem getting into the country?"

"I don't think so. I'll add the money you gave me to what I give the guards, so that should ease us into Syria with no questions."

As Kadir predicted, once the money exchanged hands they were waved into Syria without any problems. "You're in Syria, where are you going?"

"I'm going to Al-Bab."

"I'm going to Aleppo. You're welcome to continue with me to Al-Bab. I'd like the company, it's a boring drive."

"Thank you. I appreciate your generous offer."

Kadir put the vehicle into gear, and the truck lurched forward and gained speed. As they bumped along, the lush greenery disappeared, replaced by parched land. A twin-engine plane flew toward them, its landing gear dropping as it continued past. Ismet leaned out the window and viewed the craft until it disappeared over the horizon.

"That plane's heading to Al-Qamishli. Twice a day from Damascus." Kadir swerved to miss an errant goat ambling along the roadside.

"Have you been on it?"

"No." Kadir shook his head. "No desire to fly on a plane. Unless you're a pilot, you've no control. At least when I'm driving, I know where the truck's going, and I can decide what happens."

"I've never been on a plane. I'd like to one day, Allah willing."

Mile after dusty mile slipped by. Once in a while a small patch of green appeared, perhaps fed by a spring. Signs of life stirred at these locations. A few people, goats, sheep, and small, tilled fields and olive trees co-existed. Traffic was sparse, an occasional truck and a rare car. There were more animal-drawn carts than motorized vehicles.

Kadir pulled into a truck stop on the outskirts of Al Mushayrfah. As they approached, Ismet noted a swath of green stretching from horizon to horizon.

"The area is so green. Why is this?"

"We're north of Ar-Raqqa, which sits on a tributary of the Euphrates River." Kadir pointed to the south and continued his motion to the north. "A small part comes through here, turning the desert into an oasis. We'll stop for diesel and a tea before continuing to Al-Bab."

During the long ride, Ismet and Kadir exchanged stories about the Kurdish situation, once Kadir announced he was also a Kurd.

He was in complete agreement with establishing a recognized Kurdistan nation and hoped one day he'd see this happen.

"I'd also like to behold a formal Kurdistan nation," Ismet said. "In fact, I'm going to Al-Bab and later to Aleppo, to find others to help us push Syria and Turkey to agree."

"How do you plan to get Turkey to agree to such a thing?" A puzzled expression spread across Kadir's face. "I think they'd prefer to eliminate all Kurds if possible."

"A friend and I found something near Halabja we think will be persuasive. There's no other way to make Kurdistan a reality."

"What did you find?"

"Something left over from Saddam Hussein's time—weapons."

"What kind of weapons? How'll they be used?"

"I'm sorry, I don't want to talk anymore about it." *Did I say too much?*

Kadir pulled into the Al-Bab bus station. Ismet thanked him and wished him well on the remainder of the journey. Kadir said, "I'll spend the night here before heading to Aleppo. Do you have somewhere to stay?"

"No, I don't. Can you recommend a place?"

"Let's lock up the truck and we'll go to a guesthouse I use."

***

After a simple but filling meal, Kadir offered to take Ismet to meet some of his friends. Ismet, sensing some danger, was reluctant to do so, but so far everything Kadir said appeared to be true.

"Okay, Kadir. Who're these friends?"

"They're people like you and me, who dream of a Kurdistan nation. I think they'll be interested in meeting you."

After weaving through the streets and doubling back to make sure they weren't followed, Kadir knocked on the door of a nondescript building. A peephole opened, and someone glared at them. The opening slammed shut, and the door sprang open.

"Kadir! Welcome back, my friend," said the guard, a burly man holding a shotgun. "Who's this?"

"This is Ismet. He's one of us. He's from Iraq."

The guard said nothing further but motioned both men inside. After a cursory search for weapons, the guard nodded toward a closed door. When they entered the room, all talking ceased as the occupants looked at the newcomers.

One of the men asked Kadir, "Who's your friend?"

"This is Ismet, from Iraq. He also longs for a new Kurdistan nation and has something that'll help."

Ismet noticed no names were offered by any of the men. He sensed some hostility, which was to be expected, as they didn't know him.

"I'm an Iraqi Kurd, who was injured in Saddam's attack against Halabja. As you can see, I'll always bear the scars, but I was one of the lucky ones."

Ismet told his story about finding the weapons. The discussion continued until the early morning hours when the group agreed to help Ismet.

They had one condition. The group's apparent leader said, "We don't like the MSF doctors coming to Al-Bab every week. They might be foreign spies. We monitor each of them when we can. Abdel, the manager of the hotel where the MSF hold their clinics, always gives us warning of their arrival."

"What do you want me to do?" Ismet asked.

"We take turns going to the clinic with false ailments so we can look around. We also obtain medicine for our Kurdish brethren."

"Show me where the hotel is located. I'll complain of pain from my injuries."

***

Breakfast over and his tea finished, Ismet stopped his reverie about his journey from Halabja. He needed to plan his report for the meeting scheduled that evening.

He planned to tell them about Ben, the New Zealand doctor, how he met him at the Al-Bab clinic and later in Aleppo. He'd hand over the pain pills he obtained for those who needed them.

Did Ben notice me at Suq al-Medina? Should I silence him?

Chapter 24
Cappadocia, Turkey
Tuesday, March 15

Morning found Willie and Aiden in the lounge for a quick breakfast. They kept to their normal routine, discussing their plans at a corner table, away from prying eyes and ears.

Aiden spread a tourist map of the Cappadocia region on the table and pointed to his destinations. "I'll knock out two more underground cities today, Tatlarin and Özkonak."

"I'll head to Gaziemir this morning. We must resume our tourist roles for any prying eyes. How about lunch here in Avanos? Afterward, I'll prowl the streets of Ortahisar."

"I hope we find something definitive soon. I don't mind the tourist bits, but I'd rather we locate the weapons, assuming the Kurds put any here."

"Agreed. I'd still like to understand what set off the detector in Uchisar."

"Okay, perhaps we can return there this evening, eh?"

**

Aiden left the hotel for the six-mile ride to Tatlarin. Once he arrived, he noticed a lot of erosion of the cliff area, making this an improbable location for a weapons cache. Still, he needed to check it out. He parked his car and headed up a steep grassy path toward the cliff face.

**

As Aiden climbed, a cream-colored Mercedes pulled into the lot and parked next to his car. A large, fat man with gray hair got out.

The fat man pulled out his cell phone from a pocket and speed-dialed. When someone answered, he spoke in Kurmanji, the dialect spoken by Turkish Kurds. "The one I'm following is at Tartlarin. He's going inside."

"Keep an eye on him, but don't get too close. Report back if there's something of interest."

He put the phone back in his pocket and returned to his car to wait.

**

At the same time Aiden reached the entrance, an elderly gentleman stepped forward. "Hello. I'm tour guide. Read this." He handed Aiden a small leaflet written in English explaining about the underground city. "Come."

They entered Tatlarin through a narrow, dark tunnel. In some places, the low ceiling forced Aiden to crouch to avoid smashing his head. Even when the tunnel ran into wider open spaces, the ceiling rarely reached over six feet high.

As expected, Aiden noted many similarities between Tatlarin and the other underground cities. A tourist could visit several modern-day cities and find similarities among them.

They walked through the two levels open to the public, Aiden utilized the detector to scan for any substances. It remained silent. He thanked the guide when they returned outside, gave him a small tip, and went back to his car. He set off for Avanos for his lunch date.

***

Willie drank another coffee before driving to Gaziemir. After arriving, he realized Gaziemir's entrance hall was built with stone rather than carved into the mountainside. The passage was huge, with a length of over thirty feet. As he entered with other tourists, Willie reached into his backpack, extracted the headphones, and activated the detector. Throughout their tour of the underground city, the phones remained silent.

The visit itself was interesting. He viewed a bathing area, two churches dating from the Byzantine era, animal shelters, storage rooms, cooking areas and living spaces. Ever mindful of their mission, he wanted to move on to the next area, as Gaziemir appeared to be a bust.

Once the tour ended, Willie went back to his car for the return trip to Avanos. Aiden waved at him when he pulled into the village square.

"Find anything?" Aiden asked.

"Nothing, although I enjoyed the tour."

"Same for me at Tatlarin. I guess we should eat lunch. Afterward, I'll head to Özkonak."

"Let's try the *Bizim Ev Lokantasi* (Our House Restaurant)," Willie said. "I enjoyed their food the last time I visited Cappadocia."

"You're the food expert, lead on."

The men made their way to the restaurant. A large group of tourists entered the hotel in front of them, creating mass chaos for the waiters as they tried to sit fifty cackling foreigners who wandered around like lost children.

A waiter walked over to Willie and Aiden.

"I'm sorry it'll be a few minutes before a table is ready. We must organize this group first. May I suggest a drink at the bar while you wait?" The waiter gestured through a pointed arch toward the empty bar, with a bartender waiting for customers. " I'll come for you."

"Thanks," they said.

They headed to the counter, where they received complimentary thimbles of red wine. After a short wait, the waiter escorted them to a table. To their surprise, Cemil Galip sat at the table.

"Welcome back to Avanos, my friends. I saw you park in the square and figured you might come here for lunch. I'm on my break, so I thought I'd surprise you."

"It's good to see you." Willie shook Cemil's hand. "How's your family?"

"Everyone's fine, thank you. I've taken the opportunity to order a proper Turkish meal for us, along with some Tekel beer."

While they ate, Cemil asked, "So what have you seen since you arrived in Cappadocia?"

The guys gave Cemil a rundown of the underground cities, the open-air museums, and the citadel.

"Weren't you staying at the Kelebek Cave Hotel in Göreme? I thought I saw you at the Duru Hotel last night."

Aiden and Willie exchanged glances. Willie explained to Cemil about their rooms being ransacked. "We switched hotels."

Cemil and the guys strolled back to the square after an enjoyable meal and one too many Tekel beers. "Do you want to come back to the shop for some wine?"

"Thanks for the offer, but our time in Cappadocia is winding down, and there's plenty still to visit," Aiden clasped Cemil's shoulder as they shook hands. "We'll come back again before we leave."

***

Cemil waved farewell and returned to his shop. The thin man waited for him inside. "What did you find out?"

"They appear to be tourists, but I don't know. Something isn't right about them. They said they switched hotels because their rooms were ransacked. But why did it take them a few days before they moved?"

"Keep an eye on them while they're in Avanos."

"Should I follow them when they leave?"

"No, someone else will take care of it."

***

Aiden took off for Özkonak, about eight miles away. He found the underground city an interesting place to visit, but disappointing from a mission perspective. After wasting almost two hours at Özkonak, he headed back to the Duru Hotel to await Willie's return.

***

Willie headed to Ortahisar to check out the main tourist attraction, which dominated the area. With a height of 280 feet, it was a castle-like rock formation and a former strategic stronghold. The honeycombed castle had caves and tunnels while uneven, circular steps led to the top.

Willie worked his way up to take advantage of the stunning panorama. On his way down, he followed a winding tunnel. Along one side, a smaller channel branched to the right. Willie ducked under the rope cordoning the area off and entered the smaller shaft to find out where it led. He'd turned his detector on when he started down from the top, but it remained silent.

The tunnel widened into a small room. There were a couple of old Turkish carpets in the corner. *Strange. What're these doing here? Nothing else here.* Willie moved one of them and an AK-47 clattered to the floor. He continued shifting the carpet and uncovered five more weapons.

As Willie moved the second rug, the needle on his meter twitched, and a high-pitched whine almost shattered his eardrums. Two wooden crates lay hidden underneath. He pried off the tops. Ammunition filled one while the other held grenades and six small rectangles of plastic explosives.

Now we're talking!

Willie planted a tracker in each container, replaced the covers, and put everything back the way he found it. He retreated to the main stairs and headed back to his car.

***

150

That evening Willie and Aiden ordered room service so they could discuss the day's results. No bugs were found in their rooms, but Aiden turned on the TV and found a channel with Turkish music. He cranked up the volume as loud as they could tolerate.

"The underground cities were negative, but at last, we've something positive to report," Willie said.

"Yeah, about time. From the top of the castle, someone could create chaos with those weapons. There wouldn't be a way to escape if the Turkish security forces lived up to their reputation. Perhaps it's planned as a suicide mission."

"We need to put our report together and include negative searches and the weapons cache."

"Don't forget we should mention about our uninvited lunch guest. He expected us."

To: Alpha

From: Mountie and Rebel

Tatlarin, Özkonak, and Gaziemir underground cities a bust. Small weapons cache, comprised of AK-47s, grenades, and plastic explosives located in Ortahisar Castle. Trackers embedded— stationary.

Sarin gas canister tagged in Uchisar remains in original location.

Possible unwanted contact with Cemil Galip, owner of Cemil Galip's Pottery Shoppe. Volunteered he knew we switched hotels. Appears to be monitoring our activities. Request background check.

* * *

While Aiden and Willie talked inside, tourists and locals crowded the hotel's perimeter as they enjoyed the mild evening and partook of local beverages—cognac, wine, beer, raki, and ayran, a yogurt-based drink.

Two men concentrated on the hotel's entrance—Thin Man and Beady Eyes. A man left the hotel and walked toward them. Silence enveloped the three as they headed to a nearby car and climbed inside.

"Well? What did you find out?" the thin man asked.

"The two foreigners ordered room service. It appears they're in for the evening." Cemil glanced at his watch. "Can I go now? I've done as you asked. My wife and children are expecting me."

"Yes, you may go." Beady Eyes looked at Cemil. "If you run into them again, don't say anything about being at the hotel tonight. The government thanks you for doing your patriotic duty."

***

Two other men surveilled the hotel, unaware of the other group. The fat man, and a young man wearing glasses, Spectacle Man, scanned the crowd.

"I can't find them. Perhaps they're inside." The young man pushed his glasses back up his long, pointy nose. "Shall I find out?"

"No. We don't want them to catch us. We'll come back tomorrow."

Chapter 25
Mardin, Turkey
Tuesday, March 15

Afran trudged up the hill in the bright morning sunshine, taking care to check behind for any unwanted followers. The dew still clung to the high grass, making for a slippery and hazardous trek. He shrugged his shoulders, trying to shift his heavy backpack to a better position.

Fifteen minutes later, he reached his destination, a two-story rickety stone and timber barn used for sheltering sheep during the winter. Although the stone was strong and well cemented together, the wood appeared ready to tumble down during the next strong wind.

Appearances were deceiving. Afran set down his pack and opened a brand-new padlock holding a heavy wooden door snug within a steel frame on the side of the building. He pushed the door open, grabbed the bag and dragged it inside, using a shoulder to shut the door.

Taking a penlight from his pocket, he turned it on and threw three deadbolts. He pulled out a box of matches and went around the large room lighting the kerosene lanterns.

Whitewashed brick walls supported a solid wooden-beam ceiling. Scattered around the room were several workbenches, toolboxes open and ready for use.

Tap knock knock tap. Knock tap knock. Knock tap knock.

Afran went to the door and responded. *Tap knock tap.*

Thunk. Thunk. Thunk. The deadbolts slid out of the door, allowing him to pull it open. Outside, four of his men waited to enter. He stepped aside and the pack-laden men entered without a word.

Once Afran secured the door, and the men dropped their packs, they exchanged greetings. "Four others will be here in about thirty minutes, and the last group will arrive in an hour."

"I'll make tea." One of the men walked to the far wall where a table held a propane bottle and small gas stove. Next to the table stood several five-gallon containers containing water collected during a recent rain. Primitive facilities, but effective enough for their needs.

"Let's empty the packs and sort the contents so when the others arrive we can assemble our packages." Afran pointed to three tables. "Pull those tables together and put everything on them."

Over the next hour, the remainder of the men arrived, packs were emptied, and tea furnished. The tables were piled high with an assortment of needed items: sticks of dynamite, blasting caps, detonators, grenades, spools of wire, rolls of electrical tape, plastic bags, and timers.

"Tape the dynamite into three-stick bundles." A short, wiry man, missing two fingers on his left hand, stepped forward as Afran explained what he wanted. "Nasdar Kaban, our explosives expert, will attach the detonators and timers."

"How do we detonate them?" someone asked.

"When three bundles are prepared for each man, Nasdar will explain how to place the explosives and ready them for detonation."

The men concentrated on their tasks and before long, the bundles were ready for Nasdar's contribution. First, he inspected each bundle and secured the dynamite. After he added the detonators and timers, Nasdar continued to prepare the bombs while the others drank tea and ate pistachios and dates. The conversation was subdued as the men contemplated the upcoming attack.

An hour passed while the men worked.

"We're ready," Nasdar said. "What's next?"

"Gather around." Afran stood next to another table, a huge hand-drawn map depicting the Bati Raman Oil Field. It showed a rough rectangle, measuring about two miles wide and eleven miles long. Thirty-three black circles and over a hundred red circles were spread throughout the area, while ten squares dotted the perimeter. A thick black line led away from the rectangle to the southeast.

"Here's what we have. The squares represent guard towers and the black circles represent the original wells. The red circles are newer wells." He pointed at the black line. "This line symbolizes the pipeline carrying the oil to Iskenderun, about five hundred kilometers away.

"We'll split into teams of two. Five teams will place a dynamite bundle near as many of the black circles as possible."

"Why not place some by the red circles?" someone asked.

"The older wells aren't as productive now. We don't want to destroy overall production, but cause enough damage to encourage the military to deploy their forces to protect the field."

Afran pointed back at the black line. "The final team will locate suitable places along the pipeline to place their charges. They'll cause damage and force the Turks to stop pumping until repairs are complete. If we're lucky, they'll spread troops along the entire pipeline."

"I've shown the men how to set the timers," Nasdar said. "What time do you want the action to start?"

"Detonation time will be 0430 tomorrow. We'll head to the village in pairs at 2200. The truck will meet us outside the village an hour later. I've allowed two hours for us to move into position. It's about eighty kilometers to the oil field, but we'll use back roads to avoid any security checkpoints.

"Each man will carry three dynamite bundles, four grenades, several rolls of tape, a spool of wire, and wire cutters."

Earlier Afran had numbered six wells for each team. "Place the bundles in your designated areas and when finished set trip wires on your way back using the grenades.

"By 0300, this should be completed. If you aren't finished, still head back to the truck, which will depart at 0400. By detonation time, we should be out of the area."

Several men wanted to destroy the wellheads, sending countless barrels of oil into the air. Others wanted to attack the A-frames supporting the walking beams, which raised and lowered the pumps in the wellheads. Neither location was selected. Rather, Afran decided on the motor operating the entire well.

"We want to keep any environmental impact as small as possible. We don't want to see the land burning like in Iraq in 1991. The motors are the components farthest away from the wellheads. Once they're destroyed, operation of the well ceases. Any questions?"

Silence greeted Afran as several men pushed toward to examine the map. No questions.

Afran glanced at his watch. "1700. Review the map. Rest." He pointed to the rear of the room. "There's bread and fruit in the back if you're hungry. I'll meet everyone at the truck by 2300. Will the final team departing make sure the lanterns are out and the door is locked? May Allah guide us tonight."

***

At 1900, Afran joined Dersim and Serbest at a small restaurant in the village. They ate a meal of rice pilaf and grilled vegetables, along with a bowl of spicy lentil soup and fresh bread. After the meal, he gave them new instructions.

"Serbest, when you get to Akçakale, I want you to remain there and prepare for the operation I've planned." He slid an envelope across the table. "Here's a map of the town, the address of a safe house, and specific instructions.

"There's a small military contingent which could request assistance when the operation begins. They might close the border."

Serbest smiled and glanced over his instructions. He nodded when he finished reading.

"I'll be ready."

"Dersim, after you drop Serbest off, head to Göbekli Tepe. Merdem is waiting for you. We want you to create another distraction."

"It will be done."

***

At 2300, an old truck pulled out of the village. Even though it appeared the vehicle might fall apart at any minute, the well-maintained engine purred like new. This was one of the PKK's transport vehicles, with the cargo area covered by heavy canvas and enough seats to handle the twelve men. Afran rode with Nasdar, who doubled as their driver.

The truck bumped and weaved along the dusty gravel road. The truck's lights lit up the still blossoming trees, changing them into sentries leading the way forward. In the back, the men talked among themselves, keeping their voices low so they couldn't be overheard.

"This'll be our first blow in obtaining Baziyan's freedom." Afran stared out the window as he spoke to Nasdar. "I studied the American war against the British to learn tactics. They used small bands to strike and then disappear. We'll do the same."

"I agree with your plan." Nasdar rocked in time to the bumps as he gripped the steering wheel and tried to miss the larger holes. "We need to attack in many places and spread them out, to make it easier for the break-out attempt."

At 0045, Nasdar brought the vehicle to a halt. Through the trees, the lights of a guard tower at the Bati Raman Oil Field shimmered against the night sky. Afran climbed out of the cab and walked to the back. The men climbed down and passed out the backpacks. Each pack displayed the Kurdish flag in a prominent position.

The men shouldered their packs, paired up with their partners, and crowed around Afran. He acknowledged them with a nod.

"You're the lance to strike fear into the enemy." Afran spoke in a soft voice. Those in the back strained to hear his words. "Go forward and begin our assault. May Allah guide you."

The pairs separated and disappeared into the trees. Within moments, there was no sign they had been there.

Afran returned to the cab and climbed back in. "Now we wait. I'd rather be with them."

"I too wish to be with them. But we all have our roles to play."

Afran nodded and let the silence wash over them.

***

As planned, five of the teams worked their way through the trees and approached a six-foot chain-link fence. Two of the men used penlights to check the fence for electrification and intrusion sensors. Nothing was apparent, so another team cut the links with bolt cutters to create a large enough hole to slip through.

Ten minutes later, the last of the ten men was inside the fence. They peeled away in pairs toward their respective targets. As the men moved further, the trees thinned until only tall grass remained.

They spread out searching for the wells. The Turks made it easy—each one displayed a number on a prominent red and white sign bearing the logo of the company—TPAO.

Pair by pair, the men continued their quiet ingress toward their targets, mindful of possible roaming guards. The night remained calm—only a light humming from the motors and squeaking and creaking from the well action disturbed the tranquil night.

One by one, dynamite bundles were taped into position by the motors, a single package delivered to each well. When a team finished placing their bundles, they backtracked to the fence for their departure. Before reaching the fence but back among the trees, they set tripwires to slow down any pursuit.

While the teams were busy within the oil field, the sixth team located the pipeline and followed it for about a mile before finding an ideal location to place their bundles.

The three-foot diameter pipeline was suspended on concrete pillars about six feet above the ground as it left the oil field. The men placed their charges near the base of a concrete pillar and by the bracket holding the pipe.

Once finished, they headed back to the truck, taking care to place tripwires among the nearby trees.

With the men busy with their assigned tasks, Afran paced, back and forth, with nothing to do but wait. He'd stop and gaze into the distance as if he could position the charges from afar.

"Relax, my friend." Nasdar waved his open right hand in the air. "It's up to the men to complete the job."

"I know, but I should be with them."

"Sometimes the commander must remain in reserve and leave the action to the young. You've done your job, now let them do theirs."

At 0330, the first pair returned to the clearing. Eyes bright, smiles spread across their faces, they flashed thumbs-up gestures as they opened bottles of water and gulped them down. Afran gave both men a pat of the back as they climbed into the back of the truck.

By 0350, the last team walked up to Afran. Unlike the other teams, they didn't smile and inspected the ground as if they had failed in their mission.

"What happened? Did something go wrong?" Afran asked. He was anxious to hear their report.

"Gotcha!" One of the men laughed, and both grinned from ear to ear. "We were the last through the fence and closed the opening as tight as possible. We used some of our wire to keep it shut. Should anyone walk by, they won't pay any attention."

"Well done. To all of you." Afran beamed as the last man climbed into the truck. "Nasdar, let's head back to the village."

Just before 0430, Nasdar stopped the truck along the edge of the road. They were partway up a hill and could see a few perimeter lights at the distant oil field. The night remained quiet.

Two minutes later, the stillness erupted. Blast after blast reverberated across the valley. Brilliant flashes spread across the oil field, changing the night sky to daylight. Fires burned at the site of each explosion.

The men laughed, shook hands, and cheered. They had done it. The first salvo in the Kurdish operation to free their leader, Baziyan, had launched as planned.

On Halabja Day, March 16.

Chapter 26
Fort Myer, Virginia
Tuesday, March 15

Toni finished her third hot chocolate of the morning and headed to the door when the chime of the desktop VTC system alerted her to an incoming call. She returned to her desk and accepted the connection.

"Good morning, Toni." Admiral Blakely appeared on the screen, wearing his uniform. "I know we had a call scheduled for this afternoon, but there's urgent information for you to pass to the team."

"Morning, Admiral. Shoot."

"That's an interesting word choice given my information." The admiral said. "One of our sources confirmed the target for Halabja Day will be the Bati Raman Oil field near Batman."

"Wow! What're their instructions?"

"Make them aware of the target. However, since the source stated chemical weapons wouldn't be used, they're not to proceed to the area. This information is for situational awareness only."

"Shouldn't they still be in the area in case the source is wrong?"

"Negative. The identity of the source is sensitive. If any of the team members are discovered near the attack site, it could jeopardize future communications and perhaps the source's life."

"Understand, Admiral. Will make it clear. Anything else?"

"That's all for now. We'll have our regular briefing as scheduled."

"Yes, sir."

After termination of the call, Toni went to the small cafeteria, run by those with physical disabilities. A driving force behind the hiring of disabled people to operate the facility, they treated Toni like family. She grabbed another hot chocolate and returned to her desk, where she composed an email to the team.

To: Zulu

From: Alpha

FOR SITUATIONAL AWARENESS ONLY. Halabja Day target is the Bati Raman Oil Field in Batman Province.

Conventional weapons/explosives only—no chemical weapons. Do not proceed to area. Due to intel sensitivity, attack will commence as planned. Continue current mission. Acknowledge.

The task completed, Toni headed down the hall to a large room identified as the Creativity Den, where specialized gadgets were designed and assembled. This was where the trace detectors were hidden within camcorder shells now being used on the current mission.

"Hey, Charles. Okay to enter?" Although Toni and Georgia had unlimited access to the den, they always announced their presence as they didn't want to become test subjects.

"Hiya, Toni. C'mon in—it's safe." Charles laughed.

Toni ducked and weaved her way through the various benches loaded with odd-shaped components with wires hanging out like spider legs, empty equipment cases, and other strange-looking devices.

While Charles oversaw Bedlam's computer support requirements, his first love was engineering. He enjoyed turning his mind loose and creating something unique. He had five approved patents for his ideas, with another ten under review.

"Where are you? I can't see you for all the stuff in here." Toni moved a couple of roll-around carts out of the aisle as she ventured further into the room.

"I'm back by the dummies. To your right."

Toni spotted two mannequins draped in the latest lightweight armored fabric and headed toward them. Charles waved and put down a six-inch knife.

"I'm testing this fabric to see how effective it is in repelling a knife attack. The wearer will receive one heck of a bruise and perhaps a broken bone, but the knife won't penetrate into the body."

"Great. When you're satisfied with your tests, we'll get shirts made for the team." Toni glanced around. "How are the canisters coming?"

"C'mon I'll show you." He led her to the back of the room, where dozens of containers lined the wall.

"There are ten ready to go and another ten should be done by the end of the day. Thanks to the original descriptions, plus Aiden and Willie's photos, we now have replica tanks to replace those with the sarin gas." Charles picked one up and handed it to Toni.

"Not too heavy." Toni peered at the photo taped to the wall. "Appears to be the same, down to the writing."

"The writing was the hard part. Easy to copy, but I didn't want each one to be 'weathered' the same, so I wrote a computer program to modify the fading in random patterns."

"What should I tell the admiral? The next briefing is in an hour."

"Tell him we're ready to send the first batch now. Each one is fitted with a GPS tracking device. All the guys need to do is swap canisters and switch the device on." Charles gave Toni a thumbs-up. "We'll control the real canisters, and they'll have glorified misting machines."

***

Once the scheduled briefing time approached, Toni connected to Admiral's Blakely's office.

"Good afternoon, Admiral. Any further intel?"

"Hello, Toni. Nothing new."

"Okay, sir. Before I begin with the update on the team's efforts, there's good news. Charles replicated the lettering from the gas canister Mountie and Rebel photographed. He located a stockpile of the same type of canister and ten are ready to send."

"Great news. What happens if the Kurds try to use one of these?"

"Charles said the original canisters turn the liquid inside into a mist when they're opened. His canisters will do the same, except it's water."

"Tell him well done. Get those on the way to the team ASAP."

"Yes, sir. They'll be sent to Incirlik Air Force Base. I'll send another message to them advising the shipment is on the way. Rebel and Mountie asked whether to take the canister they found. Will tell them to replace it with a fake."

"Good. Anything else?"

"Yes, Admiral. They also found a weapons cache in Ortahisar Castle. Items are tagged and stationary. The gas canister is also in the original location in Uchisar.

"Rebel and Mountie also had a chance encounter with Cemil Galip, who knows a lot about their movements. They requested a background check on him. That's all regarding Cappadocia.

"Haggis confirmed his suspicions regarding Merdem Karza Dimen and requested a background check. Charles has the details. Haggis also said some of the grenades and plastic explosives were moved from the weapons cache. He's tracking them. So far they're still in the area."

Admiral Blakely scribbled on a notepad and nodded for Toni to continue.

"Kiwi's luggage arrived, so he's much happier with his own clothes. Given the increased unrest in the city and concern regarding Ismet, he obtained a weapon. He also reported no additional contact with Ismet."

"Okay. Hope he doesn't need the weapon but better to be prepared."

"Aussie continues to search for Dersim in Mardin. No luck. He said he's under surveillance by a single individual but provided no further details. Since he hasn't found Dersim in Mardin, he's heading to Diyarbakir."

"Why Diyarbakir?"

"One of Aussie's contacts indicated Dersim frequents the old city, so he wants to follow up on this. Almost forgot. Aussie confirmed Kiwi's Ismet is the same person described to him in Halabja."

"Good update. Thanks. Anything else?"

"No, sir. That's all for today."

"Contact me if anything comes up."

Toni broke the connection and prepared another message for the team.

To: Zulu

From: Alpha

Ten replacement canisters ready for shipment. Will arrive Incirlik AFB Thursday. Use credentials provided to gain access to base and obtain canisters. Trackers installed. Return active containers to AFB for transport back to BHQ.

Chapter 27
Halabja, Iraq
Wednesday, March 16

After the meeting had concluded with Mufti Tanreverdi and the others in Mardin on Sunday, Mullah Ahmed returned to Zakho, anxious to inform the committee about the target chosen for Halabja Day.

On Monday afternoon, Mullah Ahmed attended a quiet meeting with Mullah Mala and Mullah Barzan. Before arriving at the meeting place, he took a roundabout stroll through Zakho, hopped in a taxi for a short ride, and crossed a pedestrian bridge onto a small island in the middle of the Little Khabur River.

Once believed to be where Zakho began, the island offered a few trees and several benches for weary inhabitants seeking to escape the hustle and bustle of the city. Today, the three mullahs had the island to themselves. Various fruits, bread, and water were spread across a bench. They shook hands and embraced one another.

"Please sit down. Would you like something to eat? How about some hot tea?" Mullah Barzan pulled a thermos from a bag near his feet. "Nothing like a cup of hot, sweetened tea for the traveler."

"Thank you, Barzan. Yes, I'd like some tea." Ahmed took the proffered cup. He sipped the hot liquid and grimaced. "I think you forgot the sugar."

"Sorry, my friend. Wrong thermos. I can't use sugar because of my diabetes, so I brought a separate thermos for me. Here's some sugar." Barzan produced a small bag of sugar cubes from his bag.

Ahmed added two lumps to his tea, gave a tentative sip, and nodded. "Much better. Thanks."

"So what did our Kurdish brethren to the north decide?" Mala pointed toward the distant Turkish border. "I hope they selected a worthy target."

"There was much debate. Mufti Tanreverdi let everyone have their say, but I think the decision was made before the meeting. The target is the Bati Raman Oil Field. His cousin, Afran Begin Zirek, is leading the attack." Ahmed broke into a series of coughs. Barzan tapped him on the back until the coughs subsided.

"Here, have some more tea. I'll add the sugar for you." Barzan handed him a fresh cup.

"Thank you." He finished the tea, placing the empty cup on the bench. "The tea helps. I thought something was lodged in my throat."

Ahmed continued to fill the others in about the meeting and the upcoming attack. While they engaged in their conversation, two young men strolled onto the island and sat on one of the nearby benches, beyond hearing distance. They ignored the mullahs and paid attention to a pair of small pleasure craft sailing by the island.

Mullah Mala shifted the conversation away from the Mardin meeting. "Tomorrow after midday prayers, we'll head to Halabja. I've arranged for someone to drive us, and we'll spend the night with friends."

Ahmed's body heaved with a racking cough, his face turning bright red. The other mullahs helped him to stand, which eased his coughing. When it stopped, they aided him to sit.

"More tea, please." Ahmed's face had returned to its normal coloring. "The trip took more out of me than I thought." He sipped on his third cup of tea, now lukewarm.

Mala and Barzan glanced at each other. Barzan a slight nod.

"Do we need to take you to a doctor or do you want to go home? I'll ask those two men to help us." Mala pointed to the men sitting on the bench.

"Y-yes, I think I should go home." Ahmed finished the tea and set the cup on the bench. "Must be something I ate."

Barzan approached the two men. "Would you help us take our friend home? He's sick and we're not sure he can make it on his own."

"Yes, we'll help."

As Barzan returned to the others, Ahmed tried to stand and pitched forward onto the grass.

"He's fainted," Mala yelled. "Help us."

The two men ran over and assisted Ahmed back onto the bench. He wobbled in place, regaining strength as he sat with his head between his knees.

When he returned to normal, the two mullahs and the two men helped Ahmed stand and headed back across the bridge. They flagged down a taxi and took Ahmed home.

Ahmed lived on the third floor of a four-story apartment building. At one time the building glistened with a new coat of white paint. Lack of care and pollution left the color an off-white, bordering on gray.

The elevator didn't work so the four men helped Ahmed up the stairs. When they reached his apartment, he handed the key to Barzan. After they entered, the two men wished Ahmed good health and departed.

Barzan offered to spend the evening, but Ahmed refused. "No, no, it's okay. I'm tired. Perhaps you'd make a pot of tea for me before you go."

Barzan went into the kitchen and whistled as he prepared the tea.

"I hope you'll be over this for tomorrow's trip." Mala shook his head. "Of all the times to become sick."

"Allah's will." Ahmed's face bore a weak smile as he rested on the chair. "I'll be better tomorrow."

A few minutes later, Barzan brought the tea and placed it on a table within easy reach. "Is there anything else we can get you?"

"No, that's fine. I'll be better after some rest. I'll see you tomorrow afternoon."

***

Mala and Barzan left Ahmed's apartment and went down three flights of stairs before returning to the afternoon's sunshine. The two men who helped bring Ahmed home leaned against the building.

"Keep an eye on him." Barzan glanced up toward Ahmed's apartment. "If he comes out, call me."

***

The next afternoon Mullah Mala and Mullah Barzan knocked on Ahmed's door. No answer. They knocked again.

"Coming." A hoarse voice croaked. *Snip. Snip.* Ahmed slid the deadbolts back and his pale and haggard face appeared in the doorway. "Come in."

"Ahmed, you look terrible." Mala shook his head as he examined Ahmed's features. "I'm sorry but I think you need to stay here and rest. I'll pass along your thoughts and prayers at tomorrow's ceremony."

"Thank you, Mullah Mala. I drank the rest of the tea Barzan made for me, hoping it'd help settle my system. It hasn't worked. Barzan, could you make some more before you go?"

"Yes, I'll do that. I'll make a big batch for you."

An hour later, the car Mullah Mala arranged arrived outside, the driver honking the horn several times.

"We must go now. May Allah watch over you." Mullah Mala clasped Ahmed's hand. "We'll stop by when we return tomorrow evening. Get well."

***

That evening, they ate with their host in Halabja, Mullah Ziryan Raman. The food was simple—rice, cooked and raw vegetables, bread, and dates—but filling. After they finished, Ziryan suggested they move onto the veranda and have their tea in the fresh evening air.

"Too bad Ahmed wasn't well enough to make the journey." Ziryan raised his cup to eye level. "I hope he recovers soon."

After the tea, Ziryan escorted Mala and Barzan to their rooms. They were basic—a single bed, nightstand, lamp, and an armless, straight-back chair.

The following morning the three mullahs went to the Halabja village cemetery to pay their respects to those who had perished on March 16, 1988. Later, they would proceed to the Halabja Memorial Cemetery, where today's service would take place.

An hour later, the mullahs arrived at the memorial. Towering over the thousands of headstones was an immense stone and glass structure, a museum containing photographs of the men, women, and children who perished. Statutes and monuments were spread among the grounds, silent figures guarding the headstones.

The service began at 1000. Hundreds of people from Halabja and surrounding villages attended. A solemn affair, no speeches were made. Rather, silence, an occasional breeze dipping through the trees, and the muted prayers of family survivors paid tribute to those butchered by the Hussein regime.

Mullah Ziryan introduced Mala and Barzan to people he knew. Quiet words were exchanged, sympathies shared.

One by one, group by group, the crowd thinned until only the mullahs and a few survivors remained. Mullah Ziryan took the others by the arms and led them back to the car.

"It's time to leave the memorial to the families. Let us not intrude upon their sorrow." Ziryan opened the door for Mala while Barzan walked around to the other side.

"We'll have some refreshment before your return to Zakho." They nodded, still reflecting on the impact of the service and what had happened twenty-three years before.

***

When they returned to Zakho, they went to Mullah Ahmed's apartment building. They thanked the driver and trudged up the stairs to Ahmed's apartment. Barzan knocked. No answer. He knocked again.

"Ahmed, are you there? Can we come in? It's Mala and Barzan."

Silence greeted his words. He tried the door handle—unlocked. He pushed the door open, and they entered.

"Ahmed, where are you? We came to see if you're okay and if you need anything." Barzan and Mala glanced around. No sound was heard. No Ahmed.

Barzan walked down a hallway to Ahmed's bedroom. The door was closed, so he knocked, thinking Ahmed might be asleep.

"Ahmed, it's us. Can we come in?"

No response. Barzan opened the door. He saw Ahmed, lying on the bed. Dried blood covered the lower part of Ahmed's face and upper chest, and stained the pillow and sheet a dirty brown.

Barzan checked for a pulse. Nothing. He turned to Mala, shaking his head.

"He's with Allah."

"What did you put in his tea?" Mala asked. He stared at Ahmed's lifeless body.

"How did you know?"

"I said nothing, but I've never known you to drink unsweetened tea. Ahmed didn't know, so he kept drinking whatever concoction you used."

"He needed to be silenced. He wanted to betray our cause to the Americans for personal gain." Barzan said. "Now he's with Allah, a martyr to the cause."

"I know about his conversations with the Americans. I told him to do so. What did you give him?"

"Nothing exotic—arsenic."

Chapter 28
Batman Province, Turkey
Wednesday, March 16

The night remained quiet. Civilian guards positioned in the ten watchtowers surrounding Bati Raman Oil Field struggled to remain alert. The men were well trained, veterans of Turkey's mandatory military service. Yet their training didn't teach them how to stay awake in the middle of the night perched in a tower twenty feet in the air.

Shaban Volkan, the night guard supervisor for the Turkish Petroleum Corporation (TPAO), yawned and stretched. He glanced at his watch. *Three more hours. Three long hours. Nothing ever happens during the night. Well, once—the time three mountain sheep crashed into the gate. A guard open fired, missing the sheep but made sure everyone remained alert the rest of the night.*

Since he struggled to keep his eyes open, Shaban stood and walked to the office door for some fresh air. Nothing stirred. He checked the time again—0429.

Explosions rippled across the oil field. Black smoke billowed, chasing red, orange, and yellow flames fifty feet into the air. Shockwaves rolled across the compound, rattling guard towers, shaking trees, and cracking windows in the office buildings. Alarms blared, adding to the din.

Panicked, several guards opened fire, some shooting outside the compound while others shot at imaginary targets within. The fireballs abated, but flames still burned at the source of the explosions. Gunfire trickled to a halt as the guards ran out of ammunition.

Shoved backward by the shockwaves, Shaban picked himself up from the floor and staggered outside. He leaned against a low wall in front of the building, stunned.

Shaban shook his head to clear the ringing in his ears. He unclipped a radio from his belt and contacted the guard towers for status reports.

"Tower One report." Nothing. Shaban tried again—same result. When he reached Tower Eight, someone responded.

"This is Tower Eight. What the hell happened? I see fires burning at several of the older oil wells."

"This is Shaban. Can you spot any of the others? I can't reach them."

"There are a few men heading in your direction. Two are helping a third man who can't walk."

Shaban also contacted Towers Nine and Ten. The men were okay, shaken by the damage they saw. None of the wells in their sectors exploded.

"Stay at your posts until we understand what's happened," Shaban said. "Allow no one to cross the fence. Shoot over their heads."

Shaban returned to the office and picked up the phone to summon help.

"Allo? Batman Havaalani?"

"Yes, this is the air base in Batman. How did you get this number?"

"My name is Shaban. I'm the night guard supervisor at Bati Raman Oil Field. We've been attacked—many of the wells are burning. We need ambulances, fire trucks, security. Anything else you can think of." Sweat dribbled down his forehead creating a path from his eyebrows to his eyes. He slung the droplets from his eyelids, mixed with tears of disbelief. He rubbed his eyes again. "Hurry."

"I'll contact my superior. We'll send help."

Shaban called the local TPAO supervisor and explained the situation, stating he requested help from the air base.

"I'm on my way. If any media show up, keep them as far away as possible. Don't let in anyone who doesn't need to be there."

Fifteen minutes later, Shaban heard a loud *whop, whop, whop.* Two aging Turkish Chinook helicopters landed on the helipads. No sooner had the rotors slowed, than twenty armed Special Forces personnel jumped out of each one and ran toward him.

A young lieutenant led the way. He stopped in front of Shaban and saluted.

"Where do you want us positioned, sir?"

Shaban pointed toward the main gate. "Place four of your men there. The rest should start a sweep along the perimeter. There are ten guard towers around the field, with two guards in each tower. If the guards can't be found, or are injured or dead, leave replacements."

"Yes, sir." The lieutenant yelled orders at the troops who jumped to action. He turned back to Shaban. "Ambulances and fire trucks are on the way. The army will send tanks, armored personnel carriers, and troops from Diyarbakir."

"Thank you." Shaban lost his balance and stumbled against the lieutenant.

"Let's get you inside. Relax—we'll take over until the army arrives."

Over the next hour, a flurry of activity took place. Six ambulances and a dozen fire trucks arrived. The TPAO supervisor, Kemal Berk, appeared, anger etched across his brow. He found Shaban and yelled in his face.

"You fool! Look what happened. It's your fault. You and your guard force are useless."

Shaban listened to Kemal's diatribe in silence, accepting the blame as a true supervisor should. Kemal wouldn't spend the money despite Shaban's repeated calls for more guards and equipment.

While Shaban dealt with the supervisor, the lieutenant directed the fire trucks toward the most severe fires. His men found a few injured guards, all with minor injuries, and helped them to the ambulances for treatment.

By this time, the day shift arrived. The guards took over for the troops while the oil workers lent a hand to the firefighters to extinguish the blazes.

"Listen," Kemal said. Everyone ignored him. "I'm in charge, and you'll do as I say."

A tall, burly oil worker walked up to Kemal, his left arm covered with blood from a cut on his forehead. "Stay out of the way. If you'd listened to the recommendations everyone made, this might not have happened. Now, we'll fix your mess."

His words stunned Kemal, who turned and went back into his office, slamming the door behind him.

As the morning slipped past, the fires were extinguished, one by one, until at last the final one gave way under the furious onslaught of the firemen and oil workers.

The fire chief completed his rounds and went to Kemal's office. "Luck was on your side. There were twenty-eight fires but none of them reached the wellheads. Otherwise, this would have been worse than the fires in Kuwait's oil field during Saddam's retreat. We still have several fires smoldering but the situation is under control."

"What caused the explosions and fire?"

A knock on the door interrupted them. The Special Forces lieutenant entered. "Thought you should be aware. My men found several trip wires throughout the field. Also, there were two bundles of unexploded dynamite attached to motors at other wells. I've requested demolitions experts to dismantle the bombs."

Kemal walked to a map of the area hanging on a wall. "Show me."

The lieutenant pointed. "They're all at the far end of the field, between guards towers eight through ten."

A little after 1300, the sound of diesel engines thundered across the oil field. A dozen Kobra armored personnel carriers followed six transporters, each carrying a Leopard-1 main battle tank. An Akrep reconnaissance vehicle led the procession while a variety of supply vehicles brought up the rear.

As soon as the Akrep arrived inside the gate it slid to a stop. A lanky, mustachioed soldier, wearing combat fatigues and the insignia of a Turkish Land Forces colonel stepped out and spoke through a portable loudspeaker.

"This facility is now under the control of the Sixteenth Mechanized Infantry Brigade, part of the Seventh Corps from Diyarbakir. I'm Colonel Bulut Ibrahim. Martial law is now in effect."

Kemal ran out of his office. "This is TPAO property and I'm in charge."

"The oil pumped from this field belongs to the Turkish government." Colonel Ibrahim stared down at Kemal. "TPAO could not protect the facility from terrorist attack. It is now my responsibility. You may leave."

While the colonel spoke, eight troops bailed out of each armored personnel carrier and moved throughout the oil field, replacing the Special Forces troops and civilian guards at the guard towers and gates.

An hour later, the Sixteenth MIB maintained complete control. Civilian workers were removed before the Special Forces personnel returned to their base in Batman, and the ambulances and fire trucks had long departed.

Colonel Ibrahim climbed the nearest tower and scanned the oil field and the perimeter through binoculars.

"Let the terrorists attack again." The colonel thrust out his chin. "We're ready for them."

***

Afran left one person behind after the fireworks started. His task—watch how the Turks responded and report back. Xandan Yad, the twenty-two-year-old cousin of Afran, was chosen for this important assignment. He would not fail.

Xandan remained in position throughout the day, jotting notes in a small notebook as the situation changed. As dusk descended, he hopped on a trail bike they brought with them and headed toward Mardin.

At 2030, Xandan used the code to announce his arrival at the barn. Relief filled him when he received the tap-knock-tap response before the deadbolts shifted and the door opened.

Afran stood in the doorway. Seated around the room was the remainder of the men who participated in the attack. Everyone gazed at Xandan with anticipation, waiting for his report.

Afran handed Xandan a glass of water, which he gulped down in one long swallow. Refreshed, he beamed at the others.

"What did you witness?" Afran asked. Anxious as everyone else, he remained stoic.

"My brothers, we've done it." Xandan raised a hand to ward off questions.

"I counted fires at twenty-eight of the oil wells. The civilian guards fired in all directions when the explosions began. Beautiful to witness—chaos, as we wanted.

"At first Special Forces troops arrived in two big helicopters and later fire trucks and ambulances came. I could tell by the gestures some civilian was upset but everyone ignored him."

Not able to control his emotions any longer, Afran asked, "Did the army arrive and take over as we wanted?"

"Yes, Afran. In the early afternoon, six tanks, twelve armored vehicles, and many support trucks arrived. A colonel took charge. He spoke through a loudspeaker and he said the field now belonged to the army."

Cheers erupted at this news. Men slapped one another on the back and banged on the tables. Some cried, happy with the news.

"Anything else?"

"Before I left, the army put men in the guard towers and at the gate. They erected tents in many places throughout the area, set up a field kitchen, and patrols walked along the perimeter.

"I also witnessed the damage done on the pipeline. Oil gushed out, covering the ground in black goo until someone turned off the flow. More guards were positioned by the mangled pipe."

"Well done, Xandan." Afran turned to the others. "Well done to each of you. A successful attack, the first in our quest. It'll not be our last."

Chapter 29
Mardin, Turkey
Wednesday, March 16

Dersim and Serbest rose early to pray before departing from Mardin. At 0630, after a quick breakfast, they climbed into the truck and headed to Akçakale, 180 miles away.

The previous evening, Afran met with Dersim and Serbest to discuss their plans. "When you arrive in Akçakale, Serbest should remain there to prepare for the upcoming operation. Dersim, after you drop off Serbest, head to Göbekli Tepe."

On the old Mardin-Sanliurfa Road, they traveled in silence, thinking about their plans. Upon arriving in Kiziltepe, Dersim turned right onto the E90 Highway and headed east toward Sanliurfa.

Dersim swerved around a pile of rocks in the road, left over from someone's recent breakdown. "If Afran's attack proved successful, there will be new roadblocks." He glanced at Serbest.

"It'd be rather awkward trying to explain why someone who delivers dry goods is transporting illegal cargo."

"Should we spot a roadblock with enough warning, we could always turn around, and take one of the less-traveled roads along the border. On the other hand, that would make for a longer journey and closer to the border there might be even more barricades."

"Insha'Allah, things will happen the way He desires." Serbest worked his worry beads, rocking in time to the swaying of the truck.

They continued along in silence for the next hour, no signs of roadblocks. Serbest pointed as they approached a roadside café. "Let's stop for a break and tea."

"Good idea. We can listen and talk with other truck drivers to find out about the roads and the security situation. I'll top off the diesel, so there's plenty for the remainder of the trip."

Dersim parked the truck near the entrance to the café so they could keep a watchful eye on their cargo. Serbest went to the counter to order tea while Dersim found empty seats for them near a window. Several truckers sat at a nearby table, and recognizing one of their own, invited Dersim to join in their discussion.

Serbest joined the group, bringing tea for Dersim and himself plus a large plate of fresh baklava to share with the table. After discussing the continuing escalation of diesel prices, low wages, and the weather, Dersim and Serbest inquired about road conditions and the security situation.

A trucker wearing blue jeans and a red sweatshirt said, "Once you head south on the Sanliurfa-Akçakale Road you're unlikely to run into any established security checkpoints until you reach the outskirts of Akçakale."

Another driver said, "A company resurfaced the road two weeks ago, so there's been less activity. However, if you veer too close to the Syrian border, you'll encounter increased security. They're forcing drivers to unload their entire vehicle near the border, searching for contraband."

A waiter came over with fresh tea. He set the pot on the table and warned the men.

"Don't go near Batman when you leave. According to the radio, terrorists bombed the Bati Raman Oil Field. The military declared martial law in the area and killed three men who got too close."

All other conversation ceased as the truckers digested this new information. A few praised the attack, but most remained silent, contemplating what the future held.

"Do you think there'll be more attacks? Will martial law spread to other areas?" A small, gray-haired trucker grabbed his hair in frustration. "I lose money if I can't deliver goods. I don't need any trigger-happy guards checking my cargo. They'll want more baksheesh."

Several nodded at the old man's comments. Others joined in, voicing their concerns. Their snack finished, Dersim and Serbest thanked the truckers, paid their bill, and returned to their truck.

Out of sight of the café, Serbest pumped a fist into the air. "Yes. Afran did it. Now it's our turn."

Dersim nodded but didn't speak.

"Are you okay? I thought you wanted this. Our revenge is under way."

"The reality of what we're doing is sinking in now that the first attack has happened." Dersim said. He shrugged, a half-smile etched on his face. "I hope we're doing the right thing."

"Of course, we are. Remember, the Turks attack us each year. For once, we struck first."

Dersim nodded again at Serbest's words and drove back onto the road. They endured the remainder of the journey in deathlike silence, each man wrapped up with his own thoughts, until they approached a security checkpoint outside Akçakale.

"Papers, please. What're you carrying?" a young Turkish private asked while two corporals walked around the truck.

"We're bringing a load of dry goods from Mardin for one of our customers in Akçakale." Dersim handed their papers to the guard. "We come about once a month."

The private conferred with the corporals. "Okay, your papers are in order," he said. "The security fee to enter the city is sixty lira. Once you pay, you may continue."

Certain the fee would go into the soldiers' pockets, Dersim handed over the money. One lifted the barricade and Dersim pulled forward.

"Easy enough. But I hate paying that baksheesh."

"It's a small price to pay for our true cargo. As you pulled away, I saw one of the soldiers writing something in a book. I wonder … perhaps the license plate number?"

"If they check it out, they'll find the number doesn't exist. I made it in Mardin for this trip."

They continued into the city, turned right onto Mimar Sinan Street, and went to a building near the Akçakale Covered Sports Arena. The bottom floor of the building held a row of small shops while the upper five floors contained apartments. Dersim and Serbest took the dry goods into a shop.

After completing their delivery, Dersim and Serbest went to a nearby street café for an apple tea. Serbest surveyed the area. "This is a perfect location. If it's necessary to create a diversion, the sports arena will be the perfect target. With people coming and going all the time, it'll be difficult for Turkish security forces to keep an eye on everyone."

"I agree. It was a stroke of luck to rent an apartment on the top floor of this building overlooking the arena. Let's finish our tea and haul the other containers upstairs."

There was a small elevator in the building, so they didn't have to lug the heavy crates up the stairs. They propped the elevator door open until they crammed as many crates inside as possible. In true

Turkish fashion, the elevator wouldn't stop at any floor except the top one once the button had been depressed.

After getting the crates into the apartment, Dersim and Serbest checked out their rental. There was a small kitchen, a living room with a dining table, two bedrooms, a bathroom, and a large walk-in closet. The living room and one bedroom overlooked Mimar Sinan Street and gave excellent views of the sports arena.

"Let's break the weapons and ammunition into smaller parcels that'll fit into the backpacks we brought. I want to finish before I depart for Göbekli Tepe. I'll also take a loaded backpack with me."

"Okay, Dersim. Let me close the curtains first. A couple of nearby buildings are taller than this one and if someone is watching they could see us."

An hour later, Dersim and Serbest finished filling seven backpacks with weapons, explosives, and ammunition. They stored six backpacks in the closet and took the empty crates to Dersim's truck. While Dersim retrieved the last backpack, Serbest stepped into a food store to purchase a few provisions.

Coming out with two heavy grocery bags, Serbest handed one to Dersim, who placed the sack on the seat next to him.

"Remember, Serbest, keep a close eye on security personnel locations around the sports arena and along the streets toward the city center. We might need the information later."

"Good idea. I plan to take a couple of walks each day at different times to learn more about the area."

"Okay, I'll get going and will be in contact."

Dersim took off for the forty-five-minute drive to Göbekli Tepe. He hoped it'd be an easy trip, but if he ran into Turkish security personnel and encountered any problems, he was prepared to fight.

After an uneventful trip, Dersim arrived at Göbekli Tepe and headed to the Turkish workers' campsite to locate Merdem. He brought the backpack with him. Once he reached the campsite, he asked a worker if he knew where Merdem stayed. The worker took him to Merdem's tent. Merdem came out and greeted Dersim like a long-lost brother.

"Dersim, it's wonderful to see you! Come. Let's share a bottle of raki and catch up on the news."

"Hello, Merdem, it is good to see you again." Dersim lowered his voice. "Is there somewhere we can talk in private?"

"Yes, let me get the raki and a few things. We can head up the hillside. It's normal for workers to leave the campsite during their off hours, so no one will be suspicious."

Settled in a small depression on the hill overlooking the campsite, Merdem and Dersim made a toast to their cause with a glass of raki and brought each other up to date.

"I took six grenades and plastic explosives from the boxes in the cave and put them in a backpack," Merdem said.

"Good. I brought more explosives with me, along with two pistols and ammunition. If we run into difficulties, we should be able to fight our way out and head back to Mardin."

"I found a different truck for us. One of my cousins will take your truck back to Mardin so it can be used for its normal business and not draw any unnecessary scrutiny by the security forces."

"Thank you. An excellent suggestion."

"No problem. My cousin, Helmet, will leave this evening so your truck will be back in Mardin tomorrow morning. Let's finish the raki and find Helmet."

Merdem and Dersim headed back to the campsite. Helmet waited for them at Merdem's tent. Dersim hadn't met Helmet before, so Merdem introduced them. Dersim gave his keys to Helmet and asked him to take care of the truck on his way back.

"I'll take good care of it. Before I go, I need to tell you some disturbing news from Mardin. There's been a foreigner asking questions about you."

"Anything I should be worried about?" Dersim asked.

"From what our friends learned, this foreigner is following your journey from Iraq. We aren't sure who he is or who he works for. They told me to warn you to be careful around any foreigners."

"Please thank everyone. I'll be careful, but at the same time, no foreigner will be allowed to get in the way of the operation."

Helmet took his leave while Dersim and Merdem turned in for the night.

***

After Dersim left Akçakale, Serbest checked out the neighborhood. He secured the apartment and walked across the street to survey the sports arena and the surrounding area. The security guards gave him no apparent notice. He appeared like any person.

Serbest meandered through the streets and alleys, with no particular destination in mind. He made a mental note of the locations of security guards. This information could be important later if they needed to escape.

At one point he found himself near the Akçakale prison. Serbest envisioned blowing up the entrance to the building and getting the prisoners out. He had the materials, but he let the thought go, since it wasn't germane to their plans.

Before heading back, he stopped at a nearby kiosk and bought a local paper, bread, cheese, and water. He returned to the apartment, checked around to make sure nothing had been disturbed and sat to eat his meal and read the paper.

Tomorrow he'd continue his reconnoitering. He also needed to rent a garage to store the other weapons when they arrived.

Chapter 30
Mardin, Turkey
Wednesday, March 16

Jake informed BHQ of his intentions to head to Diyarbakir. He spent the previous day combing through Mardin, looking for any clues to Dersim's whereabouts. Nothing.

I'm bored shitless. You'd think I was searching the Outback for Dersim. How hard can he be to find? He opened his email. A new message from BHQ.

To: Aussie

From: Alpha

If no luck finding the target, check out Diyarbakir en route to Haggis's location.

"Guess Haggis needs my help. Time to use the shit house, pack up and leave."

Jake arranged a one-way car rental through the concierge, and an hour later he cruised northeast on the D950. The patch-quilt fields of wheat and cotton were interspersed with vineyards, flocks of sheep, and herds of cattle. A car sped around Jake before cutting in, causing him to slam on his brakes to avoid a collision. "Idiot! Nothing but idiots on the road."

***

Four vehicles back, a green Mercedes kept pace. Lt. Koray's superior at the TNIO office in Mardin instructed him to follow the Australian.

"Don't let him see you but don't lose him. We need to find out what he's up to and who he contacts."

As they approached Diyarbakir, traffic became heavier. Lt. Koray closed the gap, so only a car and a large truck separated them. *Where's he going?*

***

Jake took the airport exit and drove to the rental car parking lot. An attendant took the keys, checked over the vehicle and motioned for Jake to board the shuttle for the terminal.

Twenty minutes later, the city bus departed the terminal for Diyarbakir's bus station. Jake sat behind the driver and mulled over his options. *Guess I'll start with the bazaar. Perhaps someone will know of Dersim. If I can't find him today, I'll join CC.*

The first passenger off the bus, Jake stepped into the brilliant sunshine. Hands grabbed him. "Get lost," Jake yelled. More hands grabbed him and someone pulled a bag over his head. "Piss off." Jake said He kicked and flailed his arms as he was dragged away.

***

Lt. Koray followed Jake's bus to the terminal. Once Jake boarded the city bus, Lt. Koray waited a few minutes and followed.

Not authorized to work in Diyarbakir due to a feud between the two offices, he tapped two digits on his cell phone and connected with his boss in Mardin.

"Sir, the foreigner dropped his car at the Diyarbakir Airport and is going into the city on a shuttle. What should I do?"

"Follow him as long as possible. I'll contact the Diyarbakir office and let them know."

As Jake disembarked at the city depot, a dented, once-white van screeched to a halt. The side door opened, and two men jumped out to subdue Jake. One used a wooden club to clobber him, and he slumped to the ground. The strange men manhandled him into the vehicle, which took off, burning rubber, scattering pedestrians and sideswiping several vehicles.

Lt. Koray made note of the license plate number, 21 A 0 before a large truck stopped ahead of him, blocking his view. He slammed his hands on the steering wheel in frustration. After the truck moved, he couldn't find the van. He called his boss again.

"Sir, when the Australian got off the bus at the station, four guys grabbed him and threw him into a van. I couldn't give chase because of traffic blocking me."

"Did you get the license plate number?"

"Not much that'll help. The van was dented, an off-white color, with a Diyarbakir provincial license plate. All I got was 21 A 0 before my view was blocked. I think there were three other numbers."

"Okay, go to the office. You'll work with them until we locate the foreigner and find out what's going on."

***

Several hours later, Jake woke with a headache and gingerly touched a huge lump under his matted hair. There didn't appear to be any other injuries. *Except for the noggin, I'm as fit as a Mallee bull. Now, where am I?*

Jake's sight improved as his eyes adjusted to the low light coming through a grimy window. He'd no idea how long he'd been out, but dusk had fallen. He examined his surroundings—a bed, a bucket, and a locked door. Nothing else.

"Hello? Hello!" Silence. "Anybody there?"

A door slammed in the distance. Keys rattled outside as someone unlocked his door and stepped inside.

"About time! Where am I? Why'd you kidnap me?" The guy who came into the room was at least six and a half feet tall, coal-black eyes, and long black hair. He stared at Jake but didn't utter a word.

"Hey, dickhead! I'm hungry and thirsty. How about some service?"

The giant grabbed Jake by the shoulder and hauled him out the door. Jake scrambled to keep on his feet as he was dragged along the hallway and down a flight of concrete steps into a musty, cobweb-draped basement.

The behemoth shoved Jake into an armless chair and wrenched his arms behind, lashing them together with a black leather belt. "Hey, moron, ease up on the pressure! You trying to dislocate my arms?"

Footsteps thundered down the stairs. Three men, all wearing identical silicone masks, took position in chairs in front of Jake. A fourth man, with the same mask, switched on some floodlights and aimed them at Jake causing him to squeeze his eyes shut and make an ugly face. "Hey, turn those off or give me some sunglasses."

"Amusing, Mr. Journalist." The man chuckled and clapped his hands. "Now, why don't you tell us a story?"

"I can talk all you want, but what story would you like? How about Jake and the Beanstalk? You've got the giant. Look—you know I'm a journalist, so what're you, a kidnapper after a ransom?"

Wham! The giant hit him with a massive paw, knocking the chair over. The leader motioned for the chair to be set upright.

"Don't you have a sense of humor?" Blood trickled down the side of Jake's face.

"Let me tell you a story, Mr. Journalist. There was this nosy foreigner asking about things that don't concern him. What should be done with him?"

"Let him go? Perhaps he made a bad mistake?"

"He needs to be taught a lesson." The leader stood, nodded at the giant, and went upstairs, the other men following.

***

When Jake came to, he lay on a park bench. As he struggled to sit up, the world spun. Putting his head between his legs, he vomited. He wiped his face with the back of his hand as he tried to sit up again.

"Made it," Jake gasped. "Where am I?" He glanced around. The sky was dark, with few stars. The distant shops appeared to be closed. His bags were on the ground next to him. "Surprised they didn't do a walkabout," as he rummaged around. "Everything is still here."

Jake remembered the giant hitting him again and again after the others left the basement. Blood flew everywhere until he blacked out.

His clothes were covered with dried blood, and he winced as he grabbed his jaw, moving it left to right. His left arm ached, and when he moved, sharp pains shot up and down. "I took a beating, but I'm still in one piece, more or less." While he spoke to himself, a Turkish police officer strolled up to him.

"Can you help me? I think I need a doctor for my arm."

"Ah, foreigner. Me speak good *Englisce*." The officer beamed and assisted Jake to his feet. "I help. We go hospital."

He blew his whistle and flagged down a passing taxi. The driver helped the officer put Jake into the cab, and they hurried to the hospital.

A male nurse helped him into an examination room. Jake caught sight of his face in a mirror. "Looks like a wild horse stomped all over me." His eyes resembled two slits, with heavy black and blue bruises and severe swelling. Scratches and cuts covered his face and arms while dried blood matted his hair.

A doctor came in. "Ah. You met some of our less friendly inhabitants. Let's fix you up."

"Your English is good."

"It should be. I grew up in L.A. and went to med school at Stanford."

"Ow! That hurts, Doc." Jake grimaced in pain as the doctor poked and prodded his arm.

184

"I think the bone is cracked. We'll need an X-ray to confirm. In the meantime, I'll suture a few of those cuts. Afterward, the nurse will help you clean up."

***

The police officer paced up and down the hallway. Per protocol for dealing with foreigners, he'd stay until Jake was released.

The officer pulled out his phone, dialed a three-digit number, and connected to the Diyarbakir TNIO office. He explained the situation. Someone would join him soon.

***

An hour later, Jake's face was covered with small bandages and his arm in a cast. The nurse took him to a room for multiple patients but he was the only one.

"Doctor come soon. Stay."

When the doctor arrived several hours later, Jake rested on a bed. "We're keeping you overnight for observation. I'm concerned you might have a concussion. The police officer who brought you will be outside the room until I examine you tomorrow. Pull the cord by your pillow if you need anything and a nurse will come."

"Thanks, Doc, for putting me back together. Is it all right to use my laptop and check my email?"

"As long as you're careful with the arm and don't overdo it, I don't see a problem. I've ordered pain medication in case you need it. Good night." The doctor handed Jake his laptop as he left the room.

"Night, Doc, and thanks again."

Jake waited until he was alone and pecked a short email with one finger.

To: Alpha

From: Aussie

Taking a day off work. In hospital with possible concussion, broken arm, cuts, and bruises. Didn't find the target but think his friends found me. Doc says I must remain overnight. Will head to Haggis's location as soon as I'm released.

***

The police officer stationed outside Jake's room was dozing when someone kicked his chair. He jumped to his feet and demanded, "Who're you? What do you think you're doing?"

Two men dressed in gray stood in front of him. Lt. Koray showed the officer his badge. "We'll take over now."

Chapter 31
Aleppo, Syria
Wednesday, March 16

A car backfiring or perhaps gunfire woke Ben from a deep sleep. If the latter, the clinic would be busy today.

Ben dressed and went downstairs. Several other doctors were gathered around a large oval table. He grabbed a coffee and joined them.

Dr. Franz Friedrich nodded. *"Guten Morgen,* Ben. Did you hear the loud noises?"

"Yes. I was sound asleep and almost jumped out of my skin."

Franz laughed. "Aleppo's new alarm clock, ja? Some said a shoot-out occurred between Syrian government forces and some thugs."

"Anyone killed or injured?"

"Ja. Some died, and many sustained injuries. None of the injured came here."

Dave entered the room as Franz finished speaking. "According to the news, people were at one of the local bakeries protesting the one hundred percent increase in the price of bread. Government forces tried to break up the protest and people threw stones, bread, anything they could find, at the troops, for sure.

"The troops couldn't control the crowd and fired on the protesters. The al-Kindi Hospital administrator requested we send four doctors to help with the wounded. Any volunteers?"

"I'll go," Ben said.

"Me, too," Pierre chimed in.

"Ja," Franz said.

"That's four." Dave pointed at himself. "I'm going. We'll leave as soon as we load supplies, for sure."

Dave oversaw the loading of two vehicles with various medical supplies they might need to treat the wounded. Packed and ready to go, he led the procession through the streets of Aleppo until they reached the al-Kindi, a seven-story structure atop a hill.

First built to treat tuberculosis patients, it was Syria's oldest public hospital. Since most of their doctors were not versed in trauma/triage, they contacted the MSF.

Dave and the others rushed inside and ran through a long hallway, filled with the cries of the injured. Blood covered the floor, chairs, and gurneys as the available doctors tried their best to deal with the sea of humanity.

A Syrian doctor raised his head from a patient and recognized the MSF doctors heading toward him.

"Allah be praised. Help has arrived. It's too much—we can't cope." He took a huge gulp of air to ease his tension. "Many were brought in dead—men, women, even children. Many more were injured."

"Where should we start?" Dave asked. Ben and Pierre wandered further down the hall and identified injuries—head, stomach, extremities, and spine. Most appeared to be gunshot wounds although a few suffered blunt and penetrating trauma—clubs, bricks, perhaps knives.

"Let those two help me determine who needs surgery first." The doctor pointed down the hall. "If you and the other doctor go to the end and turn right, the operating rooms are on the left."

A heavy coppery tang permeated the air, so heavy Ben gagged. He pulled back a sheet on a gurney, only to discover the person was dead, three eyes instead of two. He moved to the next gurney. Blood continued to soak through the cover.

Ben pulled the sheet back—a gaping hole appeared, blood bubbling with each breath. The person tried to scream, but nothing came forth from a mouth stretched by horrible pain.

"Shot in the lungs—this one's first for surgery." Ben's stoic announcement covered his inner tremors. He hadn't dealt with this type of injury since Allied forces kicked Saddam Hussein out of Kuwait.

Two male stewards rolled the gurney toward the end of the hall while Ben and Pierre continued triage.

"What a mess—GSWs everywhere." Pierre shook his head at the damage humans could inflict upon one another. "I pulled part of a bottle from the skull of one casualty. There's been several with knife wounds, too."

As Ben and Pierre worked in the hallway, Dave and Franz approached the operating theaters, and the metallic odor shifted to one more stale and flat. Franz pushed open a door, the stench overwhelmed them.

"Ah, more doctors. Thank you for coming." A surgeon wearing blood-spattered scrubs and a stained mask pointed toward a corner. "Wash up in the corner. Clean scrubs are in the locker next to the sink. Grab yourself a table—plenty of people still need our help."

Once the injured parked in the hallway were identified by the seriousness of their injuries, Ben and Pierre joined the others in the operating theaters.

Ben's first surgery patient had powder burns around three horrific cavities spread along his spine.

"Shot at close range and in the back." Pierre peered over Ben's shoulder. "Let's check for exit wounds."

They log-rolled the patient up onto his side and Ben gasped.

"This isn't a man—it's a woman. Must have been running from the soldiers and they still shot her." Ben checked for exit wounds, leaving the woman's clothing in place as much as possible to protect her modesty.

"Through and through. Let's stop the bleeding and plug the holes. She'll need blood." Pierre prepared a morphine syringe while Ben soaked up blood with clean gauze. "We need a chest x-ray and an exploratory laparotomy to check for internal injuries."

Franz worked on a young boy, tears in his eyes. No more than ten or twelve, he suffered multiple gunshots to his leg. Chunks of soft tissue were missing, the lower part of the femur shattered.

Franz called Dave over to assist. "What do you think?"

Dave stared at the boy's injuries and back at Franz, his eyes grave. "It needs to come off."

Franz nodded and began the gruesome task.

***

Six hours later, the wounded had been treated. Several more died on the operating tables. Doctors and nurses cast off soiled scrubs and masks and tossed them in a nearby container. Many of the staff sank onto benches overcome by the absolute carnage.

Exhausted, the MSF doctors gathered in a small room for a short break before heading back to their clinic. Dave let out a big sigh as he sat down. "One of the local doctors told me Syrian Kurds organized today's protest. No wonder the government forces fired on them. There's friction between Bashar Al-Assad's regime and several minorities, including the Kurds, for sure."

"Do you think things will escalate?" Ben asked.

"I don't know. We maintain contingency plans in case it becomes too dangerous for us to remain in Syria. Let's head back to the clinic."

The return trip to MSF Headquarters was done in silence. Dave stopped at a traffic light near their building while Ben glanced at the crowd hurrying across.

There! That's Ismet!

Ben yelled, "I'm getting out here! I spotted Ismet again. Meet you back at the building."

Ismet saw Ben climb out of the vehicle, and he ran, pushing people out of his way. Ben gave chase, but Ismet pulled ahead and turned into a narrow side street, which ended at a tall wall. Ismet tried to find an open door to escape, but they were all locked. He turned back as Ben entered the side street.

"Stay away! Why are you chasing me?"

"Why are you following me? I see you everywhere. Stop!" Ben reached for his gun. *Bugger. Left it in the room. No help now.*

Ismet moved forward.

"Stop! I just want to help you."

Ismet stopped dead in his tracks. "Why do you care? Tell me!"

Ben slid forward, hoping to catch him. A knife appeared in Ismet's hand, and he lunged at Ben, catching him in the arm.

He screamed at the pain and threw a Jiu-jitsu kick at Ismet, hitting his hand. Ismet dropped the knife, and they both scrambled for it. The knife slid away from them, and Ismet threw a punch at Ben's face. Ben dodged the blow and countered with a series of blows, knocking Ismet to the ground.

When Ismet fell, he was closest to the knife. He grabbed it and struck again. Ben fell to the street, blood streaming from his arm and a new cut across his chest. Ismet took off, leaving Ben behind.

***

Ben woke twelve hours later. He glanced around. He was in one of MSF's recovery rooms. A nurse checking his vital signs observed his movement. "Hello, Dr. Ben. How are you feeling? You scared us." Nurse Farida moved forward to fluff Ben's pillows and tuck in a loose corner of the blanket.

"How did I get here, Farida? The last I remember was being in a fight on a side street."

"Let me call Dr. Dave. He left instructions to be contacted as soon as you woke."

A few minutes later, Dave came into the room. "Hi, Ben. How are you doing, for sure?"

"A bit groggy and sore."

"What the hell were you doing? Jumping out of the vehicle to chase someone was a stupid idea."

"I saw Ismet, the guy who's been following me. I wanted to catch him and find out why."

"Listen, I realize you've another reason for being here, other than helping the Syrian people. I understand, and we're grateful for your help, for sure. But you left your gun behind, and this is the result."

"I agree, Dave, but it's important. How bad am I?"

"You're lucky. You needed six stitches to close the gash on your arm – no big deal. The greater concern is the chest wound. It took a dozen sutures to close, but one area is deep. We'll be able to take the chest tube out in a couple of days, for sure."

"Thanks. How did I get here? The last thing I remember is falling to the street and banging my head. I saw Ismet running away as I fell."

"The attack happened not far from the clinic. Most people in the area are aware we're here, for sure. Four Syrian men dragged your sorry arse to the front door. Pierre and I patched you up and gave you something to sleep. Nurse Farida has been with you since we finished working on you."

Ben tried to sit up but groaned and fell back on the pillow. Dave shook his head, a stern expression across his face.

"Don't push it. You need to rest and stay quiet for the next few days so you can heal. Is there anything you need from your room?"

"Yes, could someone bring me my laptop? If I must remain here, at least I can catch up on my emails." *And let BHQ know what's happened.*

"Sure, I'll grab it for you. Nurse Farida will also bring you a light meal if you're up to it." He turned to leave when Ben stopped him.

"Dave, thanks for fixing me up. I owe you."

"When you recover we'll put you back to work. I'll check on you in the morning."

***

Throughout the afternoon, a procession of colleagues visited Ben. He grew tired as time passed, and the discomfort in his chest increased as the pain medication wore off. Before taking any more drugs, which would knock him out, he opened his laptop and poked an update for BHQ.

To: Alpha

From: Kiwi

Syria government forces fired on locals protesting one hundred percent increase in bread price. Demonstration organized by Syrian Kurds. Dozens of casualties.

Confronted Ismet. Stabbed twice. Not life-threatening. Out of commission for a few days. Will keep you advised.

Chapter 32
Al-Bab, Syria
Thursday, March 17

Ismet spent Monday rehearsing his speech for the meeting. Nerves twisted him into knots as the time approached. He left his room in the guesthouse and wandered to the same building Kadir had shown him.

Frisked by the guard, who found no weapons, he motioned Ismet through the door where six serious-looking men waited. One of them signaled for Ismet to sit.

"Begin."

"I met one of the MSF doctors. His name is Ben, and he's from New Zealand. I first met him in Al-Bab at the MSF clinic. As instructed, I complained of pain from my injuries, and he gave me medication."

"What happened next?" The leader leaned back in his chair, his head resting against the wall.

"I went back the following morning and complained again of pain. He gave me more pills. He doesn't speak much Arabic, so Abdel translated for me. I told him the Kurdish people deserve their own country."

"Why did you say this?"

"I wanted to find out what he'd do. He told me he was a doctor and not a politician. I explained we possessed something to make the West listen to us. I didn't mention what we'd acquired, and he didn't ask."

"Good. If he's a foreign spy as we think, we might learn about this from other sources. Well done."

"Thank you. When they left for Aleppo, I followed. I think he might have spotted me at the Suq al-Medina, but I'm not sure. "

The leader, a squat man with graying hair and piercing eyes, dressed in gray trousers, white shirt, and a black sports jacket, stood up and approached Ismet.

"Welcome. I'm Salih Shervan." He swept his right hand from side to side to encompass the others in the room. "We are the Executive Committee of the Democratic Union Party."

"Hello, Salih. It's an honor to meet you."

"We share a common goal, you and I. We both support the PKK, want autonomy for the Kurdish people, and believe one person can unite us, Abdallah Baziyan."

"You're right. I'm glad Kadir brought me here. What should I do now?"

"You've done well for our cause. Now we want you to join a protest organized for Wednesday at the bakery in the Tariq al-Bab district of Aleppo. The Syrian government allowed the price of bread to double, and we want people to complain."

"What if I spot the MSF doctor again? What should I do?"

"Silence him."

***

The next morning, Ismet returned to Aleppo. Salih had directed him to a tall apartment building on Muyassa Street. He rang the bell for apartment fifty-two.

"What do you want?" a man with a deep voice asked.

"I'm Ismet. Salih sent me."

The door buzzed open, and Salih entered the lobby. He boarded the small elevator and pressed the button for the top floor. Ismet came out and walked up a flight of stairs. Number fifty-two was on the left. After he knocked on the door, a series of clicks and bangs echoed across the landing as locks were opened and deadbolts thrown aside.

The door opened. A tall young man, with a pistol stuck in his belt, stood in the doorway. "Are you Ismet?"

"Yes."

The young man stood aside allowing Ismet to enter.

"I'm Farhad Yusef. Welcome to my home. You'll stay here until after tomorrow's protest."

"Thank you. What's the plan for the demonstration?"

"Some friends are making protest signs now. One of our people will film the rally with a video camera and post the action on the Internet. The signs will be in Arabic and English. We want people to complain about the high price of bread. If we don't generate enough reaction, several men and women will hurl stones, bread, and anything else they can find, at the police."

"What will I do?"

"We'll meet several others this afternoon for a final group meeting. I want you to be one of the people ready to throw stones."

Darkness descended as Farhad's doorbell rang. A group of men and women, all in their twenties and thirties, came into the room. Two of the men carried signs calling for the end to Assad's regime and Kurdish independence. No introductions were made.

"Down to business. The protest is scheduled to begin at 0830," Farhad said. "We need to be in position about thirty minutes before, so we can pick good spots around the area and within the crowd."

"How big is the protest supposed to be?" a women asked.

"We're hoping for at least one thousand, but would like a lot more." Farhad rubbed a hand through thinning hair. "The main thing is for us to stir up the crowd if they're too peaceful. We want the authorities to respond with force, which will be captured on video to show the harsh treatment of the Syrian people."

"So the protest is being staged to enrage people against Assad's regime?" Ismet asked.

"The regime has been trampling on people's rights for some time, the Kurds and other minorities in particular," a man said with curly hair and hazel eyes, said. "Doubling the price of bread gives us an opportunity to put pressure on the government through our protest. If it's a quiet event, no one will take notice."

"That makes sense." Ismet nodded. "I'd like the honor to confront the authorities if needed."

"Ismet, all of us here today will share the honor," Farhad said. "Others will carry the banners and wave Kurdish, Alawite, and Druze flags. With Allah's blessings, we'll raise awareness of minority suffering."

The following morning, Farhad and Ismet approached the bakery on Muyassa Street after 0800. A large crowd had gathered in the plaza. The bakery doors stood open, a long line of patrons weaving their way down the street. Clusters of people swept into the square, packing themselves into the area. Banners and flags were unfurled adding color to the scene as the light breeze brought them to life.

"Seems like we've more than the one thousand you wanted, Farhad." Ismet gawked at the milling crowd. "It appears many more are supporting the cause."

"Yes. We'll have a good day. Over there—policemen are putting up barricades." Farhad pointed to the right and beamed. "In the opposite corner, isn't that some of the al-Jaysh al-Sha'bi—the People's Army? What a joke—they support Assad's government."

As the time for the protest approached, a bespectacled young man climbed on top of a car with a portable megaphone. Making sure the system worked, he shouted, "Down with Assad! Rights for minorities! Lower bread prices! No more oppression!"

People waved their banners and flags and repeated the speaker's words while clapping their hands. A ripple of excitement coursed through the crowd. Additional police officers and the militia pushed their way into the crowded square, but so far the protest had a holiday atmosphere.

An hour later, Farhad voiced his impatience. "It's too quiet. People are acting like it's a picnic, not a protest against the government. Ismet, it's time to stir things up."

Ismet headed to his designated spot. He glanced around and observed others moving into position. Someone blew a whistle and protesters hurled rocks at the police and militia. A police officer grabbed a megaphone. "Stop! Leave the area!" The increasing noise generated by the crowd drowned out his voice.

More objects targeted the government officials. Rocks, bread, bricks, even shoes pelted the officers. People pushed toward the barricades. Another official yelled, "Stop! Depart now and go home. If you don't leave, we'll arrest you."

His comments inflamed the crowd. They pulled the barricades down, using the wood to hammer the police officers and militia. One of the militia officers ordered several of his men to fire warning shots over the crowd. The crack of their rifles rose above the din.

People screamed and continued to rush toward the militia. Two of the young militiamen aimed at the crowd—and fired! Other militiamen joined in. The police officers, not realizing what happened, thought the mob had overrun the militia and added their gunfire into the fray.

Ismet made his way over to Farhad. "What should we do?"

Farhad stared at Ismet with wide eyes and screamed, "We need to at—"

Blood spattered Ismet as a bullet tore through Farhad's throat and his body jerked backward from the blow. Ismet put his hands over the hole, trying to stop the bleeding. No use—Farhad was gone!

Screams and gunfire reverberated around the square. People ran in all directions, pushing, shoving, and trampling one another to escape the deadly fire.

Ismet crawled under a car, tears flooding his eyes. The stench of blood overwhelmed him, and he retched, once, twice, three times. He stayed underneath the car as the gunfire slowed and screams diminished. The plaza was almost empty, except for the dead and wounded.

***

Ismet remained huddled under the car, afraid to move. Sirens blared as multiple ambulances arrived. Medical personnel searched through the carnage, looking for survivors.

He wept as he prayed. "Allah, why have you forsaken us? What have we done to incur your wrath?"

The plaza grew quiet as the wounded were taken away. Some people returned to the square looking for loved ones. Screams and keening echoed across the embattled marketplace when those sought were found dead. Hope remained for others not located at the massacre site.

Ismet crawled from underneath the car and stumbled into a nearby building—the bakery at the center of the protest. He found the restroom, washed the blood off, and meandered away from the area in a daze.

He reached a major thoroughfare and paused with others waiting to cross. He glanced up—staring at him was Ben!

Ismet ran down the street, pushing people and jumping over obstacles. He gazed over his shoulder. Ben was chasing him. He ran faster and made a quick turn into a side street hoping to lose the foreigner.

Dead end. Ismet stopped and turned around as Ben entered the street. "Get away from me! Get away. Leave me alone! Why are you chasing me?"

Ismet thought Ben uttered something in poor Arabic but he couldn't make it out.

"Who told you? Stay away!"

Ismet backed up as Ben inched forward. He pulled out his knife and slashed at Ben, ripping a gash in his arm. Panic set in as Ben screamed and kicked his knife hand. Ismet dropped the knife and dove for it.

The knife slid away, and Ismet threw a punch at Ben that missed. Ismet grunted in pain as Ben hit him, again and again, knocking him to the ground. He landed near his knife. He grabbed it and swung at Ben, cutting a deep furrow across his chest.

Ismet took off, heading back to the main street. People stared at him as he hurried past them. He caught his reflection and realized why. His face frightened most people due to the scarring, and now his features were battered and bruised by the fight with Ben. His clothes were blood-soaked and torn.

Where to go? Farhad's. Someone there can help me.

Thirty minutes later, Ismet rang Farhad's doorbell.

"Yes?" a woman asked.

"This is Ismet. I was with Farhad. Can I come in?"

The door buzzed, and Ismet entered the building. When he arrived at the apartment, the door opened.

Ismet recognized everyone. The only one missing was Farhad. Someone asked, "Where was Farhad after the shooting started? Were you with him?"

"Yes. I witnessed his murder."

Weeping and curses filled the room. "What happened?" another person asked.

"When the shooting started I went to Farhad. We were talking when he was cut down in mid-sentence. I hid and waited for things to quiet down. Once I returned to the main street, I ran into Ben, one of the MSF doctors. He chased me, but I cut him twice with my knife and got away. I don't know if he's dead. I came here afterward."

"We need to leave Aleppo as soon as possible," another woman said. "If they killed Farhad they will figure out where he lives. They'll arrest anyone they find here."

"Where'll we go?" Ismet asked.

"We'll head to Al-Bab and go to the Sanctuary. They'll help us. We've two vans behind the building. Let's grab our stuff and go. Now."

Chapter 33
Mardin, Turkey
Thursday, March 17

Afran knocked three times on the ornate wooden door to Mufti Ismail's compound on the western side of Mardin. A male servant opened the door and gestured for Afran to enter. After securing the entryway, the assistant led him to the male side of the house.

The manservant took Afran to the room where he first met with Mufti Tanreverdi and the others to discuss the attack on Bati Raman Oil Field. The mufti sat at the table waiting for him.

"Welcome back, Afran." Mufti Tanreverdi stood, shook Afran's hand, and gave him a traditional man hug. "Well done. You completed your task with excellent results."

"Thank you, Mufti." Afran and the mufti sat. "I'm glad you're pleased."

"I'm more than pleased. You launched the attack beginning our operation and damaged the target. The military is now deployed in case more attacks occur. That's what we wanted."

Afran's face beamed as he realized his cousin's rare praise was meant with honest sincerity. "Are we ready for the next phase?"

"Yes." The mufti's eyes bored into Afran's, who held the gaze without flinching.

"I'm giving you the honor and responsibility for leading the diversionary attacks in Kahramanmaras Province. I want simultaneous hits on three locations to further draw out the military."

"Thank you. This is a tremendous honor. Thank you for your trust."

"You'll lead one attack. Who will you pick to lead the others?"

"My two closest friends, Jawero Paldar, and Warzan Zagros. I trust them with my life."

"Let's pray to Allah your trust isn't tested."

***

The sun's rays shimmered through light clouds as three trucks left a large, weathered warehouse on one of the western slopes of the city. Dersim's BMC truck, driven by Helmet, led the small convoy.

Two Turkish Tonka trucks followed. An armed man rode shotgun in the cab with each driver, while ten additional armed men, their weapons concealed, rode in the back.

The thirty-six PKK sympathizers headed to the Kahramanmaras Province to continue the operation to free Abdallah Baziyan from Turkish captivity. Afran was the overall commander of the group and rode with Helmet.

"At last, we begin. May Allah's blessings be upon our group. May He enlighten us and fill us with courage for the cause we're undertaking." Afran sat with his head bowed as he prayed.

"Please explain again why we're going to Kahramanmaras Province if Baziyan is held in Gaziantep Province," Helmet said.

"Simple. The Turkish Army maintains a major military presence in Gaziantep. We don't possess a force large enough to take them on head-to-head. We'll create a diversion by attacking areas in Kahramanmaras, which are guarded by the gendarmerie. Understand?"

"How will the attacks help?"

"Once we overrun the gendarmerie, the army will send units to assist, reducing their forces in Gaziantep."

"Okay, makes sense." Helmet nodded as he continued driving along the bumpy road.

"Another operation will also take place in Sanliurfa Province with the goal of further reducing the army in Gaziantep. If both operations are successful, we'll pounce on Gaziantep and free Baziyan."

"Aha!" Helmet slapped his forehead. "Now I understand why Dersim and Merdem are in Göbekli Tepe."

"Yes. Others are poised to create diversions in different areas if needed. Our main force will locate in small groups around Gaziantep Province waiting for the right moment to attack the prison."

An hour later, the three trucks pulled into a rest area outside Adiyaman. Dozens of vehicles of all descriptions were scattered around the area. The small convoy separated with each one going to a pre-determined location.

"Take a peek at the large green truck up ahead." Afran pointed at a vehicle the color of a fresh bay leaf. "Check out the driver's side of the bumper and you'll see two red circles with a white crescent in the middle. Pull up next to it."

Helmet parked next to the truck. Afran got out and went to talk with the other driver and returned a couple of minutes later.

"Back your truck up to the rear of the green vehicle. We'll transfer the cargo into this one and take off. The other trucks will catch up on the main road."

Fifteen minutes later, Helmet pulled the truck back onto the main highway. "Did we receive everything we need?"

"Yes, everything—AK-47s, grenades, and RPGs. There are also several Turkish assault rifles and two sniper rifles captured during a recent skirmish. The other two trucks picked up similar loads, so we'll be ready when we arrive in Kahramanmaras Province."

Once the three vehicles resumed their loose convoy, they pulled off the highway and used smaller roads as they approached their destination.

Afran motioned for Helmet to stop as they reached a junction. "I spoke with the drivers while we loaded the weapons. The last vehicle will stay behind when we approach Bahcelievler. Tomorrow they'll attack the gendarmerie garrison."

Afran waved out the window for the vehicles to continue. "The vehicle behind us will break away before we reach Türkoglu and will hit the nearby garrison."

"What about us? Where are we going?"

"We're going to Sekeroba. The nearest available Turkish Army unit to these locations is the Fifth Armored Brigade in Gaziantep. There's an armored unit assigned to Kahramanmaras, but it's on a temporary deployment in Silopi."

"What if the Turkish Air Force attacks instead of the Army?"

"Should that happen, they would receive a nasty surprise."

The second vehicle turned right at a T-junction toward Türkoglu. Helmet noted the departure. "There goes the other vehicle. We're on our own."

"Once you reach Sekeroba, continue through the village and take the first right into the mountains," Afran instructed. "We'll camp there for the evening."

Thirty minutes later, Helmet stopped the truck in a small clearing. Their position provided a clear view down the valley into Sekeroba. The twelve men climbed out of the vehicle and stretched their legs. "After you relax for a few minutes, we'll pitch camp." Afran pointed to a level area surrounded by trees. "Two guys on guard duty at all times, working two-hour shifts. Questions?"

"Yes, Afran," one of the men said. "When do we attack?"

"At dawn. The other two teams will do the same."

***

After the last vehicle in the convoy separated, the leader of team three, Warzan Zagros, instructed the driver to head into a forested area near Bahcelievler. They found a good location near a river about two miles from the gendarmerie garrison.

"We'll post a guard once it gets dark," Warzan said. "The river's rush is masking our movements, which is good, but might stop us from hearing anyone sneaking around."

As darkness descended upon the team, discussion of tomorrow's action took center stage. It wasn't cold, but they huddled around the small fire, bolstering each other's courage. All had fought against the Turkish military before, but never with such a small group.

***

When they reached the T-junction, Jawero Paldar waved farewell to his friend, Afran. He settled back in the seat and instructed the driver to take the second left. As they approached rolling hills dotted with sheep, Jawero said, "The gendarmerie will be like sacrificial lambs after we finish with them tomorrow."

After he'd turned left on the second road, the driver asked, "Where to now? This goes into a field."

"Continue to the end of the lane. There's a barn we'll use for shelter until tomorrow morning."

Once inside the barn and the doors were closed, the men piled out of the truck. Jawero said, "We've the remainder of the day and most of the night to check our weapons and rest. I want someone in the loft to spot anyone approaching. If you're religious, I suggest you pray."

***

The following morning, about an hour before dawn, Afran used his enemy's captured Aselsan military tactical radio to contact the other two teams. He wasn't afraid of the Turks overhearing him. The radios used Direct Sequence Spread Spectrum frequency hopping over 1,300 channels. "Du (Two), Se (Three), this is Yak (One), over," Afran said.

"Yak this is Du, hear you fine."

"Yak this is Se, we're ready."

"This is Yak. Begin."

The three teams grabbed their gear and climbed into the vehicles. The drivers fired up the engines and headed out—next stop—attack!

***

Helmet proceeded to a small bluff overlooking the gendarmerie building on the outskirts of Sekeroba. Two sentries, each wearing dark green trousers and light green shirts, guarded the pink-colored building. Light clouds floated by as the sun rose. The muezzin, a man appointed to call the faithful to prayer, began the dawn call.

Three cannon-like sounds and white contrails filled the air as RPGs hurled at the building. One took out the main gate, killing one of the guards. Another hit the roof while the third one missed everything. Soon afterward, the whizzing sounds of AK-47s filled the air, interspersed with the crack of Turkish H&K G3 assault rifles.

Smoke spread across the area like a thickening fog, and the stench of expended ammunition became overpowering. Sporadic gunfire continued from both sides. Screams were heard as rounds found victims.

***

Team Two maintained position as the call to prayer came over a loudspeaker. Jawero shouted, "Fire!" Three RPGs launched at the small red gendarmerie building, catching everyone there by surprise. One of the guards outside the building dropped his weapon and ran down the road into Türkoglu screaming at the top of his lungs, "Run! Run for your lives! We're under attack!"

Another guard fired into the air, unable to control his weapon, killing nothing but clouds. One of Jawero's men ended the guard's life, taking the top of his head off with a single shot.

As the building began to burn, thick smoke wafted upward. More shots came from the building but missed the attackers.

At that moment, the man next to Jawero screamed and grabbed his left arm. "I've been hit!"

Jawero fired his AK-47 in the general direction of the building then helped the man to the ground. He wrapped a field dressing around the ugly gash. "Squeeze tight. That'll help stop the blood loss. Doesn't appear too bad."

The man whimpered with the pain but nodded at Jawero. "Shoot them. Kill them all!"

Without warning, the gendarmerie gunfire intensified. The guard who ran into the village returned with a dozen armed men. The gendarmerie inside the building came out, and together they formed a pincer movement and caught Jawero's men between them.

"Yak this is Du. They have us pinned down. What should we do?"

"Hold on as long as possible before retreating. This isn't a suicide mission, so we need to regroup for further battles."

"Roger. Will fall back when things become too hot for us."

Jawero urged his men forward. "Keep firing! Keep firing! We need to stop them so we can leave." Gunfire from both sides continued, with the Kurds using measured bursts, which were far more accurate than the 'rock and roll' firing by the gendarmerie.

A brief lull brought silence to the battlefield. Jawero shouted, "Fall back! Fall—" A lucky round fired by one of the gendarmerie caught Jawero in the shoulder, spinning him to the ground. He yelled, "I'm hit!" and blacked out.

As the shooting ceased, the Kurds moved away from the gendarmerie post and returned to their vehicle. The troops didn't pursue them but returned to the remains of their garrison.

***

Warzan's team was in position in the woods near the Bahcelievler Garrison as dawn broke. One of the men, in his first action against the Turks, couldn't wait for the signal to fire. All of a sudden, his AK-47 went off. In his excitement, he'd pulled the trigger without realizing.

Return fire sped toward him from alert Turkish guards. He screamed in panic and dove for the ground, covering his head. Gunfire intensified as both sides engaged in a firefight, although no one had a clear target. Warzan shouted, "RPGs. Now!" Two rockets streaked toward the gendarmerie building, blowing a huge hole in one of the walls. A third rocket followed the other two, went through the building and out through the far wall.

One of the Turkish guards hopped on a motorcycle and took off. Two of Warzan's men tried to bring down the fleeing Turk but only hit a few trees.

Warzan called to his men, "Follow me! We need to move closer. Keep shooting!"

The Kurds moved forward, shooting at anything moving. Return fire slowed and stopped. Warzan put up his hand. "Cease fire! Cease fire!"

As the Kurds stopped firing, the Turks resumed shooting, hitting three of Warzan's men. Seeing their comrades fall, the Kurds stopped firing, turned and fled further into the forest.

"Yak this is Se. Good news and bad news. We damaged the garrison but took casualties. At present we're retreating to our vehicle. What should we do?"

"Pull further back for now and wait to see what the Turks do."

***

"Yak this is Chwar (four). Military units are leaving their garrison. Six tanks and fifteen Otokar Kobra infantry vehicles. About 120 soldiers are coming your way. The Kobras are moving fast so they'll arrive before the tanks do."

"Thanks for the report. Proceed to alternate location and report when possible."

"Will do. May Allah be with you."

Chapter 34
Cappadocia, Turkey
Thursday, March 17

Aiden and Willie checked out of the Duru Hotel. For the remainder of their time in the Cappadocia area, they would switch hotels every three to five days. They didn't know where they would stay but would sort the logistics out later.

As they packed their belongings into the cars, Willie nudged Aiden. "Did you read the email from BHQ? One of us should make a road trip."

"Yeah. I think we need six cans to be on the safe side."

"Agree. Gonna flip for the journey? It's over three hundred miles round trip."

"Naw, you can go, and I'll keep searching here, eh"

Willie pulled a coin out of his pocket. "Nothing doing. We do this fair and square—heads goes to Incirlik and tails remains here. Call it."

"Heads."

Willie tossed the coin in the air. Once it stopped rolling, tails showed through the dust. "Okay, I'll leave in the morning."

Aiden departed first, heading out of Avanos. Willie waited about twenty minutes before departing. They planned to meet at Derinkoyu underground city, the last one on their list, and the largest one.

After Aiden arrived, he purchased tickets and joined a group of tourists waiting to enter. Willie caught up before he reached the head of the line. "Are we going on a tour or going to wander on our own?"

"Be easier for us to activate the detectors and walk around on our own instead of following a guide with a large group of tourists."

Once inside, Aiden suggested they split up. "Let's head to the lowest level and work our way up. Eight levels open to the public, so why don't you start at the bottom one and I'll do the floor above, eh? We'll keep leapfrogging until we complete our sweep or find something interesting."

Willie and Aiden descended into the bowels of the ancient city. By Willie's calculation, when he reached the eighth level, he was about 125 feet below the surface. He activated his detector and shoved the buds into his ears. Silence so far.

Aiden walked through the seventh level as fast as possible. The tunnels were devoid of tourists, and he wanted to finish and move on. Nothing emanated from his earbuds as he bobbed and weaved his way around carved rock walls and into various nooks and crannies, and ducked his head where the ceiling lowered. *All of these underground cities are similar. The people living in them had the same types of needs, and the rock had to be hand-carved.*

"Aiden. Aiden." Willie whispered as he rushed toward his partner.

"What's up? Find something?"

"Ortahisar—I checked the tracker, and the two crates of ammunition and explosives are moving. Check for yourself."

"Okay, I'll keep searching here. Why don't you pick up the trail and follow? Once I finish, I'll call you, eh?"

"Okay, Aiden. Something's going down."

Aiden continued working his way through Derinkoyu. After he'd finished on the seventh level, he proceeded up a flight of stairs and began again. All remained quiet on this level and the next.

"Four levels done, four more to go," Aiden muttered as he made his way to the fourth floor.

***

Willie headed back to his car and drove toward Ortahisar. Only a few roads traversed the area, starting there made the most sense rather than trial and error in finding the right road.

Twenty minutes later found Willie near the base of Ortahisar Castle. He had made the correct decision. Two main roads cut through Ortahisar, and it appeared the weapons cache transited along the same road away from him. Since the trackers could be monitored from a maximum distance of twenty miles, he hoped to find the vehicle and maintain coverage without being spotted.

The road ended in a T-junction. Based on the tracker, Willie made a right. He glanced at a Turkish road map on the seat. *They're heading to Kayseri.* Willie pushed the pedal to the floor, and the little car jumped forward with sudden acceleration.

***

Dildar Sangar Zagros and Belen Azad, both PKK activists, were tasked with moving one of the weapons caches from Cappadocia to Kayseri and Malatya while hauling supplies to support assaults on the Turkish Army.

Dildar drove a red and white DAF XF truck, emblazoned with the Dunya company logo on the cab and sides. Dunya's trucks were a common sight throughout the country, except this one belonged to a PKK sympathizer. The details displayed on the vehicle were copied from a bonafide Dunya truck, with false plates attached.

Belen checked the map. "Continue on this road and follow the signs for Kayseri. We should arrive in about thirty minutes."

"Okay, but I'll need to stop soon. This truck goes through a lot of diesel."

Red flashing lights appeared in the rearview mirror. "Trouble behind us. A government security vehicle." Dildar monitored the Jeep in the rearview and side mirrors.

"Relax, our papers are in order, and the weapons are well-hidden among the cargo. They would need to rip the load apart to find them, assuming they even suspect what we're carrying."

As the security vehicle approached, they heeded the siren. Dildar eased onto the shoulder, careful not to go too far, or they might tip over. The Jeep slid to a stop next to them with the driver giving them a hard stare before accelerating past and continuing down the road.

"Nothing to worry about." Belen grinned. "Must be late for lunch."

"Well, I admit being nervous about them pulling us over."

Dildar eased the truck back on the road and continued toward Kayseri. Five minutes later, a sign indicated an upcoming rest area. "We'll stop and fill the truck up ahead."

"Okay, while you take care of that I'll use the restroom and buy some tea."

***

Aiden had almost completed his search of the fourth level when his detector activated. He ducked his head and walked into an area with five entrances, three on the same level, one higher going up to a small room, and one leading down to a tiny alcove.

As he moved toward the room on the upper level, the detector's intensity pegged as far to the right as possible. An unbearable whine screeched in his ears, so he removed the earbuds. Climbing into the small room, he spotted an area in one corner covered with soil. A small piece of burlap protruded near the wall.

Aiden swept the area with the detector. *No doubt about it. We've found something here.* Looking at the detector's settings, he smiled. *Sarin! All the search has been worth the effort.*

He brushed the soil away from the burlap. Lifting the cloth, Aiden found two canisters. *Jackpot!* He attached two of the small trackers underneath the canisters beneath a small rim. A perfect fit, the trackers were unnoticeable. He checked the meter and both devices registered.

After replacing the canisters under the burlap and soil, Aiden made his way back to the surface. When he reached his car, he called Willie.

***

Willie sped along the road to Kayseri. The monitor indicated the cache maintained position a couple of miles ahead. He passed a sign for a rest stop. It appeared those transporting the weapons needed a break or perhaps fuel.

As he pulled into the rest stop, his phone rang. Spotting Aiden's number, he answered. "Any luck?"

"Yes, found two on the fourth level. We can track them."

"Splendid stuff! I'm at a rest stop outside Kayseri. Whoever took the weapons cache is here somewhere."

"Let me go through the remaining three levels and I'll be on my way, eh?"

***

While Dildar filled the diesel tank, Belen went inside and ordered two apple teas with baklava. He returned to the truck and handed Dildar his snack. "Dildar, check over there." Belen pointed to a Jeep about one hundred feet away. "There's the security vehicle that passed us earlier. I told you … late for lunch."

"I'll be satisfied as long as they don't follow us. Ready to go?"

"Let's do it."

Dildar pulled back onto the road and continued toward Kayseri.

***

Willie waited as the suspect truck departed. The trackers showed the weapons cache on the move. He continued to hold his position until another truck and two cars headed for the exit before following. He called Aiden. "We're on the move again. I'll keep following and will update you on our progress."

"Okay, passing through Incesu now. Will be in Kayseri in about twenty minutes."

Willie continued following the target vehicle. As they entered the city, the truck took an exit toward the center. Willie followed, keeping at least two vehicles behind in case someone checked for unwanted company. "Aiden, when you enter Kayseri, follow the signs pointing to the city center. They'll say Merkez. We're going toward the center now."

"Okay, will do. I'm approaching the city."

A few minutes later the truck pulled onto Mustafa Kemal Pasa Bulvari and went to an apartment building across the street from Kayseri's Ataturk Stadium. Willie pulled over behind a row of parked cars and witnessed two men climbing into the back of the truck.

The men jumped down from the vehicle a few minutes later and carried something heavy inside.

Willie answered his ringing phone. "I'm approaching the city center," Aiden said. "Where to?"

"Follow the signs for Kayseri's Ataturk Stadium. The vehicle is parked in front of an apartment building across the street from the stadium. I'm stationed nearby."

Willie peeked at the tracking meter while he waited for Aiden to appear. His eyes grew wide. "Shit! Some of the weapons are moving. One tracker's still in the truck while the other is in the building."

Aiden pulled up behind Willie and joined him. "What's the situation?" Willie explained.

"I wonder if the stadium is a possible target? It must hold around 25,000 people, eh?"

An hour later, two men came out of the building and jumped in the truck. Aiden made a quick decision. "Willie, you stay here, and I'll follow the truck. Is the one tracker still in the building?"

"Yes, it appears to be on the top floor, which overlooks the stadium."

"Okay, if the device moves, follow. I turned my tracker on, and I'll stay behind the truck until something happens. Will keep you posted."

"Okay, Aiden, be smart."

"Will do and don't do anything I wouldn't, eh?"

"Where's the fun in that?"

Dusk drew near as Aiden followed the vehicle out of Kayseri. He called Willie. "We're on the highway heading east. Appears Pinarbasi is the next location."

"Okay, things are quiet here. It's getting dark, and right now no lights are showing on the top floor."

Willie fidgeted as his legs and lower back stiffened from sitting in the car. He got out for a quick stretch. As he did so, six tall, beefy guys walked past, heading into the apartment building. *Strange. Four of them are carrying tennis bags. They aren't tennis players, more like linemen for an NFL team.*

A few minutes later, Willie saw lights in an apartment on the top floor. Before the curtains closed, he glimpsed two of the guys who had carried tennis bags. He checked the meter—the tracker remained stationary.

Willie continued to monitor the building, but nothing of interest presented itself.

***

Three hours later, Aiden still followed the truck. The latest signpost indicated forty-five miles to Malatya. *Better call Willie.*

Willie answered on the second ring. "No change." He explained about the six men who entered the building. "The NFL guys appear to be in the apartment with the tracker. No obvious movement. How are things with you?"

"We're approaching Malatya. They maintained the same speed for the entire trip and didn't vary their route."

Forty-five minutes later, the truck pulled up to a large concrete block building. In the distance, Aiden detected military aircraft revving up their engines. He contacted Willie. "The truck and tracker entered a large warehouse. Before they entered, we passed a sign pointing to Erhac Air Force Base. From where I am I can make out jet engines. Wonder if the base is another target, eh?"

"Maybe. No change here. I'll stay for another hour or so then I'll break off. The canisters are the priority and I need to collect them from Incirlik so we can swap out the ones we know about."

"Good plan, Willie. I'll email BHQ."

Aiden found a quiet off-street area to surveil the warehouse doors. He checked the tracker again—no change. Time to update BHQ.

To: Alpha

From: Mountie

Derinkoyu a success—two canisters. Ortahisar Castle weapons cache moved. Split between an apartment building in Kayseri and a warehouse in Malatya. Two suspected targets: Kayseri's Ataturk Stadium and Erhac Air Force Base.

I'll monitor Erhac while Rebel proceeds to Incirlik to collect canisters. Upon his return, we'll make the swap. Will keep you advised.

***

Inside the warehouse, Dildar and Belen joined their colleagues from Mardin. Now twelve strong, they were ready for action.

Chapter 35
Göbekli Tepe, Turkey
Friday, March 18

The previous day, Merdem took Dersim to meet the Turkish foreman, Ahmed, to check on the part-time job availability.

"Yes, we can always use extra help. A lot of earth must be moved. Are you up to the task?"

"Yes, Ahmed. Thank you. I'll work hard." Dersim nodded and shook Ahmed's hand.

"There's room in my tent so he'll stay with me, Ahmed." Dersim gave a half salute to Merdem's offer.

"All right. I'll inform Professor Konrad we hired him."

Ahmed went to the canteen tent and found Konrad sitting with CC, Jürgen, and some others. "A new worker is joining us to help move the soil away from the excavations. Will that be okay, Professor Konrad?"

"Yes. We can always use more laborers. Do we need another tent to house him?"

"He'll stay with Merdem, the injured worker. The new man's name is Dersim."

CC was half-listening to a story being told by one of the other men at the table when Ahmed entered the tent. Since Konrad sat next to him, he couldn't help but overhear their conversation. At the mentioned of Dersim's name, CC tuned out the storyteller and concentrated on Ahmed and Konrad. *I recognize the name! Is Dersim from Halabja? I'll keep an eye on both of them.*

***

On Thursday morning, Serbest woke early and went for a walk. The pull of Akçakale prison became too much to resist, so he headed back to gaze at the facility. *Might break into this prison as a test, before trying to release Baziyan. Would a trial run help? I need to speak with Dersim.*

Pulling himself from his daydreaming, Serbest continued his reconnoitering. He still needed to find two garages to rent and check out the Turkish military compound.

On the corner, a small shop sold bread, vegetables, fruit, and a variety of newspapers. Serbest glanced through the papers. "Is there a local paper for Akçakale? I moved into the city yesterday, and I'm still learning my way."

"Welcome to my humble shop. Yes, *The Akçakale Daily*." The shopkeeper walked up to the stand and pulled the appropriate paper. "I'd be honored if you accepted a free copy as a way to welcome you to our city."

"Thank you. I'd also like to buy half a dozen blood oranges."

Serbest took the newspaper and the oranges to a nearby park and sat down on an empty bench. He peeled one of the oranges, revealing the rich crimson flesh beneath. Taking a bite, he enjoyed the sweet yet mellow flavor as the juice ran down his chin. After wiping his face with the back of his hand, he opened the paper to the want ads.

By lunchtime, Serbest rented two small garages. One was near the Akçakale prison while the other was a block away from the sports arena. His tasks finished for the day, he returned to the apartment to finish reading the paper and scan the news channels.

***

The following morning, Serbest headed toward the southern end of the city. Akçakale formed a divided city with Tell Abayd, Syria. The Turkish garrison maintained the border crossing, well-known as being porous and a favorite of smugglers.

Akçakale boasted a population of just under 100,000, and Serbest approached the border crossing within twenty-five minutes. He went to a café and ordered orange juice while he concentrated on the activity at the junction. He glanced at the Turkish garrison and the surrounding buildings. The residential block stood eight stories tall. *I need to rent an apartment on an upper floor if available.*

"Excuse me," Serbest said to the café owner. "I'm new to Akçakale. Are any apartments available in the area?"

"Yes, plenty of good ones to choose from. The best apartment is on the top floor of the building across the street if it's still available. You can see for miles. The building opened two years ago, so the electricity and plumbing all work."

"Who do I need to speak with to view the apartment?"

"Let me make a phone call and I'll be right back."

Serbest stared at the tall building again. *The top floor will make an excellent position for attacking the garrison.*

The café owner returned, face beaming. "It's all arranged. The owner will join you in the building's lobby in thirty minutes to show you around. Good luck!"

"Thank you for your help. How much is the orange juice?"

"Nothing today, a token gift for a new arrival in our city."

Thirty minutes later, Serbest met the apartment owner at the building's entrance. A short man, almost as wide as he was tall, with a huge, droopy mustache covering his mouth, approached him.

"Welcome! Welcome. I understand you want to rent my apartment? Excellent price for you. Fine view, too. Come."

The owner escorted Serbest into the elevator and took him to the top floor. They entered the apartment where a stunning vista, overlooking parts of Akçakale, Tell Abayd, and beyond greeted them. Floor to ceiling windows ran along the outer wall of the living room, giving an impression it floated on air.

"I told you it was a fine view, best in the city!" He beamed with pride. "The windows open from the side, but you must be careful not to lean too far over the low wall. We can put screens on them if you wish."

"What a view! I love it!" Serbest meant his words, not for the breathtaking scenery but because he could peer down and scope out the entire four-story Turkish garrison. The low wall would provide shelter from any return fire while the open windows will simplify their aim. "Let's do the paperwork."

After completing the arrangements, Serbest walked back through the city to the apartment on Mimar Sinan Street near the sports arena.

***

Throughout Friday, CC kept a close eye on Merdem and Dersim. They remained joined at the hip all day, which made his job easier. Nothing seemed amiss, although CC suspected something lurked beneath their calm demeanors. Merdem had been to the cave and following his visit the backpack and explosives were gone.

***

Late Friday evening, Dersim and Merdem crept out of their tent and worked their way up the hill to the cave. A pitch-black night due to heavy clouds meant they didn't need to worry about anyone spotting them, but every few minutes they stopped to listen for any followers.

They approached the cave fifteen minutes later. Dersim scanned the area again, ducked his head, and went inside, followed by Merdem. "I hid enough grenades and plastic explosives on the hillside to create panic if we need a diversion." Merdem pointed to various areas around the site. "I want to take the rest of the stuff from here and move it to Akçakale."

"Okay, I'll take a box and head back to the tent." Picking up a box, Dersim went to the cave's entrance and out into the night air.

Merdem and Dersim paced themselves coming down the hill so they didn't stumble with their loads. Once they stored everything in their tent, Dersim made a final trip, making sure nothing remained in the cave.

***

CC caught a pulsating hum emanating from the tracking meter and pulled it from his pack. Trackers in the cave were moving and appeared to be going toward the Turkish camp.

CC grabbed the meter and his backpack and rushed out of his tent. He crept between other tents toward the canteen where he viewed the laborers' area.

Against the skyline a shadow moved, then a second one.

CC crept closer to the Turkish camp and paused. He checked the tracking meter and three trackers glowed in one small area while three remained up the hill. *Merdem and the new guy, Dersim, are moving the crates from the cave.*

As he waited, the two Kurds left the tent and went back up the hill. A few minutes later, they returned carrying more crates. Merdem and Dersim made a third trip together, bringing the last of the stockpile. Dersim disappeared once again, returning a few minutes later.

CC glanced at his meter and witnessed six red blips concentrated in the same location.

Seems like they're finished.

Crawling along the ground toward Merdem's tent, CC overheard someone talking in a low voice. *Doesn't sound like Turkish. Perhaps Kurdish?*

The tent's flaps flew outward, and two men came out, lugging heavy boxes and wearing backpacks. *Merdem and Dersim!*

The two men headed to where the Turkish workers parked their vehicles. They went to an old, beat-up dark-colored car, either black or blue but hard to tell in the dark. Someone opened the trunk, and they placed the boxes inside with a dull thud. They repeated this until all six crates were moved. Next, they put the backpacks in the trunk and closed the lid.

One of the men opened the driver's door, and the dome light came on, revealing the man's features. Bandages covered part of the man's head—Merdem. Both men glanced around, got in the car, and Merdem started the engine and pulled away. The lights remained off. The only sound was engine noise and the crunch of gravel as the car departed.

When the car reached the worn path leading to the road, the headlights came on. CC hurried to his rental car, parked on the opposite side of the camp. He slowed down as he neared the foreigners' camp because he didn't want to wake anyone. CC retrieved his car and left the camp with his lights off.

***

"Well, that was easy," Dersim said. "Let's go to Akçakale. There's a checkpoint outside the city, which I understand is unmanned at night. Hope that's the case tonight."

"I've a baksheesh envelope ready in case there are guards. I also have this." Merdem raised his Glock in emphasis.

"Guns are a last resort. We want to complete our operation. However, I'm ready, too." Dersim brandished his own Glock. They both chuckled.

***

CC kept his distance. There was little traffic, and he didn't want to tip them off. He passed a road sign, Akçakale – twenty-five kilometers. He tried to stay far enough back to avoid detection, yet close enough so he wouldn't lose them in the streets of Akçakale. *Brake lights! Have they seen me?*

***

Akçakale's streetlights lit the sky ahead of them. "Slow down, Merdem. If the checkpoint is manned, it'll be around the next curve."

Merdem slowed down until he spotted the raised barrier. "No checks tonight."

"Okay, head toward the city center and I'll tell you when to turn."

Five minutes later, Dersim pointed to the right. "Turn here. Serbest is at the apartment across the street from the sports arena. If there's an open parking spot, take it. I'll call Serbest so he can help us."

When they pulled up outside the apartment building, Serbest stepped forward. The two men got out of the car, and they hugged.

"It's wonderful to see you again," Dersim greeted. "Let's pull the stuff from the trunk and haul it upstairs. Merdem, park the car behind the building when we're finished and meet us at the apartment."

***

CC used the tracking device to follow Merdem's car. He missed the right-hand turn, but thanks to the meter he realized his mistake and turned back. He gazed at the name, Mimar Sinan Street. As he pulled onto the wide avenue, lights appeared as a car pulled away from an apartment building and disappeared around the corner.

Finding an empty spot, CC parked his car and checked the meter. All six tracking devices remained active and were now in an apartment at the top of a six-story building across the street from the arena. Lights were on, but the curtains were closed, so he only glimpsed brief shadows as someone walked around.

He removed the laptop from his backpack and sent a short email to BHQ.

To: Alpha

From: Haggis

Weapons cache moved from Göbekli Tepe to Akçakale. Merdem and a man named Dersim, perhaps our Iraqi Kurd, are in an apartment building across the street from the sports arena. Tracking devices confirm weapons are with them. Will remain in the area overnight.

***

As Merdem left to park the car behind the building, headlights reflected in his mirror. A car pulled into an empty spot near the apartment building, and the lights switched off.

He parked his car and came around the building from the other side so he could monitor the new arrival. *Appears to be one person.* He edged closer, wanting a better view.

While Merdem closed on the car, the driver stared in his direction. He recognized the face—the nosy foreigner from Göbekli

Tepe. *He must have followed us*! Merdem ran toward the car, brandishing his Glock.

***

CC spotted Merdem approaching. *Shit!* He turned the key but the engine wouldn't start. *Come on baby, let's go.* He tried a second time and a cloud of smoke rifled from the exhaust as he sped away.

Damn. The last thing he needed was for Merdem to spot him. He hadn't taken a shot and CC wondered why. *I better head back to Göbekli Tepe.*

CC was heading out of Akçakale when he slammed on the brakes. *What am I doing?* This might be the opportunity they needed. He had to go back and put a tracker on Merdem's car.

An hour later, CC crept around the sports arena and found a good place to sit and surveil the building. The meter showed the trackers still in place in the apartment, now in darkness. *I better not lose them.*

***

Merdem stared at CC's car as it sped away. He wanted to scare him away, but a gunshot at this time of night would bring out nosy neighbors and too many questions. They didn't need any attention—yet.

He went upstairs to break the news. "The foreigner, CC, followed us from Göbekli Tepe. He parked outside. I chased him off but will he stay away?"

"Calm down, Merdem." Dersim patted him on the back and motioned for him to sit. "We've another apartment we can move to so even if he returns we won't be here. Thank Allah you saw him and prevented a disaster falling upon us."

Serbest made tea for the three of them to calm their nerves. After they had grabbed a seat, he filled them in on the rental arrangements he made.

"Well done, Serbest," Merdem's panic attack seemed to ease after drinking the tea. "We need to move from here right away. Do you have keys for the other apartment?"

"Yes, the lease started today so we can move in whenever we want."

"Okay, let's organize things here. I want to move at first light. Any sooner and we'll raise suspicions at the new place."

Serbest paced the room and turned to the others. "I've been checking out the Akçakale prison. Do you think we should use it as a trial and attack?"

"No, Serbest," Merdem said. "It's not as good an idea as you think. We can't do anything to jeopardize our plans."

Serbest shrugged. "Okay, I only want to be ready and thought it'd help."

"Don't worry. More weapons are arriving tomorrow." With a gleam in his eye, Merdem continued, "Sunday, after Zuhr (after true noon) prayers will be the signal we're waiting for. There will be five of us. Two will attack the sports arena as a diversion if any event is being held. I want you to lead the attack on the Turkish garrison."

Serbest nodded and smiled. Even his eyes lit up with anticipation. "It'll be done. May Allah's blessings be upon us."

Chapter 36
Al-Bab, Syria
Friday, March 18

After the disastrous demonstration in Aleppo on Wednesday, the surviving core demonstrators left Farhad's apartment in two blue windowless vans bound for Al-Bab. Three men and two women accompanied Ismet.

"Once we arrive in Al-Bab, we'll go straight to the Sanctuary," a woman said.

"What's Sanctuary?" Ismet asked.

"You've been there—the building where you met Salih. We call the residence Sanctuary in case we're ever captured. The Syrians would go crazy trying to locate our safe haven."

An hour later, the vans arrived at their destination. A guard ushered Ismet and the others into the same room as before. Salih relaxed on a green sofa. In front of him, a low table held bottles of water and a large basket of assorted fruits. "Help yourselves to some refreshment. You must be hungry and thirsty after the trip from Aleppo."

"Thank you," Ismet said. "About Farhad—"

Salih held up his hand. "We'll talk later but for now, please relax. I positioned extra guards around the building's perimeter. There are also a few surprises inside, should the Syrian authorities ever locate us."

Ismet helped himself to a bottle of water and an apple and sat down. The room remained silent despite seven occupants. Only shallow breathing disturbed the calm.

"After you're finished, please go to the basement where you'll be taken care of." Salih pointed an index finger at Ismet. "Not you. I want you to stay with me."

When the room emptied, Salih asked, "So what happened in Aleppo? It seemed to be a war zone on the TV."

"We followed your instructions to incite the people if the demonstration became too peaceful. They waved their banners and laughed, having a good time. Once we challenged the police and militia, someone told us to stop."

"Go on. How did the shooting start?"

"Well, more people began throwing stuff at the police. The police made threats and when the protesters didn't stop, the authorities open fired."

Salih nodded at Ismet's description. "The TV and radio reports blamed the shootings on the demonstrators, saying the crowd shot first. Did you recognize anyone shooting at the police or the militia?"

"No, Salih. No one shot at them. People only threw things, and all hell erupted."

"Figures. The Assad regime owns the TV networks, the major radio stations, and newspapers. No one will say anything showing the government in a bad light. We need to raise awareness outside Syria. Let me think about this."

"About Farhad—I couldn't do anything to save him." Ismet's whole body shook with sobs as he buried his face in his hands. "T-the bullet went through his throat … blood everywhere … I tried to help, but …."

"Calm yourself, Ismet. I witnessed Farhad's shooting on the TV." Salih paused, fighting back his own tears over the loss of his close friend. "We'll avenge his death. Rest assured."

"I tried—later. When I spotted Ben, the MSF doctor, I wanted him to die for what happened to Farhad." By this time tears poured down Ismet's face unabated as reality set in. "Now what do we do?"

"Right now I want you to rest. There's a room downstairs you may use. Please join me for dinner this evening."

***

Later that evening when Ismet entered the room, Salih sat with two others, Kadir, who brought Ismet to Al-Bab from Turkey, and Abdel, the manager of the Hotel Dar al Kanadil.

"Welcome, Ismet. After a quiet dinner, I want to discuss something with the three of you." As Salih finished speaking, a house servant entered the room and bowed.

"Come, the food is ready. Let's enjoy ourselves while the night is still young."

Over a meal of lentil soup, grilled mutton, rice, and vegetables, Abdel regaled the group with stories about various foreigners who had stayed at the hotel.

"Imagine this one couple from France. They couldn't believe we didn't serve alcohol. The woman said she couldn't eat anything without her evening wine."

"How did you respond?" Kadir asked.

"I told them if they wanted alcohol they should have remained in Europe. The man said we're uneducated heathens who understand nothing about looking after guests." Abdel harrumphed and rolled his eyes.

"What happened next?" Ismet asked.

"They both stood up, and the man said they were checking out of the hotel. No idea where they went nor do I care. I was glad they left."

After they finished eating, the four men returned to the living room where coffee and baklava awaited. Once everyone helped themselves, Salih said, "I'm not happy with how the Syrian government suppressed details of the slaughter at the demonstration in Aleppo. We need to do something."

"What do you propose?" Ismet asked.

"We filmed the demonstration to post on the Internet. However, the government has blocked all Internet access so we can't show our side of things."

"What about taking the video to Turkey or another country?" Kadir asked.

"We can try to do that. I'm not sure the Turks would allow it to be aired on TV, but perhaps it could be uploaded to the Internet." Salih turned to Abdel. "How soon are the MSF doctors supposed to return?"

"Tomorrow. Dr. Dave, the head of MSF in Aleppo, and Dr. Pierre from Paris. They're supposed to spend one night here."

"Good. I want to kidnap one of them. We—"

"What? How'll kidnapping a doctor help?" Kadir asked.

"We'll hold the person until the MSF agrees to air our video. Once it is aired, we let the person go."

"What if they refuse to do this?" Ismet asked.

"The good doctor will remain a hostage until the video is shown."

"How do you want this done?" Kadir asked.

"Abdel, what rooms will the doctors be in?"

"Rooms two and three."

"Okay. Ismet, Kadir … tomorrow night after the doctors are asleep, I want you to kidnap one of them. Abdel, you need to stay clear of this. We don't want anyone to learn about your connection to us."

"Once we kidnap one of the doctors, where do we take him?" Ismet asked.

"Bring him here. He'll stay in the basement out of sight while he's with us."

* * *

Late Saturday night, two men entered the hotel via a back door Abdel left unlocked. Decked out in black—hoods, shirts, trousers, shoes, and gloves—only their eye movements broke up the darkness. "Shut the door," Ismet whispered. "We don't want someone to come by and take notice."

Kadir pulled the door closed behind him as their eyes adjusted to the dim light emanating from a single overhead bulb farther down the corridor. Pointing to his left, Kadir motioned with his right hand. "This way. The rooms are down here. The dining room is to the right."

They crept along the corridor, each carrying a small bag. When they reached the guest rooms, Ismet found room two. "Abdel said Dr. Dave took this room," he whispered. "Let's do it." Ismet inserted the passkey supplied by Abdel, and the door unlocked with a gentle click.

"Ready?"

Kadir nodded and moved forward. They entered the room and tiptoed to the bed, one on either side. Dr. Dave appeared to be sound asleep, snoring lightly.

Ismet pulled a leather-bound length of pipe from his bag. He used his homemade sap on Dave's head. *Thud.* He hit him again, and they heard a squishy sound.

"Don't kill him! Salih wants him alive."

"He's not dead, but I want to make sure he doesn't make any noise while we move him. Help me get him up."

Ismet and Kadir dragged Dave from the bed and put him in the room's caster chair. Kadir pulled some clothesline from his bag and bound the doctor to the chair.

Satisfied he couldn't break loose and they could move him, Ismet opened the door to make sure the coast was clear. "Let's go. No one's watching."

They pushed the chair into the corridor and headed toward the outer door. Every time the chair made a slight squeak, they paused and listened for pursuit.

When they reached the outer door Kadir leaned on the crash bar. Ismet gave a hefty push, and the chair sailed through the opening, tipping over as one of the casters caught on the doorsill.

Their van was parked right outside the building, with the sliding door propped open. Manhandling the chair with Dave still strapped to it, they pushed him into the van. The chair tipped over as Ismet shut the door. Kadir started the engine, and after Ismet climbed in, he took off through the streets of Al-Bab.

***

An hour later, after a circuitous route through the city to ward off any possible followers, Kadir pulled up at the back of the building referred to as Sanctuary.

They both got out of the van. Kadir went to a side door and opened it while Ismet propped the van's sliding door open and hauled the chair out. Dr. Dave remained bound in the chair but appeared to be coming around.

"Guess I didn't hit him hard enough," Ismet said. "I wanted him out cold until we got him downstairs."

"Never mind. Let's finish this."

They half-dragged, half-carried Dave and his chair down the stairs, banging each step as they descended. Once they reached the bottom they took him into a small room. A low wattage bulb cast eerie shadows on the once-white concrete walls. The room contained a bed with a dirty pillow and gray, woolen blankets. An empty bucket stood in the corner. Nothing else.

Ismet pushed the chair to the bed. Kadir cut the braided rope binding Dave, and together they lifted him up and tossed him onto the bed. His head hit the wall as he collapsed in a heap.

"This job's done. We better report our guest is here," Ismet said. "Wonder what's next."

Kadir slammed the door shut and locked it behind them.

***

Dave had faked some of his unconsciousness, but when his head hit the wall, he blacked out again. Sometime later, he realized his surroundings. Had a whole day passed or was it still night?

Grime and cobwebs covered the small window in the upper part of the concrete wall. Little light filtered through so he couldn't determine the time.

He staggered from the bed, almost passing out from the pain in his head. He probed with a finger and found a huge lump where one of them clobbered him. His hand came away wet as the area around the lump still seeped.

Dave relieved himself in the bucket and returned to the bed, sitting on the edge as he checked out his surroundings. *Like a dungeon without the medieval torture tools. Who took me? Where am I?"*

***

Salih remained in the living room waiting for Ismet and Kadir to return. "How did it go? Did anyone see you bring him here?"

"It went as planned. We brought Dr. Dave. Right now he's in the basement conked out," Ismet said.

"Because you hit him twice," Kadir said. "More than enough."

"I said to use force only if necessary. Was it?"

"Yes, to keep him quiet and not alert any others. He'll have a headache, but he'll live."

***

That afternoon, Salih donned a mask and went to talk with their hostage. When he unlocked the door, Dave was perched on the edge of the bed.

"How are you feeling?" Salih asked. "Are you hungry or thirsty?"

"What am I doing here? Who are you? What's going on?"

"Relax, we mean you no further harm as long as your organization cooperates. One of the men who brought you seemed overzealous, but I assume you're recovering."

"What do you want?"

"We require your organization's help in delivering word to the outside about the Syrian government's role in the massacre at the Aleppo bakery demonstration. The press reports indicate the demonstrators started the incident, and the police and militia needed to protect themselves."

"What can MSF do that you can't?"

"We filmed the entire demonstration but because the Assad regime shut down the Internet we can't show the truth. We need for you to contact MSF and explain what they need to do to win your release."

"And when they refuse? They won't be happy with you kidnapping me, for sure."

"If they refuse, your body and a copy of the videotape will be dumped at MSF's facility in Aleppo."

Dave rushed at Salih. A sickening crunch echoed throughout the room and Dave collapsed to the floor, a pool of red spreading out from his face.

Chapter 37
Diyarbakır, Turkey
Friday, March 18

Jake had suffered a simple fracture to his left arm. Both of his eyes remained bruised, and his head was smothered with various bandages to protect the sutures. He waited for the doctor to stop by so he could be discharged. He hoped. The slow process irked him.

"Good morning, Mr.—" the doctor paused while he studied the charts. "Jake. How are you this morning?"

"G'day. I've felt better, but the doc fixed me up pretty good on Wednesday. Where's he? Can I leave now?"

The doctor laughed. "He's not working today. Let's check you over. If everything appears okay, I don't think there would be any reason to keep you longer."

"Let's get cracking."

Fifteen minutes later, the doctor finished his examination. "Your vital signs are okay, and the sutures are holding. The small cast on your arm seems fine. I think we can let you go."

"Many thanks, Doc."

"Did you hear about the terrorist attack on the Bati Raman Oil Field? Terrible—but the military will respond soon."

"What happened? Did someone claim responsibility?"

"Kurdish terrorists damaged several oil well pumping stations. The army is protecting the field now. No one claimed responsibility but everyone assumes it's the Kurds."

"Isn't that unfair to blame the Kurds for every problem?"

"Perhaps, but this is Turkey. No love lost between the Turks and Kurds." While he talked to Jake, the doctor scribbled on a notepad and handed him a bottle.

"Here are some painkillers and a prescription for more if you run out. The instructions are written on the bottle. Take the prescription to any pharmacy and they can fill it for you."

"Thanks again, Doc. Appreciate your help."

"Don't overwork yourself for a few days and you'll be okay. A nurse will arrive soon to assist you on your way."

Forty-five minutes later, Jake walked out of the hospital. As he left his room, he realized the police presence outside his door was gone.

Jake went to a nearby taxi stand. He needed a car, so he asked the taxi driver to take him to a rental agency.

Not able to secure a foreign-made vehicle, Jake rented a three-year-old blue Turkish Kartal station wagon. The car was dented in multiple places and had two cracked side windows, but the engine started the first time and purred like brand new.

Jake hopped in the car and drove to Sanliurfa. According to the latest BHQ instructions, he'd rendezvous with CC at the airport where a package awaited them. The trip would take about two hours, assuming the engine worked as promised.

About sixty kilometers from Sanliurfa, Jake stopped in a layby to send CC an update on his arrival time.

To: Haggis

From: Aussie

Will be at Sanliurfa Airport by 1430. Meet me at the cargo services. If I arrive first, I'll collect the package and wait for you. Driving a blue Kartal station wagon.

Jake arrived at the terminal a few minutes late due to unexpected slow traffic caused by three overloaded Turkish Tonka trucks trying to pass one another without success. He followed the signs for cargo services, parked in front of the building, and went inside.

"Hello, mate. I want to pick up a package." Jake leaned on the chipped counter and stared at a young Turk seated at a small table.

"Do you have a receipt with the shipping number?"

"No, I'm picking the box up for a friend. He was supposed to meet me here but hasn't arrived yet."

"Well, I'm not supposed to hand over anything without the receipt to show the correct person took the parcel."

Jake frowned, pursing his lips. He tried another tack.

"C'mon, mate, who'll find out? I won't tell anyone. It's a carton for Mr. CC, who's working at the Göbekli Tepe dig."

The clerk's eyes lit up. "Why didn't you say? We receive packages all the time for Professor Konrad. I guess I can help …."

"You'd help me a lot by finding the parcel before Mr. CC arrives so we can go meet with Professor Konrad."

"Okay, come with me." The clerk lifted part of the counter top for Jake to enter. "Your box will be in the back."

Ten minutes later, they located the package. The clerk examined the name and the customs form.

"Mr. CC, yes?"

"Correct."

He grabbed the package and headed back to his desk, Jake following. The clerk set the parcel down and opened a customs book.

"I need to figure out the customs duty and tax. It'll take me a few minutes, so please sit down."

The clerk continued to flip through the book, stopping a couple of times to jot down some information on a note pad. He closed the book, checked the customs form again and began calculating. While the clerk figured out the cost, Jake examined the sender's address, knowing it was fictitious.

"Okay, you owe me one hundred forty-nine dollars."

"Say what, mate? How did you figure that amount?"

"The book told me. No duty on camera equipment, but there's eighteen percent tax on the shipment."

"So how did the cost become one hundred forty-nine dollars? Should be closer to one hundred."

"The book says eighteen percent. The amount is based on the value listed on the customs form, plus on the cost of shipping and insurance. You can pay me in US dollars or Turkish lira."

Jake shook his head. "Highway robbery, mate."

"No pay, no parcel. Perhaps you need to wait for your friend."

Jake reached into his front pocket and pulled out a worn wallet. "No, I'll pay now. I need a receipt." He handed over the money.

The clerk, face beaming, wrote out a receipt. "Here is your receipt and your box. Thank you. Have a nice day."

Jake walked outside, unlocked the car door, and placed the package on the seat. Before he could climb in, he heard a whistle, followed by his name.

"Hey, Jake. Thanks for collecting the container. Sorry, I'm late but the drive took longer than I thought." They shook hands while Jake explained about the costs associated with picking up the box.

"Submit the receipt when we return and you'll be reimbursed. BHQ are the ones who sent the parcel so they can pay the relevant costs."

"Okay, mate, you're the boss."

"Aye, and don't forget it, you wally!" Both men laughed as they climbed into the vehicles for the drive to Göbekli Tepe.

Midway back to the dig, CC pulled into an empty rest area, Jake following. They parked and got out of their cars.

"Thought I'd fill you in on what's going on before we arrive. Professor Konrad thinks you're a friend of mine stopping by for a visit. After I'd told him you work as a freelance journalist, his eyes lit up. He might want some publicity."

"Not a problem. Would help to explain my presence and allow me to hang around for a while."

"Aye. There are enough things going on. Merdem and a new guy named Dersim took the weapons cache to an apartment in Akçakale. No idea if they'll be back. I hope so, as I'd like your opinion."

"For something as old as Göbekli Tepe, you'd think things would be quiet."

"We also uncovered a body while excavating. Wasn't dead long, either. Not sure if there's any connection or only a coincidence."

Jake nodded and pointed at the package.

"So what's in the box? The customs form indicated photography equipment."

"Let's open it and find out."

Jake opened the box, and they found two-dozen trackers and two tasers. Each man took half of the shipment and stored the items in their backpacks.

"If there's nothing else, let's get back on the road. We'll be there in about twenty minutes."

"Lead the way, boss." Jake laughed and waited for CC to pull back on the road and followed.

When they reached the camp, CC and Jake headed to the canteen tent since work would stop soon for the day. They grabbed a cup of coffee and sat at a table when Konrad and Jürgen entered.

While CC made the introductions, Konrad couldn't contain himself.

"At last! We've wanted a journalist to help us update our website regarding our efforts, but it needs a professional's touch."

"I'll do my best to help while I'm here. I'll also be going around the countryside to gather additional background information for my story."

Konrad nodded. "That's fine—we won't take too much of your time. CC took new photographs for us."

"Ja, Jake, now we need someone who can write." Jürgen pointed at Jake's bandages. "What happened to you?"

"I ran into some guys who didn't like Australians."

Konrad changed the subject. "Ahmed told me Merdem and the new man, Dersim, didn't show up for work today. CC, did you see them last night or this morning?"

CC cast a quick glance at Jake. "No, I didn't notice either of them after we finished work yesterday. I wonder where they are?"

"I don't know but the police returned this morning, wanting to speak with Merdem. I suppose they'll show up sooner or later and Ahmed will inform Merdem about the police."

After finishing their coffee, CC and Jake headed for a walk around the dig. CC pointed out where he worked with Jürgen and the body's location.

"Up the hill over the rise is where the weapons cache was found."

"Everything was gone?"

"Aye. That's what delayed me meeting you at the airport. I skirted around the dig so no one would spot me and then checked. Empty."

"I wonder if something will happen in Akçakale?"

"Aye. I do too. As part of your information gathering, would you check out the apartment? I'll write the directions and give you some details."

"No problem. I can go tomorrow."

"Good idea. Let's head to the tent so I can send BHQ an update."

To: Alpha

From: Haggis

Aussie arrived as scheduled. Collected package from Sanliurfa Airport—thanks. Confirmed entire weapons cache removed. Aussie will check out Akçakale tomorrow using his cover while I continue my duties.

CC closed down his laptop and they headed outside. The afternoon's brilliant blue sky stood aside to let shades of purple, red, and indigo take over as the sun sank toward the horizon. Heading to the canteen tent, the tantalizing aroma of shish kebap set their mouths watering with anticipation.

"Hey, mate, what's that fantastic aroma? Dinner, I hope."

"Aye, Charlie hinted earlier about a special chicken shish kebap he planned to serve, stuffed with goat cheese."

"Let's go!"

They joined the line making its way to the serving area. After piling their plates high with shish kebap, grilled vegetables, pilaf rice, and fresh bread, they grabbed an empty table.

No sooner had they settled down, when the main oil lantern shattered, plunging the tent into darkness. Small fires ignited, caused by spilled oil as smoke filled the tent. Charlie ran over with a bucket of flour and doused several, covering him and others with powder.

Gunshots echoed across the dig. People yelled and pushed their way to escape from the tent. When the echoes died away, the sense of peacefulness, which had existed before the attack, didn't return. All remaining lights were extinguished.

CC and Jake made their way outside, keeping as low a profile as possible. They crawled to a small dip in the ground, which offered a semblance of protection.

"Hey, mate, is this how you welcome visitors?"

"Aye."

Jake shook his head as explosions rippled around the site's perimeter. Ancient walls, which had stood the test of time, collapsed. Clumps of rock, stone, and earth rained down upon the fearful men. Cries erupted from those injured by the fallout.

After a few moments, silence descended across the camp as everyone held their breath and kept quiet, fearing another barrage.

Chapter 38
Cappadocia, Turkey
Friday, March 18

Willie continued to monitor the apartment building on Mustafa Kemal Pasa Bulvari across the street from Kayseri's Ataturk Stadium. A few minutes after midnight, the final light in the apartment of interest disappeared, placing the top floor in complete darkness.

About an hour later, with no further activity, Willie started the car and eased away with the lights off. Two blocks away, he turned on the lights and began his journey to Incirlik Air Force Base.

Three grueling hours later, caused by winding roads through the Taurus Mountains, Willie approached the base. Armed Special Police standing adjacent to the barricade motioned him to a stop while two others monitored his approach from an armored vehicle. A German shepherd poked its head out a window, staring at him.

Willie stopped, rolled down the window, and presented his passport and an entry authorization letter.

"Morning, ma'am. Is this here where I'm supposed to go? I was told there would be some housing I might borrow for a spell before going to a meeting."

She examined his passport and entry letter before nodding at the other SPs. Stepping into the security booth, she returned a moment later with a placard for his vehicle and a map.

"Hang this from your review mirror as long as you're on the base. Before you drive off-base, remove the placard and secure it out of sight, but when you leave for the final time, drop it off here."

"Yes, ma'am, I'll do as you say."

"Here's a map to the Air Force Inn. Show them your entry letter and they'll give you a room if there's space."

"Ah thank ya kindly, ma'am."

By the time Willie obtained a room, it was almost 0500. His appointment at the armory wasn't until 0900, so he climbed into bed and shut his eyes.

Four hours later, Willie entered the amory after showing his passport and a separate authorization letter. An airman took him into a hermetically sealed room where his cargo was located.

"Do you need the code?" The airman pointed at a keypad to the left of the door. "I can dig it up somewhere in the safe."

"No, I'm set."

Willie pressed four buttons on the keypad, and the door hissed open.

"Good luck. I'll be at the desk if you need anything."

Willie nodded his thanks and entered the room. Several beige and black Pelican Storm cases sat on the floor next to a gunmetal-gray desk.

He grabbed a pair of wire cutters from a nearby workbench, cut two crisscrossed cables around one of the beige boxes, and opened the lid. This case contained rolls of duct tape, compression bags, special gloves, and disposable chemical masks.

Willie pulled out what he thought they would need, shoved it in an empty backpack, resealed the container, and turned to one of the black cases. After verifying the contents, he placed the entire container on a dolly and headed for the exit. After securing the room, he returned to the desk. The airmen helped him take the box to his car and load it in the trunk.

"Anything else you need, sir?"

"No. Many thanks for your help."

Willie hopped in the car and placed a call to Aiden.

"Collected the package and on my way back."

"Okay, I reserved a room at the Zumrut Hotel in Nevsehir for two nights."

"Thanks. I should arrive about 1500."

***

Aiden had maintained coverage of the warehouse in Malatya while Willie made his run to Incirlik. No one ventured out of the building, and as dawn approached, he began his return trip to the Cappadocia area. Despite the potential for an attack on Erhac Air Base, the Cappadocia gas canisters were their priority.

Aiden made the three-hour trip from Malatya to Nevsehir with no difficulty. Once he arrived in the city center, he followed signs for tourism information. He parked the car and went inside to inquire about hotel rooms.

"Here is a good hotel for you—not expensive." The tourism clerk pointed out a window. "Right across the street."

"Okay, would you reserve two rooms for two nights? I'll head over now."

"Yes, sir. I'll do so before you reach the desk."

As promised, the rooms were reserved by the time Aiden reached check-in. He signed for both, collected the keys, and headed back to his car.

Aiden left the city center and drove to the airport where a package awaited them. He found the cargo area and went inside to collect the parcel.

Ten minutes later and one hundred forty-nine dollars poorer, Aiden returned to the vehicle, put the box in the trunk, and made his way back to the hotel to await an update from Willie.

***

Aiden was sitting on the hotel's veranda when Willie arrived. He grabbed a bottle of water from the table.

"Here, you'll want this, eh?"

"Thanks." Willie twisted the cap off the bottle, tipped his head back, and poured water down his throat, gulping each mouthful until the bottle was empty.

"I needed a drink. Thanks. No problem at the base, and I brought a box of four with me."

"Good. We can go after the others tonight. I also picked up the package from the airport. Georgia sent tasers and more tracking devices."

Willie nodded. "I'm hungry. Is the hotel restaurant open?"

"You're in luck. They serve meals all day during tourist season."

"Give me a half-hour to have a shower and change. I'll meet you in the restaurant."

After a light meal by Turkish standards, Willie and Aiden went for a walk to work off the extra pounds they piled on with the exquisite fare.

"We've got our work cut out for us tonight. We need to hit Derinkoyu and recover two cans." Willie yawned and stretched his arms over his head as they continued along a quiet street. "Also the one in Uchisar."

"Don't forget we need to go back to Mazi and complete our search. I think that should be our first stop, eh?"

"Why not pick up the cans we found before?"

"In case we're stopped, I'd rather have the fake ones in our possession. We can pass them off as a humidifier system."

"Good point. Okay, let's do Mazi first."

Their stroll had taken them around a wide circle back to their starting point. They found an empty table on the veranda and ordered two Turkish coffees from a passing waiter.

Aiden and Willie killed time as they nursed their coffees. Turkish tradition meant no one would shoo them away from the table. Finally, Willie pointed at his wrist. "Time to go."

The two men returned to their rooms and prepared for their evening excursion. A short time later, they met at Willie's car, dumped their packs in the back seat, and climbed in. He put the vehicle in gear and their journey to the Mazi underground city began.

An hour later, they found a place to park. Unlike many other underground cities, Mazi's entrance was not in a village but on the west side of a slope making nighttime access easy.

They grabbed their packs and approached the gateway, watchful for any potential observers. An iron bar gate secured the entrance.

"This won't take long to open." Willie pulled a set of lock picks from his pack and a minute later, eased the gate wide enough for them to enter.

Aiden pulled on an iron bar and the gate closed with a squeak.

"Okay, which direction?"

"Turn on your detector and follow me." They both clicked on their flashlights. Ahead were three tunnels. Aiden took the one to the right, which headed further underground. A few minutes later, both detectors emitted faint beeps.

"Got something, Aiden."

"Me, too. Same as before. Let's keep going, eh?"

"Over there—one of the ancient ventilation shafts." Aiden used his flashlight to focus attention on a hole carved in the ceiling and walked toward it.

As they approached, the intensity of activity on their meters increased.

"Where's the canister?" Aiden poked his head over the edge of the shaft, pointed his light, and stared down. "Can't see far enough."

Willie dug in his pack while Aiden checked around the area. He pulled out a six-foot bungee cord and slipped it through the detector's handle.

"Lower this down the shaft. If the intensity increases, we'll have confirmation."

As the detector descended into the shaft, the beeps grew louder. Willie pulled the detectors back up. "Guess we need to go down a level."

Aiden led the way, and they dropped a level in a couple of minutes. He continued to where the shaft was located, and as they approached both meters pinged to the maximum.

They searched but couldn't find anything. Willie lowered his detector down the shaft as before, but the beeping diminished. Pulling the cord back up, the intensity returned.

"The canister must be here someplace. But where?" Willie glanced around but couldn't locate anywhere to hide something.

"Willie, above your head." Aiden had focused his flashlight up the shaft. Beyond eye level, the bottom of a backpack was highlighted in the beam.

Willie shifted position for a better view.

"I'll be damned. There's a tan backpack hanging on a hook driven into the stone about three feet up the shaft. Help me up."

Aiden gave Willie a hand to climb onto the edge of the shaft, about four feet off the tunnel floor. Willie reached up and grabbed a strap hanging down the side of the pack. A few tugs and the bag tumbled toward him.

"Whoa! Don't drop it!" Aiden reached up and helped Willie control the backpack. Grabbing the straps and the back of Willie's shirt, he guided them to the floor.

"Whew! That was close." Willie shook his head. "Might have ruined our day."

"Turn off your meter and let's find out what's inside." Aiden turned the bag around to face him. "Check out the Kurdish flag on the cover. Hand-sewn like the others, eh?"

"Yep, seems we've a winner."

Aiden flipped the cover open. Inside were two Glocks, four hand grenades, and what they wanted—a gas canister.

"You stay here and I'll grab a fake from the trunk."

"I won't go anywhere." Aiden pushed the backpack against the wall and leaned back, stretching his legs out.

Ten minutes later, Willie opened the trunk. He popped the latches on the case and grabbed one of the fakes. Before shutting the trunk, he pulled out a telescoping pole with a hook on one end and returned to the entrance without any further problem.

They worked together to lower the sarin container into a compression bag. Afterward, Willie went over the seal area with duct tape to ensure it remained sealed, while Aiden placed the fake canister back in the backpack.

Aiden grabbed the pole and hoisted the bag back on the hook in the shaft. Satisfied with their work, they headed out of the underground city and back to the car.

Once the canister was secured in the trunk, they took off for their next stop—Derinkoyu.

Unlike Mazi, Derinkoyu's access was inside a town. They drove past the entrance, noting several cars were scattered around the parking lot. After turning around, Willie slowed when they approached the lot as they both scanned for people. Not spotting anyone, Willie pulled into the parking lot and squeezed between two cars not far from the entrance.

"Coast is clear."

They hopped out of the car, carrying their backpacks. Before leaving Mazi, they had placed a fake canister in each of their backpacks so they could proceed as soon as they arrived.

Willie worked the lock on the gate, similar to the one at Mazi. In moments, they were inside and headed along a tunnel leading to their destination.

"The cans are on level four." Aiden pointed to where they needed to turn. "Down here. Turn on your detector, eh?"

A few minutes later, Aiden shifted to the right when the tunnel split into two. As they walked along the corridor, their meters beeped, continuing to increase as they proceeded.

The tunnel ended in a larger area with four additional entrances other than the one they were using.

"Up there—it's a small room." Aiden took off his pack and climbed. He scrutinized the northeast corner.

"Appears they're still here. Hand up the fakes."

Willie took the containers they brought and hoisted them up into Aiden's waiting arms. Aiden shifted some of the soil. Pulling the burlap aside, the two gas canisters sat, waiting for someone to return.

While he uncovered the containers, Willie climbed into the room to lend a hand. Together, they made short work of the effort, and within minutes, the real canisters were replaced with the fake ones.

Fifteen minutes later, they emerged from the passageway. Giving the perimeter a careful scan and not spotting anyone, they returned to the vehicle and secured the canisters in the container.

"Two locations down, one more to go." Willie pulled out of the lot, heading for Uchisar.

Once they arrived at the main square, Willie parked near the storm drain. A few people were still milling around as they decided where they were going.

"I'll grab the jack and spare tire. We'll pretend we've a flat." Willie headed to the trunk, grabbed the items he wanted, and placed them near the rear driver's side tire, about four feet from the drain cover.

Aiden joined Willie at the back of the car. "Let's take our time with changing the tire. No point rushing while people are loitering."

An hour later, the square was devoid of people, except for Willie and Aiden.

"After midnight. Now or never." Willie raised the car while Aiden scanned the area as he collected the final fake canister from the trunk and put it in his bag.

"Willie, help me lift the drain cover. I'll head down and make the swap while you keep watch."

They pried the cover out of the drain's rim and pushed it aside. Aiden began his descent as soon as there was enough space for him to shimmy past the cover.

"Be back as fast as I can. Keep an eye out."

While Willie waited, he verified the tire's lugs were tight, lowered the car and replaced the items in the trunk. When he shut the lid, the face of a Turkish police officer appeared.

"Allo, what you do?" The police officer glanced around.

"We had a flat tire on the way to our hotel." Willie spoke louder than normal in the hopes Aiden might overhear the conversation.

"Before two. Where friend?"

"Down the drain."

"W-what that mean?"

Willie pointed to the open drain hole on the other side of the car.

"My friend dropped his keys while we changed the tire. Without the keys we can't leave."

The policeman nodded. "I understand. Find keys and go hotel, right?"

"Yes, as soon as my friend finds them."

"Hey, Willie, I found the keys! I'll be back up in a couple of minutes."

Willie pointed with his right hand toward the drain. "He found them and is coming up. We'll put the cover back before we leave."

"Okay, I go building now. Come if you need help." He pointed at the nearby government building.

"Thank you. We should be okay."

Two minutes later, Willie heard Aiden approaching the top of the drain's ladder.

"Come on up—the coast is clear."

"Here, take care of this and I'll replace the cover." Aiden handed Willie his backpack.

"Good idea about the keys." Aiden patted Willie on the shoulder and returned to packing the final canister.

"I checked the tracking meter and we've eight canisters registering. Four right here, and the other four where they should be." Willie dipped his head shoulder-to-shoulder and grinned. "Now what?"

"Now we head to Incirlik and drop these off. While you're driving I'll send a note to BHQ, fill them in and request instructions."

Five minutes later, they left Uchisar behind.

To: Alpha

From: Mountie

Successful extraction of four sarin containers, two from Derinkoyu, one from Mazi, and one from Uchisar. All replaced with Charles's cans and stationary per tracking meter. Proceeding to Incirlik for transfer to storage. Will return to Nevsehir hotel tomorrow evening. Confirm completion of Cappadocia assignment and request next task.

Chapter 39
Ft. Myer, Virginia
Saturday, March 19

Georgia sifted through a batch of emails that had arrived over the past three days. Toni took the weekend off, so it fell to her to prepare the report for Admiral Blakely.

At the appointed time, Georgia connected via secure VTC to Admiral Blakely's office. Two men sat with the admiral.

"Good thing I'm prepared," Georgia mumbled before turning the sound on. *Why didn't the admiral's staff warn me others would attend today's session?*

"Good afternoon, Georgia. As you're aware, we've visitors. The distinguished gentleman is Sir Alexander "Alex" Jackson, the British National Security Advisor. The tough-looking guy is Harrison Robertson, the Australian NSA."

"Good afternoon, Admiral, gentlemen. This is a good day to be with us because there's plenty to report."

"I say, Georgia, nice to put a face to the name." Sir Alex spoke with an upper-class English accent.

"G'day. Hope you're keeping my Jake busy." *His voice is the same as Jake's.*

"Georgia, Sir Alex and Harrison came to Washington to discuss other matters, but as members of the Bedlam oversight committee, I asked them to join us for today's session."

"Thank you, sir." *I hope I can handle the pressure without looking like a fool. Why did I swap weekends with Toni?*

"Let's get the ball rolling, shall we?" the admiral said.

"I'll begin with Cappadocia. Rebel and Mountie completed their sweep of the six underground cities on our list. They located several weapons caches and tagged various crates.

"Of importance to our primary objective, they identified four sarin gas canisters. All were replaced with the phony cylinders fabricated by Charles. The real ones are en route to Incirlik."

"How did they find the caches? Are you sure these are what we're after?" Sir Alex preened his goatee with one hand while adjusting his monocle.

Moron.

"The detectors used are sophisticated and can detect trace amounts of over forty threat substances. Furthermore, each cache contained the same type of tan backpack, all sporting hand-sewn Kurdish flags.

"Once Rebel and Mountie identified the canisters in Derinkoyu underground city and a storm drain in Uchisar, they were tagged and left in situ."

"Why didn't they remove the canisters as they found them?" Harrison asked. "The objective is to recover the chemical weapons, right?"

"Yes, sir. However, we wanted all initial disclosures tagged and tracked until we've located more caches. We don't want to tip our hand too soon."

"Quite right, quite right," Sir Alex said.

"We also needed the replica cylinders to swap with the real ones so anyone returning to the cache wouldn't spot any difference."

Georgia stopped for a sip of water. Her mouth seemed like sandpaper, and her presentation skills didn't match Toni's. She took a deep breath and continued.

"Mountie and Rebel also tracked one of the weapons caches from the Cappadocia area to an apartment building overlooking the Ataturk Stadium in Kayseri. Based on tracker locations, the individuals moving the cache also took part to a warehouse near the Erhac Air Force Base in Malatya.

"Our assessment is the stadium is a feint while the base would be a legitimate target in the Kurds' eyes."

"Have the Turkish authorities been notified?" Harrison directed his question to Admiral Blakely.

"No. As much as we'd like to inform them, they would want details we can't share. They might jeopardize our primary objective—the sarin canisters."

"Sirs, at this point no one is monitoring the Kayseri apartment or the Malatya warehouse. Mountie and Rebel are escorting the canisters to Incirlik for safekeeping. They requested instructions for their next move."

"We'll decide at the end of this session." The admiral made a rolling motion with his right hand for Georgia to continue.

"Yes, sir. Two men relocated the weapons cache Haggis uncovered in Göbekli Tepe. It's now in an apartment overlooking a sports arena in Akçakale.

"You may recall, sir, the cache also contained hand-drawn maps, including one of a Turkish military compound near the Syrian border. We believe the military post is the primary target, with the sports arena secondary."

Admiral Blakely nodded and scribbled on a pad in front of him.

"Aussie traveled to Göbekli Tepe since he lost Dersim's trail. Haggis introduced him as a freelance journalist to the foreign team conducting the excavation, and they want him to write a story about their latest activities."

"That's my Jake, getting himself sorted." Harrison nodded his approval at Jake's efforts. "I need to make sure *The Daily Telegraph* and the *Brisbane Times* will be ready to post his articles, both on the Halabja survivors and the Göbekli Tepe excavation. We'll also spread his reports across a number of other newspapers and magazines."

"As part of learning about the local environment, Aussie will make a trip to Akçakale and will scope out both areas." Georgia said. She added a word of caution. "He's still recovering from his Diyarbakir run-in so we need be cautious how much he takes on."

"What happened in Diyarbakir?" Harrison turned to Admiral Blakely with an inquisitive expression.

"Sorry, Harrison. With your travels, I couldn't give you an update. Georgia?"

"Yes, sir. We aren't aware of all the details yet, but several individuals grabbed Aussie as he left a bus in Diyarbakir. He was beaten and threatened before being dumped on a park bench, with a concussion, a broken arm, as well as cuts and bruises. He spent a couple of nights in the hospital before he joined Haggis."

"Okay. Jake's a hard one, so he'll bounce back quick." Harrison nodded several times as if he needed to convince himself.

"Now to Kiwi. He encountered Ismet, which resulted in a fight between the two. Ismet stabbed Kiwi twice and escaped. Kiwi's injuries are not life-threatening, and he says he'll be on his feet again in a few days."

"He should understand the extent of his injuries since he's a doctor." The admiral pursed his lips as he came to a decision.

243

"I thought at first we should pull both him and Aussie from the field. It's easier to second-guess them from afar. Tell the team to continue the mission. I think Mountie and Rebel should clear up any loose ends in the Cappadocia area and stand ready for a quick reassignment."

"Yes, sir. That's all regarding the team, but we compiled an assessment of Kurdish activity against the Turks.

"On March 16, a series of explosions rocked the Bati Raman Oil Field, destroying at least twenty-eight pumping stations. The pipeline to the coast also sustained some damage."

"How did the Turks respond? Heavy handed, I assume." Sir Alex glanced toward the ceiling and rolled his eyes. "They always overreact."

"Yes, sir." Georgia scanned her notes. "According to available information, the Turks declared martial law in the region and moved part of the Sixteenth Mechanized Infantry Brigade into the area. Leopard-1 main battle tanks and Kobra armored personnel carriers now protect the oil field.

"On the same day in Aleppo, a protest at a government-controlled bakery turned ugly when police and the militia fired into the crowd. The demonstrators protested the 100 percent increase in the price of bread. Syrian Kurds appeared to be the instigators of the protest.

"The following day, three simultaneous attacks were carried out in Kahramanmaras Province against gendarmerie posts, resulting in several deaths and injured personnel. The Turks dispatched tanks and Otokar Kobra infantry vehicles to the attack areas. As far as we can determine, they're still deployed."

"Excellent report, Georgia. Well done." Admiral Blakely turned to Sir Alex and Harrison. "Any comments?"

"Yes." Sir Alex removed his monocle before continuing. "A couple of things. I regret to report we've lost one of our sources. According to our information, someone poisoned him.

"I won't provide his name, but he was an Iraqi mullah with inside information. He informed us about the sarin gas. We're working to establish another source. However, there's a looming question—he reported there were forty gas canisters. We've recovered four. Where are the rest?"

After a moment of silence as everyone realized the impact of Sir Alex's words, Harrison offered a glimmer of hope.

"One of the reasons I flew all the way to Washington was to share information about a source we acquired a few months ago. Until recently, his intel didn't break the threshold for reporting. He's embedded in southern Turkey as a shepherd and also part-time smuggler. On March 2nd, he witnessed several men, whom he believed to be Kurds, hide a weapons cache in a cave the shepherds used for shelter in the Sanliurfa area. He said the stash contained weapons, grenades, explosives—and six cylinders."

"Georgia, pass this latest information to the team. Instruct Mountie and Rebel to wrap up Cappadocia within twenty-four hours and proceed to Sanliurfa."

As the connection broke, Georgia overheard Sir Alex, "I say, I don't like it …." *Wonder what the pompous ass doesn't like?*

To: Zulu

From: Alpha

Good work according to Alpha-One. Continue mission as planned in Aleppo, Göbekli Tepe, and Akçakale.

Mountie and Rebel—wrap up Cappadocia within twenty-four hours. Proceed to Sanliurfa area. New Alpha-Three source indicates six gas canisters are hidden in a cave. Will attempt to isolate location.

Alpha-Two source contaminated. Recovery not possible, cause unknown. Further information might be compromised. Proceed with caution.

Chapter 40
Mardin, Turkey
Saturday, March 19

Now is the time to expand our efforts. Mufti Tanreverdi examined the map spread across the table, pointing to each successful venture with an extended finger on his gnarled right hand.

Black circles surrounded Bati Raman Oil Field in Batman Province, and Bahcelievler, Türkoglu, and Sekeroba in Kahramanmaras Province. The mufti pulled a red marker from his pocket and drew an ornate red cross through each of these locations.

Satisfied with the new markings, he nodded. *Plenty more to do.* Tanreverdi continued to study the map, tapping the marker against his chin. He picked up a black marker from the table and circled several locales.

A light tap on the door interrupted his thoughts. The door opened, and a manservant appeared.

"Mufti, as you requested, Afran is here." He stood aside for Afran to enter and pulled the door shut as he left.

"Please join me." The mufti motioned for Afran to sit next to him. "Well done with Kahramanmaras Province. I understand things went well, and the Turks responded as we hoped."

"Thank you, Mufti. Yes, the attacks worked. What's next?"

"Let me show you." Tanreverdi stood, motioning for Afran to join him at the map.

"Here's what I want. Before moving closer to our objective, we need to spread out the military even more." He gestured at the map, indicating several areas. "Put together a plan to hit Diyarbakir Province, perhaps four or five locations. Also, I want several of the gas canisters spread along the southern provincial border."

"Mufti, I thought you didn't want to use the gas."

"I don't, but we must make provisions. Take five cylinders from the stockpile."

"Yes, Mufti. Anything else?"

"Are the men ready in Kayseri? How about Malatya?"

"All we need to do is give them their orders."

"How many men are in Kayseri?"

"Six."

"Instruct four of them to go to Cappadocia and set up a feint. They should place some of the explosives around the area and use the weapons to shoot over the people. They must be careful—no foreign casualties, only scared ones."

"Yes, Mufti. We'll do as you desire."

"How many canisters are in Cappadocia?"

"Four."

"Okay, move them to Malatya. After the men finish their operation in Cappadocia, they can move them along with any remaining weapons to the warehouse."

"How soon do you want this to happen?"

"Tomorrow. This'll force the Turks to respond. Activity began in Göbekli Tepe last night. Serbest will also engage the enemy in Akçakale."

Afran nodded. "When do you want my plan for Diyarbakir and when should we carry out the attacks?"

"Brief me this evening and begin Monday morning."

***

An hour later, Afran entered a cramped, seedy bar in the center of Mardin. He glanced around the room and located his friends at a small table in the rear. Before joining them, he stepped to the bar and ordered an ayran, a watery yogurt mixed with salt.

He grabbed his glass and weaved through the tables, stopping to talk with other friends and acquaintances. At last, he sat down with Jawero and Warzan, the other team leaders during the Kahramanmaras attacks.

"How did the meeting go with Mufti Tanreverdi?" Jawero nudged Afran as he took a large gulp of ayran.

Choking and gasping for air, Afran pushed him back. "We achieved success so I thought he'd be pleased. The mufti gave us new instructions. First, who's the better planner?"

Fingers pointed across the table. Jawero aimed his digit at Warzan while Warzan's unwavering pointer targeted Jawero. Everyone laughed.

Afran waved his hands to quiet his friends. "I'll decide. Jawero, go to the Kayseri apartment on Mustafa Kemal Pasa Bulvari across the street from the stadium. Six men are waiting for instructions."

"What're they to do?"

"Pick four of them to return to Cappadocia. They're to plant a few explosives around the area and find a good position to shoot over the heads of people. They're not to hurt anyone.

"Do this tomorrow. Once the people are scared and fleeing, the men are to grab the remaining weapons, including the gas canisters, and take them to the warehouse in Malatya."

"Yes, Afran. What about the other two?"

"They're to find out when the next football match will take place in the stadium. They're to shoot at the lights only to instill panic among the people. Afterward, they're to proceed to the warehouse and wait for more instructions. After you finish, return here."

"What about me, Afran?" Warzan raised his right hand, palm up as if waiting for spiritual guidance.

"You, my friend, will help me plot more mayhem. This time, we're going after Diyarbakir."

***

During the evening, Afran and his two friends joined Mufti Tanreverdi for a light supper in his designated chamber. The senior manservant led them into the room, while another servant entered through an archway carrying an oval platter with steaming bowls of soup—spicy lentil, from the aroma. Mounds of fresh bread waited in front of each place setting.

"Sit down, sit down. We'll eat before we begin." Tanreverdi, always the gracious host, beckoned the others to join him.

After they finished, Afran motioned for Jawero to speak first.

"Mufti, I met with the men in Kayseri. They're delighted with their mission. Four headed to Cappadocia this evening while the other two are removing all signs of their presence in the apartment. A football match is scheduled for late tomorrow afternoon. Once they disrupt the game, they'll move to the Malatya warehouse."

Tanreverdi nodded his acceptance of this information.

"Good. Three attacks for tomorrow, counting Akçakale. It remains to be seen if the Turks also head to Göbekli Tepe to safeguard the excavation."

He turned his attention toward Afran, who stood and walked to the desk to use the map as he spoke.

"Mufti, Warzan and I spent several hours choosing ideal spots to attack in Diyarbakir Province. We picked three locations in the northern part of the province: Ergani, Egil, and Kocakoy. But—"

"What's the matter, Afran? You're pale." Tanreverdi wore an anguished expression as he guided Afran to a chair. Warzan poured some water and handed the glass over.

As Afran drank, his coloring returned. After a few minutes, he stood and walked back to the map.

"I'm sorry, Mufti. Only a bit of lightheadedness. I started to say we had identified three locations and went to the barn to confirm what weapons are available. I don't understand what made me check, but I went into the inner room—the one where we stored the gas canisters."

"Please continue. This doesn't bode well."

"I counted the canisters. We were sent forty. I had four transferred to Cappadocia, and six to Sanliurfa. Thirty should remain. I counted three times—ten are missing."

Tanreverdi paled at this news. *I knew the gas would become a hazard. Now, what do we do?* He thought for a few minutes, and nodded, his decision made.

"We continue as planned. An investigation must be conducted to find the culprit and bring the canisters back. Investigate this after the Diyarbakir attacks."

"I'm sorry, Mufti. I thought the barn was well-secured."

"It's done, Afran. We'll figure out what happened and deal with the culprits. In the meantime, please continue."

"I'll find out, no matter what it takes." Afran took a deep breath and exhaled, easing his built-up tension. "Warzan and I selected the three locations north of Diyarbakir to draw the military further away from Gaziantep Province. We also recommend including Adiyaman. Not only is this town closer to Gaziantep, this is also an area we've attacked before. There is a small garrison we should be able to overrun, forcing the army to move in."

"I understand your logic and accept your proposal. Will you be able to attack on Monday morning?"

"Yes, Mufti. The three of us will each lead one of the assaults. Helmet, a cousin of Merdem, returned a few days ago from Göbekli Tepe and will lead the fourth."

"I knew I could depend on the three of you. Now, it's getting late, and an old man needs his rest. Contact me tomorrow if you need anything. Otherwise, may Allah guide you to victory."

***

While Afran and the others met with Mufti Tanreverdi, four men left the apartment in Kayseri, climbed into an old but serviceable van, and headed to a safe house on the outskirts of Avanos in Cappadocia.

The leader, a heavy-set man, sat in the front passenger seat smoking a cigar, and a young man wearing thick glasses drove. The other two climbed in the back. They all carried tennis bags with them and had the stature of NFL football players. They rolled the windows down to diffuse the cigar smoke.

As they neared the turn-off into Avanos, Fat Man, also called Felek Xabat, pointed straight ahead with the remnants of his cigar. "We must collect our supplies. At each stop, we'll take everything: weapons, ammunition, explosives, and canisters if there are any. Nothing is to remain behind. Whatever we don't use tomorrow, we'll take to Malatya.

"We also should keep an eye out for those two foreigners who seemed to be everywhere we went. If they follow us, you know what to do."

Palan Olan, nicknamed Spectacle Man, nodded while the craggy-faced twins in the rear grunted their acknowledgment.

Throughout the night, the four men hurried with their tasks. Everything stashed around Cappadocia by the Kurds now sat in the back of the van, except the backpack hidden in the drain—a police vehicle straddled the location.

The men finished placing six remote-controlled explosive packages around Cappadocia as the first prayer call echoed across the valleys. At last, the men entered the Avanos safe house for a few hours sleep before the action commenced.

At 0930, Felek strode into the kitchen and started breakfast. In no time at all, the odor of fresh coffee and burned toast wafted through the house. Combined with the clattering of plates, the other three men woke and traipsed into the kitchen table.

A bowl containing a dozen boiled eggs commanded the center of the table. Platters of fresh fruit, various cheeses, beef salami, and toast stood guard. Pitchers of fresh-squeezed orange juice held end positions along the square table, while two coffee carafes, steam floating toward the ceiling, occupied space on either side of the platters.

After they filled their plates and ate, Felek motioned out the kitchen window toward a teetering wooden shed.

"Our Cappadocia transportation will be four Kuba KB-150 motorcycles out in the shed. We'll leave the van here and use the bikes. After you finish your part of the plan, return here, put the bike away and wait inside the house. Once we're all back, we'll load up the van and head for Malatya."

The others nodded as they continued to shovel in the food as if this might be their last breakfast.

"I'll trigger the first explosion at 1300, with the others coming in five-minute intervals. Fire any time after but head back here before the final explosion."

"Okay, Felek."

Palan stretched and resumed eating while the twins responded with healthy burps.

"Ten minutes and we depart."

Felek drained the last dregs from his coffee cup and went to one of the bedrooms to retrieve his tennis bag. The other three followed moments later.

***

Felek dialed the cell phone controlling the detonator hidden about a hundred meters from the entrance to the Göreme Open Air Museum. Moments later, his second phone rang.

"Allo."

"Success."

Perched on a hill high above Uchisar, Palan anticipated the detonation and focused his binoculars on the location. From this position, he'd spot every detonation and inform Felek.

One of the twins, resting on top of a fairy chimney overlooking the center of Göreme, fired as soon as the explosion registered. Careful to avoid casualties, he shot out several car windows. Switching his sights, he resumed shooting at windows along the top floor of several buildings.

After he'd reloaded, he targeted a well-stocked fruit stand, his shots ripping apart melons, as patrons screamed and pushed at each other to escape. Finished, he packed his weapon in the tennis bag, made his way to the ground, and headed back to the safe house.

Five minutes after the first detonation, Felek triggered the second one, this time between two ancient rock churches in Cavusin.

As before, he received a one-word call from Palan—success.

In the meantime, the other twin climbed to his position overlooking Ürgüp. As soon as he reached his destination high above the road winding down to the town square, he began shooting.

A devout Muslim, he abstained from drinking any alcohol, so he aimed at several open-air stalls selling wine. Bottle after bottle shattered, splattering glass shards and the local red wine across vendors and patrons alike.

As he finished his task, a mammoth explosion rocked the area, sending a thick plume of black smoke above the town. Flames leaped skyward, blown by a steady breeze. Secondary explosions filled the air, generating more flames and creating more clouds of smoke.

"Oops. Too close to the gas station."

He packed his weapon away and fled the scene as the scream of sirens blocked out the panicked screaming of the townspeople and tourists.

Palan didn't need to inform Felek about the third explosion. The plumes of smoke kept climbing into the sky, marking where a Turk Petrol Ofisi gas station once stood.

On schedule, the fourth bomb exploded as planned. With no one assigned to Ortahisar, Palan confirmed this one, which exploded near the small rock castle in the city center.

A moment later, he took shots at various buildings around Uchisar. When the fifth bomb exploded, the city's water tower swayed as one of the support legs shattered, sending a mighty flow down the main street, flooding stores and washing away stalls.

Palan packed his weapon away and peered over the edge of Uchisar's castle. He spotted the police and fire department heading towards the chaos. The car blocking access to the drain was gone.

The shots and the explosion emptied the square, leaving him alone. He ran to the drain, tugged the cover away, and scurried down the ladder. Grabbing the backpack containing a gas canister, he raced back up to the square, straddled his bike, and sped away.

As the time for the final detonation approached, Felek changed positions to gain a clear view of the Avanos Park. His target—the balloon vender.

Pop. Pop. Pop.

People screamed, grabbed their kids and ran away. The vendor released his balloons. As they floated high into the air, the remainder exploded as a flurry of shots hit their mark.

All of a sudden, a huge geyser shot into the air as the final bomb exploded. Water from the Red River shot into the air, and cascaded over vehicles passing across the bridge. Felek disappeared.

An hour later, Felek, Palan, and the twins finished sanitizing the safe house, packed everything into the van and took off for Malatya.

***

The Kurdish objective was achieved. Throughout Cappadocia chaos reigned, overwhelming emergency services and the civil administrations. Calls flooded military switchboards with demands for assistance. The military would respond but hours would pass before help arrived.

In the meantime, townspeople and tourists alike pitched in to help one another. Shops and restaurants opened their doors, offering free food and water. Those needing first aid received treatment at the scene. Despite six explosions and the sporadic gunfire, there were few injuries and only one person died.

***

By 1600, Felek's van wormed its way through the crowded streets of Kayseri. Horns blared, cars crawled along the main thoroughfare as supporters of Kayseri Erciyesspor and Sivasspor pushed and prodded their way to Ataturk Stadium.

Police wearing riot gear maintained a keen eye on all supporters while water cannons waited in strategic locations. Not wanting a repeat of the 1967 disaster in which forty-three followers of these teams died and three hundred were injured, the police weren't taking any chances.

Thirty minutes later, the traffic thinned out as the majority of the vehicles turned onto Mustafa Kemal Pasa Bulvari and continued toward the stadium. Clear of the traffic jams, Palan picked up speed, and they soon left Kayseri behind them.

***

Game time approached. Every possible space was filled in the 25,000-seat stadium. With all the seats taken, hundreds of fans crowded into standing-only areas. At 1730, everyone stood for the Turkish national anthem.

Before the end of the song, heavy caliber rounds shredded the cleats and halyards holding the Turkish flag in place. The flag fluttered to the ground as a huge gasp erupted around the stadium.

Lights popped, dumping glass shards on spectators. The shots weren't audible over the crowd noise, and no one witnessed from which direction they came. Pandemonium erupted as everyone in the stadium rushed for the exits. People fell, stampeded by the masses.

Across the street, two men slipped their weapons into tennis bags and made their way to a car hidden behind the building. A few minutes later, a yellow taxi with Malatya license plates turned right onto the main street and headed east.

The driver stared in the rearview mirror and smiled.

"They're running like ants. We brought fear to their lives, giving them a taste of what the military does to Kurdish villages."

***

By 2200, the taxi and the van joined other vehicles inside a warehouse in Malatya. The twelve became eighteen. All were ready to attack their next objective.

Chapter 41
Incirlik Air Force Base, Adana, Turkey
Sunday, March 20

Late Saturday evening, Willie and Aiden approached the closed gate at Incirlik Air Force Base. Two armed Security Police stepped out of the guard shack, one clutching a leash attached to a growling German shepherd.

"Yes, sir?" The senior airman lowered his weapon while his partner, a staff sergeant, maintained his aim in the general direction of the vehicle while he kept the dog under control.

"We're authorized visitors. Here's our passports and entry letters." Willie held out the documents.

The airman stepped through a side gate and approached the vehicle. Using a small flashlight, he examined the passports and compared the photographs with the vehicle's occupants. Afterward, he scrutinized the entry letters.

"Wow! Signed by the Air Force Chief of Staff. You guys important, huh?"

"No, but our boss is. Are we okay to enter?"

"Let the staff sergeant take a trip around the car with Bruno, and you'll be set."

Bruno and the sergeant circled the car. Satisfied, he nodded. "Okay, sir, you're cleared to proceed. Need any directions?"

"No, thank you. We're heading to the Air Force Inn." As soon as the gate opened, Willie pulled onto the base and followed the signs toward the base guest quarters.

"Okay, Willie, turn right here." Aiden gestured to the upcoming intersection. "The building is manned around the clock so let's dispose of the container before claiming our rooms."

A security guard examined their identification again at the armory. Satisfied their documentation authorized entry, an airman grabbed a dolly to help them with their package. Two armed senior airmen escorted them to the same area Willie visited before.

After they had entered, Willie counted more black containers than when he first visited.

"Seems Charlie's been busy. Now all we must do is find the other canisters."

"Let's dump this stuff and grab our rooms. I'm beat." Willie attempted to stifle a wide yawn without success.

Twenty minutes later, they headed to adjacent rooms in the Air Force Inn. After securing the outer doors, they unlocked the linking one.

"Let me send a note back home." Willie powered up his laptop and checked out the accommodations while he waited.

"Hey, new marching orders from BHQ." Aiden stepped into Willie's room and read over his shoulder.

"We can head back in the morning. Let's leave after breakfast. We should arrive at the hotel in Nevsehir around 1300." Willie nodded as Aiden grabbed a map to plot the route to their next destination.

To: Alpha

From: Rebel and Mountie

Four live canisters now secured at Incirlik. Will return to Cappadocia in the morning. ETA 1300. After final area check will travel in two-car convoy to Sanliurfa for next search.

***

By 0700, Willie and Aiden dug into their breakfast.

"Willie, I don't understand how you can eat this stuff. It looks awful and doesn't smell much better, eh?"

"Y'all don't know what you're missing. Grits are from heaven." Willie steered another spoonful toward his mouth, anticipation looming in his eyes.

"All I can say is, yech. Rather drink sour milk."

"Add in a bit of salt, butter, and cheddar cheese. Stir in a fried egg, over easy and crumble some bacon over the top—heaven!"

Aiden lifted the spoon and took a tentative bite. "Hmm, not bad at all. Hell of a lot better than oatmeal, eh?"

An hour later, Willie surrendered their vehicle pass at the gate and headed to the highway for their journey through the Taurus Mountains to Nevsehir.

After an uneventful trip through the mountains, Willie nudged the sleeping Aiden.

"Check this out. Wonder what happened?" Willie pointed at the upcoming checkpoint. "This is new. Three tanks and three armored personnel carriers. Those troops don't look too happy, either."

Willie stopped at the barricade. Soldiers surrounded the vehicle, glancing inside while holding their weapons in a menacing fashion.

"Passports." The demand came from an unsmiling corporal. Willie handed over their documents.

"Where go?" The corporal glanced through their passports before giving them back.

"To Nevsehir—our hotel." Willie handed the documents to Aiden. "Okay?"

The soldier checked them over again and nodded. "Go."

"Oh, what fun." Aiden watched in the side mirror as Willie maneuvered along a narrow channel created by the tanks.

"When we arrive at the hotel, we can be the nosy tourists and ask what's going on."

A few minutes later, they approached the city center. Military vehicles seemed to be everywhere. Willie pulled into the lot next to Aiden's car.

***

"Hey, aren't they the two guys the office made us follow?" a thin man asked a beady-eyed man sitting next to him.

"Where?"

"Going into the Zumrut."

Beady Eyes picked up his binoculars and focused on the two men heading into the lobby.

"Yeah. Remember, I ransacked their rooms and placed an electronic unit in each one. Aydin at the Drug Enforcement Administration voiced his unhappiness in following a Turkish family to Ankara after the guy ditched the device."

"They should do their own work. Not all foreigners are involved in drugs. Let's leave them be. Nothing came from the electronics or the ransacking, and they didn't visit any known drug dealers in the area."

***

After Willie and Aiden retrieved their room keys, Willie inquired about the military presence.

"Yesterday, someone set off bombs and fired many, many bullets around Cappadocia." The clerk's head bobbed as he spoke. "The news blamed the attacks on the Kurds. Now the military is deployed to make Cappadocia safe."

"Can we still go to the tourist places? We wanted to do more sightseeing before we leave." Aiden pointed to his map to indicate where they wanted to go.

"You're foreigners. Stop for the roadblocks and show your passports. We want tourists so the army will let you visit. Are you going to stay longer with us?"

"No. We'll pick up our things and check out. First, we'll stop and visit a friend in Avanos and afterward we're going to Alanya."

After checking out of the hotel, they returned to their cars and headed toward Uchisar. As they approached, Willie slowed down and signaled for a right turn. He pulled into a scenic pull-off.

Aiden jumped out of his car and ran forward. "What's the matter, eh?"

"Is your meter on? I turned mine on before we drew near, and the things we tagged in Uchisar aren't registering."

"Are you sure?"

"The reason I stopped. I wanted to find out if anything registered on yours."

"Let's check." Aiden walked back to his car, Willie following. He grabbed his detector and turned the device on—nothing.

"We only tagged one item here—the fake gas canister."

"We tagged it on Friday, two days ago. Still within the battery life of four to seven days. Even if the tracker fell off, we should still find a transmission."

"Unless ..." Willie said. "Unless someone discovered the tracker or moved the canister outside beyond twenty miles."

Over the next three hours, they crisscrossed the area, searching for traces of any of the trackers they planted. Tanks, armored personnel carriers, and recon vehicles maintained a watchful eye over everything. Foot patrols abounded, augmented by gendarmerie and police officers.

Established roadblocks and roving patrols stopped Willie and Aiden several times during their travels, but a quick check of their passports ensured a speedy release. No matter where they traveled, none of the trackers registered nor did their detectors identify anything new.

Exhausted and finding themselves at the end of their search grid, they pulled into the Hotel Avanos, overlooking the Red River.

"I'm hungry and tired. Let's grab rooms here." Willie nodded toward the hotel.

"Best idea all day."

Twenty minutes later, they commandeered a table overlooking the river. A cold Efes beer sat in front of each of them as they munched on chicken döner sandwiches.

"I want to do one more run in the morning before we head to Sanliurfa. We activated the first device five days ago, still within parameters." Willie swallowed the last of his sandwich and took a big swig of beer.

"Okay, one last run. Finished? C'mon, let's head back to the rooms. My turn to update BHQ."

To: Alpha

From: Mountie and Rebel

Completed check of Cappadocia. Suspected Kurdish attacks occurred yesterday. Multiple explosions and possible sniper fire. Army moved in tanks, armored personnel carriers, and recon vehicles. Ground troops, augmented by gendarmerie and police patrolling all towns within the area.

Disturbing news. All tagged items are now out of range or the trackers failed. Primary concern is the fake canisters tagged two days ago. No additional chemicals identified through use of the detectors.

Will make final sweep through area in the morning en route to Sanliurfa. Will advise any new information.

On Monday morning, Willie and Aiden ate a light breakfast before checking out of the hotel. With the army presence, they didn't want to begin their last run until more tourists became active.

By 0900, they decided they had waited long enough and circled through the Cappadocia towns one last time. Results remained the same—negative.

They stopped to fill their gas tanks at a nearby station. An army recon vehicle sat at the pumps. A major got out of the passenger seat and walked toward them.

"Hello. Passports please." Willie and Aiden offered them to the major, who gave them a cursory check before handing them back.

"Have you visited Cappadocia? Where are you going now?"

"Yes, we finished our tour of Cappadocia and now we're going to Alanya." Aiden nodded to support Willie's explanation.

"Ah, Alanya is a good place. You'll enjoy. Sorry to bother you. Some Kurdish terrorists are causing trouble right now but come back again soon. The problem will be fixed."

"Your English is good." Aiden complimented the major, hoping he'd let them leave.

"Thank you. I learned from Turkish-American Association in Ankara. When I went to Ft. Benning in Georgia, many Americans helped me. Now I must return to my duties. Have a nice day."

After they filled their tanks and paid, Willie walked by Aiden with a sour expression on his face.

"What's bothering you, eh?"

Willie stopped and turned back to Aiden. "I'm worried about not finding any of the trackers. We no longer know where the weapons are."

"You might be right, but think positive. No matter where the four gas canisters are now, they can't hurt anyone, eh?"

Willie's face brightened at Aiden's words. "Yeah. We did achieve our objective here, didn't we?"

"You bet, partner. Let's go find some more."

***

As they approached Sanliurfa, minarets and apartment blocks dotted the skyline, while the city itself sprawled across hillsides and valleys. Willie pulled into a rest stop on a nearby hill. An ancient castle dominated the center while trees and parks colored the otherwise drab appearance of the stone and brick buildings.

"I think conducting our search here will be more difficult." Aiden swept his right hand across the expanse. "Fewer tourists, and even more places to hide, eh?"

"Yep. Let's head to tourist information and find a hotel. Afterward, we can lay out a recon plan."

An hour later, Willie and Aiden were ensconced in adjoining rooms in the Edessa Hotel, a three-story structure, with various storefronts along the street. A perfect spot for them, as it commanded a corner position, making an approach easy from different directions.

Willie stuck his head through the doorway into Aiden's room. "Y'all ready? Let's head downstairs. I want a beer."

"Won't be happening here. Sanliurfa is a dry city."

"Never mind, let's go."

Soon they were seated in a small booth in the lobby, and the staff offered them an apple tea and baklava. As the waiter returned with their snack, the ground shook and a crescendoing rumble filled the air.

"What's the noise?" Willie stared at the man.

"Nothing." The waiter shrugged his shoulders. "Army tanks—they're reminding the people who controls the country."

"But why?" Aiden glanced at him with a puzzled expression.

"With the attacks at the oil refinery, gendarmerie facilities, and the Cappadocia area, the army wants to demonstrate to the people they're strong. This happens every year. Nothing to be alarmed about."

The rumbling faded as the tanks moved along the street. The men finished their snack and headed back to their rooms so they could send another update to BHQ.

To: Alpha

From: Rebel and Mountie

Completed final sweep through Cappadocia—still negative results. Now holed up in Sanliurfa. Tanks are rolling through the streets as a show of force. Will commence search tomorrow.

Chapter 42
Akçakale, Turkey
Sunday, March 20

Merdem, not satisfied with trying to scare CC away from the Akçakale safe house, had returned to Göbekli Tepe on Saturday in time to catch the foreigners in their canteen tent. Using a high-powered rifle borrowed from Serbest, he fired multiple rounds into the tent, hoping to scare them into departing. He also triggered the explosives lining the hillsides. He became disheartened when the ancient walls collapsed, as he didn't want to cause any damage to the excavation itself.

After triggering the last of the explosives, Merdem worked his way back to his car, parked a distance away from the dig. When he returned to the apartment, everyone was asleep. Horrendous snoring thundered from each bedroom. He went into the kitchen, grabbed a bottle of water and returned to the living room. After taking a swig, he kicked off his shoes and stretched out on the sofa. Minutes later, his snores joined the chorus.

Once dawn broke, sunlight streamed through the blinds, waking Merdem from a sound sleep. Not a morning person, he staggered into the kitchen and put a kettle on the stove to heat water.

"How did things go?" Serbest stood in the doorway, yawning and stretching to work the nighttime kinks out of his body.

"Okay. I shot into their community tent." Merdem said. "I hit a lantern, starting a fire, and a breeze carried their screams. After I finished shooting, I set off the explosives and returned here."

"Belen and Dildar arrived last night. We're ready to conduct our attack. No event is scheduled at the stadium because the team is playing elsewhere, so we'll attack the garrison."

An hour later, the five men left the apartment. Merdem and Serbest occupied one vehicle, while Dersim, Belen, and Dildar took another. Each man carried a stuffed backpack. Before heading to the apartment building overlooking the garrison, the two teams went to the garages Serbest rented earlier in the week, and grabbed additional ammunition and rifles, hidden inside tennis bags.

They parked the vehicles in the underground parking area and hauled their equipment to the elevator. Once inside the apartment, Serbest walked to the windows and glanced down at their target.

"Seems peaceful. Not for long." He turned back to the others and issued orders. "Merdem, take Dersim and go into the bedroom overlooking the compound. We'll begin in fifteen minutes. Belen, you're with me. Dildar, your job is to retrieve the elevator, prop the door open and keep everyone away. We'll want the elevator fast when we finish."

A final glance over the wall revealed two guards at the main gate. Two others stood beneath a tree toward the rear of the compound, their smoke signaling their location. A fifth person leaned against a narrow pedestrian entrance, weapon slung over his shoulder.

At the same time Serbest sighted on one of the main gate guards, the chatter of an AK-47 exploded throughout the apartment, followed by a scream of delight.

"Look at them run." Merdem laughed. "Not so tough now. No tanks to protect them or run over helpless people."

"Merdem!" Serbest's voice dripped with anger. "What're you doing? We must take out the guards one at a time, not spray the compound like terrorists."

"Not like this." Dersim tried to grab Merdem's weapon. "You don't have any idea who might be inside those rooms. Our fight is with the Turkish military and security forces. What if women and children are inside the building?"

"Trust them to hide behind their families." Merdem pulled away from Dersim as Serbest stormed into the room.

"Merdem. Enough." Serbest pointed out the door. "Trade places with Dildar."

"Not until I'm finished." Merdem leaned out the open window, searching for his next victim. A single *crack* resounded throughout the room. The back of Merdem's head mushroomed, decorating the room with bone, brains, and blood. His lifeless body, now balanced on the window ledge, swayed like a teeter-totter.

Without warning, Merdem's remains plummeted eight stories to the ground, bouncing off the side of the building before smashing onto an asphalt pad. Blood seeped out of his fractured body, running into the grass.

More shots rang out. Glass shattered, sending shards into Dersim and Serbest, drawing fresh blood. Bullets ricocheted around them, ripping into walls and furniture, adding to the destruction. Return fire began from the other room, as Belen identified targets firing from various windows in the four-story garrison.

Dersim wiped gore from his face and crouched next to the window ledge. He raised his AK-47 during a lull in incoming fire and let loose a long burst toward the main gate. The guards ducked at the incoming fire. Serbest rejoined Belen, who maintained a better angle at the compound.

"Don't spray, pick your shots. After you run out of ammunition, join Dildar. I'll grab Dersim, and we need to head to the basement."

"I'm hit." Serbest grabbed his arm after a ricochet burned a furrow across his arm. He stepped into the corridor. "Dersim, we need to get to the vehicles."

"I'm coming." Dersim fired a final burst and ran to the apartment's outer door where he joined Serbest and Belen.

"Where's Dildar?" Dersim helped Belen wrap Serbest's upper arm.

"He's holding the elevator." Belen pushed the door open. The hallway remained empty. The three men scurried toward the elevator.

"Hurry," Dildar yelled, motioning with his arm for them to move faster.

At last, the door closed, and the elevator headed to the garage. While they waited, Serbest gave orders to the others.

"Dildar, you and Belen take one vehicle and head to the apartment across from the stadium. We'll take the other and will meet you. Grab any weapons left behind when you arrive, and use the bleach under the kitchen sink and wipe down as many surfaces as you can. Once you're finished, head to the Sanliurfa cave."

"What about you and Dersim?"

"We'll monitor the military compound from a distance and delay any pursuit."

Thirty minutes later, Dersim parked a block away from the apartment where they might spot anyone coming and going. Dildar had stopped in front of the building. He spotted no obvious signs of surveillance, but after the gunfire exchange, they couldn't be too careful.

Sirens continued to blare in the distance, and emergency vehicles continued to flow to the military compound. Serbest kept an eye on the apartment while Dersim walked to the corner and joined a growing crowd of onlookers.

"What's going on?" Dersim stretched up on his toes to peer over shorter gawkers.

"A terrorist group attacked the military compound by the border." An old man next to Dersim nudged him. "The military killed ten terrorists and captured three others."

"The terrorists blew up the barracks." Another elderly person pushed forward. "They came from Syria."

Dersim turned to go back to the car when three military vehicles zoomed down the street, horns blaring to clear the way. Ambulances followed.

"What did you learn?" Serbest gestured to the corner with a thumb. "Anything to worry about?"

"Confusion—terrorists blew up the barracks. The military managed to kill several terrorists and captured some, too." Dersim's eyes twinkled, extending his smile from ear to ear. "They came from Syria."

A few minutes later, Serbest spotted Dildar and Belen returning to their vehicle. "Give them a couple of minutes, Dersim, and follow them."

Once they headed out of town, the traffic grew heavier. Rumors created panic and people with the means moved away from the border, anticipating more terrorist activity.

The regular military checkpoint outside the city was abandoned, with the barriers raised high. The unanticipated convoy expanded as vehicles merged onto the major thoroughfare from every direction.

At last, they turned onto the Sanliurfa Road and headed north. Two miles along the road, the slow-moving traffic ground to a halt. Red lights flashed in the distance.

Serbest, who drifted in and out of a light slumber, awoke when Dersim stopped. "Why are we stopped?"

"Might be a problem ahead—see the flashing lights? Perhaps an accident." Dersim rolled the window down and leaned out, attempting to identify the delay. Traffic stood still, so he stepped out of the car, returning moments later.

"Did you see anything?" Serbest winced as he scraped his injured arm against the car door.

"Yes, a military roadblock. They're stopping vehicles in both directions."

Thirty minutes later, they had worked their way forward. Now only six cars separated them from the roadblock. A slew of tanks, armored personnel carriers, and other military vehicles covered the approach to the checkpoint.

Troops armed with G3 assault rifles examined the identification of every individual. Whenever they cleared a vehicle, one of the armored personnel carriers would reverse off the road long enough for the car or truck to pass, before resuming its earlier position.

"To the right. Aren't those guys Belen and Dildar?" Serbest pointed to where two men stood in front of a car, legs spread wide and hands on the hood. Soldiers continued to frisk them as Dersim pulled forward until motioned to stop.

"Identity cards." A burly sergeant first class held out his hand.

Dersim reached out the window with their documents. The sergeant scrutinized the cards before returning them.

"Destination?"

"Sanliurfa—to visit his cousin." Dersim directed his thumb toward Serbest, who stared out his window.

"You may go." The sergeant waved his right hand, thumb extended upright and the vehicle blocking the road lumbered backward, allowing them to pass.

Once on their way, Dersim exhaled a sigh of relief. "I wonder why the Turks singled out Belen and Dildar. I hope they're released soon."

Serbest nodded but didn't speak. A sheen of perspiration dampened his face. He moved his right arm to wipe his brow and winced at the effort.

"Head to the cave. I need some painkillers from the medical supplies and my arm must be cleaned and bandaged."

When they arrived at the cave, Dersim parked the car underneath several trees and helped Serbest inside. He took him to the back and adjusted several crates, creating a makeshift seat and eased Serbest down and searched through the containers for the medical supplies.

Dersim found some Vicodin tablets. Grabbing a water bottle, he handed two pills to Serbest.

"Here, take these. They should help with the pain."

Serbest took the pills and water. After swallowing the tablets, he drained the bottle.

"Thank you. Now find the bandages and the antibiotic powder. A minor graze but still painful."

After finding the items, Dersim helped Serbest remove his shirt. A reddish-brown furrow, about three inches long, decorated his arm.

Dersim sprinkled Quickclot powder along the injury and wrapped Serbest's arm with a gauze bandage. Satisfied with the dressing, Serbest struggled back into his shirt.

"Grab me a blanket and heat up some food. I'll rest after I eat."

After Serbest fell asleep, Dersim rummaged through the supplies, making a mental note of everything. Toward the rear of the cave stood two crates, similar to the others, except for a crude black crescent painted on each side.

Prying off a lid, he gasped. He pulled out a cylinder for a closer examination. Sarin. He opened the other crate and found three more canisters.

Where did these come from? Who brought them? Dersim pondered these questions as he checked on Serbest—still asleep. He put the crates to the side and rearranged the other containers to conceal his theft.

Dersim hauled the first crate outside, searched around the area, and found a faded path headed into the brush. He followed the trail through a mixture of tall grasses, thorny bushes, and stunted trees for some distance before finding a perfect hiding place—at least for now.

Four massive evergreen trees, with trunks intertwined, and engulfed by six-foot-tall thorny bushes, acted as a beacon. He spotted an opening to the side and pushed the crate in as far as it'd go.

Stepping back to the path, Dersim moved back and forth to ensure the crate was hidden. He returned to the cave, noted Serbest was snoring, and grabbed the second container. Once stowed with the other one, he pulled some additional thorny branches to close off the opening.

Dersim set up a small camp stove when he returned, and heated water for coffee. As he drank his coffee and munched on some lamb jerky, Serbest stirred.

"That smells like heaven. Would you give me some?"

"Sure. Want some jerky, too?"

"Yes. Any sign of Belen and Dildar?" Serbest stretched and moved his injured arm around, testing its mobility.

"Not yet." They sat in silence, drinking and eating.

As the sun set, a car approached. Dersim peeked out—Belen and Dildar.

The two men entered the cave, and everyone shared a man-hug. Both accepted a bottle of water and some jerky and sat on a blanket strewn across the ground.

"What happened at the checkpoint?" Serbest nodded in the general direction of Akçakale. "We recognized you spread over the front of the car."

"Those Turkish soldiers." Dildar spit onto the ground. "My identity card was faded and crinkled. I told them it went through the wash. They thought it was a fake."

"At first, I thought they pulled us over for a baksheesh shakedown. But one wanted to look in the trunk." Belen belched and drank some water. "I protested, and they made us move the vehicle over. When we got out of the car, they frisked us for weapons and checked inside. Afterward, they forced us to open the trunk."

"Where did you put your weapons and backpacks?" Dersim stood, grabbed more coffee, and returned to the blanket.

"We had removed the spare tire and put everything in its place. After we put the cover back, the weapons and packs were concealed. When we opened the truck for the Turks, they couldn't find any contraband, so they let us go."

"Allah guided and protected you. Now, we must rest. Tomorrow, I'll contact Afran for instructions."

***

A shepherd paid close attention while Dersim removed the two crates from the cave and hauled them into the brush. While he remained occupied, the shepherd used a small digital camera to capture several images.

As dusk fell, the shepherd returned to his hiding place—the same spot where Dersim concealed the crates. If Dersim had crawled inside, he'd have found the shepherd's bedroll, meager rations, and a satellite phone.

Chapter 43
Göbekli Tepe, Turkey
Sunday, March 20

Friday night's attack took everyone by surprise. An hour after the echo of the final blast faded, they remained hunkered down under available cover, fearful of another explosion. The cries of the injured softened, now more like whimpering.

CC crawled over to Jake. "C'mon, whoever attacked us must be gone. Let's help the injured."

"Right you are, mate."

They both dug into their backpacks and pulled out penlights. CC searched for Konrad while Jake headed into the remains of the canteen. Others followed suit, turning to those nearby who required assistance.

CC found Konrad a short distance away, propped against a boulder, holding a handkerchief to his head.

"Konrad, let me check you out."

"Oh, CC, I'm glad you're here. People will need help, but I'm afraid I'm in no condition to lend a hand."

"Aye, you've a goose egg aboot yer heed."

"*Mein Gott*, CC. Speak in English."

"Sorry, professor. Sometimes under stress, I slip into my old habits. There's a big lump on the back of your head. The bleeding stopped, but we need to keep an eye on you. Might be a concussion, too."

CC tended to Konrad while Jake pulled open a flap of the collapsed canteen and ventured inside. He shined his light around the tent. Crushed tables, smashed chairs, and the remnants of last night's dinner were strewn everywhere.

"Mmmmm."

Jake swung his light in the direction the sound came from. Nothing.

"Errrgggh."

A white shape moved in the far corner, almost hidden from view by one of the overturned tables. Jake crawled over as the person continued to stir. It was Charlie, the cook. He eyed Jake with a glazed stare.

Jake pulled the table away. He lay on his side, and Jake eased him over, careful not to apply too much pressure.

"Ohhhh." Charlie's eyelids fluttered and then focused on Jake. "What happened? I remember throwing flour on the fires."

"Take it easy, mate. Your hands are burned and so is part of your face. The tent collapsed, and you ended up under a table."

Jake helped Charlie crawl to the exit. Once outdoors, they headed to a nearby area where Turkish workers erected several tables and chairs. Injured personnel straddled the chairs, while others pitched in and applied basic first aid.

Jürgen ran over to help Jake. "*Mein Gott*, Charlie. You're a hero—your actions put out the fires. Let me see your hands."

Jake rummaged through the medical supplies heaped on the tables, finding gauze, burn spray, and several Dynarex instant cold packs. When he returned, Jürgen had finished cleaning the minor burns on Charlie's face and worked on his hands and forearms.

"Here, mate. I brought some stuff to help."

Jürgen finished cleaning the burned areas, and Jake activated four of the cold packs by giving each a single squeeze. Together they placed the packs over the blistered areas and secured them with the gauze.

"Charlie, you're one lucky fellow, mate. Your hands might be painful, but there isn't any burned flesh. Red blotches and blisters, but you should feel better soon."

"Charlie, open your mouth." Jürgen held two painkillers in his hand. "Take these for the pain. Here's some water to wash them down."

Blue and red flashing lights lit the sky as a stream of ambulances and police cars poured into the area. Emergency crews jumped from their vehicles and scurried over to assess the medical requirements. Several armed police officers staged themselves around the perimeter, on the lookout for additional attackers.

For several hours, the excavation teams, both Turkish and foreign, assisted the responders in taking care of the wounded. Once the last ambulance departed, an uneasy calm descended among those remaining.

Someone passed out water bottles and cups of tea. Others gathered blankets and checked on everyone else. By unspoken mutual agreement, they returned to their tents and retired.

***

CC and Jake bolted out of their cots just after 0900 on Saturday morning. A loud rumbling of machinery woke the entire campsite and people wandered outside as a military convoy approached. Two tanks and several armored personnel carriers, led by an Akrep recon vehicle, stopped near the excavation's gates.

The Turkish workers cheered while the foreigners viewed the activity with interest.

"A bit late, aren't they, mate?" Jake shook his head.

"Aye, but their arrival will give us an excuse to slip away and continue with our mission. I'll inform Konrad later. In the meantime, I better notify BHQ."

CC returned to his tent and composed a brief message.

To: Alpha

From: Haggis and Aussie

Dig came under attack last night. Sniper fire and multiple explosions. No fatalities but various injuries. Aussie and I are fine.

Turkish military now present. We'll assist as needed today and proceed to Sanliurfa in the morning to commence search operations. Will link up with Rebel and Mountie when they arrive on Monday.

CC closed his laptop and headed outside. Jake approached, carrying two steaming cups.

"Here, mate. Some hot coffee. Breakfast is being rustled up now. The military brought a field kitchen with them and will feed us."

After simple, but nourishing food, and thankful they didn't have to put up with pre-packaged meals, CC and Jake tracked down Konrad. They found him talking with the commander of the military force, so they waited until he finished.

"Ah, CC and Jake. I need your help."

"How's your head this morning?"

"Much better, thank you. With the military here, we must put up markers to keep them from trampling over the excavation."

"We can help. Jake and I can spend the rest of today and tomorrow helping around the site. Monday morning we'll be leaving. My company wants me to return and Jake is tagging along."

"But, Jake. I thought you'd write an article about our work here?"

"Yes, professor. I'll still do the story. CC took plenty of photographs and I made notes. I'll rustle something together and send the article to you for review."

Throughout the rest of the day and the next, CC and Jake helped others set up new tents, and cordon off areas to keep the military from destroying any artifacts.

***

On Sunday, they spotted Jürgen staring at the wall that had toppled during the explosions.

"What's the verdict, Jürgen?" CC stared at the wall's remains. "Good, I hope."

"Ja. It'll take time, but most of the stones are undamaged. The ancient mortar crumbled from the force of the explosions, but we'll rebuild the wall almost as good as new."

"Do you want to start today? We're leaving in the morning, but will help as much as possible."

"Ja. We must clear the soil and move the stones out of the way. Before we move them, I want to write some small numbers on the bottoms so we can keep track as we work."

"Good idea."

Throughout the day, the work progressed but at a slow pace. Jürgen numbered the stones as CC, Jake, and several Turkish workers struggled to reposition them on the side of the hill for later reconstruction.

As the sun sank beyond the horizon, two portable generators kicked on, triggering a dozen klieg lights, and illuminating the perimeter with artificial sunlight. Eerie shadows descended into the camp while beyond the reach of the lights darkness loomed.

"We're finished for tonight." Jürgen extended a dirty paw to each of them, shaking their hands. "*Danke.*"

"I feel better now. Everyone's night vision is shot." Jake raised his hand to block the intense light as he and CC headed to the Turkish mess.

"Aye."

***

The first recognition reaching CC's consciousness on Monday morning was one of silence. With the rising sun, the camp no longer required the klieg lights and soldiers turned the generators off.

"What a racket. All night long. I didn't sleep." Jake yawned and stretched.

"Aye."

"That's what I like about you, mate. A man of few words."

"Aye." CC grinned. "C'mon, Jake, let's move. Breakfast, pack, and goodbyes. We need to hit the road."

Their preparations took several hours before they finished and departed. CC led the way from the excavation, turning right on Sanliurfa Road. Before entering the city, he reached into his backpack and turned on his detector.

They continued through the city, weaving through the main streets and slipping onto smaller ones. CC had plotted and memorized a surveillance detection route, doubling and tripling back on themselves before proceeding to their destination.

By 1530, they pulled into the parking lot for the Elruha Hotel, a stone-built, multi-story facility resembling a palace. After obtaining their room keys, they ventured onto the terrace for a Turkish coffee and baklava.

CC sent a text message to Aiden: *Leave hotel 2000. Turn right, head to the traffic circle. Will find you. Confirm.*

Five minutes later, CC received a one-word response from Aiden: *Confirmed.*

Coffee finished, Jake stood. "Going for a shower and a snooze. Join you later."

"Aye. Will sit here a while longer and then do the same."

CC grabbed another coffee as a distant rumble rolled across the city. The sky was a deep blue without a cloud in sight. No plane departed from the nearby airport.

"Hmmm. I think the army is on the move."

For the next hour, the rumbling escalated and diminished as if someone played with a volume control. As he stood to return to his room, a waiter appeared to clear the table.

"What's that rumbling?" CC gazed at the sky. "No clouds—no rain."

"Yes, *efendim.* Turkish Army is coming. Terrorists attacked Göbekli Tepe and Akçakale. The military will deal with them."

Right before 2000, CC and Jake left their hotel and headed toward the traffic circle. A main battle tank sat in the grassy area of the circle, capable of swinging its turret in any direction to respond to threats.

Three armored personnel carriers augmented the tank. Military police checked identification cards of the motorists. The city police erected barricades on the sidewalks and performed random pedestrian inspections.

A police officer recognized CC and Jake as foreigners and moved the barrier, and they slipped through.

"No problem. Enjoy your stay." The officer turned and stopped two locals who tried to sneak by. He continued to shout at them while CC and Jake crossed the street and headed for their rendezvous with Aiden and Rebel.

They walked past the Edessa Hotel toward the corner where another tank stood guard. Crossing the street, they headed back toward the Edessa as two familiar faces stepped out and strolled in their direction.

"Hey, Aiden, Willie. What're you guys doing here?"

"Hey, CC. What brings you here? Who's your friend?"

CC made the introductions while the four men maintained a slow circular motion, checking for surveillance.

"Clear, mate."

"Same here."

CC nodded and moved toward the traffic circle. "Why don't you come to our hotel for dinner? We booked a table big enough for four."

"If it's not too much trouble, we'll join you, eh?"

Conversation during their meal alternated between raucous laughter and chitchat interspersed with softer, meaningful discussion of the situation. They agreed to work as two independent teams. Thanks to a source, they realized six canisters remained hidden somewhere nearby.

Without warning, a huge explosion rocked the hotel. Chandeliers swung, plates and cutlery slid off tables, patrons screamed, and the lights went out. A small candle burned on each table and the waiters brought more. Before they finished passing out the extra candles, the lights returned, glowing so bright the bulbs seemed like they might explode before they settled down.

A waiter appeared with a metal triangle and small rod. He ran the rod along the triangle, attracting everyone's attention. After the noise had diminished, he announced: "Terrorists attacked several locations outside the city today. The Turkish Air Force's response caused the explosion."

Cheers erupted at the news. Local patrons stood and danced, arms in the air. The four men left their table and headed outdoors. Sirens reverberated off buildings while the flashing lights of emergency vehicles crisscrossed the city center.

A small dark-colored Murat sedan sped by CC and the others as they stood on the sidewalk. The driver ignored the instructions to halt and rammed his way through the traffic circle.

The tank's turret tracked the vehicle as it raced away. Smoke billowed from the tank's main gun as a single round hit the car. Through the flames and billowing smoke, it was clear the vehicle no longer existed. A heap of twisted metal smoldered in its place.

Chapter 44
Diyarbakir, Turkey
Sunday, March 20

"Stop here." Afran, dressed in the uniform of a Turkish Army major, pointed to a long, flat stretch of road. A few minutes after midnight, four Mercedes Unimog all-terrain vehicles slid to a halt between two rows of leafless trees, buds ready to open.

Black and tan camouflage patterns interrupted the olive green color of the ATVs. The Kurds had confiscated them from various army compounds over the previous two years. A common sight throughout the countryside, they were the perfect platform for attacking the Turks.

Fifteen men wearing tan armbands exhibiting a small Kurdish flag jumped from the rear of each vehicle. Several broke out cigarettes while others headed into the trees. The drivers and team leaders climbed from the cabs.

Afran raised his right hand and with his index finger extended, made a circling motion. The other leaders, all dressed in captain uniforms, jogged to his position.

"We'll take a ten-minute break and continue toward our targets. Synchronize our time, as I want all attacks to begin together. It's now 0015."

The other three men adjusted their timepieces.

"Jawero—you attack Ergani. Warzan, Egil is your target. Helmet, proceed to Adiyman. I'll take Kocakoy."

"When we finish, what's next?" Helmet bounced from foot to foot, eager to begin.

"When you complete your mission, head to the village outside Sanliurfa. The military compound is our next target. Any more questions?"

The men shook their heads.

"Okay, let's move out. We attack at 0430."

Someone blew a whistle, and all four teams remounted their vehicles. Three vehicles headed north while the fourth went in a southwesterly direction.

***

When Felek Xabat and Palan Olan finished their mission in Cappadocia, they brought the sarin gas canisters with them, not realizing they were fakes. None of the others in the Malatya warehouse perceived their plan.

Mullah Abdul, a fierce advocate of using the gas, had argued with Mufti Tanreverdi, whom he considered too timid to lead the Kurdish endeavor. After multiple debates threatening to expand into serious arguments, Tanreverdi caved to Abdul's demand for his supporters to lead one of the attacks.

Before leaving for Cappadocia, Felek and Palan met with Abdul and received their marching orders.

"Be cautious with the attacks in Cappadocia—there are too many foreigners. When you commence the attack in Malatya, don't hold back. Use the cylinders. We must demonstrate to the Turks we're serious about our demands."

Felek and Palan would each lead five men. Their primary objective from Tanreverdi—destroy Turkish F-4E fighters and RF-4E reconnaissance aircraft at Erhac Air Force Base. Abdul gave them a secondary mission—deploy the four gas canisters near the pilots' barracks.

Their attack would begin at 0430 as preparations for dawn patrols commenced. The teams planned to attack from opposite sides of the base, merging into one group as they approached the barracks.

Felek and Palan monitored the second hands sweeping closer and closer to launch time. They gave a whistle. Eight men focused their RPG-7s on their targets. Another whistle. Clouds of grey-blue smoke appeared when high explosive anti-tank grenades streaked toward the aircraft. As one, the eight rounds exploded.

A tremendous *boom* filled the air. Towering fingers shot upward, the flames reaching for the heavens, as thick smoke billowed around the burning aircraft. Smaller explosions erupted when onboard munitions detonated, a result of the intense heat and flames.

Men screamed and shouted, air raid sirens blared, and chaos descended over the base. The eight men thrust aside their RPG launchers, and grabbing their AK-47s, raked the responders with an intense hail of lead, adding to the carnage.

The remaining men, including Felek and Palan, shouldered their backpacks and made their way to the barracks, utilizing vehicles, small sheds, and trees to mask their progress.

Each man entered a different building. According to hand-drawn sketches of the interior provided by a Kurdish member of the cleaning crew, large wooden storage lockers stood like sentries on either side of the entranceways. Ventilation holes in the doors were perfect for releasing the gas into the corridors.

The men opened the closets, placed their backpacks on the floor, reached inside, and twisted open the cylinders' caps. The liquid would soon vaporize after contact with the air, and strike anyone who came near—according to their plan.

Thirty minutes later, ten of the twelve attackers returned to the warehouse. The men readied a truck and two cars for their departure.

Felek stared at his watch—again. "Where are the other two? We must depart before the area is sealed."

"They must be dead." One of the men pointed toward the air base. "One fell after being shot by a security guard. The other grabbed his injured arm but kept running. We don't know where he went."

"Why didn't you help them?"

The man lowered his head in shame. "I-I was scared—I ran."

Felek shook his head in disgust. "We must go. We'll meet as planned outside Sanliurfa."

One-by-one the truck and two cars departed. The last car stopped for the person closing the doors. The first glimpses of dawn shimmered above the horizon while they sped away, leaving Malatya behind them.

***

Three Unimog ATVs continued along back roads around Diyarbakir and toward their destinations. Coming around a bend in the road, the convoy approached a military checkpoint. An armed soldier waved his hand up and down for them to stop. Two sandbagged machine gun positions overlooked the site, perched upon opposing hills.

Afran stepped from the lead vehicle. Upon recognizing his rank, the soldier snapped to attention and saluted.

"Why are you slowing us down? Can't you tell we're in a hurry?" Afran pointed at the lead truck's bumper, signifying the vehicle belonged to the intelligence detachment of Seventh Corps, headquartered in Diyarbakir.

"I-I I'm sorry, sir. No one informed me. Please continue your journey." The soldier raised the barricade and saluted as the vehicles stormed past.

The convoy shrank as vehicles turned onto side roads leading to their destinations. By 0400, the teams reached their positions. The attacks, designed to further spread the military throughout the area, began on time.

The military in Diyarbakir used trains to move heavy equipment and supplies throughout the area due to narrow, twisting roads traversing around hills and mountains. With the destruction of the tracks and switching station, repairs would be required as well as sending a force to secure the area.

Along the tracks, ten bundles of explosives positioned every ten meters erupted in a consecutive string, tossing rails, ties, spikes, and gravel into the air, spreading a dusty cover as they returned to earth. The Ergani railway switching station collapsed as RPGs stormed through the wooden structure and out the other side.

Mission accomplished, Jawero's team boarded their truck and turned south, their destination—the rendezvous point outside Sanliurfa.

***

Warzan's team had the easiest target of the three. Egil, a small village, possessed a single government building. No permanent gendarmerie post, only an occasional visit by a team passing through. Afran chose this location due to the mayor being a relative of the provincial governor.

Their target, constructed of red, sun-baked bricks, crumbled under the attack. By the sixth RPG round, the roof collapsed inward as the walls pancaked. When the dust settled, the former building resembled a construction site, waiting for work to begin.

Warzan blew on a silver whistle to end the attack. All eyes focused on him as he waved his hand in the air, motioning for the others to gather on his position.

"Well done, brothers." He nodded toward the ruined building and smiled. "We've completed our mission. Time to depart."

***

When Afran's team arrived in Kocakoy, the only building with noticeable activity housed the local mayor and a small gendarmerie contingent. At first, he wanted to level the building using RPGs. However, he changed his mind and instructed the team to maneuver as close as possible. Once in position, he wanted them to use explosives, hand grenades, and AK-47s.

"What about the RPGs?" One of the men held up his RPG and pointed ahead. "I could hit the building from this distance."

"I understand, my friend. However, I've another target to exploit before we arrive in Sanliurfa."

Ten minutes later, the team held positions along the western and southern perimeters of the building. To avoid friendly fire, they left the remaining sides clear.

One man rushed forward with a satchel charge and placed the bag near a door. Stolen from a Turkish Army supply depot, the pouch contained ten pounds of C-4 and a timed fuse.

The man returned to his position as the C-4 detonated, blowing the door inward. Black and white smoke streamed out the entrance and muffled screams echoed from inside. Two windows opened, and the assault team hunkered down as a blistering storm resonating like angry bees searched for them.

The courageous response from within the building wounded two of the attackers. Uninjured team members responded with their own withering fire. All of a sudden, a hush descended upon the area.

Afran's team withdrew without any urging. Once they climbed back on the truck, they pulled away. Like their counterparts, they headed west.

***

When they separated from the others, Helmet's team traveled the farthest distance. Adiyman lay in a valley, divided in two by one of the tributaries of the Euphrates River.

Helmet instructed his six snipers to shoot at the top of the bridge. He reminded them to only scare people, not cause casualties. The team also carried AK-47s and RPGs, but they would be used for the next mission.

The men found suitable positions while the rest of the team remained near the truck. At 0430, they found little traffic, a few trucks, and the occasional car. The snipers selected their targets and fired at the front of each vehicle. Two errant shots took out front tires, causing the unsuspecting drivers to collide with the side of the bridge.

Another shot shattered a windshield as the driver swerved to miss one of the crashed vehicles. Scared by the sudden loss of the glass, the driver wrenched the steering wheel in desperation, applying pressure to the accelerator. The resultant momentum caused the vehicle to flip on its side, further blocking the road.

Each man fired three rounds before returning to the Unimog. Once everyone returned, Helmet gave the order to depart.

***

Afran's driver turned onto the Adiyaman-Sanliurfa road. They followed the signs for the Atatürk Dam, straddling the Euphrates River between the two provincial borders. After finding a quiet place to park, the team disembarked.

"We'll break into pairs, one RPG for each team. Position yourselves as close as possible to the dam, and aim along the upper ten feet. We want to cause disruption, which will force the military to respond. Shoot once and return to the truck."

Fifteen minutes later, eight projectiles hit their target, throwing rock and earth upwards. The dam held, but in three locations, small rivulets of water cascaded downward, joining the river below.

***

Two hours later, Afran's team joined the others outside a small village in the valley adjacent to Sanliurfa. While the rest of his team shared their exploits, Jawero, Warzan, and Helmet joined Afran, along with Felek and Palan.

"Were you successful?" Afran glanced around the small group. "Any problems?"

The first three men gave a thumbs up to Afran's first question and shook their heads at the second.

"We achieved our mission—but at a cost of two men." Felek half-raised both hands with open palms. "Both were hit by return fire. One died at the base and I don't know what happened to the other. He never made the rendezvous at the warehouse."

Afran stood silent for a moment, using his fingers to help with a calculation. "We have seventy-four men to carry out our next mission. Verify the number of sniper rifles and RPGs remaining with your teams. If you require ammunition or grenades for the launchers, we brought extra supplies. Everyone must check their weapons, eat, and rest."

The men nodded and wandered back to their groups. Afran pulled a worn hand-drawn map of their target from his pocket and studied the layout again, committing all details to memory.

At 1530, Afran called for the team leaders. When they arrived, they joined him on a blanket. In the middle, rocks pinned down the corners of Afran's map.

"The compound is surrounded by a ten-foot-tall chain-link fence, topped with strands of concertina wire. Two entry points." Afran pointed to the gates at opposite ends of the rectangular compound. "The Turks are helping us out. Their tanks are parked in straight rows, easy to aim, shoot, and move onto the next one."

Everyone laughed and nudged one another.

"My team will take the main gate. Warzan, Jawero, and Helmet, you'll each take a side." Afran explained their targets. "Felek and Palan, your team will be in reserve." He glanced at his wristwatch. "We depart in fifteen minutes, giving everyone plenty of time to move into position. We'll attack at 1900 but wait for the signal."

"What will be the signal?" Warzan glanced around at the others, who nodded at his question.

"The main gate blowing up."

***

A few minutes before 1900, Afran peered at the main gate through binoculars. He shifted his view to the left, following to the end of the fence and back to the right before ducking into the brush.

"Hmmm. More guards than I expected." He mumbled to himself and used the binoculars again. "They seem alert. Allah will guide us if we're to be successful."

Afran raised the RPG-7, aimed at the portal, and pressed the trigger. The projectile streaked toward the opening, slamming through the double wooden gates. Each section bounced against the fence and whiplashed back into position before falling off their hinges. The signal given, automatic weapons fire commenced around the compound. Additional RPGs screamed through the air, adding to the carnage as tanks burst into flames.

The turret of a Turkish tank transited to the left and fired into the telltale smoke cloud left by two RPGs. The two men were pulverized, their remains scattered over their teammates.

A group of Turkish soldiers ran out of a low concrete building, firing as they headed to the fence. Several Kurds were strafed by the heavy response and fell to the ground, out of the fight.

The intensity of the counterattack increased. After the attacks in Göbekli Tepe and Akçakale, the Twentieth Mechanized Brigade maintained a high alert level. The Kurdish attack faltered as the Turks gained the upper hand. One of the Kurdish teams panicked and retreated to their truck, leaving their leader stranded. The driver tried to start the vehicle without success. After several attempts, the engine kicked over, and the driver backed away from the fight. Another Turkish tank spotted the truck and took appropriate action. The resultant shot flipped the truck, killing a dozen Kurds.

Afran realized his men were taking a severe beating. He blew a whistle to signal immediate withdrawal. The remaining men withdrew to their vehicles and departed, with Turkish APCs in pursuit.

Witnessing the counterattack's ferocity, Felek and Palan abandoned the reserve team. Felek pulled a fellow Kurd from behind the wheel of a dark blue Murat sedan and jumped inside. Palan ran around to the passenger side and repeated Felek's action.

Gunning the engine, Felek skidded through the grass but maintained control of the car. They fled, leaving others to their own resources.

Fifteen minutes later, Felek entered a side street in Sanliurfa. He sped along the street, missing pedestrians while scraping several vehicles. A barricade stretched across the street blocked the way ahead.

Felek mashed the accelerator and demolished the wooden barrier. Soldiers and police officers raked the Murat with their weapons, blowing out the back window. Palan's head twitched and blood splattered him as several rounds entered the vehicle, nicked Palan's left shoulder and neck, and exited through the damaged windshield.

Screaming in panic, Felek veered around stopped cars and trucks and continued along the thoroughfare toward a traffic circle. Palan managed to open his door and rolled out of the car, ending in a heap in the gutter.

Another barricade loomed—Felek screamed again and smashed his way through, the front of the car now mangled, with pieces scraping the asphalt.

He breathed a sigh of relief when he realized his escape route remained clear—no vehicles or roadblocks in sight. *I must steal another vehicle and return to Mardin.*

A moment later, a tank's projectile turned the car into a pile of twisted metal, immolating Felek.

***

At the same time, the remainder of the Kurds limped away from the Twentieth Mechanized Brigade's compound. Of the seventy-four men who began the assault, the few uninjured included Afran, Jawero, and Warzan. Helmet and at least twenty-five others were killed or missing, while another thirty-five sustained various wounds, some minor, some life-threatening.

The Turkish Army rolled out of their barracks in Diyarbakir, Adiyaman, and Sanliurfa Provinces, spreading themselves throughout the cities, towns, and villages.

Chapter 45
Aleppo, Syria
Monday, March 21

Dr. Pierre returned from Al-Bab on Sunday morning. He called the entire team together as soon as he arrived.

"I've bad news. Someone kidnapped Dave yesterday morning from his room at the hotel. They also grabbed another foreigner."

The room filled with stunned chatter. Pierre motioned for calm, but no one paid any attention. He pursed his lips and let loose with a sharp whistle, bringing the room to dead silence.

"The police are investigating. So far there aren't any leads. Abdel, the manager, said they found a rear door unlocked and—"

"*Mein Gott*!" Dr. Franz pulled a smoldering cigar stub from his mouth and waved it around, causing several people to cough. "How can we help? Does anyone understand why they took Dave?"

"The police said foreigners are sometimes kidnapped for ransom." Pierre shook his head. "Anyone have any ideas about what action we should take?"

Voices increased in volume as several people made suggestions. Ben stood and joined Pierre.

"I'll search for Dave." Ben spoke in soft tones to keep others from hearing. "No one else speaks Arabic. The team can spare me but not some of the others."

Pierre nodded his agreement. "*Oui*, but what about your injuries? You're still healing."

"I'll be okay. Will you drive me over?"

"*Oui*, but let's wait until morning. Perhaps more information will be available."

***

After a restless Saturday night, tossing and turning, and unable to find a comfortable position to sleep, Ismet rose early. A disturbing dream haunted him every time he drifted into slumber.

Ismet checked on the prisoner, Dave, the MSF doctor. He grabbed some fruit from the kitchen and headed to the basement.

He walked along the corridor and opened the lock when a loud crash came from farther down the hall. Ismet pulled a peg from the hasp on the door where he thought the noise originated.

"Le. me … f here. C'mo.." A muffled voice spit out English words as another thud resounded against the wall.

Ismet stepped into the room. A man with sandy-colored hair, pale complexion, and long limbs lay on the bed, his legs poised for another kick. Bungee cords secured his arms and legs, and a piece of duct tape covered his mouth and wrapped around his head.

The man wore torn jeans, tennis shoes, and a somewhat white sports shirt. Now bloodstains, dust, and grime covered his clothes. Black and blue bruises highlighted his eyes, almost swollen shut.

Sensing someone in the room, the man stopped kicking and maneuvered into a position to squint at the intruder.

Ismet unwound the duct tape, giving a final tug to remove the gag from the man's face.

"Ow. That hurt! Shukran, I think. Who're you? Where am I?"

Ismet realized the man spoke passable Arabic. "I'm Ismet, and you're a prisoner. What's your name?"

"Nathaniel Webster. I'm a freelance journalist from California."

"Why are you here?"

"I wanted to write a story about the government's poor treatment of its people. I witnessed the demonstration near a bakery in Aleppo and followed a van to Al-Bab and found a hotel. Someone knocked me unconscious when I peered out the door, and I awoke here."

"Who'd read your story?"

"Lots of people. All over the world. Not everyone condones the treatment minority groups receive from larger or more important organizations."

Ismet nodded. *Might I be wrong? Do others care?*

"I must go now. I'll come back later and bring you some food."

He closed the door and returned to Dr. Dave's room. When he entered, he found the doctor asleep, at least he appeared to be. Bloodstained and tattered clothing covered his body. Deep scratches adorned his face and arms.

Ismet put the fruit on the bedside table, left the room, and returned upstairs. He needed to speak with Salih. Walking into the dining room, he found him dressed in stylish clothing, enjoying a late breakfast.

"About time you joined me. Where did you go?" Salih motioned to a chair. "Take a seat and eat some breakfast."

"I went to visit the MSF doctor. I heard a noise coming from another room and found a young man. Why is he here?"

"I planned to tell you about him. I had you and Kadir followed when you went to kidnap the doctor. After you pulled away from the back of the hotel, this man appeared in the doorway. While he wrote your license plate number, the guys I sent grabbed him and brought him here."

"Why?"

"At first, because he spotted you. Now we realize he's a journalist, and he might be valuable. If the MSF doesn't air our video, perhaps we can persuade his employer to do so."

The remainder of the day passed as Salih issued orders for another demonstration. Ismet sat and listened but didn't participate in the planning. His fervor for demonstrating had waned.

At dinner, Salih sensed something bothered Ismet. After desert and once the room emptied, he broached the subject.

"Ismet, you've appeared dejected all day. Is there something we should discuss?"

"Yes. When Kadir brought me here, I thought we were working for the greater good of all Kurds."

"We are, Ismet. Can't you understand?"

"At first, I thought I did. Perhaps I was caught up in the excitement of doing something important. But I fail to understand how inciting a riot at a peaceful demonstration will further the Kurdish cause."

"Ismet, sometimes events overcome us or are more complicated than they appear. You must trust me."

"We kidnapped the doctor because your words made sense. But, what about the journalist? Someone tortured them. How does beating those men help our cause?"

"You don't understand the bigger picture. We'll assist the Turkish Kurds after we deal with Assad. Don't forget, you also stabbed one of the MSF doctors."

"Stabbing him seemed appropriate. Now, I-I'm not sure."

"I think you must rest and decide whether you're with us or not. We will increase our pressure on Assad's regime, and I rely on everyone's support."

"Okay, Salih. I'll talk with you in the morning. I didn't sleep well last night, and I'm tired."

***

Ismet tossed and turned. At last, he fell asleep.

"Ismet." A voice whispered.

He shook his head, trying to dislodge the soft voices, which seemed to come from above.

"Ismet." Another whisper. A female voice. One he recognized.

"Momma? Is that you?" Ismet bolted up, tears welling in his eyes.

"Yes, Ismet. It's Momma."

"I can't see you. Can you come closer?"

"No, darling. I can't."

"Where's Papa? Is he with you?"

"Yes, he's here and sends his love. Only one of us may speak with you. Ismet, why are you hurting people?"

"They deserve to be punished."

"Didn't our people endure enough pain and suffering in Halabja? The doctors, what did they do? They're only trying to help others."

"What about the Kurdish nation?"

"Ismet, people who attack our homes should be punished. But stabbing the doctor and kidnapping and beating another person is wrong."

"What should I do?"

"You should help the doctor to escape. And the journalist—he'll tell our story. Fight against those who oppress us, but leave innocent people in peace."

"Yes, Momma."

"Ismet, I must go now. I love you."

"I love you, Momma. Papa, too."

"I love you."

His mother's voice faded away. Ismet glanced around the room. He remained alone. Sliding under the covers and adjusting his pillow, Ismet fell into a deep sleep, the first since leaving Halabja, several weeks ago.

Ismet opened his eyes and focused on the clock—0400. *Was it a dream or did Momma visit me?*

He climbed out of bed, dressed, and opened the door a couple of inches. The hallway seemed empty. Ismet yanked the door wide open, and stuck his head out of the room, checking both directions. Still clear.

Ismet grabbed his backpack, shut the door, and snaked along the corridor. Sconces cast strange shadows upon the walls, acting as sentries as he tiptoed toward the stairs.

Creak. A thud. *Creak.*

Silence.

He reached the staircase and headed down. When he stepped onto the landing, he glanced around—no one else. After walking through the living room and into the kitchen, he opened the door to the basement. Cold air pulsated around him as he descended, causing involuntary shivers.

Ismet pulled a flashlight from his pack, thumbed the switch on and made his way to his first destination—Dr. Dave's dungeon.

He opened the door and stepped inside. Once he closed the door, he touched Dave on the shoulder. No response. He shook his shoulder and Dave's eyes popped wide open, a fearful expression on his face.

"What do you want? Haven't you done enough?" Dave shifted away from Ismet, watching for any sudden movement.

"I-I sorry." Ismet spoke in halting English. "I help. Come."

Ismet put out his hand out. After hesitating for a moment, Dave climbed out of the bed.

"Where are we going?"

"Free ... dom. Come."

As they crept out of Dave's room, Ismet put his index finger to his lips.

"Shhh."

They turned right and stopped at another door. Ismet pulled the peg from the hasp and they went inside.

Nathaniel lay curled in a ball on the bed, his arms and legs still secured. Ismet woke him and motioned for Dave to speak.

"I think this lad had a change of heart and wants to help us escape." Dave tapped on Nathaniel's bonds. "Let's take these off and find out where we're going. I hope this isn't a trick."

Ismet helped remove the bungee cords and together they assisted Nathaniel to his feet.

"Come. Follow."

Ismet waved his hand as he coaxed the door open for a peek. Not spotting anyone, he led the way, farther to the right until they came to a flight of three steps leading to a bolted door. He motioned for quiet, opened the door, and stepped outside.

"Quick. No guard. Follow."

Ismet loped across the grass toward a tall brick wall. Dave assisted Nathaniel, and they joined Ismet a couple of minutes later. As they reached the wall, Ismet ducked into the shadows. The two men followed his example and glanced in the direction Ismet pointed.

Two armed guards came around the corner of the building. Their AK-47s hung by the straps over their shoulders and they puffed away on cigarettes. They stopped, laughing, and finished their smoke break before strolling around the far end of the building.

As soon as they left, Ismet grabbed a wooden ladder he'd placed in the grass during the afternoon and leaned the rickety frame against the wall.

"Up. Fast."

The three men climbed onto the top of the wall, pulling the ladder up to assist going down the other side. Clearing the wall, Ismet led them to a small, white Kartal car. Ismet started the vehicle, and they headed away from their prison. He drove down one narrow street after another through a run-down neighborhood.

Fifteen minutes later, Ismet stopped in front of a ramshackle garage. After they had opened the doors, he drove inside. Ismet found a thin cord hanging from the ceiling and pulled, snapping on a single light.

"You ... stay. I come ... back."

"When'll you be back?" Dave glanced around, searching for something to use to protect himself.

"Soon. Bring ... help."

Ismet walked along back streets and through alleyways until he reached a position to monitor the Hotel Dar al Kanadi. He couldn't enter the building—Abdel would inform Salih.

***

Pierre and Ben left the Aleppo MSF building early for the trip to Al-Bab. This time, Ben carried his Beretta. The drive passed in silence, each man wrapped up in his own thoughts.

As they approached the hotel, Ben monitored their progress, searching for anything out of the ordinary. After Pierre parked the battered blue Land Rover, they climbed out and went inside. Abdel met them at the main desk.

"Welcome back, my friends." He shook their hands and motioned them to a nearby table.

"Any news?" Pierre cut off any attempts by Abdel to delay them. "Do the police know where Dr. Dave is or who's holding him? If not, we'll check around."

"No need, my friends. Let me call them and find out the latest."

Pierre and Ben shared glances. Abdel went to the desk and picked up the phone.

"I think he's stalling." Ben motioned toward Abdel. "I wonder who he's talking with?"

"*Oui*, something is fishy. Perhaps we should leave."

As they stood, Abdel finished his call and rushed over. "The police don't possess any new information. They want you to leave the investigation to them."

"I don't think so, Abdel." Ben pursed his lips and shook his head. "It's over forty-eight hours since the kidnappers took Dr. Dave. Nothing in the papers or on the TV. I don't believe the police are doing anything."

"*Oui*, I agree with Ben." Pierre nodded toward the door. "We brought flyers with Dr. Dave's photograph and our contact number. We'll put them in the stores and hope we can find him. Let's go."

They walked across the street and went into a corner store. Ben asked if they could leave one of their flyers. The man recognized them as MSF doctors and placed the paper in the window. They walked outside, and stood for a moment, deciding which way to continue.

"Psst. Ben." Spoken in Arabic.

Ben glanced around and caught a hand waving from an alleyway. He pulled out his gun, and ventured forward, Pierre following. They turned the corner. Ismet stood alone, a knife in his right hand. Ben raised his weapon, preparing to shoot.

"No, no. Peace. I come in peace." Ismet lowered his hand and bending down, placed the knife on the ground. He kicked the knife toward Ben, making no effort to close the distance.

"I'm sorry." Ismet jabbed at his own chest and arm, the same areas where he'd stabbed Ben.

"What do you want?" Ben picked up the knife, maintaining a careful eye for any sudden movement from Ismet.

"Dr. Dave."

"What about him?"

"Come. He safe. Also another man."

"Who's the other man?"

"Journalist. Other people kidnapped him."

"Pierre, bring the vehicle over so Abdel doesn't spot Ismet joining us. How far do we go?"

"By vehicle, about five minutes."

Pierre nodded and went for the Land Rover. Pulling up to the alley, the others joined him and they departed.

Ismet gave directions and in a few minutes, they reached the garage.

"Inside. Hurry. I must go."

"Ismet, what changed you?"

"My mother. She came in a dream and guided me. I'm sorry for hurt. After you take the men away, I'll leave here."

"Where'll you go?"

"I'll join my friend, Dersim. He in Turkey but working for a worthy cause, not like the Kurds here."

"Where's the sarin?"

"In Turkey. None in Syria."

Ben nodded as they entered the garage. Dave spied them and rushed over, giving Pierre and Ben a huge hug. Laughter and smiles broke out among the three men who had become friends. Dave broke away and motioned for Nathaniel to come forward.

"This is Nathaniel Webster, a freelance journalist kidnapped by the same organization which took me. We'll take him with us, for sure."

"Thank you." Tears welled in Nathaniel's eyes as he realized he was safe. Ben turned around to thank Ismet.

He was gone.

***

Ninety minutes later, the doctors and Nathaniel entered the Aleppo MSF building. Pierre and Ben gave the two men thorough examinations and pronounced them healthy although battered and bruised.

After joining them for a light meal, Ben excused himself and returned to his room to send an update.

To: Alpha
From: Kiwi

Unknown person(s) kidnapped Dr. Dave, the head of the Aleppo MSF group in Al-Bab two days ago. Surprise benefactor assisted in his recovery—Ismet Timur.

Ismet plans to join Dersim. Stated the sarin is in Turkey but not in Syria.

Suggest I proceed to Turkey and join the gas hunt. Please advise.

Ben returned to the group to monitor Dave and Nathaniel's condition. Two hours later, he retired to his room for the evening. New orders awaited.

To: Kiwi

From: Alpha

Travel to Adana tomorrow morning. Upon arrival, collect reserved rental car. Proceed to Incirlik. Obtain three black Pelican Storm cases from armory and join remainder of team in Sanliurfa. Contact instructions forthcoming.

***

After leaving the garage, Ismet made his way to the bus station where he obtained a one-way ticket to Tell Abayd, on the Syrian-Turkish border. He should be at the safe house in Akçakale within a few hours.

Chapter 46
Sanliurfa, Turkey
Tuesday, March 22

Afran selected Nizip, forty-five kilometers from Gaziantep, as the next rally point for the Kurdish operation. Trucks, ATVs, cars, and motorcycles converged on a block of buildings in the city's industrial district. Numerous car repair services surrounded the old, but serviceable warehouses.

He climbed out of the lead ATV, walked to a side door and beat the PKK code against the wooden frame. A moment later Nasdar Kaban, their explosives expert, opened the door. They embraced each another and strolled to a long wooden table heaped with various cold dishes, fruit, and sweets.

"Many others arrived earlier." Nazdar gazed out a window. "We've set up cots in another warehouse behind this one for everyone to rest."

"Well done." Afran smiled as he grabbed an apple. "Over 350 men will be present in a few hours. I need to rest. Wake me when everyone's here. I must meet with the leaders to discuss our plans."

Three hours later, Nasdar woke Afran.

"My friend, everyone has arrived. The men will eat and sleep while the leaders will join you when you're ready."

"Let's begin."

Afran approached a table where a large map of Gaziantep Province dominated the available space. A smaller one of Gaziantep City also lay on the table. He glanced at the assembled leaders, nodding at several.

"Over the past six days, our attacks have created chaos and spread the Turkish military across the area as we wanted. Several men were martyred for our cause.

"We're in the final stages of our efforts to free Baziyan. We must now draw elements of the Fifth Armored Brigade from Gaziantep before we attack the prison."

He leaned over the provincial map and circled five areas: Araban, Islahiye, Karkamis, Nurdagi, and Yavuzeli.

"The Turks demonstrated in Sanliurfa they're ready for our tactics. We'll change how we hit the areas by using hit-and-run techniques. No RPGs or explosives. AK-47s and grenades only. Use cars and motorcycles. The trucks and ATVs will be used within the city."

Afran paused before asking an important question. "Who wants to lead?"

The leaders nodded in unison. Every hand shot into the air.

"You'll draw straws later. Shortest ones will attack these locations tomorrow. You may begin anytime you choose as long as you return before dark. Ensure the townspeople are aware of your departure so they'll spread the word to the security forces."

Serbest half-raised his hand.

Afran nodded for him to proceed.

"Do we aim high or shoot to kill?" Several others nodded agreement with the question.

"I'll leave the targets up to the team leaders. These aren't tourist areas so there shouldn't be many foreigners, but we also don't want a bloodbath. Create enough of a scene so they reach out to the military for assistance. Any questions about tomorrow's operations?"

The leaders glanced around the group. One-by-one they shook their heads.

"Good. Now for the final operations. They'll take place on Friday. Our ultimate goal is securing Baziyan's release. We might lose men because the Turks will be ready.

"We'll use a three-prong approach. One team of fifty will hit the Fifth's barracks in the Sahinbey district, and another fifty will hit their barracks in Sehitkamil. You'll decide among you who will lead these attacks. I'll lead the rest of our men against our primary objective, the prison in Oguzeli. They'll begin when the muezzins call for Salat."

"When Baziyan is freed, where'll he go?" Belen, one of the leaders asked, as he stared at the maps.

"Only Mufti Tanreverdi and I will be aware of his destination."

"What weapons should we use on Friday?" Belen turned to Afran as everyone waited for the reply.

"Everything. The gas canisters hidden in Sanliurfa will be brought here. I also transported ten more from Mardin."

A hush settled over the group as the enormity and severity of their final efforts gripped them.

"We'll meet again in an hour to determine who leads tomorrow's attacks. Dersim, will you join me?"

Once the others departed, Afran guided Dersim by an elbow farther away so no one could overhear.

"Dersim, I want you to return tomorrow to Sanliurfa. Bring the gas canisters and any other weapons here."

"Okay."

When they regrouped, Nasdar brought a small basket containing varying lengths of straw, plucked from a discarded broom.

He held the basket high so no one could view inside. After everyone had taken a straw, comparisons determined the shortest. Those with longer straws tossed them on the floor.

Dildar, Jawero, and Xandan were among the lucky ones. Erdelan Karmran always referred to as Happy because of his positive disposition, and Robin Yado also drew short straws.

Afran met with the five winners to provide their final guidance.

"Pick your men—no more than twenty per team. Each of you proved your worthiness multiple times so I won't give a pep talk. Once you select your men, proceed with your mission. Return by dark tomorrow evening so we can prepare for the final operation."

Over the next three hours, the five teams departed to the raucous cheers of their fellow Kurds. When the last team slipped away, Afran addressed the others.

"We're on the brink of our destiny. In two days, we'll raid the prison holding Baziyan. Allah willing, we'll achieve our objective."

The warehouse erupted with cheers and shouts of their leader's name. Men climbed onto tables and chairs, waving their weapons and Kurdish flags in the air in time with the chants. Serbest and Warzan approached Afran while the others celebrated.

"Afran, we want the honor against the Fifth Armored Brigade compounds," Serbest motioned toward Warzan. "We understand what's at stake. Men will fall to ensure you and the others succeed."

The three men embraced. Afran nodded his agreement with their offer, unable to speak.

***

Ismet waited until the last possible moment to enter Turkey from Tell Abayd, Syria, before the crossing closed for the evening. He hurried through the quiet streets of Akçakale, keeping to the shadows.

He turned left on Mimar Sinan Street, crossed over, and headed toward the indoor sports arena. Two police cars commanded a noticeable presence in front of the apartment safe house. He paused behind a tree, leaning to the side to check for activity.

Two men paced by the police cars, smoking and laughing. The front door of the building opened and two more men strode down the steps, joining the others.

The apartment is out.

Ismet continued to the end of the street, turned right and stopped beneath a street light. Pulling out the notes he made when he spoke with Dersim via cell phone, he determined the garage Serbest had rented should be around the next corner.

He identified the correct garage among a row of them. Ismet tried to open the front door—locked. He scurried around the back, counting, to ensure he selected the correct garage. The rear wall contained a small door, half glass, half wood, and a separate window. The doorknob wouldn't turn when he tried, so Ismet found a rock and broke the glass. Careful not to cut himself, he reached inside and opened the door.

As advised, a red car took up most of the area within the small confines. Ismet checked under the driver's seat and located the keys. The engine cranked over first time. The gas gauge indicated full, so he opened the garage door and backed out.

After closing and securing the front, Ismet returned to the car and drove out of Akçakale, heading for his next destination.

***

Dersim found his truck among those hidden around the warehouses. With a sense of normality being back in his own vehicle, Dersim started the engine, weaved his way out of the industrial site, and headed toward Sanliurfa. Dry, dusty fields, waiting for the spring rains, encroached upon the roads' edges.

Ahead, red and blue flashing lights indicated something amiss. Dersim slowed and pulled onto the shoulder as a military convoy sped toward him. A Kobra reconnaissance vehicle led the procession followed by six large transporters, each struggling under the weight of a Leopard-1 battle tank. Another Kobra served as the convoy's caboose.

After they passed, Dersim resumed his journey. Arriving at the cave, he spotted a red Tofas Sahin sedan tucked into the trees. He parked and walked toward the cave's entrance, glancing around for any potential trouble. To the side of the opening, Dersim stopped.

"Allo." He listened for a response.

"Dersim?" A familiar voice echoed within the cave. Someone shuffled toward the entrance.

"Ow. Stupid rock." Ismet stuck his head out the opening and glanced around while rubbing his right ankle.

"Ismet, I'm glad you found the cave." Dersim grabbed him in a bear hug, happy to be reunited with his friend. "Did things go well in Syria?"

"Not as I thought things would be. They offered to help us but used me for their personal goals. Until Assad is gone, they aren't ready to work with us."

"The attempt to free Baziyan will be soon." Dersim pointed inside the cave. "I must bring the remaining weapons to Nizip. You can help load and follow me back."

When they finished loading the truck, Ismet boiled water over a sterno can for tea. During their break, Dersim pondered how to explain about the canisters he hid.

"Ismet, help me load the weapons and supplies. Remember those gas canisters we found? Six are nearby. I moved them—I'm having second thoughts about anyone using them."

Ismet nodded. "Life seemed easier when we only scavenged."

"Let's grab the canisters." Dersim led the way along the dim path to the four intertwined evergreen trees. He pushed aside several branches so he might reach inside. Nothing. He crawled through the narrow opening until he banged his head against something solid. The canisters. He dragged them out one-by-one, pushing them into the opening for Ismet to retrieve.

Dersim backed out of the hiding place, pulling the last canister.

When he turned around, a familiar man stood next to Ismet, holding an AK-47, pointed in Dersim's direction. They stared at one another and grinned. The man handed his weapon to Ismet and rushed forward.

"Dersim. Good to see you."

"Babir! What're you doing here? Who's minding the stores, Gewran?"

"My mind's been in turmoil ever since our meeting with Mullah Mala. I couldn't let him lead you astray. We might provide the PKK with guns and ammunition. Those canisters though—nothing but pure evil."

Dersim and Ismet both nodded and stared at their feet, like children being scolded for doing something wrong.

"Dersim, you're like a son to me. I followed my heart."

"What did you do?"

"I met a man, a former member of the Australian Special Air Service Regiment. His team came to northern Iraq in 1991 to provide aid to Kurds who lost their homes during the Gulf War. They came to my store to purchase blankets, tents, and water containers. We became friends."

Dersim and Ismet listened in silence, wide-eyed with mouths dropping to their chins.

"I called him for help. A few days later, someone from the Australian Embassy came to visit me. I explained about the canisters. He arranged for me to travel to Turkey to monitor the activities of a Kurd named Serbest Pawan Rohat, an aide to one of Baziyan's closest friends, Mufti Mehmed Salih Tanreverdi.

"I followed Serbest here when he brought a load of supplies and discovered the cylinders. I passed this information to the Australians, and they wanted me to remain here and report."

"What do we do now?" Dersim pursed his lips and stroked his chin, deep in thought. "Afran wants me to bring the canisters to Nizip tonight. Ismet will return with me."

"Do as Afran requested."

While Dersim and Ismet loaded the truck, Babir grabbed his gear and wandered further into the bushes. He placed a call to his Australian contact and explained the situation.

"I'll pass your information up the chain. Expect a call back in the next twelve hours with instructions. Follow normal contact procedures."

"I'll be waiting." Babir disconnected the call and shut the phone down. He'd check in four hours for any messages.

Babir helped the others with the last few items and waved them off.

"Can we give you a lift?" Dersim asked.

"No, no. I'm okay. I'll go into Sanliurfa and will be in Nizip tomorrow."

After Dersim gunned the engine, they headed away from the cave and turned onto a road leading east.

When they were out of sight, Babir grabbed his gear and walked behind the cave. Secreted in a small grotto stood his transportation—a Turkish Kuba 100cc motorcycle. He stuffed his belongings in the saddlebags and departed for Sanliurfa.

***

Throughout the day, remnants of the five teams returned to the warehouse. Weary, dirty, but wearing big grins, four returned unscathed.

The fifth group was another matter. Of the twenty courageous men who set out on their mission, eight came back, all bearing various injuries.

Afran met the leader, gave him an embrace, and led him to a small table and chairs in the corner, which he used as his office.

"What happened, Robin?"

"Th-they were waiting for us. I split the team into two groups, one to attack from each side of Yavuzeli." Robin gulped for air, tears dripping from his eyes as he relived the action.

"We coordinated our movements by radio. As we entered the town, all I remember is a flash and a loud boom. The next thing, the car next to me no longer existed. Four men snuffed out in an instant."

Afran nodded, but kept silent, allowing Robin to share his story without interruption.

"They used tanks—American ones. I don't remember the type but not the Leopard. With only grenades and AK-47s we couldn't fight back. Twelve men died, and everyone else is wounded."

Robin's head collapsed onto his arms, his body racking with sobs.

"I'm sure you did your best. The fault is mine for not allowing you to take any RPGs. Tend to your team and their injuries. Eat and rest. You'll join our planning in the morning for the final operation."

Robin nodded, staggered out of the chair, searching for the remainder of his team.

***

Dersim and Ismet arrived at the warehouse as the sun dipped behind the horizon. Hungry and tired, Dersim solicited volunteers to help unload. Finding a couple of men willing to assist, they returned outside.

When they finished unloading, Dersim searched for Afran, Ismet in tow.

"Afran, this is my long-time friend, Ismet. Mullah Ahmed sent him to Syria. His mission is finished and now he joins us."

"Welcome, Ismet. We're in the final stages. I want you to help Dersim tomorrow placing the canisters around Gaziantep. With what you brought today, we've sixteen."

Dersim and Ismet exchanged glances and nodded.

"We'll go over the locations in the morning."

***

Babir powered up his phone for the third time. A text appeared.

Someone named Haggis will contact you tomorrow. He can be trusted. Follow his instructions.

Chapter 47
Sanliurfa, Turkey
Tuesday, March 22

After the Turkish tank demolished the car on Monday evening not far from their hotel, CC recommended they go back inside.

"I imagine the street will fill with troops and security personnel. We don't want to be caught up in any round-up."

The four men trudged back inside and returned to their table. A waiter brought them fresh coffee and baklava.

"On the hotel. From management." The waiter beamed as he served the sweet dessert as if a car being turned into a pile of twisted rubble occurred every day.

Most of the other tables remained empty after the excitement. Once they finished, Jake suggested they go to the rear courtyard.

"Okay guys, we must still sweep the area for the sarin despite what happened tonight." CC motioned from the courtyard toward the traffic circle where the incident took place. "This might make our jobs harder. Recommend we work in pairs rather than alone, one driving and the other monitoring the detectors."

The others nodded and maintained silence.

"Make sure you take your passports and cameras. Don't forget to act like tourists. Any other questions?"

New sirens screeched across the city, along with the cracks and pops of gunshots. Shrill whistles added to the din.

"We'll meet at Willie and Aiden's hotel for breakfast at 0730. I'm turning in for the night but will send an update to BHQ."

Willie and Aiden returned to their hotel while Jake and CC trotted upstairs. CC powered up his laptop and flipped on the TV while he waited. An enterprising camera crew captured the moment the tank fired on the car. Knowing the Turkish penchant for showing gory and explicit details, he switched the TV off.

To: Alpha

From: Haggis

Aussie and I met with Mountie and Rebel. Will commence coordinated canister search in the morning.

Efforts might be hampered by increased military presence in the city. Turks appear to be trigger-happy so we'll work in pairs, posing as tourists. Will advise.

On Tuesday morning, CC and Jake left their hotel, hopped in CC's vehicle, and drove the short distance to join Aiden and Willie for breakfast.

After helping themselves to the buffet, the four men grabbed a table on the terrace. The air temperature remained chilly, as the morning sunshine hadn't risen far enough to reach over higher buildings. They controlled the veranda, at least for a short time.

"Jake and I will work our way around the west side of the city. We'll also check two miles north and south. Suggest you do the same on the east."

"Sounds like a plan." Willie glanced around the table before continuing. "Should we keep in regular contact?"

"Aye. Recommend the two non-drivers send text messages to each other. Call in an emergency."

The two teams departed for their respective areas. They followed the main thoroughfares through the city on the first pass. The return trips shifted to side streets, as they speculated anything hidden would be in a quieter area. Nothing. Nada. Zilch.

"This is worse than a stake-out." Aiden yawned as he whipped the wheel to avoid a collision with a *dolmus* making a sudden stop for a passenger. "Shit. Where did they learn to drive, eh?"

"At least, they don't speed, just weave around and stop whenever and wherever they want." Willie laughed as Aiden gripped the wheel tighter as two motorcycles cut in front of them. "Relax, enjoy yourself. As long as we don't crash, today will be a good day."

Throughout the morning, both teams crisscrossed the city. Still nothing. As CC came toward a traffic light, a man jumped in front of the car.

CC blew the horn and stomped on the brakes. The vehicle lurched to a stop, tires squealing. Jake and CC jumped out as a policeman ran to the front of the car. Before they approached, the officer bent down, grabbed the man by his collar, yanked him up, and threw him face down on the hood.

He pulled out his cuffs and secured the man, who sported shoulder-length black hair, glazed eyes, with a sickly grin, showing several missing teeth.

The policeman shoved him at another officer who appeared and stepped over to CC.

"I'm sorry, sir. This imbecile loves to jump in front of cars and scare the drivers. One day he'll make a mistake and meet Allah."

CC shook his head, a relieved expression on his face. "I thought for certain I hit him."

"Don't worry, sir. Please, return to your car and continue your journey."

CC and Jake nodded, climbed back in, and waited as the officer held up his hand while traffic cleared. As soon as an opening appeared, the policeman motioned them forward and gave a half-salute as they passed.

"What a nutter," Jake said. "If he makes a mistake, he's a bloodstain."

"Aye." CC nodded, breathing a sigh of relief.

They continued along Sanliurfa's streets and into the countryside without any success.

***

Willie finished his fifth text to Jake, all containing the same message: *Nothing.*

Both men became bored with the monotony of driving around without having any positive results. They even switched drivers to break up the tedious transits.

"Hey, check the group out. Perhaps they'll allow me to take their photograph." Willie pointed at the villagers climbing out of the back of a dump truck near a beige-colored building. A Turkish flag flew on a nearby pole.

Aiden stopped the car. Willie hopped out, and ran to the group while waving his camera. He didn't speak Turkish, and they didn't speak much English, but he pantomimed taking their picture.

The crowd of about twenty, all from the same family based on resemblance, pushed and prodded one another to form a semi-circle, with the taller members in the rear and the smallest children in the front.

Willie stood before them and took several photos of the smiling horde. He shifted position to take the last picture when a booming voice caught his attention.

"You. What're you doing?" A burly policeman, wearing a holstered pistol on a white web belt and carrying an ancient rifle stormed up to him. "No photos of the building."

"I'm not taking … Let me show you." Willie clicked back to the first photograph and stepped through them so the officer could verify for himself.

"No building. Only the family."

"Family okay, building—no. Security." One of the older family members spoke to the policemen in Turkish, and he responded.

"They asked for copies of their photographs. They think you might take their souls away with you but if they receive a copy everything will be okay." The officer smiled at the villagers' simple logic.

"Tell them yes." Willie nodded. "I'll provide enough copies, so everyone receives one."

During Willie's conversation with the officer, the family climbed back in the truck and drove away.

"Wait, where should I send the photos?" Willie shook his head.

The policeman laughed. "Once the pictures are ready, send them here. I'll give you the address. The family comes every week."

Frustration levels continued to rise. Approaching a familiar-looking traffic circle but from a different direction, they noted a barricade being erected. Aiden slowed the car as both readied their passports for inspection.

"Stop. You came before. Why back?" The soldier challenged them in broken English.

"We're lost. Where's our hotel?" Willie handed over a brochure from their hotel.

"Ah. That way. Go." The soldier gestured to a side street leading away from the circle.

Aiden nodded and pulled away, going down the street the soldier suggested.

"Is this the right way?" Willie stared at the map on the back of the brochure and shook his head.

"No, but I didn't want to argue. Easier to do as he said. Let's find the hotel, eh?"

"Good suggestion. I'll pass the word to Jake."

An hour later CC and Jake caught up with Aiden and Willie at their hotel. Sitting on the veranda, they enjoyed the last rays of the sun before they disappeared for the evening.

"What a bust. My backside's sore and nothing to show for the effort." Jake pulled a face. "My detector went crazy at one point. I checked for the substance which triggered the alarm, but nothing registered."

CC laughed. "Aye. I glanced out the window and realized the problem. We drove past a chemical company."

"Now what?" Aiden sat back in the chair, stretched, and crossed his arms.

"We finished our searches in the city. Tomorrow morning, I suggest we expand further out. If we aren't successful, I believe we should split, one team going to Gaziantep and the other to Mardin."

Everyone nodded, somber expressions etched upon their unsmiling faces.

***

After CC rose the following morning, he checked for incoming messages. After reading the single new entry, he smiled.

"Aye. Some progress. Good."

The four men ate breakfast at their respective hotels and met in a park across the street from where the tank maintained its position in the once pristine flowerbed.

"Excellent news. Ben is flying to Adana this morning and will be with us by 1300. We're to wait for him to join us."

"What happened to Ismet? I thought Ben was chasing him, eh?" Aiden pondered this new development, his index finger and thumb rubbing his chin.

"Ismet had second thoughts about the direction he took. He's on his way to join Dersim. All we must do is find them."

***

Ben arrived at Aleppo's airport at 0600. When he entered the terminal, a thin, bald man with bushy eyebrows waved a sign with Ben's name. The man motioned for Ben to follow and they left the terminal via a side door.

"Hello, name's Vince. I'll be your pilot, steward, and tour guide to take you from your comfortable Aleppo surroundings to Adana."

"Kia Ora. What type of plane are we using?"

"A Cessna 421, Golden Eagle. Should arrive in Adana about forty minutes after takeoff."

Less than an hour later, Ben waved farewell to Vince and headed into a customs building used by those entering the country via private aircraft. A cursory check of his passport and a quick entry stamp saw him on his way. After collecting the rental car, he headed to Incirlik Air Force Base.

By 0830, Ben departed from the base. Before leaving, he placed four Pelican Storm cases in the trunk, each holding four fake canisters. Although instructed to collect three cases, a fourth one fit.

When Ben reached the Adana-Sanliurfa Highway, he headed east. With dual lanes, the smooth road differed in sharp contrast to those in Syria. Fertile fields abounded, green shoots reaching for the sun. Mile after mile, Ben sped along, encountering sparse traffic.

Four hours later, he entered Sanliurfa and followed the directions to CC's hotel. They met in the parking lot, and CC helped Ben with check-in before escorting him to the terrace where the others waited.

"Welcome, stranger." Willie grabbed Ben and pushed him into his seat. "Glad you're with us."

"Aye. Good to be together but the mission awaits. I want to explore the areas further out in the south first. Suggest we do this together as two teams. Ben, you'll ride with Jake and me."

Three hours later, the teams returned to the hotel, dejected. Once again, their efforts didn't turn up the canisters. They sat down for a coffee when CC received a text message: *Check email—urgent.*

CC hurried upstairs, grabbed his laptop, and returned to the others. As soon as the system booted, he logged in to find one email.

To: Haggis
From: Alpha-One
URGENT
Contact number 090-881-192837465. Contact name is Babir. Will provide information related to your mission. Use callsign as introduction. He's expecting contact. Call ASAP. Acknowledge.

CC sent a one-word response: *Acknowledged.*

He spun the laptop around for the others to read the missive.

"Hey, mate. I met a Babir in Zakho." Jake closed his eyes, his index fingers waving in the air, as he appeared to be sorting something out. "Got it. Babir is Dersim's cousin."

Everyone grew excited at Jake's news. CC raised a hand for silence. The number rang and moments later, a male answered.

"Allo?"

"Am I speaking with Babir? This is Haggis."

"Oh. Yes. I didn't expect a call so soon."

"Where are you now?"

"I'm at the Asian Guest House in Sanliurfa. The address is 12 Eylul Caddesi. I'm in room four."

"Okay, I'll arrive in about an hour. I'll bring a friend you met before. His name is Jake."

"I met a man by the same name two weeks ago. A journalist who spoke funny."

"Aye. He speaks with an Australian accent."

When CC ended the call, the others laughed, poking fun at Jake's funny speech.

At the appointed time, CC knocked on the appropriate door. They detected a click, and the door opened.

Jake needed a single glance to confirm identity. He turned to CC and nodded.

"Babir? I'm Haggis. This is Jake."

"Yes. Please come in. May I offer you tea, water, juice?"

"Nae, thank you. My office instructed me to meet with you because you've important information for us."

"Yes. I met with Dersim and Ismet yesterday. They loaded weapons and six gas cylinders into Dersim's truck and went to Nizip.

"I told them they were wrong to use the gas. They of all people should understand. Mullah Mala led them astray."

Babir stopped speaking, grabbed a piece of paper from the desk and handed the slip to CC.

"This is his cell phone number. He's expecting your call in the morning. Wait until after 0900. They're to place sixteen gas canisters around Gaziantep tomorrow. You must stop them before it's too late.

"The operation to release Baziyan takes place on Friday afternoon."

Chapter 48
Sanliurfa, Turkey
Thursday, March 24

CC returned to Babir's hotel on Thursday morning. They agreed the previous night he should be on hand in the event Dersim wanted verification.

The second hand passed twelve, and the time read 0915. CC dialed the number Babir provided.

"Allo?"

"Allo. This is Haggis speaking."

Silence.

"Allo, Dersim?"

"Yes, I'm here. Is Babir with you?"

"Aye. One moment."

CC handed the phone to Babir.

"Dersim, this is the man who will help you. Listen to him and do as he says. Your life might depend upon your decision."

"Give him the phone."

Babir nodded at CC as he returned the handset.

"Dersim, I understand you require assistance. Where and when may we meet?"

Another pause before Dersim replied. "On the Gaziantep-Sanliurfa Road, follow the road signs to a nearby village. Gunbulur. Between the road and the town is a truck stop. Meet me in the parking lot as soon as possible. My time is short."

"Aye. Two others will be with me. They both speak Arabic. Will Ismet be with you?"

"Okay. Bring Babir to vouch for you."

Click. The dial tone returned.

Ten minutes later, CC, Jake, Ben, and Babir piled into Ben's car. Prior to meeting with Babir, the team thought it best to use Ben's vehicle because the fake canisters remained in the trunk.

Minimal conversation occurred during the drive. Immersed in their own thoughts, each man contemplated about their current situation.

Babir pointed out the window as they approached the rest stop. "Dersim is here. His truck is behind the trees near the building."

CC parked near Dersim's vehicle. Once they climbed out, two men sauntered around the side of the nearby red-brick facility.

"Dersim, Ismet," Babir called their names as he rushed forward. "Come, these men will fix your problems."

Babir introduced them to the others. They all shook hands and stepped back.

CC stared at Dersim for a moment, gathering his thoughts. "Babir tells me you realize using the sarin gas is a mistake."

Both Dersim and Ismet nodded.

"We will help you. In return, you must help us."

"We still believe in the Kurdish cause." Ismet nodded at Dersim's declaration.

"We won't try to change your beliefs. We're after the canisters before mass genocide occurs again."

"Afran instructed us to place the containers in several locations around Gaziantep. We must obey, or he'll kill us."

"Aye. I understand. We developed a plan to allow you to keep your word and help us, too."

Babir, Dersim, and Ismet glanced at one another, puzzled expressions evident on their faces. They refocused on CC, waiting for an explanation.

"Before I explain, what're you planning to do after Baziyan is freed?"

Ismet glanced at his feet, deep in thought.

"I prefer to remain with Baziyan. My personal family is gone so I want to help the Kurdish people." Ismet raised his eyes. "If I might be of assistance to him, that is my desire."

CC nodded, accepting Ismet's ideals. He turned to Dersim. "What about you? What will you do?"

"What I must do. My wife and two children are in Halabja. I want Kurdish unity, but I also must provide for my family. After Baziyan is freed, I'll return to them."

"Help us recover the canisters, and I'm prepared to take you and your family to America. Ismet and Babir, the offer is also for you."

"Thank you, no. When we're finished, I'll return to Zakho and my stores." Babir nodded his thanks and pointed to Dersim. "Protect my cousin and his family—if he accepts your offer."

"One day I might like to visit America." Ismet rubbed his face. "Perhaps a doctor might do something with my ugly scars."

"I'm sure a good surgeon would help you, Ismet. Dersim, what're your thoughts?"

"Will you make sure my family is safe if I help you—take them to America even if something happens to me?"

"Aye. The future is settled. There are forty canisters. We found four in Cappadocia. Where are the rest?"

Dersim glanced at the others. He didn't realize the Cappadocia cylinders were missing.

"We've sixteen with us. Ten remain in an old barn outside Mardin." Dersim said. "Another ten are hidden."

Everyone stared at Dersim when he dropped his bombshell.

"Aye. Let's begin with the ones here. Ben, would you swing the car around, so the trunk is near the back of Dersim's truck?"

After complying with CC's request, Ben popped the release. He reached inside and removed one of the transit cases. Propping the container on the edge of the trunk, he snapped the clasps and opened the lid.

Nestled inside, sat four gas cylinders. The Kurds stared at them, shaking their heads.

"How … where did these come from?" Dersim shook his head, closed and opened his eyes, not believing what he witnessed.

"My office made them. Grab one of yours so we can compare. They should be identical."

Dersim hopped into the truck and uncovered the canisters. He pulled one out of a box and presented the cylinder for the others to examine. They scrutinized both canisters—identical except for serial numbers.

The Kurds stared in awe while CC, Jake, and Ben smiled.

"Let's swap."

The Kurds climbed into the truck while the team members opened the remaining cases. A few minutes later, they finished.

"Jake, would you do the honors?" CC pointed at Jake's shoulder, over which a disguised detector hung on a strap.

"You bet, mate."

Jake ran the detector over the canisters now positioned within the Pelican cases. Sarin registered for each one. He climbed in the truck and repeated the examination. The meter remained unresponsive.

The Kurds appeared to be puzzled. Dersim spoke first.

"How? What will happen if they're used?"

"Your new canisters are filled with treated water which will form a mist when the cylinder is opened. The same as the gas-filled ones. The difference is no one will become sick or die."

"What should we do now?"

"Place the canisters where Afran directed you. Return to Nizip and join the others. During the operation tomorrow, leave and work your way back here. One of us will wait to take you away."

"I must speak with you before we leave," Dersim requested. "Alone."

CC and Dersim walked away from the others.

"Mr. Haggis, if I go to America, will you help me find a job? I don't want handouts. I'm a scavenger and always will be. Perhaps I might work in America's recycling business."

CC chuckled and patted Dersim's shoulder. "A job will be easy to arrange. Anything else?"

"Yes, I'll help you obtain the canisters from the barn in Mardin. Also, I hid the others and will show you where. One last thing. Fourteen cylinders remain in my house in Halabja. Ten are the same as the ones here. Four are different."

CC stood rooted to the spot, stunned to learn about the additional cylinders.

"Aye. We want your help. Go now and deliver your canisters. We'll meet here tomorrow."

Dersim and Ismet embraced Babir and jumped in the truck. After they had driven away, he wiped away tears dripping down his face.

"I'm proud of them. They made the correct decision. Will you take me back to my hotel? I'll collect my things, and I'm going to Gaziantep. Contact me at the same number if you require my assistance."

The four men climbed into the car and drove toward Sanliurfa. After dropping Babir off, they returned to their hotel. Jake and Ben checked out while CC maintained an eye on Ben's vehicle.

The two men came out to the parking lot, carrying their backpacks, which they dumped in their respective cars.

"After you secure the canisters, grab another six Pelican cases to be on the safe side. If you're up for a return trip tonight, please advise and I'll send a text with the hotel information in Gaziantep. We'll stay as a tourist group in the same place."

Jake and Ben departed, and CC headed back to his room. First, he sent a text to Aiden advising them to check out of their hotel and be ready to leave in an hour. He opened his laptop and composed a message to BHQ.

To: Alpha

From: Haggis

Successful meeting with Kurds. Acquired sixteen sarin canisters in exchange for ours. Contents verified and are en route to Incirlik in two-vehicle convoy, Aussie and Kiwi.

Remainder of team will proceed to Gaziantep and commence search operations in case we've been misled.

Dersim advised knowledge of location of additional twenty canisters. Put forward relocation proposal. Dersim interested as long as his family is included. Babir and Ismet declined.

CC shut off his laptop, grabbed his belongings and went to the lobby to check out. Formalities completed, he hopped in his car to meet up with Aiden and Willie.

***

Once they left the truck stop, Dersim and Ismet headed closer to Gaziantep. The first location for emplacing a canister was near a police barracks on the outskirts of the city.

Afran wanted the canister placed within a garage he'd rented. He sought and identified a volunteer to grab the cylinder from the garage and enter the compound, triggering the gas.

"I'm glad we met the foreigners." Ismet stared out the garage window after setting the canister in position. "The police might be a target, but not this way."

"I agree, Ismet. We're doing what's in our hearts. We must help the cause but still maintain our dignity."

"Yes. I realize I wanted to hurt people, but no one deserves what happened to our village."

"Let's continue placing the canisters as Afran instructed and return to the warehouse."

Two hours later, the last cylinder was in position, all near government facilities. Dersim and Ismet realized volunteers would be required to move and activate all the canisters at the appointed time.

"I wonder how many lives we've saved by working with the foreigners." Dersim shared a glance with Ismet before putting the truck into gear. "Might be thousands."

***

Jake and Ben arrived at Incirlik by 1500. Their documents were in order and within an hour they prepared to rejoin the others. Each trunk contained three Pelican Storm cases. They both hoped the twenty-four canisters would be sufficient.

Prior to departure, Jake sent a text to CC. *En route.*

A couple of minutes later, he received a response. *Acknowledged. Rooms confirmed Dedeman Gaziantep Hotel, northwest of city. Advise ETA.*

After a brief discussion with Ben, Jake replied. *ETA 1900. Meet in lobby.*

***

Aiden and Willie met CC in their hotel's parking lot. In a loose convoy of three vehicles, they headed west toward Gaziantep.

After claiming rooms at a hotel on the outskirts of the city, they activated their detectors and began a rolling search. The team concentrated on areas where their objective might be hidden— industrial sites and warehouses in close proximity to government buildings and installations.

Two hours into their search, Jake stopped his car. Something triggered his detector. He glanced around the area. Nothing but multi-story apartment blocks interspersed with rows of garages. No government buildings.

Willie reversed the car, monitoring the intensity level on the meter. He stopped the vehicle where he thought he received the strongest reading.

"What do we have here?" Across the street from Willie's position stood a row of eight whitewashed garages with up-and-over doors.

"Third garage from the left. Ammonium nitrate. Wonder what kind of business is someone up to? Would make a nasty bomb."

Willie marked the location on his map and continued his search through the neighborhoods.

A mile away, Aiden worked his way through an industrial site. Within a few hundred yards stood a four-story brick building with the words *Emniyet Genel Müdürlüğü* emblazoned on the front.

"General Security Directorate. The building would make a super diversionary target, eh?"

Aiden continued a slow crawl up and down the rows of warehouses. Some of the buildings appeared on the verge of collapse while others resembled model showrooms.

As he reached the end of a row and turned for another pass, his detector emitted a low-intensity alarm. Aiden completed the turn, and while he continued along a row of dilapidated buildings, with most windows boarded over, the intensity shot to maximum.

"Hmmm." Aiden confirmed the readings and checked what chemical triggered the reaction.

"Two chemicals. Hydrogen cyanide and phosgene. Both can kill, eh? But it'd take an enormous amount to cause mass casualties."

Aiden also made note on his map of this location and resumed his journey, working his way through the narrow streets.

Of the three operatives, CC traveled the farthest away from their hotel. His detector remained silent for most of his journey through residential areas, near a row of light-colored stone buildings housing the provincial governor, police, and other administrative organizations.

"Nae a thing. So frustrating."

CC continued along the route drawn on his map. Up and down streets with nothing registering. He turned right onto a narrow, cobblestoned street lined with pastel-colored apartment blocks, each trying to outdo the others. When he approached the last building, his detector activated. After determining the approximate location of what triggered the meter, CC realized he sat in front of a light-blue colored building next to the last one on the block. He checked for the chemical, which initiated the alarm. There were two.

"Aye. About time. Not what we're after but still interesting."

Glancing back at the display, he reread the results: TNT and Semtex. Both useful for explosions but wouldn't provide the same mass casualty results as sarin.

The three men continued their travels through the city with no additional triggers. As dusk settled, they returned to their hotel.

***

The five travelers regrouped in time for dinner. After consuming a satisfying meal, they headed into the hotel's gardens, away from other guests so they could converse without interference.

Aware the Kurds planned their operation for the next day, they pondered their moves.

"No luck today finding any gas canisters. Perhaps Dersim and Ismet are being honest with us. The chemicals we identified will be left in position." CC glanced around the group but no one objected to his directive.

"We must continue searching tomorrow in the city. But, I'm concerned we might become accidental targets."

"If Dersim provided accurate information, we can avoid where the Fifth Armored Brigade compounds and the prison are located." Aiden scratched his head while speaking. "We can't be everywhere."

"Aye, that's true enough. Two of us must also be at the truck stop to rendezvous with Dersim when he arrives."

"When or if?" Willie's forehead scrunched as his eyebrows lifted.

"Aye."

The dark sky turned as bright as daylight.

Boom! Boom! Boom!

Explosions rippled across the city. Even though the hotel sat eight miles from the center, the team felt the eruptions. Interspersed between the eruptions of smoke, flames, and debris, the *rat-at-tat-tat* of machine guns, *cracks* of rifles and *pops* of pistols mixed with whistles and sirens.

Miniature explosions similar to cars backfiring added their unique rhythms to the symphony. Whole sections of the city plunged into sudden darkness as if someone flipped a light switch. Minor tremors reached their hotel, rattling glasses, and shaking chandeliers fixed along the covered veranda.

Gaziantep was under siege.

Chapter 49
Gaziantep, Turkey
Thursday, March 24

Afran shared a light breakfast with Dersim and Ismet. After their meal, he led the men to his makeshift office. A map of Gaziantep covered the table, with numerous red circles and three black squares.

"Study the map. These ten locations are where I want the canisters placed. One container at each spot." Afran tapped on the black squares. "These three, Security Directorate Headquarters, and the two Fifth Armored Brigade compounds, receive two apiece."

Dersim and Ismet both nodded at Afran's instructions but remained silent.

Afran handed Dersim a single sheet of paper. "The map remains with me. Here is a list of specific addresses where the cylinders must be placed. Each is a garage or an apartment we rented last week. Here are the keys." He tossed a heavy key ring toward Ismet.

"Use your truck for the job, Dersim, but change to Gaziantep provincial license plates. Less chance of being stopped. Once you finish, return here. Any questions?"

Dersim and Ismet glanced at each other and shook their heads.

"Okay. Good luck and may Allah watch over you."

Ismet grabbed a bag of food and water to take with them while Dersim scrounged around in the supply area for the license plates. Satisfied with the installation, they climbed into the cab and departed.

Twenty minutes later, Dersim's cell phone rang. He glanced at the number—unknown. He tapped the green button to establish contact.

"Allo?"

***

Throughout the remainder of the morning, Afran huddled with Nasdar, Serbest, Warzan, and the five team leaders from Wednesday's skirmishes. They referred to another map of the city, marked with two red circles, representing the military compounds, and a black circle for the prison.

"I mentioned before, that tomorrow's operation will be a three-pronged approach. Serbest, you and fifty men will hit the Fifth Armored Brigade compound in the Sahinbey district. Warzan, you'll take another fifty and attack their compound in the Sehitkamil district."

"What weapons shall we use? Any restrictions?" Serbest rubbed his injured arm, the result of action in Akçakale.

"No restrictions. You both must keep the units confined to their compounds. Should things become desperate, two gas canisters will be in each area for your use. Dersim and Ismet are placing them into position today. I'll give you the location information later."

"Afran, I thought Mufti Tanreverdi didn't want to use the gas?" Serbest glanced at the others before staring back at their leader.

"That's true. However, he's not the decision maker. I am."

Serbest rolled his eyes, shook his head, but kept his mouth shut. Others gave slight shakes of their heads but didn't want to rile Afran.

Slamming a fist on the table, Afran jumped to his feet, his chair crashing to the floor. He ran his hands through his hair and took a deep breath.

"The pressure—sometimes it's too much. This might be our only chance to free Baziyan. I overheard the prison reconstruction on Imrali Island is almost complete. The Turks will send him back as soon as they can. We must be successful. Now!"

Afran sat and glanced around the table at the team leaders.

"Serbest, if you or Warzan require any special explosive devices, talk with Nasdar."

He pulled a hand-drawn diagram from under the table and spread the document across the map.

"This is the prison where Baziyan is being held until his return to the island. The building holds three hundred sixty-eight prisoners. There are two floors with one hundred sixty-two cells."

"Where's Baziyan's cell?" Dildar pointed at the drawing's second floor, covered with small squares.

"The larger squares represent cells holding three people. Baziyan's kept in one of the one-man cells. We're unaware of the correct one—there are fifty-nine possibilities."

"How many entrances into the prison?" Happy stared at the diagram and pointed to a separate square adjacent to the building. "What's this represent?"

"The chain-link fence around the perimeter is ten feet high, with concertina wire spread along the top. There's one pedestrian entrance and one for vehicles. Once inside the compound, there are four guarded entrance points into the building, one on each side. The square is an enclosed exercise yard."

"What's on the first floor?" Xandan pursed his lips, rubbed his hand over his thinning hair.

"Administrative offices, guard quarters, and eating areas." Afran paused for a sip of water before continuing. "There are also four interrogation rooms and eight isolation chambers."

"How many guards on duty at one time?" Jawero scratched an ear, his mouth twisted into a grimace, one lip extended over the other.

"Fifty. There are six guard towers, each with two men, and four machine gun posts on the roof. The towers are always manned, but the rooftop positions are only filled when trouble is expected."

Afran gave the team leaders a few minutes to consider the information he provided. He stood, and jogged around the warehouse to stretch his legs, stopping at the food table for a handful of black grapes.

Glancing at his leaders, he noted an intense discussion underway, with several pointing at the diagram and referring to the notes. Afran returned to the group and resumed his seat.

"Any questions?"

"Who provided the document?" Robin pointed at the chart to emphasize his questions. "How accurate is the information?"

"Fair questions. Mufti Tanreverdi uses a roundabout means through trusted aides to reach Baziyan. Old-fashioned but more secure than electronic methods. He provided the details based on where he's been in the prison. The information might not be 100 percent correct, but better than going in cold. Any other concerns?"

The men glanced around the table at one another. Serbest shook his head first, followed by Nasdar, and the others.

"Good. If any arise later today, by all means, ask. Okay, here's the plan. Speak up if something isn't clear. Lives will depend upon our success.

"Serbest and Warzan. At the first muezzin call for afternoon prayers, commence your attacks. We'll begin fifteen minutes later. The rest of you'll be with me.

"Once we break through the fence, Nasdar, Happy, and Robin remain by my side, and we'll tackle the front door to the building. Dildar, Jawero, and Xandan, cover the other entrances in a clockwise fashion."

"How many men will attack the prison?" Xandan, the cautious one, shifted to obtain a better view of the diagram.

"Not counting the men who'll be with Serbest and Warzan, about one hundred fifty for the prison attack. We'll break for now and meet again in an hour. Prepare any additional questions."

Once everyone left, Afran pulled the city map to the forefront. He stared at the various markings placed around attack and supply points. Satisfied with the preparations, he sat back in the chair, propped his feet up, so no one became offended by direct view of his soles, and dropped into an uneasy slumber.

When the eight men returned, they kept their voices low so they wouldn't wake Afran. As soon as the last one took his seat, Afran popped up, ready to continue.

"Serbest and Warzan. I want you both to infiltrate your men into the city this afternoon and evening. Don't place everyone near the compounds yet. Use three or four snipers and find suitable shooting locations. Once it's dark, shoot into the compounds.

"It doesn't matter if there aren't specific targets. This is supposed to be harassing fire. We want them to enjoy an uneasy evening."

Everyone grinned at Afran's plan, with those next to Serbest and Warzan slapping the men on the shoulders.

"Dildar, Jawero, and Xandan. I want each of you to take ten men and go into the city. Nasdar will fix up some satchel charges. Use AK-47s, sniper rifles, and grenades.

"Your task is to cause unrest. Shoot at crowded areas, toss grenades into empty locations. Use the satchel charges to blow up a few power transformers and knock out the electricity. Don't kill anyone unless necessary, only shake them up. Commence your activities after darkness falls."

"At last!" Dildar's fist punched the air. "Let's stir things up."

The others laughed at Dildar's infectious attitude, knowing tomorrow would be the turning point.

"Everyone must be in place late tomorrow morning. If nothing further, eat, rest, and gather your men and supplies. Good luck to each of you and may Allah protect you and guide you to success."

Throughout the afternoon, men left in small groups, carrying weapons and other supplies. Trucks, cars, and motorcycles propelled the Kurdish forces toward their destiny.

Darkness descended, and stars popped out in a cloudless sky. The lunar cycle began a new phase, so moonlight wouldn't be a help or hindrance.

Thus began a night of turmoil and sleeplessness.

***

Early the next morning, Afran jumped into the cab of Dersim's truck. Ismet, Nasdar, Happy, and Robin, along with several others, filled the rear with weapons and supplies. With an unintentional grind of gears, Dersim eased off the clutch, and sputtered their way to Gaziantep and their destiny.

After the warehouse was emptied everyone climbed aboard an available vehicle and followed.

The call to prayer echoed across the city:

Allah u Akbar, I bear witness that there is no divinity but Allah. Hasten to the prayer. Allah u Akbar.

Before the last echo died away, loud explosions thundered over Gaziantep. In the Sahinbey district, four of Serbest's men launched an RPG attack against the main gate of the Fifth Armored Brigade's compound. The four grenades streaked toward their targets, leaving smoky contrails in their wake.

Flames and smoke shot into the air, along with the remains of the gate. Through the debris, return fire ensued. A Leopard-2 battle tank, supported by two APCs roared forward. Smoke belched from the behemoth as a projectile spewed forth, reducing one of Serbest's ATVs to a smoldering piece of junk.

Heavy machine guns, AK-47s, and assorted weapons added their chatter to the din. An RPG round skimmed past the edge of the tank and smashed against one of the APCs, diminishing the open space at the gate.

High-pitched screams added their voices to the battlefield. The ground became slick with the blood and viscera of shredded bodies.

Quick bursts of gunfire spread out from the compound seeking retribution against the invaders. The *clank, clank* of treads increased as two more battle tanks approached the gate. One shouldered the burning APC out of the way, its turret seeking revenge for the affront.

Moans and screams raised their cries to the heavens as brave men fell on both sides.

A fierce maelstrom continued from the Kurdish ranks, but they were no match for the ferociousness of the Turkish defenders. Serbest witnessed his fearless men falling so others might gain success elsewhere. Two men rushed forward, each carrying a gas canister.

"Go. Twist the top open and throw the cylinders into the compound."

The men carried out Serbest's command. The canisters sailed into the compound as concentrated Turkish gunfire cut the men down. A fine mist spewed into the air. Men from both sides of the conflict ran through the spray, unaware of what might have been.

Twenty minutes into the fight and a handful of Kurds remained on their feet. Tears streaming down his face, Serbest blew a whistle—the signal to retreat. They gave their best, but would their sacrifice be enough?

***

Warzan's men commenced their assault on the Sehitkamil compound at almost the same moment as Serbest's team. Two gates controlled access to the facility. He split his men into two groups for a coordinated attack.

Eight men fired RPGs at the same time, four at each gate. As with the attack in Sahinbey, heavy wooden planks reinforced the main gate. While the smoke cleared away from the shattered entrance, two Leopard-1 tanks erupted, their rounds seeking to punish the perpetrators.

One missile missed an ATV by scant inches. Luck disappeared for the truck Warzan used as his commander's platform. A second round whistled toward the vehicle, transforming Warzan, his driver, and several others into a thick bloody paste as the tank round immolated everything in its path.

The team hitting the rear fared better. After they had destroyed the gates, two of their ATVs inched forward. AK-47s chattered away as the vehicles climbed over the remnants of the wooden barrier and entered the compound.

The dead and the dying created a dangerous pathway for the vehicles. Without warning, through a pall of black smoke, a turret appeared.

A round sizzled forth from the M60 Patton tank, obliterating one of the ATVs, killing everyone inside. The other ATV turned tail, shooting out of the compound and down the road.

***

Forewarned of the pending Kurdish operation, CC and the rest of the team stayed away from the possible attack positions, returning to their hotel minutes before prayer call.

The rest of the team sat around a table on the hotel's terrace, waiting for CC's return. While he parked the car and joined the others, two plumes of smoke wafted upwards. Even to those located outside the city, it became evident the Kurdish operation was afoot.

"Who's coming with me to wait for Dersim?" CC pointed at Jake. "Mind a ride? Your Arabic might come in handy, although Dersim's pidgin English is understandable."

"You bet, mate. Let's finish our coffee and be on the way. Hope you figured out how to bypass Gaziantep. Don't think we want to return through the city. Might be a few trigger-happy Turks."

"Aye. Our route is sorted. Will take longer but safer."

They climbed into CC's car and headed east along back roads. The drive to Gunbulur would take about an hour, assuming no roadblocks.

***

Afran waited, impatient for the final phase. The call to prayer resounded over the area. As the last words faded, explosions erupted in the distance.

He glanced at his wristwatch, a gift from Mufti Tanreverdi. The countdown commenced. Nerves grabbed him and he shook with excitement and some trepidation.

Time. Afran took a deep breath, and exhaled into a whistle, launching the attack.

Men piled out of hidden trucks, ATVs, cars, and jumped from motorcycles. A pre-positioned team carrying sniper rifles and RPGs, working as a cohesive unit, annihilated the guards protecting the entrance, with RPG rounds smashing the gates backward, paving the way for the Kurdish advance.

Men on both sides bellowed their war cries, crushing each other. The Kurdish freedom fighters held the upper hand—armed with heavier weapons and outnumbering the overall guard force by three to one.

Despite bodies falling by the wayside, the Kurds advanced through the gate. Three groups of twenty-five men each headed to the left. Four men ran forward to the building's main doors. Two carried satchel charges while the other two tagged along to carry on the mission should the satchel bearers falter.

The outer doors parted, blown to bits. A hail of bullets reached out to the attackers, with defenders shooting through gun ports behind an inner wall-to-wall bullet resistant barrier.

Men fell, never to move again. Thick smoke filled the inside of the building, making it difficult for both sides to find targets.

A gut-wrenching shriek pierced the air. Nasdar ran forward, a special package in his hands. As bullets ripped into his body, he used the last of his strength to toss the device at the door.

An horrendous concussion wave pelted attackers and defenders alike. Although dead, Nasdar's life didn't end in vain. The door through the inner barricade hung open, one hinge obliterated, leaving the defenders exposed.

Sensing an opportunity, Afran gave a single word shout to rally his men.

"Baziyan!"

The shout generated the desired effect. Over 100 men followed Afran into the building, taking out guards who didn't surrender. But their effort was only beginning. They must still find their prize.

Dildar, Jawero, and Xandan scurried around the left corner of the building, followed by their teams. They came under fire from a guard tower and the rooftop.

A single RPG reduced the guard tower to rubble but the angle to respond to the withering fire from the machine gun nest made it impossible to overcome. Two courageous individuals approached Dildar.

"Order everyone to shoot toward the rooftop. We'll run out farther and fire RPGs at them."

With AK-47s raised toward the rooftop, one of the men nodded. As one, the men let loose a barrage. The two men raced into the courtyard. Several rounds ripped through the back of one man before he turned to fire. The other launched his grenade, smashing the machine gun and killing the guards.

Momentum in their favor, the three teams continued toward their designated positions. Satchel charges made short work of the outer doors and cruel efficiency met those who resisted. If a guard laid down his weapon, he lived, bound and thrust aside. If he refused—death.

"Happy, take half the men and search through the rooms on this floor." Afrin grabbed Happy's arm. "We must hurry before the Fifth Armored Brigade and other security forces respond."

Happy nodded and ran forward leading his men.

Afran turned to Robin and motioned toward the stairs.

"Take a group of twenty and clear the stairwell. We'll follow as soon as you signal."

At a cost of half of his men, Robin controlled the stairwell and gained access to the upper floor. Afran and the others packed the stairwell, waiting to search for Baziyan.

"We must go cell to cell. Baziyan will be in one of the individual cells. Check the others. If the prisoners speak Kurdish, release them. Otherwise, leave them behind."

Screams and gunshots echoed throughout the building as Afran stormed down the hallway, searching for the individual cells, Ismet by his side.

They checked in each cell—no Baziyan. Frustrated, Afran pushed himself to search faster. Faces became a blur, but no one resembled the man they hoped would unite the Kurdish factions.

He dashed past a cell and slid to a halt, Ismet so close he crashed into Afran.

An aged man, thinning white hair replacing the once proud black mane and thick mustache, stood gazing out of the cell. His dark piercing eyes still exhibited the fire of his youth.

"Baziyan," Afran whispered. The man nodded once.

Ismet fell to his knees, tears streaming down his face. Afran motioned for Baziyan to step back and used a piece of plastique to open the door. Moments later, the man believed to control Kurdish destiny, stepped into the hallway.

Up and down the corridor, men realized they stood in the presence of their champion.

"Baziyan."

"Baziyan."

"Baziyan."

Cheers burst forth and some unthinking souls fired into the ceiling.

"Abdallah, we must make our escape. Please come with me." Afran grabbed one arm and Ismet the other.

Making their way out of the building and through the open perimeter fence, they returned to Dersim's truck. Ismet climbed behind the wheel while Baziyan sat in the middle and Afran by the passenger door. Twenty followers climbed into the back, weapons ready.

"Where's Dersim?" Afran asked Ismet. "I thought he'd drive us away."

"H-he didn't survive. Dersim died when we assaulted the inner barrier."

Afran let out a deep sigh. He bowed his head as if in prayer.

"We must go. Head to Mardin. The team leaders will remain with the others to attack any resistance."

"Afran, I heard the Fifth Armored Brigade wiped out Serbest and Warzan's teams, with only a few surviving. We also lost many men here."

"Serbest and Warzan realized their attacks would be suicide missions. They wanted the honor to take the fight to the Turks and allow us to free this man." Afran pointed at Baziyan. "We must now take him to a safe place, so their sacrifices weren't needless. We'll mourn later."

**

About the same time as Ismet drove away with Dersim's truck, a Kuba 100cc motorcycle slid to a halt in a cloud of dust. A man jumped off the bike, allowing it to fall over. CC and Jake approached him.

"Dersim, I'm glad you made it." CC grasped Dersim's shoulder and led him toward the car. "Let's head to the hotel. You can rest and we'll grab food for you. We need to plan our next move."

**

Sirens blasted the air as the remaining Kurds prepared to battle with responding security forces. Several tanks approached, along with a dozen APCs and troop carriers.

The Kurdish force, reinforced by almost one hundred PKK sympathizers after raiding the cells, prepared for a final battle.

For over an hour, the Kurds held their own against superior forces before melting away, grabbing any available vehicle for their escape.

Throughout the afternoon and into the evening, small clusters of battle-worn men returned to the warehouses in Nizip. Of the 275 men who began the operation the previous day, plus the Kurdish prisoners they freed, by the end of the night, 125 survived.

Battered, beaten, injured, but not subdued, every man standing in the warehouse realized they had obtained victory.

Abdallah Baziyan was free.

Chapter 50
Mardin, Turkey
Saturday, March 26

The Bedlam team rose early on Saturday morning. CC, Aiden, and Willie drove to a nearby grocery store and loaded up with provisions while the others sanitized the rooms and pored over road maps.

Once the three men returned to the hotel, everyone met in the parking lot. Opening the trunk of each vehicle, they distributed the supplies.

"Hey, mate. Whose army are we feeding?" Jake grinned and motioned with his arm, encompassing the five cars. "Even I can't eat that much."

"Aye. Perhaps we can find a kangaroo for you." Everyone chuckled at CC's comment. At first, though, Dersim didn't understand, until Jake explained. The air rippled with snorts and guffaws as Dersim buckled over in fits of laughter.

"Okay, mate. Enough. Not funny."

Jake's comment and his indignant expression caused a further eruption of merriment.

"Aye, good one. The provisions will fill the trunks and cover the Pelican cases. We must assume we'll run into several roadblocks on our way to Mardin."

After checking out of the hotel and loading their belongings into the cars, they hit the road. CC led the convoy, Dersim riding with him. The trip on the regular highway would be about three hours. They added an extra hour since they planned to use back roads whenever possible.

They approached the Gaziantep Ring Road and turned left. A short distance away, the shuttered prison stood as a testament to yesterday's fierce fighting. The men watched security forces comb the grounds, searching for anything to identify individual terrorists.

"Their work is cut out for them. Not sure what they expect to find in the grass." CC gazed at the investigative operation as they slowed for the first checkpoint.

"Papers." A burly gendarmerie sergeant stuck out his hands to emphasize his demand. Three other sergeants trained their weapons toward the vehicles. A Leopard-1 tank and two APCs also maintained vigilance over the civilian convoy.

CC handed over two passports. The sergeant stared at the photos and again at their faces.

"Foreigners. Why here?"

"Vacation. First time in this part of Turkey. What happened?"

"Kurdish thugs attacked yesterday. Many peace-loving Turkish people died. Dozens suffered injuries. Many terrorists escaped, including Apo."

"Aye. We listened to the fighting from out hotel. May we pass now?"

The sergeant glanced at CC's passport photograph again and nodded.

"You may go. I learned from movies, 'Have a nice day.' " His face burst into what passed for a smile, and he waved the entire convoy through.

"Mr. Haggis, Apo is Abdallah Baziyan's nickname. It means uncle in Kurdish." Dersim's face broke into a broad grin. "He's free."

When they reached the other side of Gaziantep where they would head east, another roadblock loomed. Unlike the first one, the Turkish Army maintained control.

After showing their passports, two soldiers raised the barrier's double arms so they could continue their journey.

"So far no problems." CC glanced in the rearview mirror. The other guys followed, close as possible, like a snake sneaking through the grass.

They approached a major truck stop thirty minutes later. Dersim squirmed in his seat.

"Do you want to stop?" CC motioned toward the building. "Toilet?"

"Yes. Tea and baklava, too."

The six men scurried inside. While Dersim provided the impetus, everyone followed suit. Finished, they claimed a large round table near the main windows.

Dersim laughed as he watched the others drink their tea. He clapped his hands to attract their attention and set his tea down. He grabbed a single sugar cube from the saucer, placing it between his teeth. Picking up his cup, he drank, the cube serving as a strainer.

"This is the proper way." Dersim drank again and choked, his eyes bulging and his face reddening with the effort. Jake slapped him on the back a few times until Dersim raised his hands.

"That isn't the proper way." Dersim continued to cough until his airways cleared.

Everyone laughed as they finished their snack and headed back to the cars.

"In one mile the road shifts." Dersim used his hands to indicate a V-shape. "We go left through the mountains. Safer. Less military."

"Aye, good idea. Let's mount up."

"First, Mr. Haggis, we go to the garage." Dersim pointed to a row of well-maintained huts, almost big enough to park their cars inside.

"Why? What's in the garage?" CC led the procession as requested.

"Stop here." Dersim said. He pointed at a tan-colored garage.

"Look, at the bottom. On the right."

CC focused on the area. As they slowed to a stop, a small Kurdish flag covering the bottom right corner came into focus.

"Okay, now what?" CC turned his attention back to Dersim.

"Inside. What you want. What I hid. Gas."

"Here?"

"Yes. Truck drivers rent garages all the time. So I did, too. Ten canisters inside."

"Hey, mate. What's the bizzo?" Jake approached first, followed by the others.

"Dersim told me the sarin he stole from the others is in the garage. Back two of the cars up so we can shift the fake ones inside and grab the real canisters."

Dersim fumbled in his pockets for the key, found the appropriate one and unlocked the padlock securing a hasp. The door screeched open, and he stood aside.

"See? Canisters."

The wooden hut was empty except for ten tan backpacks lined up in two rows along the back and a large wooden crate.

"Take the fake canisters out of the cases and replace those in the packs. Not enough room for both types."

"Okay, mate. What's in the crate?" Jake turned to Dersim. "Anything we might use?"

"Yes. Eight pistols and ammunition."

Once they finished the swap, the men jumped back in their cars, each carrying a Glock-19 and eight fifteen-round magazines. CC turned to Dersim.

"Thank you."

"This feels … good. The right thing. My heart tells me." Dersim placed his hand over his heart as he spoke.

"Aye. Let's collect the ones in Mardin and we'll begin our journey to America."

Dersim's eyes glistened at CC's words.

CC turned left onto the back road and maneuvered through a series of hills and valleys. Spring sprouted, the countryside's drab winter colors giving way to a variety of shades of green. Buds threatened to burst open on nearby trees, adding their foliage to the seasonal change.

"Soon we'll come to Mardin. I must tell you where to turn. It's not a tarmacked road." Dersim signaled to slow down.

They traveled in silence, the five vehicles eating up the miles during a peaceful drive.

"Stop! Back up." Dersim ducked his head to peer through CC's window. "Sorry. I've always come from Mardin."

CC stuck his head out, waving for the others to reverse. Like a well-synchronized machine, they backed up about 100 yards. To the left, a faint trail wandered through the winter grass up a sloping hill covered with several grey-colored rock formations.

"The barn is out of sight on the other side of the hill. We must stop before the top." Dersim motioned toward a splintered rock outcrop. "Park by the rocks."

The six men bailed out of the cars and crept past the rock barrier to a spot overlooking the barn. At first glance, it appeared to be derelict.

"Hey, mate. Are you sure this is the right place?" Jake glanced at Dersim and shook his head after viewing the barn. "Seems like a strong wind will knock it down."

"Yes, the right one. On the one end is a heavy wooden door. If there's a padlock, no one is inside."

"Dersim, come with me." CC started over the ridge. "We'll find out if anyone's at home."

The two men worked their way down to the edge of the barn and followed along the side to the corner. They peered around the edge of the building and stepped out of sight.

Moments later, Dersim and CC dashed up the hill and joined the others.

"The padlock's gone but the door's locked from the inside. No head count." CC turned to Dersim. "Do you have a code to alert those inside?"

"Yes, and a response."

"Aye. Jake, Ben, and Aiden, go around the far side and work your way to the door. Dersim, you and Willie come with me."

Once the men positioned themselves, CC nodded at Dersim. He approached the door and initiated the code.

Tap knock knock tap. Knock tap knock. Knock tap knock.

A moment later, someone inside responded.

Tap knock tap.

Deadbolts slid back, and the door opened.

"Dersim! Someone reported you died at the priso—"

Jake kept his Glock ready after giving the man two quick taps.

"Is he dead?" Dersim stared at the man lying on the ground in a heap.

"No, mate. I gave him a love tap. Twice."

Dersim led the way into the barn.

"Allo? Anyone home?"

Silence greeted Dersim's call. Several lanterns spread around the room cast eerie shadows in the dim light.

"Where are the canisters?" CC pressed Dersim. "We must grab them and run before the guy wakes up, or anyone else appears."

"They're in the back room in a closet. No locks."

"Let's move, people." CC issued orders, urgency clear in his voice. "Grab the canisters, hoof them to the cars and pick up replacements. Might as well leave the fakes for these guys. They won't know the difference but we'll save lives."

The six men worked as fast as possible, and in total silence. Dersim returned to check on the unconscious man as the last canister joined the others in a case, latches locked, and trunks shut.

Chug, chug, chug.

Glancing down the hill toward the road, an old Turkish Tonka struggled over the gently rolling hills and stopped near the track through the grass.

"Shit." Aiden called to the others. "Company. Hurry, eh?"

Jake ran to the barn, ducked inside, and helped himself to several AK-47s. Dersim mirrored Jake, filling a bag with full magazines before Jake grabbed him by the arm and hustled him back to the others.

Rounds pinged off the rocks, sending granite shards into Willie and Aiden. Both yelled but continued to leapfrog from rock to rock, striving to close the distance to use their Glocks with better accuracy.

Jake handed out the AK-47s. Unlike the sporadic fire coming toward them from the truck, the team's response overwhelmed their attackers.

The air roiled with multiple crackles like lightning as both sides let loose. Two Kurds collapsed, each with a third eye.

"Damn." Jake jerked back as a round nicked his left arm. Dersim moved to help him and fell as a random shot demolished the heel on his boot. Both men scrambled to safety behind the rocks.

Three Kurds emptied their magazines and ran down the hill, disappearing over a rise toward Mardin. Gunfire ceased and an uneasy calm spread over the impromptu battlefield.

"Aiden and Willie, use the rocks to scoot as close as possible." CC ordered the two men to move while he headed toward the truck. "Eight men attacked us. Three more remain. Use caution."

As they approached, another Kurd took to his heels. The team allowed the man to escape.

They reached the vehicle and examined the cab, under the vehicle, and in the back for anyone hidden. A third body lay scrunched between the seat and the dash.

"Dersim, please join us." CC made a quarter circle with his arm to summon the others.

"I don't recognize the two men in the back of the truck." Dersim shook his head and motioned to the cab. "The man inside is Mullah Abdul."

"Aye." CC checked the team over. A few nicks and scrapes, plus Jake's graze. A still functioning team.

"Time to roll before anyone comes to investigate the racket. We'll meet at the truck stop before the main highway."

Once they arrived, CC sent the team, including Dersim, to purchase food and drinks for their onward journey. He opened his laptop and composed a message.

To: Alpha

From: Haggis

Successful trip to Mardin. Twenty sarin canisters swapped. Skirmish left three team members with minor injuries. Three opponents terminated.

Proceeding to Incirlik. ETA six hours. Require base access for Dersim and three two-man rooms for the evening. Request transport to CONUS for six plus Pelican cases and other items.

Finished with his message, he shut down the laptop. The others returned to their cars and he joined them as they approached.

"We're heading to Incirlik. I've requested rooms and extraction orders. Let's move."

The five-vehicle procession headed west, keeping to the back roads. Little traffic and half-decent roads allowed them to move at a consistent pace. After skirting around Gaziantep, CC turned onto the main road and further increased their speed.

In the distance, they noted a roadblock, their first encounter since leaving Mardin. As they approached, two Leopard-1 tanks trained their turrets on the middle of the convoy. Soldiers approached the vehicles from both sides as the cars halted.

A Turkish lieutenant strolled toward CC's car as if he hadn't a care in the world. He glanced at CC and Dersim, and continued sauntering along the line of cars. Finished, he turned and marched back to CC's vehicle where he stared at Dersim for several moments.

"All foreigners?"

"Aye." CC nodded and gestured toward Dersim. "Him, too."

"Where are you going?"

"Adana. Our vacation is over and we're returning to America."

The lieutenant glanced back along the row of vehicles, pulled off his sunglasses and once more stared at Dersim. The silence thickened, as they waited for a decision. The officer replaced his glasses and flicked his hand forward, signaling for the convoy to continue.

A loud sigh escaped from Dersim.

"Nae worry. The lieutenant only wanted to show us he's in charge."

Before entering Adana, the convoy stopped at a small rest area. While the others stretched their legs, CC checked for incoming instructions from BHQ.

To: Haggis
From: Alpha

Dersim's access documentation waiting at Incirlik main gate. Secure cases for the evening with others. Rooms obtained as requested.

Air Force personnel will assist moving cargo under your supervision. Hand over rental car keys before departure.

C-17 Globemaster en route CONUS from RAF Mildenhall rerouted to Incirlik, ETA 0600. ETD 0800, bound for Andrews AFB. Welcome committee arranged.

CC shared the contents with the team members. While the majority acknowledged the information with silent nods, Willie couldn't resist a whoop and a rebel yell, similar to a cougar's screech. Everyone laughed, except Dersim, who appeared puzzled by the team's reaction.

"Dersim, tomorrow morning we're flying to America. That's what the excitement is all about." CC patted him on the shoulder. "Ever been on an airplane?"

Dersim shook his head.

"We'll all be with you. Easy."

Formalities for entering Incirlik concluded without difficulty. After securing the cases for the evening, the team headed to the Air Force Inn. First they stopped at Burger King, where a stupefied Dersim gazed at the food pictures.

"Too many choices, mate?" Jake nudged Dersim's arm. "I'll order for you—trust me."

They took their food to the cars, registered at the inn's front desk, and checked into their rooms. CC handed Dersim his food, still in the bag.

Dersim opened the package and sniffed. He pulled out the fries and tried one. Hot and salty.

"French fries. Might not be healthy but they taste great."

Dersim pulled out his sandwich and unwrapped the burger. "What's this?"

"Whopper—a big hamburger."

"I can't eat this, no ham."

"Dersim, nae problem. I'm not sure why they're called a hamburger but no ham, only beef."

Dersim bit into the sandwich. As he chewed, his smile grew and grew.

***

The C-17 departed Incirlik as scheduled. Six men, forty sarin gas canisters, plus assorted items, including additional fake cylinders, detectors, and tasers. They turned over the AK-47s and the Glocks to the Security Police before boarding the mammoth aircraft.

Once the plane lumbered down the runway and clawed its way into the air, shouts of delight echoed throughout the cargo area.

"Wheee!" Dersim shouted. "Yee-haw!"

Chapter 51
Fort Myer, Virginia
Friday, April 1

CC led his team into Bedlam's conference room where the support personnel waited. Toni stood, followed by the others, and clapped as the team strode down the aisle to their places. Georgia, Toni, and Charles, rushed toward them before they grabbed a seat. Amidst hugs, handshakes, and pats on the back, the VTC system chimed, alerting everyone to an incoming call.

Once the connection synchronized, Admiral Blakely's beaming face appeared on the screen. Before everyone stood, he said, "Sit down. Well done Bedlam Alpha, and to the support team, too." He waited while everyone resumed their seats.

"It's been a hectic month. Excellent result for your first mission. So far we've not received any questions or comments from Iraq, Syria, or Turkey." The admiral said. "Your original mission was to locate and recover the chemical weapons and disrupt the Kurdish plots without either the Turkish or Syrian governments realizing the threats. I'd say you achieved the desired outcome."

"Sir, we returned with forty sarin canisters. We substituted a fake for each of them." CC glanced around the table. "The assignment required a cohesive effort. Toni, Georgia, and Charles responded to every request and exceeded every expectation. The guys in the field did everything required. Well done to all.

"The chance meeting with Babir and his efforts to introduce us to Dersim made the difference. He's why we succeeded, but—."

The admiral nodded. "Babir became one of the original sources and agreed to go after his cousin when the Australians asked him."

"Aye, sir. We caught a lucky break. What about those Dersim claimed he hid in his house in Halabja?"

"Good news. Nate Webster, Bedlam Bravo's temporary boss, is in Halabja now with the rest of the group. The permanent team leader remained behind because his wife is in labor with twins.

"Bravo secured the canisters. They found some in the attic and the remainder in a bolthole. Dersim was correct. Ten contained sarin and the four he said appeared to be different held tabun, another chemical agent. The team and canisters will be shipped to a secret location tomorrow."

"Sir, what about Baziyan? Is anyone cognizant of his whereabouts?"

"The Kurds' luck held. Four days later, and they would have missed him. The Turks had completed the repairs to the prison on Imrali Island and planned to return him, as the only prisoner. No confirmed word on his location, but he's believed to be in Hakkari Province."

The admiral glanced at this watch and stood. "Ladies and gentlemen, excellent work. I speak for our partners as well, when I say, well done. Now, I must leave to brief President Burns in thirty minutes."

"A celebration is in order." Jake glanced around the group. "Who wants to join me for beer and steaks? My treat."

Everyone stood and prepared to leave when CC stopped them, several hundred-dollar bills nestled in his hand. "I'm afraid I won't be able to join you this time. I must meet with Dersim."

***

An hour later, CC knocked on the door of a two-story townhouse in the D.C. suburbs. An innocent outward appearance, the property bristled with electronic and physical security measures. Once inside, he stepped to a retina scanner. Recognized by the device, the inner door clicked open, and CC entered.

Two guards met him. They acknowledged CC and led him into the library where Dersim sat watching a basketball game.

Once he spotted CC, he jumped to his feet and rushed forward.

"Mr. Haggis. Thank you for putting me in this house. All the TV channels. It's amazing! Did you see the shower? Running hot water, whenever I want, and no fire required. The food, strange but delicious."

"Aye, Dersim, this is a grand place to stay. Once others debrief you, you'll be free to go. First, you must do something for me."

"What, Mr. Haggis?"

"Call me CC. All my friends do."

"Okay Mr. H—I mean CC. Thank you," he said. A slew of questions followed.

"Where'll I go? How do I find a job? What about my family? May my children go to school? Will someone help my wife and children learn English?"

"Aye. Reasonable questions, but slow down. All will be answered in good time. The reason I'm here is I thought you might like to go for a drive, and we'll grab a hamburger."

"What about fries? And a strawberry shake?"

CC chuckled. "Dersim, anything you'd like. Take your jacket and let's go."

They climbed into CC's Ford Explorer and departed. CC drove through the quiet neighborhood, heading toward the Capitol Beltway. He merged into the heavy traffic and remained in the right-hand lane.

"May I buy a car?"

"Of course." CC swore and blew the horn as an errant driver cut in front of him. "You must pass a test for a driver's license."

"Why do I require a license? I drive better than the person who went through your lane to the exit."

CC laughed again and shook his head. "I don't make the rules."

Leaving the beltway, they headed toward Dulles Airport. Dersim admired the scenery as they sped along the highway. Once they turned into the parking lot and found an empty slot, Dersim turned to CC.

"Why are we here? Who're you meeting?"

"Friends. I think you'll like them."

"Are they going to Burger King with us?"

"If they want. Perhaps McDonald's or Wendy's."

They entered the terminal, and Dersim stood with his mouth wide open. He scrutinized the well-dressed men, women, and children scurrying about the terminal, heading to departure gates or waiting for inbound travelers. People pushed forward, seeking their friends and family.

The doors closed. No one had come through for a few moments.

They slid open—at first, no one appeared.

Dersim concentrated on the entrance, curious about who would be meeting the new arrivals.

A woman dressed in traditional Kurdish attire, accompanied by two children in Western clothing, walked forward. They jumped as the doors closed in front of them. Moments later, the opening cleared and they hurried past the doors.

Dersim gave them a brief glance. He looked again, stared, then rushed toward them.

They spotted him and he scooped his children into his arms. The family reunited, tears streaming down everyone's face as they hugged each other and talked in excited voices.

CC stood back, allowing the family a moment together in the middle of the busy hall.

Dersim appeared to sense CC's approach. He spoke to his family in Sorani. After they formed a straight line the boy stepped forward, offering his hand.

"CC, may I present Qesem, my son." They shook hands, Qesem staring up at him before returning to his place.

The young girl stepped forward without any encouragement, following her brother's example.

"This is my pride and joy, Pakan."

Dersim turned and urged his wife forward.

"This is my wife, Xalan." After a moment's hesitation, she put her hand out.

CC took her hand. "Aye. Welcome to America."

Chapter 52
Hakkari Province, Turkey
Friday, April 8

Until two weeks ago, Baziyan remained incarcerated in Gaziantep. Except for the four guards, no one else was allowed in the rec area as he paced around the square for fifteen minutes each day, breathing in as much fresh air as possible.

Hiding in the Cilo-Sat Mountain range in Hakkari Province, Baziyan walked out of a small makeshift wooden mosque. Hunted but free, he made his way to the cave which served as his new home, until the completion of a one-room log cabin. No electricity and no running water, but after twelve years in solitary confinement on Imrali Island before his temporary transfer to Gaziantep, he now lived in hope, not for himself but for the Kurdish people.

He'd address supporters in an hour, but first a rest. He climbed onto the hammock spread between the walls, ropes anchored by railroad spikes hammered into the rock. Baziyan pulled up a blanket to ward off the cave's chilly air.

"Apo. It's time." Mufti Tanreverdi stuck his head in the cave's entrance and called upon his friend.

"Okay, coming. Are many supporters assembled?"

"Yes, Apo. At least one thousand. Perhaps more."

"Good. Let me speak to them."

When Baziyan stepped out of the cave, Afran and Ismet took a position on either side, the mufti leading the way.

They marched onto a flat rock outcropping, large enough for the four men. Below, followers waited for their leader. Not the one thousand mentioned by Tanreverdi but closer to five thousand.

"Apo."

"Apo."

"Apo."

The chants grew stronger as men stomped their feet on the ground. Mufti Tanreverdi raised his hands for quiet. Five minutes later silence reigned over the assembly.

"My friends, I give you our guiding light, the man to unite all Kurds—Abdallah Baziyan!"

More cheers erupted as Baziyan strode forward. He used both hands, open-palmed, in a downward motion, requesting quiet. After the crowd grew silent, he dropped his hands by his side.

"My friends, I thank everyone involved in obtaining my release. But, I'm saddened by the loss of life to gain my freedom." Baziyan paused, bowing his head.

"We must ensure their lives weren't taken in vain. We must continue our struggle against Turkish oppression."

Shouts of Apo and Baziyan burst forth. Several men fired weapons into the air while others waved banned Kurdish flags.

Once Tanreverdi restored order, Baziyan continued.

"Before the Turks can descend upon us, we'll attack, with everything in our arsenal. Gather your weapons. We'll send word when we're ready." More shouts and gunfire resumed as Baziyan turned and walked away, Tanreverdi by his side.

Embroiled in a heated debate, Afran and Ismet were unaware of their approach.

"Ismet, you lied to me. Dersim didn't die in Gaziantep. Where is he?"

"Yes, I lied to you. He's my friend. He wanted to return to his family without loss of face. So, I helped him to escape."

"What happened to the missing canisters? Did he take them?"

"None of your business."

Afran pulled a pistol from under his jacket and leveled the weapon at Ismet's stomach.

"I should kill you now. No one makes a fool of me."

"Afran, what's the meaning of this?" Baziyan stepped between the two men. "Didn't you experience enough fighting over the past month? I'm ashamed of you. Kurds don't fight Kurds."

Afran dropped his arm holding the gun. His head sank to his chest as he suffered Baziyan's admonishment in silence.

"Leave us."

Afran hesitated as if he planned to challenge Baziyan.

"What's wrong with you?" Tanreverdi thundered at his cousin. "How dare you act this way. Leave now and return to Mardin until we require your services."

Bowing his head in shame, Afran turned and walked away.

"Ismet." Baziyan put his arm around Ismet's shoulder. "Tell me about these canisters."

As he explained, Baziyan shook his head but remained silent, allowing Ismet to finish his explanation.

"I'm happy you and Dersim came to your senses. I never would use a weapon like this against anyone. The mufti is aware of my thoughts. But, fake canisters, hmmm." Baziyan stroked his moustache as he contemplated this new information.

"I don't have a problem using dummy cylinders to bolster our forces."

"Apo, when you're the leader of the Kurdish nation, would the West be angry about the canisters?" Ismet shrugged his shoulders.

"First, I don't want to be the leader. I prefer to be a puppet master and work behind the scenes. We'll leave politics to the politicians. Second, who will inform the West?" Baziyan smiled at Ismet and Tanreverdi. " I won't."

The mufti whispered into Baziyan's ear, who nodded. Tanreverdi turned to face Ismet.

"I'm too old to keep running around with Apo. The puppet master requires a younger aide. Are you up for the job?"

Ismet nodded, eyes glistening. "Yes, Mufti. Apo, I'm honored to be your assistant."

COMING FROM MOONSHINE COVE
IN 2018

THE NEXT MIDDLE EAST THRILLER
FROM
RANDALL KRZAK

DANGEROUS ALLIANCE

READ CHAPTER ONE BEGINNING ON
THE NEXT PAGE

Chapter 1
Port Rashid, Dubai
United Arab Emirates

The target floated in the harbor's dark water, anchored fore and aft in the moonless night. A faint hiss broke the silence as climbing ropes and grappling hooks sailed into the air from Plumett NS50 Silent Launchers. Within moments, a sharp tug secured each hook to a quarterdeck railing on the cruise ship, two each on the port side, the starboard, and from the stern.

The men, dressed in black, facial features distorted by brown, black, and green camouflage paint, raced up the lines using ascenders. The whisper of their rubber-soled shoes on the ship's sides, the only hint of their invasion.

With a single click of his radio, each man signaled he was in position. They readied their TGR2 rifles and waited for the command.

Colonel (Ret.) Trevor Franklin anticipated the go-ahead from Craig Cameron, Bedlam Alpha Team Leader, and senior commander of this mission. He performed a mental review of their intel. *Ship in port for routine maintenance. Crew spending time with family and friends. Seven hostages, attending a private onboard dinner arranged by the ship's owner, taken hostage by at least ten terrorists. Threatening to kill them if their demands aren't met. Maintain silence and minimize casualties—use stun guns.*

Craig watched the seconds tick away and nodded to Trevor.

"Go."

Trevor, leader of the new Bedlam Bravo team, issued the order as he positioned his ATN night vision goggles and slithered through the stern rail. Craig slipped through the stanchions ten feet away.

Calm. Dark. Perfect time for a raid.

Trevor's eyes swept the decks above. By now the other men should be at their designated search areas on decks one through seven. He located the stairwell leading to the signal deck. From behind he felt Craig's hot breath on his neck.

They mounted the steps, listening for the creak of movement, the striking of a match, anything indicating a terrorist. Quiet greeted them. As they reached the bridge, Trevor lifted his head to peer inside. A tall man with shaggy brown hair stood in front of a control panel.

Trevor turned to Craig and raised a finger. One occupant. *Need more intel.*

He reached into his pack, grabbed his Double Trouble stun gun, and worked his way to the door. It gave a light squeak as he pulled it open. The man turned at the sound. Trevor lunged at the hijacker, pressed his stun gun against the man's chest and zapped him.

Convulsing as electricity surged through his body, the target collapsed. The wriggling stopped, Trevor flipped him over and secured his wrists with plastic zip ties.

"Where are the hostages?"

"Go to hell." The thug turned his head and tried to spit.

Trevor shoved a gag in the man's mouth and secured his ankles. "Don't go away, mate."

Trevor rejoined Craig. "One tango captured. He won't be giving any trouble."

"Aye. Good job. Don't forget to swap your stun gun's batteries."

"Thanks." After Trevor replaced them, he returned the gun to his pack and grabbed his radio. He whispered to his team: "One tango down. Continuing search."

***

Built like a wrestler, Koning Badenhorst's bulk belied his ability to move with silent speed. Wall-to-wall carpet muffled his movements. Former Gurkha Sergeant Agam Bahadir Pun, a stealthy shadow behind the huge man, his TGR2 at the ready.

Tasked with investigating decks four through seven, they hurried down the stairs, checking each passageway before continuing.

Once on deck seven, the men peered into the lounge and the well-equipped gymnasium before working their way through areas off-limits to passengers. They cleared possible hiding areas in rapid succession before returning to the staircase.

The acrid smell of antiseptic on deck six told Koning and Pun they had entered the ship's medical facility. Koning stood guard while Pun slid a fiber optic cable under each door for a peek before moving on.

A slither of light appeared underneath a door labeled 'Doctor.' Koning listened as he grasped the knob. Silence. He twisted the handle to the open position and pushed it with his hand, keeping his body to the side of the doorframe. Pun wormed inside to the right while Koning veered left.

A shadow flew past Koning's face. He dropped to the floor, kicked out with his feet, and connected with something solid. Someone grunted. As Koning scrambled to his feet, a solid punch to his stomach knocked the wind out of him, forcing him back to the floor.

The assailant kicked at Koning's head. Missed. Koning landed a side thrust kick to the nerve point above the man's right knee, causing it to buckle. He grabbed his attacker in a chokehold, pressing on the carotid artery until the man became limp.

After binding his hands and feet, Koning slapped the man until he regained consciousness.

"No *dossing*. Where are the hostages?"

"Huh?" The man shook his head.

"*Ag, man*. Are you *dof* (stupid)? Where are they?"

The dazed thug raised a shaking arm and pointed to an inner door. Koning grabbed the man and propelled him into the wall, knocking him out.

"*Lekker droom* (sweet dreams)." Koning turned to Pun. "Why didn't you help me?"

"You didn't need any."

After securing the intruder, they approached a wood-paneled door. Koning heard a muffled moan from inside and eased the door open.

A woman, long blond hair falling over her face, sat bound to a chair with strips of elastic bandages. Gauze held her hands together while a piece of tape covered her mouth.

Pun scanned the room. "Clear."

Koning freed the woman. "You okay?"

"I will be." She heaved a sigh and flexed her arms to return the circulation, rubbing at her chaffed wrists. "Who are you?" She inhaled several sharp breaths and appeared to calm down.

"*Ag*, no one. Stay here until I return."

"What about the guy who snatched me?"

"Asleep—guy fought with a wall. He lost." Koning smirked. "He won't be bothering anyone for a few hours."

***

Koning and Pun climbed the stairs to deck five. They moved from cabin to cabin, using master key cards to gain access through locked doors. Each room appeared the same: bed, side tables and lamps, dressers, and two easy chairs, a coffee table snuggled between them. A small bathroom completed the amenities.

Each room shared another similarity—empty.

After inspecting the last cabin, Pun returned to the staircase. As he placed a foot on the first step, an arm snaked over his shoulder.

His instincts kicked in. Pun jumped on the next step, yanked his *kukri* from its wooden scabbard on the back of his belt, swinging to face his opponent.

"Shh." Koning pulled his hand back. "Ag, man, put your toy away before you *steek* someone."

"Why you grab me?"

"Ag, to check your reflexes."

Pun grinned and replaced his blade. "This deck is clear. Deck four now."

Koning nodded. "Let's go."

A man of few words, Pun tilted his head toward the stairs. Together they crept up to deck four, each taking a side of the hallway to check the cabins.

No activity until they reached a small corridor on the right between two inner cabins.

They scooted along the short hallway. Straight ahead, three cabins. Pun went left, Koning to the right. Moments later, they returned to the corridor, shaking their heads. Koning stepped to the middle door and tried the handle. Locked.

He pointed to himself, giving a high sign and indicated Pun should go low. Koning reared back and kicked the door with his foot.

The door flew open. They powered into the room. Four men sitting around a card table jumped to their feet. With no weapons in sight, Koning hauled out his stun gun, and pressed it against the chest of a man, a purple snake tattoo running down his arm. Koning pulled the trigger. The man dropped to the floor in apparent agony while two others rushed at him.

348

He flipped one thug over his shoulder. The man crashed through the card table to the floor, stunned. The other terrorist grabbed Koning's arm and tried to force it behind his back.

"You fight like girl." Koning chuckled, twisted his body, and fell to the floor. He stomped his right foot on the man's ankle, placing the other in the back of his calf. The assailant fell face-first to the floor, knocking himself out.

Pun launched himself through the air at the fourth terrorist as the man grabbed his pistol.

They struggled for control and the gun discharged, smashing a nearby lamp. Pun leveraged himself and thrust his opponent into the air and against the wall, where the terrorist collapsed, the pistol spinning out of his hand.

The men trussed and gagged, Pun and Koning searched the remainder of the cabin. They stood on either side of the closet doors, grabbed a knob and tugged.

A man and woman sat on the floor, tied back-to-back, their eyes covered with blackout masks. Koning and Pun released the couple from their makeshift prison. Both captives were shaking, rubbing their wrists where ropes had cut into them.

"You're safe now." Koning glanced at Pun, who helped the couple back to chairs.

"We were playing chess when the door burst open." A young man with bright orange hair and blue eyes pointed at the table. "They knocked us down and tied us up before dragging us into the closet."

"What did they want?" Koning asked the questions, leaving Pun to stand guard.

"They never spoke." The woman, about five feet tall, with black hair, shook her head for emphasis. Her hazel eyes remained wide with fright.

"We'll move you to another cabin before we continue our recce of the ship. Pun, take them to a room by the stern stairs. I'll retrieve the hostage from deck six. Meet you there."

The three passengers now safe in one location, Koning turned to Pun. "Let's go help Nate and Fergus."

***

Nathaniel 'Nate' Webster scampered along the passageway on deck three toward the stern. He threw an occasional glance over his shoulder.

As Nate approached the stairwell, a faint shoe scuff on the rich pile carpet gave warning. He ducked around a corner and dropped into a crouch, his TGR2 ready.

Two shadows appeared—Pun and Koning. Nate waved for them to follow and the three men entered the launderette.

Koning glanced around. "Where's Fergus?"

"We decided to split up. He should be on deck two."

Koning shook his head but kept silent.

"You guys find anyone?" Nate gazed at Koning, knowing Pun's aversion to speaking.

"*Ja.* We found five baddies and three hostages. We moved them to a cabin on the deck below. What about you?"

"I found one in the chapel. He's wrapped up, lying on the floor."

"Why didn't you bring him?"

"Forgot to mention. Four terrorists with him. Two, maybe three, I'd have gone in. Four is too many."

"We help." Pun raised his kukri in the air.

"This way." Nate headed for the port hallway while the others zipped down the starboard passageway. Once in position, Nate crawled along the wall of the synagogue to the glass-partitioned doors. He snaked a miniaturized camera through a gap to verify the terrorists' positions.

The device removed from under the door, Nate pointed to the left and raised one finger. He motioned to the right, with three upright fingers. He removed his stun gun from its holster and waved at the others, who nodded and retrieved theirs. Koning swapped out the batteries before nodding he was ready.

Nate tried the doorknob. It turned, and he raised three fingers again, counting down. His hand now a fist, he thrust the door open and dove for the deck, reached out to make contact, and sent an electrical charge into the single terrorist.

From the right, bullets chewed into the doorframe above the heads of Pun and Koning, who hugged the floor. When the firing stopped, they charged forward, two terrorists receiving a single charge from their stun guns. Pun reached the shooter. He pressed his gun against the man's shoulder and fired. The man's body seized in violent spasms.

While Nate undid the ropes around the hostage, Koning and Pun bound the four terrorists with tape from their backpacks.

"I think we should consolidate the people we've freed in one spot, perhaps the launderette." Nate pointed toward the stern as he spoke. "Since we're using the staircases for movement between decks, it'll be easier to collect them when we finish."

Koning stuck his head out of the doorway. "Ok, all clear. I'll bring the three up."

"I guard."

Nate nodded at Pun's offer. "Good. I'll head to deck two. Tell Koning to follow once he brings you the others."

***

Fergus Mulligan, the newest member of Bedlam Bravo, pushed long reddish hair from his forehead and finished clearing the starboard side of deck one. As he turned the corner to work through the port side cabins, a scream echoed along the passageway. A woman with long brown hair in a ponytail ran out of a cabin midway along the hallway and headed away from Fergus, a turbaned man brandishing a knife followed in close pursuit. He let loose a shot from his TGR2. Missed. They turned into another passageway and disappeared before Fergus could fire again.

He ran to the cabin's door and peeked inside. A man lay on the floor, the remnants of a red ceramic flowerpot scattered around him, clumps of earth and roses spread along his back. Fergus rushed back into the corridor and continued pursuit.

He reached the stern and turned toward the staircase, skidding to a stop. The turbaned man lay motionless on the floor. The tall woman, brown hair in a ponytail, leaped across the body, flinging her arms around Nate, holding on to her savior.

"You're a chancer. Why do you always get the girls?" Fergus laughed. "One day you must clue me in."

"All about being in the right place. Being handsome helps, too."

"Don't forget modesty. I'll take a gander for the others, give you time to introduce yourself to the young lady."

"That's okay, boys." She gave Nate and Fergus a peck on the cheek. "You rescued me, and I'm thankful. Now, how do I get off this tub?" A wary smile had surfaced on her lips before she screwed up her face. "I've had enough excitement for one evening."

A few minutes later, the rest of the team and the freed hostages arrived. Stashed in a cabin, Pun stayed with them. The others headed up the stairs to deck one.

***

Trevor and Craig moved from the signal deck to the sun deck. They cleared the few suites in rapid fashion, and headed to the cinema. Craig eased the door open far enough to squeeze in, Trevor followed.

In a crouch, they waited for their eyes to adjust to the dim light. Craig remained by the door while Trevor glanced around the room seeking anything out of place.

A shadow moved up front. Trevor ducked and crabbed along a row of seats. He peered through the gap between two backrests toward the figure.

More movement—someone's head lolled on the back of a seat. Trevor crept forward for a better view. A TCR rifle across the man's lap, he appeared to be asleep.

Trevor snuck behind the terrorist, grabbed him in a chokehold, and subdued him. After securing the man to the cinema seat, he motioned to Craig and they continued. Not finding anyone else, they moved to the stern and proceeded to the boat deck.

Picking up their pace, they circled via the promenade, ducking as they came along a row of windows. Craig raised his head above the ledge. A gold placard on a window read: Queens Grill Lounge. Sprawled across the bar, a gagged man lay bound by several strands of rope.

"One man tied on top of the bar," Craig whispered. "You go and I'll cover."

Trevor nodded, glanced around for any further movement, and crept forward. After Trevor had untied the cord around the man's hands and ankles, the freed captive slid off the bar and stumbled into a chair.

"Thank you. My friends—a couple—the terrorists took them away after they trussed me up like a chicken. Find them, okay?"

"Don't worry. My team's clearing the other decks. Remain here with my partner until I return."

The man nodded. Craig reached over the bar, grabbed a glass, and pulled a pint. He handed it to the still shaking man, who sucked air in with great gulps.

"Here, this will help. Try to relax. You're safe now."

The man downed the pint in two swallows and held the glass out, smacking his lips. "Couldn't have another one by any chance?" He stood, twisted his body to work out the kinks and rolled his shoulders before sitting.

"Aye." Craig grinned at the man's audacity and got him another pint.

Trevor cleared the remainder of the deck and grabbed his radio. "Team, this is Black, report."

"Black this is Red. I guard five hostages. Rest of team on quarter deck."

"Confirmed. Haggis tending to one hostage. Proceeding to stern end of the upper deck. Rendezvous with hostages."

"Black this is Green. Ag, man, as soon as we clear the upper deck, we'll join you."

"Roger, Black out."

***

Trevor and Nate took the port side, Fergus and Koning proceeded along the starboard. As they searched, a clinking sound came from the direction of the bow.

"What's that?" Nate stopped to listen.

Fergus laughed. "A fruit machine."

"What?"

"I think you Yanks would call it a slot machine."

They hurried forward, the sound growing louder with each step. An alarm triggered and bells rang, the clinking became a rush.

"Casino," Trevor mouthed to Nate.

Nate grabbed Trevor's arm and pointed to starboard. The other pair gave a thumbs-up. The four men rushed the casino, weapons leading the way.

"Down, down down," Trevor shouted. Three thugs, crowded around a slot machine, one with his hand poised to pull the lever, froze in position. One glanced at his TCR on a nearby table. Koning moved forward, his TGR2 aimed at the terrorist's stomach.

Hands in the air, they sank to their knees as the team swarmed over them. A terrorist, his arm hidden behind one of the others, raised his pistol and fired.

"Ow! Bastard winged me." Fergus grabbed his ear, blood seeping through his hand.

Nate spun, his TGR2 sighted on the shooter and nailed him in the chest. The man collapsed. The team secured the terrorists and continued their search for the final hostage.

They located their goal in the cruise director's office on the upper deck ten minutes later. Once the team removed his gag and bindings, a distinguished-looking gentleman in a Saville Row suit, trimmed black beard, and manicured hands stood. He gazed at the team.

"I say, about time you arrived." Sir Alexander 'Alex' Jackson, the British National Security Advisor, glanced at his watch. "Only an hour and forty-seven minutes to find me. Not bad on a ship the size of the QE2.

"CC, what's your assessment? It was entertaining to watch on the monitors."

"Aye, Sir Alex. The team did a good job for their first training scenario. Some of the terrorists overplayed their parts when they were hit with non-working stun guns, but their actions helped add some realism. Same with the hostages, too—great acting.

"When Bedlam Alpha held their first training mission, we used Tipmman Tactical Compact Rifles and TiPX pistols. More realistic using the TGR2s for the team giving the terrorists TCR rifles and TiPX pistols for returning fire."

After each man had stripped off their Kevlar vests, extra protective padding, and helmets, Sir Alex shook their hands. "The exercise is concluded. Release the Navy volunteers who played our terrorists and hostages. I hope you didn't pound them too hard. I'll meet you at Whitehall in a week."

Ingram Content Group UK Ltd.
Milton Keynes UK
UKHW010139010423
419458UK00003B/18